The Nobody Man

The Nobody Man

Steven Jenkins

Victorina Press
www.victorinapress.com

The Nobody Man
©Steven Jenkins

First published in 2019 by
Victorina Press Ltd.
Wanfield Hall
Kingstone
Uttoxeter
Staffordshire, ST14 8QR
England

*The right of Steven Jenkins to be identified as author of
this work has been asserted by him in accordance with
sections 77 and 78 of the Copyright, Designs and Patents
Act 1988.*

Typeset and Layout: Jorge Vásquez
Cover Art and Design: Fiona Zechmeister

British Library Cataloguing in Publication Data
A catalogue record for this book is available from the
British Library.

ISBN: 978-1-999-3696-1-3 (paperback)

Typeset in 11pt Minion Pro
Printed and Bound in the UK by 4edge Ltd

This book is dedicated to the brave men and women of the Police and Armed Forces who do a difficult job in some very unpleasant places. They put their lives at risk every day in order to keep the rest of us safe in our beds at night.

Prologue

Welchy spat blood and teeth onto the floor and looked up at the man now sitting watching him. 'Fuck you,' he said through painfully gritted teeth. He strained against the cable ties around his wrists, forearms and ankles that were pinning him to the chair.

His captor leaned back in his chair opposite. 'I'll ask you once more, politely. Then things get interesting. For me. Not necessarily for you, matey. Where do I find Deano?'

'Fuck you. I don't know no Deano. And if I did, I wouldn't tell you, you fuckin' queer. Let me go – now. Might not go so bad for you. Don't dis me any more, man. You in deep shit now, know what I'm sayin'?'

His captor smiled. 'Where did you learn to speak like that? You're in Walsall. Not the Bronx. Not Los Angeles. Not Jamaica. You're a young white man from a shitty English town in the Midlands. So why the affected accent? Does it make you feel hard? Powerful? Cos from where I'm sitting, you don't look like either. You look weak, and in a world of shit, matey. Or can I call you Welchy?'

'How you know my name, man? You don't know me.'

'Oh, but I do. I know you, your piece of shit father and his father too.'

'Bullshit. You know nuffin. Nobody. You a nobody. You dead when I get out of here.'

The captor leaned forwards until his face was inches away from the young man. 'Welchy, I'm guessing you're the son of Larry Welch, grandson of Richard Welch. All trash. None of you ever worked a day in your scavenging, thieving lives. You're useless feeders. Parasites on the skin of society.'

'Don't you dis my family, man! They'll kill you! Fuckin' untie me!' He thrashed around, his heavily muscled arms straining at the cable ties, but the pain in his splinted left leg was too much and he slumped back against the chair.

'Now I've told you I know your name, I should introduce myself. But I won't. I would say pleased to meet you, but,' he shrugged, 'you know.' He turned around to the workbench behind him. On the immaculate surface were a few select items. He picked up the nearest. 'Do you know where you are, Welchy?'

'What? What you talkin' about, man? No, I don't know.' He eyed the tool the man had just picked up. 'What you gonna do with that? You full of shit, man. You won't do nuffin!' He spat blood again. 'You is a nobody man, dat's all.'

'That's where you're wrong, matey. A month ago, you may have been right. But now, sadly for you, you're wrong. You see, as humans, supposedly civilised humans, we constantly weigh up actions and consequences.' He stood up and kicked Welchy squarely in the chest, knocking the air out of him. The wall behind Welchy prevented the chair from toppling over. 'Like that, for instance. My action will have no consequence. Because I am now beyond the reach of the law. You and your family, and your scumbag friends, have always been beyond the reach of the law, haven't you? So your actions never had consequences. Unless they were actions against someone else who was also beyond the reach of the law. So you never took on that sort of opponent. On some subconscious level you know that actions against a person like that will have consequences for you, so you only choose law-abiding victims. It's like picking a fight with someone half your size with their hands tied. That's how your kind function in this country.'

'What bullshit you talkin' about?' Welchy wheezed, confused by so many multisyllabic words.

'No, I suppose you wouldn't really understand. Now.' The man crouched down next to him. 'Where do I find Deano? Last chance.'

'Fuck you.' Welchy spat blood in the man's face.

The lump hammer came down with full force on Welchy's right hand, instantly shattering carpals and metacarpals. He screamed, more in surprise than pain. The hammer came down again, on the left hand. This time he screamed in pain and terror. He knew then that this man was for real. No empty threats here. The sudden realisation that he was indeed in deep shit hit him as hard as the hammer that was shattering his bones.

'In some so-called uncivilised countries, Arabs will cut off the hands of thieves. Did you know that? It stops them thieving again. Of course they only get two chances, then they probably starve to death. No welfare system there to keep them fed, housed and supplied with new cars. Stops them thieving though.' He brought the hammer down again on Welchy's right hand, completely shattering the complex group of carpals, rendering his hand useless. It would take many bouts of serious surgery to return even minor function to that hand. Welchy slumped to the side, apparently unconscious from the pain. Even so, the man didn't hesitate and slammed the hammer down on Welchy's left hand. Instantly, Welchy screamed. Tears streamed down his face.

'No more thieving for you, matey. No more punching defenceless people. No more stabbing. I doubt you'll even be able to hold your own limp dick.' He put the hammer back on the workbench and picked up the next item. Turning round, he showed it to his snivelling captive. 'Recognise this?'

Welchy's eyes widened. He shook his head and cried, 'No, man, no. I'll tell you. I'll tell you. Deano, he's living with the crew. At the crib.'

The man hefted the item in his hand. 'I found this in your trouser pocket when I threw you in the car. Stungun, isn't it? A Taser? I heard that's how you're getting away with a lot of muggings. Zapping victims in nightclubs then pretending to help them while telling other people they're having a seizure and that you're their brother. Thieving their purses and wallets while they're lying helpless on the floor.' He switched the unit on. 'So I thought I'd give you a message for this ... Deano. That's what you called him in your Flashpic video, right?'

'Yeah, man, Deano. Andrew Dean. That's him. It's him you want. He lives in da crib, man. Kalvin Lewis, as well. He's like another leader of the Keepers, next to Deano. Half-caste nutcase, though, you don't wanna mess with him. They always at da crib, man. Go find them, see what happens.'

'The house. Not "da crib". You are not American.' He touched the tip of the stun-gun to Welchy's neck without activating it.

Welchy screamed in anticipation, tears streaming down his face.

The man sat back. 'So where is this house?'

Welchy whimpered. 'I'll tell you, but don't tell them it was me. They'll kill me. Please?'

'Strange how you caved in so easily. Not such a hard man, are you, when faced with your own level of brutality? What's the address?'

'Bedders Road. Number ten.'

The man touched the stun-gun to Welchy's neck and gave him a half-second shot, causing him to emit a high-pitched keening sound and his legs to spasm, dislodging the splint. The crotch of his tracksuit trousers grew dark as his bladder voided involuntarily.

'That's so much bullshit, matey. Old Man Wallace lives at number ten, has done for years. You trying to stitch me up, sending me to the wrong house? Thinking that I'll walk in and get beaten up by the whole Wallace family? Think again.' He leaned forwards with the stun-gun.

'Fuck, fuck, fuck,' Welchy snivelled, snot and tears

mixing on his face. 'Number twenty. It's twenty. Got a black steel front door. Garage door is reinforced metal as well. It's twenty, man. Dat's the truth.' He lowered his head and whimpered.

'Thank you. Wasn't so hard, was it?' He leaned forwards and zapped him again.

When he recovered, Welchy sobbed, 'What was that for? I told you, didn't I? What do you want from me?'

'You stole a motorbike. Yesterday. An old bike. Remember?'

Welchy looked up hopefully, nodding. 'Yeah, man, I remember. I still got it, you can have it back. No probs, man, it's yours.'

The man zapped him again. 'More bullshit. You see, I watched your funny little social media video where you set it on fire.'

'It was an old knacker. Fuckin' ancient. I'm sorry, man. I didn't know it was yours. I'm sorry, alright?' Welchy sobbed and tried to curl into himself. His not-so-splinted left leg was painfully twisted.

'It wasn't mine, matey. It was my dad's. He'd owned that bike since 1968. He bought it with hard-earned wages. You stole it without a second thought. Set fire to it. Left it on waste ground like a piece of litter.'

'It's just a bike, man. I'll get you the money for another if it means that much to your old man.'

'Unlikely. See, the shock of that, with other … recent events … was too much for him. He had a heart attack, never regained consciousness. You killed him.'

'He died? Cos of an old fuckin' bike? Dat ain't my fault. He have dementia or sumfin?'

'Wrong answer, matey.' The man stood up. 'You see, I'm looking for a shred of humanity in you, but you couldn't give a shit. You've never worked for anything, so nothing matters to you. If you want something, you steal it. Then it's not important to you, so you don't want it. Well, I'll never teach you anything, but you can give this message to Deano, Lewis and the rest of your scumbag friends.'

'Why you after them, man? Good fuckin' luck with that – they'll kill you.'

The man looked down at Welchy. 'Someone robbed and killed my wife over on the waste ground behind Ryecroft Cemetery.' He stared Welchy right in the eyes. 'I reckon it was one of Deano's little gang, and he'll know who did it. I want him, or this Lewis, to tell me who it was, and I'll leave you all alone after that.'

'Yeah? They'll fuckin chew you up, like your wife. Make you disappear. They'll fuck you up. Nobody man.'

'I'm already fucked up, matey,' he whispered, then held the Taser to Welchy's neck, pressed the trigger and watched his body thrash around. After about ten seconds, Welchy emptied his bowels into his trousers. Another fifteen seconds and he lost consciousness. Twenty seconds after that the smell of burning flesh filled the air, but still the man pressed the Taser hard into Welchy's neck. He kept on squeezing the trigger until the batteries died.

<u>**Chapter 1**</u>

Eighteen days earlier

Janice was walking the two dogs along the old disused railway line behind Ryecroft Crematorium. Known by locals for years as the Yellow Mess, it was actually once part of the London Midland and Scottish Railway. Teenagers used to spend most of their adolescence over here, riding dirt bikes, doing their courting, walking their dogs. Some of them had less constructive pastimes. Disused plastic bags full of glue once littered the tracks and pathways, evidence of attempts to gain a chemical high without the cost of buying drugs. Some went on to harder stuff; most of the locals knew well enough where not to go to avoid getting a needlestick injury. It was all part of the joy of growing up in this area in the eighties and nineties.

Janice thought how much better the LMS looked now that it was overgrown with greenery. The two dogs ran in front, chasing each other in and out of the dense woodland and waist-high grasses. The path she was on meandered between the two raised banks of the old railway line. She recalled how in her and Dan's youth, these banks and tracks weren't overgrown like this but were covered in myriad paths and tracks made by dirt bikes and pushbikes. Sadly, there were no children playing here now. The overgrown greenery was testament to that.

The old tracks all had names. Dan had broken his collarbone when he fell off his Maico 250 dirt bike trying to ride up the Crooked Tree route. He was fifteen years old at the time, rebellious, wild, a loner even then. He managed to push his bike home, and then walked to the hospital. No mobile phones to call for an ambulance in those days.

The two dogs continued to chase each other up and down the steep banks. Bryn was Janice and Dan's collie, and Maisie belonged to Dan's father, Pete. It was strange to be here again, albeit just for a short time. Dan and Janice had moved away to Shropshire years ago when crime in Walsall had become unbearable. Pete, a widower of ten years, had stayed in Walsall, more from habit than necessity. These days Pete struggled to walk with Maisie for very long. His breathlessness made walking slow and challenging, so whenever they visited, Janice walked the dogs while Dan and Pete sat in the garage and talked about motorbikes for an hour. Dan had said that he wanted to speak to Pete and Janice together, that he had something he wanted to discuss with them, but she thought she'd let them get the bike talk out of the way first.

Talking of motorbikes, she could hear one coming along the track behind her. She called the dogs to her to clip them on their leads. She didn't have a problem with kids using the waste ground for riding bikes, but she wanted to keep the dogs safe and out of the way. As the motorcycle came along the track, she stood to one side, trying to keep the dogs behind her, but Maisie lunged forwards as the bike roared past. Not far enough to interfere with the bike or rider but he stopped anyway. Skidding to a halt, he turned round on the seat.

'Hey bitch, keep your fuckin' mutts off me. I'll kill 'em, if they do that again.'

Janice stared at the young man in disbelief. He was about twenty-five years old, shirtless and heavily muscled. The motorcycle wasn't an obvious choice for a dirt bike. She recognised it as a Suzuki GSXR, a fairly modern sports bike. Probably stolen, she thought. No owner in their right mind would bring a bike like that over waste ground. Bryn and Maisie reacted to the aggressive voice and strained on their leashes, barking furiously.

'Fuckin' dogs want putting down. They don't show no respect to people.'

The irony of his statement wasn't lost on Janice. Nor the incongruity of such an affected accent in the middle of a Black Country town in England. Feeling the weight of her fifty-one years, Janice turned away without saying a word. A few years ago, she would have given him a piece of her mind, but times change. Discretion being the more sensible part of valour these days, she made to walk off in the opposite direction, dragging the furious dogs with her.

'Hey, don't fuckin' ignore me, bitch. I'm talkin' to you.'

Janice heard the bike rev hard and turned to see the young man trying to turn the bike round on the narrow path. He couldn't handle it and dropped it in the grass, rolling away from it as he did so. In spite of herself, she laughed. Both herself and Dan were motorcyclists with years of experience but they wouldn't have tried that manoeuvre there. Being laughed at for his obvious lack of skill only served to infuriate the rider. He yanked the bike upright and jumped back on it. Pointing the right way now, he sped towards Janice. She tried to step back off the track but the brambles got in her way. She pulled the dog's leashes tight but Maisie was incensed. The dog lunged forwards as the bike sped past and the rider kicked her hard. Maisie flew through the air, the leash yanked out of Janice's grip. The jolt threw Janice to the floor, where she landed heavily on her knees.

As she stood up she saw the rider turning the bike round again at a wide point in the track. Scared now, she looked around for Maisie but she was nowhere to be seen. She thought to run back up the track to the alleyway that went up the side of the cemetery grounds. There was a metal gateway there that she knew wouldn't allow a bike past. Her right knee felt wrong as she stood up, and it gave way as she tried to run. Falling, her head collided with the motorcycle as it sped past. Her vision was a blur of sun, grass, sun, then nothing. She heard Bryn furiously barking and growling and tried to hold on to his leash as she lost consciousness.

# # # #

Dan and Pete were sitting in the garage with a mug of tea each, after refitting the back wheel on Pete's 1968 Triumph

Bonneville T120. It was his pride and joy. He'd owned it from new and had done a full restoration on it five years ago. After his wife had died ten years ago, Pete had become ill with a heart problem. Since then he hadn't ridden the bike all that much but he loved to admire it and polish it and take it out on occasional sunny days. He'd been out on the Bonneville last week and unfortunately got a puncture, which he and Dan had just successfully repaired.

As they sat there, good-naturedly arguing the originality of the new Triumph motorcycles against the older Meriden models, they heard a scratching at the garage side door. Pete leaned over and opened it and Maisie limped in. She was trailing her leash behind her and holding up her front leg, whining and distraught. Dan jumped to his feet and opened the garage door but could see no sign of Janice or Bryn.

Steven Jenkins

Chapter 2

Dan stood outside Ryecroft Crematorium after the funeral service, trying not to appear ignorant when people spoke to him, but not really wanting to speak to anyone either. He could feel a rage building inside, and he knew that at some point it would vent outwards. This was not the time or place. Janice wouldn't have approved. Truthfully, Dan didn't want to be at the funeral, wasting time with people that he barely knew any more. Most of them, he hadn't seen for over a decade and he felt completely detached from their lives, their families and their interests. Still, he understood and appreciated on some deeper level that they had come to show respect and affection for the woman he had loved so much, and he was grateful for that.

After this was over, he wanted to go home alone and relax in the garden that he still thought of as Janice's garden. He had buried their dog there a couple of weeks ago. It already seemed like months. Janice would have wanted Bryn to be there, in his own place where he could be remembered fondly. Dan's eyes teared up as he thought how their loyal dog had probably died trying to protect Janice, a task that should have fallen to Dan. Angrily, he wiped the tears away and stared off into space, shoving his hands into the pockets of his trousers to stop them from shaking with rage.

Pete was speaking to friends and relatives as they all stood looking at the flowers and wreaths on the floor outside the crematorium.

'We found her straightaway,' Pete explained to his niece Christine. 'Over the Yellow Mess, where she and Dan always walk Bryn and Maisie when they come to visit. She was in a terrible mess. Her head and chest were bleeding, she was unconscious, her breathing was ragged, all over the place. Dan knew as soon as he looked at her that she was past helping. He's seen it so many times, but it's different when it's your own family.'

'How's he doing though, Pete? Is he coping?' Christine asked. 'They've been together forever. What will he do?' She was looking over at Dan with concern.

'Honestly? I don't know. He's hardly spoken two words since. Wouldn't speak to the police. The only people he spoke to at the time were the paramedics. He knew one of them and he just switched into emergency mode, started dishing out orders, managed it like it was any other incident, travelled into hospital with her in the ambulance and wouldn't leave her side. He punched one of the doctors when he wanted to stop resuscitating her. Had to be taken outside by the police but it took bloody four of them.'

Pete looked at Dan. 'He won't go back to work, I know that. How can he go back to being a paramedic, dealing with this sort of thing all the time? It'll drive him barmy.'

He shook his head. 'He was talking about early retirement anyway. He'll have his Army pension before long and nearly fifteen years of NHS pension saved up that he can take early. He should be alright financially, but what will he do? He'll just dwell on things.'

'I'll talk to him,' Christine said. 'We were close growing up.'

Christine squeezed Pete's hand reassuringly and walked over to Dan, who was standing alone. She laid her hand on his arm. 'Hey.'

Dan looked at her, seeming to come out of a trance. 'Hey Chris, how are you?'

'I'm fine.' She smiled. 'What about you? Stupid question, I know. I don't even know where to start, what to say.'

Dan took Christine's hand. 'It's OK, I know it's awkward.' He looked around. Janice's family, the Crosslyn clan, were all there. Some looked drunk already. He knew if he stayed, things would inevitably get messy. He sighed. 'Shall we go? Find somewhere to have a drink?'

'OK. Sounds like a plan.' She followed Dan's gaze to the Crosslyns. 'Have they spoken to you yet?'

'No, but they will. Full of threats and plans of revenge, trying to find out who did it. You know what they're like. I can't be doing with it today. I've just put my wife to rest, I want to sort my head out.'

'Come on then. We'll go to mine. It'll be quieter there than a pub or a café.'

Dan nodded and they walked to the car park.

On the way to Christine's home, Dan looked out of the

side window of her car at the streets of Walsall. It was as if he were seeing the place for the first time, and he didn't like what he saw. He noticed that the first thing Christine did as they drove away was to lock the car doors. As they slowed down at junctions or traffic lights, Dan saw groups of listless youngsters hanging around. At a large crossroads on the main Wolverhampton Road, Dan saw one such group, some barely more than children, run up to a Jaguar that was waiting at a red light and grab the door to try and open it. When they found the door to be locked, they hurled abuse at the elderly couple inside as they kicked the panels of the car in frustration. They reminded Dan of a group of feral animals.

'Silly buggers must have left something valuable on show,' Christine said. 'Happens all the time along here.'

'Don't the police do anything?' Dan asked, incredulous.

'What can they do? If the police manage to get out of their cars, which would be a miracle, they wouldn't catch them. And even if they did, the courts let them off. The kids think it's all a game, they enjoy the chase. It gets worse every day. Last week, middle of the day, they dragged an old man out of his car and ran over his legs as they drove off with it. Happened down on the Green Lane traffic lights.'

'But that's where the police station is!' Dan couldn't believe what he was hearing.

'Yeah, I know. They haven't caught them either. Probably never will.' Christine shrugged. 'Should've locked his doors, silly sod.'

Dan shook his head in disbelief. Since when had the

blame shifted onto the victims? How had society changed so drastically that adults were terrified of children?

As they turned off Wolverhampton Road, Dan heard a loud bang, sounding uncomfortably like the sharp crack of a gunshot, right behind him. Startled, he turned around in his seat. He saw a group of children, the oldest probably no more than twelve, standing defiantly in the road behind them.

'Bait,' Christine explained. 'They throw stones at passing cars they don't recognise from the estate, then if the driver stops to have a go at them a gang of older kids appear and mug the driver or steal the car. Best to just ignore them. It's because I haven't had this car long, they don't know it yet. Once they realise I'm from the estate, they'll ignore it.'

Dan could only stare at the children in disbelief as Christine drove away.

She carried on, regaling Dan with stories of the lawlessness in the town nowadays. 'You remember the Wilsons? Used to knock about with us when we were kids?'

'Yeah, I do. Nice family.'

'Yeah, they are. Rita Wilson has got kids of her own now, always brought them up right, kept them out of bother. Always polite, they are. One of them, the eldest girl, she was in a night club in town last month, suddenly collapsed and started fitting. Witnesses saw a young man who said he was her brother rush to help her. He said she was epileptic, and she wouldn't need an ambulance or anything. As she came round, he helped her outside where he robbed her. I dread to think what would've happened if the bouncers hadn't been suspicious and gone after her to check it out. Apparently it happens a lot. She's never had a fit in her life, but some lunatic is going round with a Taser or something and zapping girls in packed nightclubs, making it look like they're having a fit, then robbing them.' She looked at Dan. 'Or worse.'

Half an hour later they were sitting at Christine's kitchen table drinking coffee. Dan put his cup down and rubbed his face with both hands. 'I don't know what to make of it, Chris. If I thought it was an accident, that would be bad enough, but this? How bad has this country got? What is going on? She was just walking the bloody dogs.'

Chris held his hands in hers. 'I know, it's horrible. Do the police know anything yet?'

Dan shook his head. 'They're not telling me much. I told them to piss off after they started asking me for a bloody alibi. Useless bastards. As if they could miss the tyre tracks and bits of bike debris next to her body. Maybe they should be looking for who is riding stolen bikes around Coalpool these days. It used to be the Waynright family, and the Bortons. They're all dead now though. Who should I be looking for? I'm out of touch. Who does the thieving round here these days?'

'You shouldn't be looking for anyone, Dan. You'll get into trouble. You know what the law is like in this country. You'll end up being the bad guy.'

Dan looked up at her. 'Do you think I care? They killed Jan. Someone ran her over, stabbed her, and robbed her while she was dying on the floor. Bryn was still on the lead.

If they'd walked away, he couldn't have hurt them. The lead was still wrapped around Jan's wrist. Instead the bastards stabbed him.' He hung his head. 'Bryn was lying across Jan's body. He died trying to protect her. That was my job. I should have been there. I bloody wasn't though, was I?'

'Dan, you can't do this. It's not your fault, you can't blame yourself. How many times have you and Jan walked over there? Christ, we all grew up on the Yellow Mess. Spent more time there as kids than we did at home. No one's ever been killed there before. How could you know this was going to happen?'

'Maybe not. But it's happened now, hasn't it? There have to be consequences. Even if the police catch them, they'll do a couple of years in nick and come out and do it again. What's the bloody point?' He took a sip of his coffee. 'No, someone did this, and they'll pay for it. I left Walsall a long time ago, but it stays in you, doesn't it?'

Chris looked at Dan, worry creasing her face. 'What do you mean? What stays in you?'

'The violence. It's always there, just under the surface. Waiting, wanting an excuse.'

'Come on, Dan, it's not like that. You were never like that.'

'Really? Remember when Alex Chambers got beaten up on the Sandhole field? Had his head staved in with half a house brick. He had to have a metal plate put in his skull. He was thirteen years old, for Christ's sake. Just having a kickabout on the field. That happened because we were on the wrong football pitch on the wrong day. The Roscoes wanted the pitch and did that to Alex. When Alex's brothers caught up with the Roscoes, I went with them. I pointed the Roscoes out, and I helped the Chambers brothers when they dished out their revenge. Kelvin Roscoe didn't walk for six months. Clyde Roscoe was eating through a straw for the next ten years till he died, so I heard. I was thirteen years old. And the stuff I did in the Army … I've never been a saint, have I? It's always there, simmering under the surface.' Dan's fists clenched on the table.

Christine stood up and turned to the window. 'Maybe so, but you've spent the last fifteen years helping people, haven't you? Fighting back was never a crime when we grew up, it was never a choice. It was a bloody necessity. I never knew you to start a fight. Don't start this one now, please.' She sat down again across the table from Dan. 'Stay with us for a bit. The kids haven't seen you for ages. Let me help for a while. Malcolm would love to have you around too. We've been married nearly as long as you and Janice, we all grew up together. He's always on about those times. Come on, what do you say?'

Dan smiled at her and shook his head. 'Thanks, Chris, I know you mean well, but what sort of company would I be at the moment? I don't think I'd be a good influence on your kids. Besides,' he stood up and drained his coffee mug, 'I've got to look after the old man. He's not well. All this is hard on him too. You know how he doted on Jan. There's other stuff I need to speak to him about, but that'll have to wait. Thanks for the chat. I appreciate it, honestly.'

Christine gave Dan a lift back to the crematorium. On

the way, they both sat in a comfortable silence, lost in their own thoughts. At the crematorium car park, Dan looked over to where the service had been held for Janice but he couldn't bring himself to walk over there. Turning to Christine, he thanked her, they hugged and Dan promised to stay in touch, but neither of them believed it. Janice was always the one that kept the social group together. Dan was a loner, always had been. As she watched him drive away, Chris muttered a quiet prayer. 'God help you, Dan. And God help those bastards if you catch up with them before the police do.'

Chapter 3

After leaving the wake, Pete pulled his car up onto the driveway. Looking at his house, he could see something wasn't right but couldn't put his finger on it. Getting out of the car, he took a moment to steady himself and catch his breath, and grabbed his walking stick from the front seat well. As he closed the car door and turned towards the house, he realised what was wrong.

'Bastards!' He strode towards the up-and-over garage door. The top padlock was in pieces on the floor and there was damage around the central key slot. He grabbed the door and lifted it up, grunting with the exertion. Fumbling inside for the light switch, he hesitated before switching it on, the sick feeling in the pit of his stomach telling him what he would find. Or not find.

The light flickered on, and he slumped against the wall. 'Thieving little bastards.' He stumbled into the garage, kicking aside his tools that had been scattered over the floor. His bike was missing. The padlock and chain lay useless on the floor, cut with his own electric grinder, by the looks of things. His motorcycle was missing. In its usual space was a piece of A4 paper with writing on it: *£2000 or its burnd. Look on FLASHPIC we wil tel you when + wher to pay ☺ KEEPERS.*

Pete spun around, slammed down the garage door and walked up to his gate, looking up and down the road as if he could still catch them, but he knew it was too late.

Clenching his fists, Pete said to himself, 'Little scumbags, thieving little scumbags. I'll bloody kill 'em if I get my hands on 'em.'

He took a deep breath and fumbled in his pocket for his phone to call Dan. As he did so, he felt suddenly weary. He put out his right arm to the gatepost to steady himself. His left arm pulled across the left side of his chest as pain rumbled around his chest like thunder. He gasped and half fell, only the gatepost keeping him upright. Slowly he slid to the floor. He fumbled in his pocket for his phone again, but couldn't stop his hands from shaking. It felt like someone was hammering his ribcage from the inside, trying to get out. His left arm was heavy, and pain shot up his neck and into his jaw.

As Pete slipped onto his side, he heard gravel crunching on his driveway. He looked up and saw Dan's black 110 Land Rover pulling in.

'Too bloody late, son. Too bloody late,' he muttered as he slipped into blessed unconsciousness.

Dan jumped out of the car and dropped down next to Pete. 'Dad! Dad! What happened? Dad, can you hear me?' For the second time in his life, Dan dialled 999 as an off-duty paramedic. After giving the details to the call-handler on the other end of the line, he threw his phone down and ran to his car to grab his response bag.

Returning to his father, he took in the scene. Pete lying on the floor, unconscious, blue lips, shallow breathing, clammy skin. Known history of heart problems. Dan knew that the most likely cause of the collapse was a heart attack. He quickly assembled his oxygen set and put a mask over his father's face, talking to him all the time. He needed him to regain consciousness so he could give him some aspirin and spray some GTN under his tongue, but Pete remained unresponsive. His breathing slowed perceptibly, and Dan desperately looked around for the ambulance.

He could hear sirens in the distance and he prayed they were for his call. He had rolled Pete onto his side, but he could see that his breathing was very shallow now. He felt for a radial pulse at Pete's wrist but couldn't feel one. He checked the carotid pulse and could barely feel a rhythm, but he could tell that the rate was too slow. He counted the pulses and measured the gaps between them. One beat every three seconds, which meant a heartrate of twenty beats per minute. That wouldn't sustain life for long.

Dan rolled his father onto his back and began to carry out chest compressions to stimulate the heart into picking up its own rhythm again. Having done this for so many patients in his fifteen-year career as a paramedic, he knew that the outcome was usually poor. Few patients who suffer a cardiac arrest outside of hospital survive to tell the tale. Dan counted out the thirty compressions and used his inflated bag-valve-mask from his response kit to deliver two breaths. Then he was straight back on the chest for thirty more chest compressions. 'Come on, Dad, fight. Come on, don't give up.'

He heard an ambulance pull up next to his car. The crew jumped out of the vehicle, automatically kicking up a gear when they saw the situation in front of them. The lead paramedic knelt down next to Dan. He looked at him as recognition dawned. 'Shit, Dan, what happened? Let me take over, mate, while you tell me.'

'Let me manage the airway, Sam.' Dan grabbed his bag and grabbed an endotracheal tube and laryngoscope. 'Who are you with?' he asked as he slid the tube down Pete's throat into the trachea, inflating the tube balloon to hold it in place. He fitted the mouthpiece that secured everything and listened to the chest to check the tube was in the right place.

'Mickey Jones – he's just grabbing the defib.' Sam started chest compressions as Mickey arrived and attached the defibrillation pads to Pete's chest. He nodded in recognition at Dan, but remained professionally detached. Dan appreciated the reaction as he knew that Pete's best chance lay in the hands of these two experienced colleagues, and he allowed them to do their job, trusting in them completely.

'VF rhythm. Charging defib, 120 joules,' Mickey advised. Sam carried on with chest compressions, while Dan switched off the oxygen. A high-pitched continuous beep announced that the machine was fully charged.

'Stand clear,' Mickey ordered. Dan and Sam sat back on

their haunches, lifting their hands to show they were clear. 'Shock now,' Mickey said, and pressed the red button on the front of the machine. Pete bucked off the floor and Dan and Sam immediately continued with their tasks. Mickey fitted a long red needle into the intraosseous drill and pushed it to Pete's leg, into the tibial plateau bone just below the knee. Dan heard the whirring as the drill twisted the needle deep into the marrow, to allow the intravenous drugs to be administered. 'Line in,' Mickey confirmed. He pushed a saline flush through the needle and pressed the call button on his radio. '5698 to Control, confirmed cardiac arrest. Do you have estimated time of arrival of second crew, please?'

'Whiskey Mike Control, ETA second crew one minute. Out,' came the crackled reply.

The second crew arrived as Mickey was delivering the second defibrillation shock. 'Stand clear, 150 joules.' He looked around to confirm no one was touching the patient and delivered the second shock. Again, Pete arched and flopped to the floor. No sign of any change.

The lead paramedic from the second crew came over at a jog, took one look at the scene and asked, 'What do you guys need?'

'Scoop stretcher, straps, set up a bag of saline in the back of our truck,' Sam replied.

She nodded and ran back to the ambulances, telling her colleague what was needed. As she returned with a scoop carry stretcher, Mickey advised it was time for the third rhythm check.

'Still VF, charging 200 joules now,' he said after checking

the monitor screen.

Dan looked up at the waiting second crew. 'We'll move him after this shock and drugs, OK?' Seeing their hesitation at taking instruction from a civilian, he turned to Sam. 'That OK with you, matey?'

Sam nodded in confirmation and told Mickey to push in 1 mg of adrenaline and 300 mg of amiodarone through the intraosseous needle. The second crew started to fit the scoop stretcher around Pete, ready for the move.

Before long, Dan was travelling in the back of an ambulance, blues and twos wailing, en route to Walsall Manor Hospital Emergency Department, for the second time in a month. He sat in the passenger seat in the back and watched numbly as Sam and Mickey worked hard to save his father. One of the second crew was driving the ambulance, to allow more clinicians to help the patient in the back.

As he watched his colleagues, Dan knew it would be futile. There had been no changes, except that Pete's heart rhythm had now switched to asystole, or flatline. Unlike on television, there were no more defibrillation shocks needed. A flatline heart was a dead heart, and more defibrillator shocks only fried it. Repeated doses of intravenous adrenaline and good CPR provided the only hope now.

At the hospital, Dan jumped out of the back of the ambulance and motored the ramp down as the paramedic crew rolled the stretcher down, still managing to continue CPR as they hurried into the Resuscitation Room. Dan hung back outside. He already knew. He'd been here too many times over the years. He knew that everything had been done that could have been done, but there had been no changes, no return of a pulse, no response. Sitting on the bench outside the Emergency Department, he wondered who he should call. When Sam came out to find him fifteen minutes later, he barely heard his words.

'Sorry, Dan … did everything … no changes, no response … They called it just now. So sorry, mate.'

He nodded up at Sam, mumbled some words of thanks, and turned to make his way back to his father's house.

Mickey was drying his hands on a piece of paper towelling as he came out and stood next to Sam. They watched Dan walk across the car park to the hospital exit.

'Shit, he's had a rough deal lately. Should we go and get him, see if he wants to sit and talk it through?' Sam said.

Mickey just shook his head. 'I've known Dan a long time. He's more comfortable in his own company. Sociable enough when he needs to be, but keeps his distance from people. I don't think talking will do much for him right now. The police haven't found out much about what happened to his wife, and that must be destroying him. It was no simple accident, that's for sure. You know Dan used to be in the Army? If he ever finds out who murdered his wife …' He tossed the paper towel into a nearby bin. 'I wouldn't want to be around when all hell breaks loose.'

Chapter 4

Dan walked away from the hospital and back to his father's house in a daze. First Jan, now Dad. 'What the hell is going wrong with my life?' he wondered aloud. For the first time in what seemed like ages, he craved company. He called Christine and asked her to meet him at his Dad's house. After she had agreed and he hung up, he realised that she wouldn't know about Pete. 'Christ!' He stopped and leaned against the railings, traffic on the Wolverhampton Road crawling past in the usual gridlocked fashion. He watched a few of the cars going by for a minute or two, their occupants busy with a hundred different things, some of them even concentrating on driving. Watching people like this, from a short distance, he was shocked at how aggressive everyone seemed to be. Seeing everyday people driving too close to each other, accelerating into the path of other cars, just so they could be offended and sound their horns loudly, waving arms and hands out of car windows in obscene gestures, their faces scowling and contorted with rage, Dan was saddened by how society was changing. Eventually he carried on walking, just placing one foot in front of the other, trying to gather his thoughts before he met up with Christine.

He had the sudden realisation that if it wasn't for Christine, he would have absolutely no one in the world and he felt guilty that he had neglected his relationship with her over the last few years. Janice was his wife, and his father was the only other person that Dan had any sort of regular contact with, outside of work. He had thought little, if at all, of his family outside of his immediate circle.

And what of work? How could he go back now? Dan felt, rightly or wrongly, that he had failed to save the two people in his life that he cared most about, so how could he go back to working in a profession that existed to do the same for complete strangers? He would miss the camaraderie of his work colleagues, although there were very few that he considered friends, and none of them close friends. Dan had felt himself slowly becoming separated from the comings and goings of those around him in the Ambulance Service. When he first started in the Service, he would return to station after a call-out and be met with banter, chit-chat, a brew and general socialising. Nowadays, returning to station was generally a quiet affair. If there were any ambulance crews on standby, they would invariably be sitting in silence, noses buried in their mobile phones, finding companionship in a virtual reality that Dan did not understand, nor have any desire to. He realised that he would not miss his work colleagues at all. And as he was not on the virtual reality network of social media, he doubted that they would even realise he was gone.

As he crossed the road just before the M6 Junction 10 roundabout, an old Renault car stopped just behind him and the driver sounded the horn. Whirling around, ready to find an excuse, any excuse, just to vent some anger, expecting a loud-mouthed driver who was irritated by him crossing the busy road, he saw instead that Christine had pulled up next to him. She wound down her window. 'What's up, Dan? Where's your car?'

Dan took a breath, steadied himself mentally and got in the car. Ten minutes later they were pulling into Pete's drive, Christine barely able to drive through her tears. They got out of the car and Dan saw the debris left behind from the paramedics' Advanced Life Support kit. Paper wrappings from sterile kit, a torn-off printout from the defibrillator, a length of oxygen tubing. He picked it all up and walked over to the bin to dispose of it. 'Dad would hate this crap lying around his drive, you know what he's like,' he said to Christine. They both looked at each other as they realised the futility of what he had said, but Dan just shrugged and dumped it all in the bin. As he walked past the garage door, he noticed the pieces of padlock on the floor and the damaged door lock. He lifted up the door and stepped inside, seeing the usual immaculate garage but noticing the huge gap where Pete's pride and joy normally leaned on its side-stand. Dan picked up the piece of A4 paper and read the message.

'What's this mean?'

Chris took the piece of paper off him, read it and looked at Dan. 'This must have been what did it to him. The heart attack. This pushed him over the edge.' Tears welled up in her eyes again.

Dan nodded, his eyes seeming to darken. He looked at the paper. 'What's this "Flashpic" stuff?'

'Let's go inside. I'll tell you what I can.'

They sat at Pete's kitchen table, sipping coffee. All around them was spotless order with a place for everything and everything in its place. Pete always knew how to keep a clean house and he never understood how single men could sometimes be so damned slovenly when keeping things clean was much easier. Christine tapped fingers on her phone, quicker than Dan could try to keep up with.

'It's this local bunch of thugs and thieves we've got problems with now. They call themselves the "Keepers", as in finders keepers. They claim that if they "find" something that belongs to someone else, they can keep it, or sell it back. They're a pain in the backside. The police aren't doing anything, as usual. They're all over the internet. Can you believe they've got followers and fans?'

Dan shook his head. 'Why? Who would look up to scum like that? What's wrong with this town?'

She shrugged. 'It's been rotten for a long time, we both know that. Don't be fooled into thinking it's just here either. It's a nationwide problem. But it's worse lately. It's as if the internet and bloody social media has sent crime out of control. But even worse than that, it's made it respectable, almost compulsory behaviour. Last week they stole a dog from someone's back garden and threatened to hang it off a railway bridge unless the owner paid them a grand. They posted a video of the dog tied up on Mill Lane railway bridge with a rope round its neck. That sick video actually attracted a hundred and twenty "likes" online.'

'Jesus.' Dan looked horrified. 'What happened?'

'It was in all the papers. That time, they left the dog tied up so the owner could fetch it back in one piece after she'd left the cash in a bag where the old dog pound used to be. They have to keep their side of the deal every so often or no one will pay up.'

'Scumbags,' Dan spat. 'They think this is acceptable behaviour? Stealing from old men? Killing pets? Taking whatever they like?' He stopped. 'Wait. Hang on a minute. Are they a big gang?'

'I'm not sure. Probably. All the kids talk about them like they're legends. Why?'

'Who else would be riding stolen bikes over the Yellow Mess?'

Chris realised where Dan was going with this. 'No, Dan, you can't. You're not in the Army any more. You're one man, they're a violent gang, with no rules, no conscience, nothing to lose. They're evil. They're beyond the law.'

'No, Chris. They're yobs and bullies. And they have plenty to lose. And who mentioned the law? Now.' He pointed to her phone. 'Show me how this Flashpic works. I want to pay them for the bike.'

Chris sighed, knowing that if she didn't show him, he'd do it himself anyway. And deep down, she knew he had to do this, or he would literally go insane. Part of her wanted him to take them on, teach the scum a lesson. She just prayed he hadn't lost his edge. She found the Keepers' Flashpic page and looked for the Triumph.

'There. That's it, isn't it?'

Dan peered at the video on the screen. A young man, heavily muscled and tattooed, was riding the old Triumph across a dirt track. In the background was a building covered in graffiti surrounded by a mesh fence that obviously wasn't keeping graffiti artists out. The young man had his shirt off and was grinning at the camera as he revved the old engine hard and tried to pull a wheelie. He skidded, dropped the bike and rolled off into long grass, reappearing into shot a couple of seconds later. The person filming him could be heard laughing.

'You fuckin idiot, Welchy, you're useless!'

The hapless rider, now identified online for all to hear, just laughed.

'Piss off, Jonah, it's a piece of crap. It's got no fuckin power, man.' He kicked the bike. 'Fuck it, I'm gonna torch it anyway.' He reached into his pocket.

'Nah man, don't do that. Deano told us this is worth two G and he's the boss. He'll fuck you up if we don't get that cash.' The camera pointed to the floor and erratically showed angled images of both young men as they argued, then it lifted up as Welchy flicked lit matches at the petrol tank, which was leaking fuel due to the bike lying on its side. It didn't take too many attempts before one of the matches had the desired effect and flames whooshed up around the Triumph. Welchy jumped up and down near the bike, then turned to the camera, pumping his fist in the air.

He shouted, 'Fire 'em up, fire 'em up!' Then, staring straight into the camera and snarling, he warned, 'Dis is what happens when you don't pay the Keepers.'

'Welchy. I know that name.' Dan wracked his memories of his formative years, growing up in Walsall. 'We knew the whole family. They're from the Goscote estate, remember, Chris? Larry Welch is the same age as me, and Richard Welch was the dad. They're all thieves, dole dossers, troublemakers. Useless feeders, as the old man would have called them.' Tears quickly formed in his eyes. Wiping angrily at his face, he had a sudden thought. 'Hang on. Is this live?'

'I think so. Looks like it. Usually they leave stuff on as they film it, then they delete it. It's untraceable that way.'

'Can't trace them? How much more info do they need, for Christ's sake? I've been watching it for less than a minute and I've got a description, three names, and a location.'

'A location? What do you mean?'

Dan stood up, grabbed his Land Rover keys and headed for the door. 'That's the Black Track. From Mill Lane in the Butts. It runs along the back of Borneo Street. That power sub-station with the graffiti? That graffiti has been there for years, since I was a kid. I know where they are. Here.' He threw the house keys to Christine. 'Lock up for me and I'll be in touch soon.'

'Wait, Dan. Hang on …' Chris started to say, but Dan was gone. She heard his Land Rover roar out of the drive. She got up and made herself another coffee. 'Serves 'em bloody right. That's what I reckon.' She thought about calling her husband and asking him to go and provide some backup for Dan, but changed her mind. Her husband had always been the gentle one in the group when they were kids, that's what had attracted her to him then, and he hadn't changed as he'd grown older. Besides, whatever Dan had planned, she knew he wouldn't want too many people knowing about it. 'Probably best to just let him deal with it. He'll be fine,' she muttered under her breath as she sipped her coffee. 'It's everybody else that won't be.'

Chapter 5

The day before Janice's death

Dan sat in the waiting room, reading an old motorcycling magazine he'd picked up from the pile in the corner, not really taking it in, just skimming through the pages, wanting the appointment over and yet not wanting to go into the consultant's room. Years spent working in the NHS had given him a sixth sense about when news wasn't going to be good. He was debating whether to just leave when one of the receptionists called him in.

'Dr Jeffreys will see you now, Mr Travis.' She smiled and returned to her computer screen. Dan always wondered what the receptionists in places like this found to look at all the time on their computers. He guessed that eBay and Amazon did a roaring trade during working hours. Dropping the bike magazine back onto the pile, he walked to Room 4.

'Ah, Dan, come in, have a seat. How are you feeling?' The consultant stood as Dan entered the room, another indication that news wasn't good.

'I don't know, Dr Jeffreys, I was kind of hoping you could tell me how things are going to be feeling?' He smiled as he sat in the uncomfortable NHS chair.

'Quite, quite. Yes. I meant how are things since I saw you last month? You'd suggested that you were about to retire early from the Ambulance Service and return to lecturing?'

'Well, I applied for early retirement last year as soon as I turned fifty. These things take time though. You know how the wheels of the NHS turn slowly. It came through this week, so I'm on leave now for a month, using it all up till my finishing date. I've been offered a lecturing position at Wolverhampton University on their Paramedic Science programme, and I can start in August, ready for the September intake. But, it all depends on what you're about to tell me, really, doesn't it?'

Dan had been referred to Dr Jeffreys, Consultant Oncologist after finally going to see his GP about his recurring headaches. His GP had referred him to the Neurology Department for head scans and MRIs, then out of the blue a letter had arrived from the Oncology Department at the local hospital. Dan knew right then that it wasn't going to be a great result. Strangely, the headaches had improved since the letter arrived.

Of all the consultants to be referred to, he had landed with Jeffreys. He'd known Jeffreys for years, since treating him as a patient when he'd had a heart attack while hillwalking on the Wrekin. As always happens, Jeffreys had collapsed right at the top of the hill. Dan had managed to get to him in time, giving lifesaving thrombolysis drugs before getting him flown by air ambulance helicopter to University Hospital North Staffs for specialist treatment. Dan's rapid diagnosis and treatment was most of the reason that Jeffreys was still sitting here now.

'Well, the tables are turned for us now, Dan. You know how much I appreciate what you and your colleagues did for me a few years ago, and I want you to know that I will do everything I can for you. But the news isn't good.' He leaned forwards on his desk, clasping his hands together. 'I know you're a direct person so I'll tell you straight. You have a GBM, a glioblastoma multiforme, which I'm sure you're aware is a type of brain tumour. It's still in early stages, and there are treatment options that we need to consider and get started on immediately.'

Dan reeled. He was prepared for bad news, but this was way more than he had expected. 'Are you sure? I mean, of course you're sure but …'

'I have personally overseen your scans and tests. There's no doubt. I'm sorry.'

Dan knew that this type of brain cancer diagnosis was as bad as it could get. From what he recalled, GBM meant that the tumour spreads tendrils into the brain tissue, making it difficult to fully remove.

'We have to discuss treatments. Right now. No pussyfooting about. Every day counts with this diagnosis. You do understand what I'm saying to you?'

Dan struggled to focus. All of his and Janice's plans, up in smoke. Finishing with the Ambulance Service, no more night shifts, no weekends, no dealing with drunks trying to fight the world. They'd made plans to travel, recently bought a dog from the local rescue centre, Janice had cut her working hours right down. Now this. How was he going to tell her?

He picked up on what Jeffreys was saying.

'There's an experimental treatment. It's been trialled in the States and Eastern Europe but only just gained approval in the UK. I've been to Poland for conferences about this, and I think that it's a good option for you. It's not guaranteed, but results have been promising so far.'

'Go on. What do I need to do?'

'Well, we have to go through the options, informed consent and so on.'

'Forget that crap. You're the expert. I'm not one of your patients who's going to backtrack and sue you when the treatment doesn't work. It's experimental. I get it. It's not guaranteed. I get it. I might still die. I get it. Let's get on with it.' Dan leaned forwards and put his hand on Jeffreys' desk. 'Where do I sign?'

'Hold your horses!' Jeffreys smiled sympathetically. 'At least let me tell you what it is. Then if you agree, we'll start things rolling.' He pulled out some documents from a desk drawer. 'Initially we take a biopsy. We use the cells we remove to develop a vaccine. That's the experimental part. It's not a simple case of surgical removal of the tumour, as it lays roots in the brain cortex. Trials have suggested that there is no benefit from chemotherapy treatment, and the plus side of that is that there are no horrible side effects. With me so far?'

Dan nodded, his professional brain taking over now, detaching himself from the terrifying personal consequences.

'The vaccine we create is injected back into the tumour. Tests have shown that initially this can increase the tumour size but then it rapidly shrinks. Combined with radiotherapy and steroids, the tumour shrinks and doesn't grow as aggressively.'

'Sounds like a plan.' Dan clenched his fist. 'Let's start.'

'There are complications, and restrictions on the evidence. You should be aware of these.' Jeffreys took Dan's nod as assent, so he carried on. 'There are very few trials with GBM as the primary cancer, due to the rarity of the condition and the rapid decline of patients. But I think you are in the optimum stage of the diagnosis, thanks to your GP picking this up early. Also in some patients, the initial increase in size of the tumour is non-reversible. It continues to expand, then metastasises and the cancer spreads. This is always fatal. It usually happens with bone cancers, but there are no guarantees.'

'OK, you've given me the statutory spiel, now let's cut to the chase.' Dan fixed Jeffreys with a direct stare. 'If you were the patient, what would you do? I asked you once to trust me. Now I'm trusting you.'

Jeffreys leaned back in his chair. 'With conventional treatment, GBM kills most patients in less than a year. Even successful treatment rarely extends life past two years. If it were me, I'd grab this treatment with both hands. No question. You're an otherwise very fit and strong man with a positive mental state. I couldn't find a more suitable patient for this treatment. I'm so sorry, Dan.'

'Not your fault, matey.' Dan smiled. 'Let's get on with it then.'

Chapter 6

Dan drove down Mill Lane, the waste ground of the Yellow Mess on the left and the Monkey Hills on the right. At the bottom of the hill used to be a dog pound, but it was demolished in the 1980s and replaced with a car park, which was now full of illegally dumped household waste. No one in their right mind would leave a car there and go for a walk. The end result would be vandalism or theft. Yet there was never a soul in sight. So where did the vandals and thieves come from? It always reminded Dan of one of those old horror movies where the monsters scented humans and crawled out of hidden places. The Monkey Hills used to be a freight train loading and shunt yard, demolished in the 1950s. It got its name a few decades later. Two air raid shelters, still left in place on top of the hills, provided refuge for all sorts of unsavoury events and goings-on, and the noise that came from the area at night sounded like incessant monkey chatter.

As Dan drove past the Monkey Hills and up to the railway bridge, he slowed down. From this vantage point he could see along the length of the Black Track, named after the dark gravelly soil that formed the track. It was actually slag from the mining waste of the area but formed a hard-wearing track through the waste ground of the urban forest. At the far end, he could make out two young men jumping around next to a fire. They were in plain sight of the houses in Borneo Street that backed onto the Black Track, but no one came out to interfere these days.

He carried on over the bridge and down the other side, taking the turn off onto the Black Track. Some locals used this as access to their back gardens so it wasn't unusual to see cars driven along it. He drove slowly at first, making no sudden moves or appearing like he would challenge the young men. As he got closer, he could see that the object on fire was a motorcycle. The flames were too intense to make out any detail, but he guessed it was his dad's Triumph Bonneville. 'Bastards,' he growled. As he drew level with the rear of the last house on Borneo Street, he slowed further as if he was going to turn into the driveway at the back of the house. Of course, the house had strengthened and padlocked rear gates, and so he stopped the Land Rover as if he was going to get out and unlock them.

This piqued the interest of the two young men and they started to walk towards him, sensing something else to steal or rob. Dan pretended to fumble with his keys, then looked up and noticed the men. He made a move to get back in his Land Rover and the two young men started to sprint towards him, as he had guessed they would. What they weren't expecting was a two-tonne Land Rover to suddenly do a U-turn and accelerate towards them.

Unwilling to believe that someone would actually confront them, they stood still, confused for a couple of seconds. It was all the time Dan needed. He aimed for the larger of the two, the muscular one identified in the video as Welchy. The other one, a weaselly individual who lacked the confrontational aggression of his friend, but possessed slightly more street sense, dived out of the way at the last second, while Welchy stood in a "come and have a go if you think you're hard enough" stance as the Land Rover roared straight at him.

As the front grille of the Land Rover connected with the man's waist, the look on his face was sheer disbelief. The front of the Land Rover struck his upper legs, instantly shattering one of his femurs. His head bounced off the bonnet and he was flung backwards onto the dark shale of the Black Track. The three injuries – abdominal injury, head injury and fractured femur, known as Waddell's triad – caused instant loss of consciousness and Dan slammed the brakes on and skidded to a halt before he ran over the inert body.

The other scumbag was away on his toes and pumping his arms madly as he ran. Dan got a good look at his face as he turned round in a panic to see if he'd escaped, and muttered, 'I'll see you soon, matey. You can count on that.' He turned to Welchy and dragged him to the back of the Land Rover. He dumped him unceremoniously in the back, then rolled him over into a recovery position. 'Don't want you choking on me just yet, I've got plans for you.' He slammed the back door shut and spun the Land Rover around, kicking up a dust cloud of shale that he hoped would shield his registration plates from prying eyes. He exited the Black Track where he had joined it, turned left and headed out towards Walsall town centre, and then onto Wolverhampton Road where he joined the M6 motorway at Junction 10.

Miraculously the traffic was moving at a steady pace, so Dan joined the flow of traffic and calmly headed home. He knew his passenger wasn't going to wake up any time soon, so he drove carefully, not attracting attention to himself. Home was less than an hour away, and he mulled over his plans en route.

Chapter 7

D an reversed his Land Rover into his garage and parked
it next to Janice's small Peugeot. He and Janice had
moved to this secluded barn conversion about ten years ago.
As he dragged Welchy out of the back of the Land Rover
and into the garage, he fought back tears as he remembered
Janice's first look when she saw the place. She had loved
it from the start, as had Dan. It was surrounded by fields
on three sides and the Wrekin hill to the front. They had
demolished the farmhouse that used to stand nearby five
years ago due to subsidence, which the converted barn had
luckily avoided. They also owned two derelict outbuildings,
which Dan had renovated and now used as a garage and
a workshop. The nearest neighbour was about half a mile
away on Gluddley Farm. Unless someone was watching
Dan's home from the old disused shooting ranges on the
north side of the Wrekin, it would be very unlikely that he
would be observed, but he took no chances. Pulling the
garage doors closed, he set to work on his patient.

Most paramedics have an unauthorised and not
entirely legal response kit that they maintain at home for

emergencies. Known about but mostly overlooked by the Ambulance Service management, these range from Basic Life Support kits for use in a cardiac arrest situation only, to the type like Dan's. He had almost a full range of emergency Advanced Life Support and Trauma equipment, and most of the drugs needed, except for the controlled drugs like morphine and diazepam.

Dan placed a sturdy old wooden chair he and Janet had been meaning to sell on top of a tarpaulin and, with a little difficulty, dragged Welchy from the car and set him down in it. He then set up an oximeter to measure his pulse and oxygen levels, then did a quick set of observations to establish overall status. A clear airway and no serious damage to the chest wall or lungs meant that the patient was breathing normally. But his blood pressure was a little low and he had a pulse of one hundred and thirty per minute, which Dan knew were indications of an internal bleed somewhere. That needed controlling if he was going to get information out of this thief.

Welchy wasn't wearing a shirt (he liked to show off his steroid-induced muscles to intimidate people) and Dan could see that there was no bruising around the liver, no rigidity or swelling of the abdomen that might indicate internal bleeding. It must be the femurs, Dan though. He cut Welchy's trousers off with a pair of Tuff-Kut scissors and looked at his legs. Sure enough the left thigh looked swollen and deformed. A probable fractured femur and maybe a shattered pelvis. Acting quickly, Dan wrapped a pelvic splint around Welchy and pulled it tight. That would help to control the bleeding inside the pelvis, which was often hidden but could leak enough to kill a person if not corrected. Next he applied a splint to the left leg, stretching it first, applying traction to the long bones of the femur. This was sometimes all that was needed to stem the blood loss, allowing the body's own clotting mechanism time to staunch the blood flow. Applying traction must have been painful, as even in his unconscious state, Welchy groaned.

Next Dan slid an intravenous catheter into Welchy's antecubital fossa, a thick superficial vein in the crook of the elbow favoured by drug addicts the world over, and indeed Welchy's arms bore the scars of old track marks. He set up a bag of 0.9% sodium chloride to replace the body fluid lost so far, then prepared some tranexamic acid to inject through the cannula. This would coagulate the blood and promote clotting. He pushed one gram slowly into the cannula, as administering the acid too quickly could cause the blood pressure to drop. After about five minutes, he rechecked the blood pressure and pulse rate. Both seemed to be holding steady, and ten minutes after that they showed signs of improvement.

There was a large bruise and swelling on the left side of Welchy's face, but if there was a serious head injury there, Dan knew there was nothing he could do about that at the moment, except take him to hospital. And that wasn't part of his plan.

Lastly, Dan took several zip ties from a drawer in his workbench and went about securing Welchy's wrists, forearms and ankles to the solid wooden chair. Satisfied that he had done all he could for now, he leaned against the tyre of the Land Rover and closed his eyes. If the pulse rate measured by the oximeter machine dropped below fifty, or raised above one hundred and thirty, an alarm would sound and he would wake up, but for now, Dan knew he needed sleep. He planned on having a chat with his patient when he woke up, and he needed to be rested before then. His eyes closed and he slipped into a peaceful doze. The sun set on the western horizon behind the garage and the light slowly dimmed inside, leaving Dan and his patient peacefully awaiting events of the next morning.

<u>Chapter 8</u>

Janice's Peugeot crawled slowly along Bedders Road with Dan at the wheel and Welchy slumped across the rear seats, still unconscious and snoring heavily. Every time Dan drove the small car over one of Walsall's ubiquitous speed bumps, Welchy grunted as his head lolled. Dan could not recall ever driving in any place that had so many speed bumps. It was probably to dissuade joyriders, which Dan suspected was unsuccessful. Normally Dan wouldn't really notice speed bumps, but the Peugeot wasn't quite wide enough to straddle the tarmac-raised sections of road, and the suspension wasn't as forgiving as the Land Rover. Still, the little French car served a useful purpose. Small, dark and with the number plates removed and stowed in the boot, the Peugeot was about as non-descript as a car could get.

The streets of the estate were quiet at that time of morning, the drudge of workers heading off to the daily grind not being a significant feature of this community. Looking around at the houses as he drove along the road, Dan didn't think that they looked that much different since his childhood; in fact, if anything they had changed for the worse. Drab red-bricked semi-detached houses were mostly surrounded by ill-tended yards that were once gardens, now strewn with car tyres and plastic children's garden toys, broken and weather-faded. Some yards had caravans rotting away slowly, obscuring any light that might have sneaked into front windows. Wheelie bins stood next to front doors, as if on guard.

Most households here used side or back doors as the main entrance anyway, a habit that Dan had noticed in many similar housing estates in various towns, but one which he could never fathom. As a paramedic he had often responded to emergencies in houses like these, knocked on the front door ready to administer instant lifesaving treatment, only to be greeted with a shout of 'Go around the back, we don't use that door!'. This street looked no different to those areas, except that from his own experience of growing up around here, and subsequent recent events, this area was inexorably linked in his brain to violent memories and feelings of depression. He wondered how kids growing up here nowadays were ever supposed to make anything of themselves. The very buildings that they lived in seemed to set the scene for the rest of their lives. Most had red-and-white flags of St George hanging out of upstairs windows, still left in situ despite the national football team's poor efforts that summer, tattered and threadbare now.

Dan noticed a few mopeds and scooters leaning against the walls of some of the houses and thought that these must belong to members of the Keepers, otherwise they would have been stolen. Not for the first time, Dan contemplated how many young men around here considered themselves to be Keepers. The task of finding out which of the gangsters and thieves were responsible for Janice's death suddenly seemed immense and overwhelming. These streets seemed to sap all strength and determination out of his bones.

Mentally shaking himself out of his morose thoughts, he drove on. As he approached the crossroads of Rutland Street, he stopped the car, left the engine running and applied the handbrake. Wearing jeans, baseball cap and a hoodie, Dan got out and walked round to the rear passenger door. He opened it and pulled out the unconscious Welchy, leaving him lying on his side in the gutter. Easing himself back into the driver's seat, Dan glanced around then slowly pulled away. As he suspected, no one was about. Even if there was, he guessed that they would look the other way. Getting mixed up in violent affairs was never a good way to live a peaceful existence in a place like this. People would just go back into the house and wait until whatever was happening had finished happening, or go out the back way and walk around the block to avoid it. Calling the police had never been an option here, as in many inner-city estates in England. Being known as a grass or a snitch was worse than being labelled a paedophile.

The chances of being seen by police as he drove away with no number plates on his car was negligible, virtually zero. They didn't patrol here usually, in case of 'stirring up negative emotions of persecution in the populace', to quote a local council official. Dan drove out of Walsall and stopped in a transport café car park to refit the number plates. Circling back on his route a couple of times, he kept an eye out for any vehicles that may have followed him, but he saw no evidence of pursuit. Finally, he headed towards Shropshire and home.

As he drove at a steady sixty-five miles per hour, he mulled over recent events. He hadn't had a chance to discuss his diagnosis with either Janice or his father, and now it had been overshadowed by their deaths. He knew that he should just allow the police to get on with their job and find the people responsible, but he also knew the likelihood of that happening was virtually nil. The police were operating in an over-restrictive bureaucracy that impeded their investigations, and even when they caught the perpetrators, the courts would inevitably release them with petty fines or a not-guilty verdict.

No, this had to be handled his way. What did it matter now? He had already decided that he wouldn't place much hope with the treatment for his brain tumour. The chances of recovery were too slim, and he had lost most of the fight in his heart. All he cared about now was getting the people responsible for Janice and his father's deaths, and dealing out some rough justice. He balked at the methods he would have to employ, but he reasoned that the ends justified the means. It wouldn't be the first time he'd had to use force in his life. His Army career had sent him to many hostile places, including Belfast, Iraq and Sarajevo, and he had felt no compunction at that time in applying force, even deadly force when necessary.

Was this so different? Those times had been officially sanctioned conflicts and he had operated within the law. Mostly. Again, those ends had justified the means. Why did this feel so different now? Should he feel any sympathy or remorse for the enemies that he was now hunting? He certainly didn't fear the repercussions. By the time the wheels of the British justice system had turned, his condition would have done its worst. And he didn't intend to get caught. People turning a blind eye could as easily work in his favour as against him.

But still, using brutal and violent methods against civilians did not sit comfortably with him. He shrugged off his doubts. This was no time to go all philosophical and soft. His enemies had chosen him, had started this war by killing the two most important people in his life. They had shown no doubt, no mercy, no sympathy. They offered no apologies, no excuses that the deaths were accidental. No, they had joked about it online, spreading their message of fear and lawlessness. In Dan's mind, he considered the Keepers to be terrorists. True, they did not use fear and intimidation to achieve political aims, but they used those methods to achieve their own social agenda. Whatever they wanted, they took. They thought they were beyond the reach of the law, and they were probably right, but that didn't mean they were beyond the reach of some form of justice.

Dan had spent most of his adult life trying to avoid Walsall and forget that he had grown up there. His formative years had been spent in a violent, lawless and deprived town. Aggression, poverty and unemployment were the main qualities of life then, and he figured that things hadn't changed that much, except the welfare state benefits seemed to pay better nowadays. He had been lucky in many ways. His dad had kept him on the straight and narrow, unlike most of his friends. He had avoided drugs and joined the Army as soon as he could, like his father had done. The Army had given him a sense of belonging and a way out of the town and he had never looked back. When he completed his time in the Army, he had settled in Shropshire and loved it there. Sure, like every area it had its problems, but not like Walsall. As far as Dan was concerned, nowhere was that bad. He had felt safer patrolling the streets of Belfast than he had walking back from a night out in Walsall.

Janice and her family, the Crosslyns, had also grown up around Walsall, albeit with a different background and different values. She came from a travelling fairground family based in the area, and she and Dan had known each other since they were children. They had encountered a lot of resistance from her family when they had started dating seriously. Dan had fought one of her three brothers just to earn the right to take Janice out on a date. Even then, he had to watch his back in case any of the Crosslyn clan decided that he wasn't welcome any more. Janice had also fought, but she wasn't allowed to answer back to the menfolk in her clan, so she had fought by leaving with Dan as soon as she could. He had joined the Army at eighteen, proposed to her six months later, and they were living in married quarters six months after that. It had been tough as they were both so young, but it meant they were out of Walsall and out of reach of the Crosslyn clan and their interference, so it had all been worth it.

Now Dan thought that the Crosslyns would want a piece of him. They had come to the wedding, and made it very clear that if he wanted 'their wench', he had better look after her. Old Man Crosslyn had been dead now for over twelve years, but her brothers still expected him to honour that deal. And he felt that he had let her down. She had died a violent death and they would expect him to take responsibility for that. They didn't need to blame him though, he was already doing enough of that. The Crosslyn brothers had already made it known that they were after the people responsible, but Dan thought they were all talk. The old man had been different, but Dan didn't have much time or respect for Janice's brothers. They had always rested on the laurels of Janice's father, who had been a bare-knuckle fighter of some fearsome reputation. And he had worked hard all his life, growing up in a travelling fairground family, earning his way as a ring fighter in the fairground, where young men coming to the fair would try and knock him down in a boxing ring. Usually they were full of beer and bravado and soon gave up when Crosslyn caught them with a couple of jabs and a few body shots. He had always been careful not to seriously hurt the challengers, preferring to humiliate them and force them to quit, but occasionally he came up against stiffer opposition, usually from the traveller gypsy clans. These bouts would always draw a crowd, and some heavy betting. Old Man Crosslyn had lived and worked in this hard environment well into his late forties, when eventually this sort of fairground entertainment was outlawed due to 'health and safety' concerns.

Putting all thoughts of the Crosslyns and of Walsall out of his mind as he pulled into his driveway at home, he thought about taking Bryn for a walk up the Wrekin and then remembered – damn their souls. He would make them pay for every single crime against him, and more. Leaving Janice's car next to the garage, he went inside. He had work to do, and a mission to plan.

Chapter 9

Christine sat at her dining table, sipping a cup of tea and reading the local paper. She skimmed through news of car thefts and reports of people convicted of assaults. She shook her head at interviews of local councillors and police chiefs who were telling the people of Walsall that 'crime is on a decline while reported crimes are increasingly being solved'. Political bullshit. Then something caught her eye.

Police are asking for witnesses to an incident in Bedders Road in Walsall yesterday. A young man was found lying in the road, unconscious with severe injuries after what is thought to have been a hit-and-run incident. Police have not ruled out the possibility of inter-gang rivalry, as the victim is thought to be a member of a local gang – the Keepers – although this is yet to be confirmed. The young man's injuries are thought to be life-threatening and he is under armed guard in the Queen Elizabeth Hospital Birmingham's trauma unit. Police confirm that he has not yet regained consciousness and they are waiting to interview him. Anyone with any information can contact police on an anonymous incident telephone number ...

Christine put the paper down and finished her tea. 'It's started,' she thought aloud. 'I hope you know what you're doing, Dan.'

She thought about phoning him, but would it be wise? Would the police be looking at him for this? No, there's nothing to link him to this yet. They think it's a gang thing. She looked out of her window. She couldn't see anyone in the street. Maybe if Dan had been careful enough in Bedders Road, there would be no witnesses. Even if anyone had seen, would they speak up or just keep their heads down and their mouths shut? She thought that most people would do the latter. Probably more than a few people would be glad to see at least one of the local hooligans out of action for a while. Christine had no doubt that this incident was down to Dan, absolutely no doubt at all. She was just a little surprised that the 'victim' was still alive. Was that part of the plan? To send out a message? Time would tell, she supposed.

She stood, threw the newspaper into the recycling pile and washed her teacup. As she stared out of her window, she realised that deep down she wanted Dan to get this gang, wanted him to hurt them and get rid of them. Her own kids were growing up fast and she didn't want them to live in a place ruled by fear and violence. It was a terrifying thought. She felt a mother's protective rage building as she thought of what had become of the local area and how dangerous it was becoming for her girls. Surely it hadn't been this bad when she was growing up? If it was, she hadn't noticed. Sure, there were always bad lads, kids who got into trouble, kids who loved to fight, adults too. But they generally used to keep their fighting between themselves. They went out together, got drunk together, then fought each other on the way home from the pub, only to sober up next day and go out again the next night to continue the cycle. Thieving and burglary was common, and most people saw it as the victim's fault if they were daft enough to not leave something locked, chained up or hidden away.

Looking back, Christine couldn't remember anywhere near the level of crime and underlying fear of violence that persisted now. The modern drugs problem didn't help either, she supposed. There had always been gangs, though, and if you were caught in a different gang's patch, or even just in a different street, woe betide you. It seemed crazy when she recalled how Malcolm had been beaten up once when he was about fourteen years old, just because he had got off the bus early one day and walked across the estate. He had got too hot in the crowded bus, he'd said, and fancied a walk. That walk cost him three teeth and a fractured jaw. No way for a boy to have to live, she thought now. But at the time, they just accepted it, blaming Malcolm for being stupid enough to walk through the estate on his own. The housing estate where he had always lived, where his family lived, where he would one day get married and raise his own kids. When had this level of violence towards children become the normal standard?

Dan always said how much he hated the place, how he couldn't wait to get out. It was ironic how he had chosen to leave Walsall to live as a soldier, patrolling the streets of Northern Ireland and later in the Middle East, to get away from the violence and crime in his own home town in England. But she and Malcolm never saw it in quite the same light, until recently. They had even talked last night about moving away but they couldn't afford it, and besides, the girls were at a difficult stage in their schooling. Exams looming, Christine and Malcolm didn't want to uproot them at the moment. And jobs weren't easy to find, so they couldn't move too far away. They were trapped, and they knew it, like so many other people in the town. But one day, maybe?

<u>Chapter 10</u>

'Deano, man, it's fucked up. Welchy's messed up, man. Who did this shit? Who's messin' with us?'

Kalvin Lewis sucked his teeth, looked at Jonah in disgust and punched him hard in the side of the head, knocking him sprawling onto the floor. Deano looked on, appearing bored.

'What's dat for?' Jonah whined. 'Why you beatin' on me?'

Lewis leaned back on the sofa. 'You make me sick, white boy. Talkin' like a black boy. Who you are, huh?' He leaned forwards and raised his fist again. Jonah cowered. 'Who the fuck is you?'

Deano lazily intervened. 'Leave him, Lewis. Ain't his fault. He's right. Somebody messin' with us. Somebody out there, he thinks he can fuck with Keepers. We need to find dis fucker and put him down.' He subconsciously ran his hand over the pistol sitting on the sofa next to him, which he'd bought last year when he'd travelled to London to meet up with one of the East London gangs. With the boom in cross-county drugs trade, Deano intended to take full advantage of the situation. While he was there, he picked up a 9 mm Baikal pistol. Originally manufactured in Russia and designed to fire CS cartridges for anti-mugging self-protection after the Berlin Wall came down and Soviet draconian rule disappeared overnight, they were now illegally exported to Lithuania and converted to fire Czech bullets. Deano had one for himself and fondly referred to it as his 'pit bull'. Other local gang members had pit bull dogs to look hard; Deano had his Baikal and his reputation. He left his hand resting on it, looked at Kalvin Lewis and said, 'Call a meeting. Get as many Keepers as you can round here. One hour.'

Lewis nodded, picked up his stolen iPhone and accessed the Flashpic app. He would put a call out now and the other Keepers would receive it instantly. It would be up to them to attend or not – there were no hard and fast rules to being in the gang. Generally, members acted independently of each other, only relying on each other for muscle, intimidation and to sell stolen goods. The only things they weren't allowed to deal with independently were firearms and drugs. Deano had full control of all local drug trade on the estates, and he came down hard on any trespassers, and that included his own gang members. Last year when he found out that one of the Keepers was trading Spice and not cutting him in, he had Lewis blind him in one eye. Lewis took great delight in carrying out his orders if it involved violence or intimidation. He had allegiance to no race, colour or creed. He had a grudging respect for Deano, and knew that without the gang leader, he wouldn't have the network of people to run his local scams, schemes and rackets.

Lewis had grown up as the youngest of seven brothers, and despite being the youngest he had quickly earned the reputation as the most violent and ruthless. He had hospitalised and crippled his Jamaican father when he was only twelve years old after his father tried to show him the error of his criminal ways with a leather belt. As everyone was scared of his family, Lewis had grown up accustomed to getting his own way and no one would fight him, or show any resistance. So he had learned that violence was easy and had no repercussions or deterrent. No one had ever stood up to him except one or two of his older brothers, and nowadays they avoided him rather than confront him. He enjoyed violence, relished the adrenaline kick that he got from it, and he nurtured his notoriety. When people crossed the street rather than walk past him, Lewis took that as a compliment and a mark of respect instead of an insult. Many an innocent person had been attacked by Lewis as he walked past them. Sometimes for gain, as he took whatever money they had, and sometimes just for the hell of it. The only other Keeper who was anywhere near as vicious was Deano. Deano took aggression and violence to a whole new level, and even Lewis thought twice about taking him on directly. Even so, Deano wasn't naïve. He knew full well that Kalvin Lewis would knife him in the back without even blinking if he thought it would benefit him. Honour among thieves had always been a Disney fairy tale and never more so than in present-day street gang life in England.

Within the hour, other gang members drifted into Deano's house, which was his home as well as the main headquarters, drugstore and stolen goods store for the Keepers. He didn't have to pay for it, of course. That privilege went to the taxpaying, law-abiding citizens of Great Britain. It was an ex-council house, sold off to a privately owned Housing Association, who couldn't care less what went on in the house as long as they received their rent on time, which of course they did as the welfare state paid it. Deano claimed state disability benefit, and all he had to do to keep a roof over his head was submit his forms on time. He could afford to pay private rent, but then the authorities might want to know where his income came from, and that would complicate matters.

The gang members arrived in various ways, some on foot, some in stolen cars, some on stolen bicycles, mopeds or motorcycles. These were all left outside in the secure knowledge that no one would dare steal them, a white K painted on the fuel tank, seat or frame. Heaven help any owner who recognised his or her stolen bike and tried to reclaim it. Better to just take the loss on the chin and buy another. One of the Keepers who arrived on such a bicycle left it leaning against the side of the house, pushed his hands deep into his hoodie pockets and went inside. He sat near the back of the room, near the door, until he was sure of the reason for this unusual call to a meeting. He was around twenty-five years old, one of the older members, but looked a lot younger. Lean and trim, to the point of being skinny, he blended in well, never catching anyone's eye, never speaking up or out of turn. To honour his place in the gang, he brought in a good revenue in stolen goods, mainly from burglaries, with the occasional stolen car thrown in for variety. Pulling his hood up and leaning against the wall next to the back door, he nodded a greeting at a couple of the others as they acknowledged him.

'Hey Benton,' said one of the younger Keepers, a pasty-faced white boy of about eighteen. 'Still not got an engine in dat bike? What's up with you, man? Can't you ride a real bike?' He sniggered to his cronies, who had all arrived on stolen motorbikes and mopeds. Benton just smiled and shrugged, neither aggressively or submissively. No need to rile things up, but no need to let the little fuckers walk all over you either.

'Nah man, just keeping my head down. Got things cookin', know what I mean? Don't wanna bring heat down on me right now. You know how it is.' Suggesting that the younger member was also a major player was a useful method of deflecting banter without rising to it.

'Yeah man, I hear you.' The teenager strutted away with his cronies and found a seat where Deano would see him. Benton was quite happy to stay near the back, observe proceedings and not be noticed too much. He knew full well that Deano and Lewis had clocked who had arrived and who was missing, and that was enough contact for him. After a few more minutes, Deano started speaking. There was no call for hush, no introductions, just an immediate silence as his quiet voice started to make itself heard.

'If you all don't know why we're here, you must be walking round with your heads up your arses.' Some sniggering from the younger members of the gang soon settled. 'Some fucker is messing with us. Welchy is in hospital. He ain't gonna make it, by the sound of things. If he does, he ain't no more use to us. He's fucked. I wanna know who did this, why, and then I want to meet this wanker. Anybody know anything?'

There was some shuffling around, some of the younger members postured and swore, but no one had any useful information.

'None of ya?' shouted Deano. 'Some fucker comes onto our turf, runs down one of our gang, in full view of another fuckin' Keeper, and not one of ya knows fuckin' anything?' He picked up an empty beer glass from the table next to his chair and flung it across the room, where it smashed against the wall a couple of feet from Benton. He didn't flinch, he knew it wasn't aimed at him personally. 'Jonah,' Deano snapped. 'You were there. What fuckin' happened?'

Jonah looked around, aware that all eyes were on him. Some people loudly accused him of doing nothing while one of their own had been nearly killed.

'He came out of nowhere, Deano. Driving his car like a madman, trying to run us both over. Welchy just stood there, didn't fuckin' move, just stood his ground, and this bastard just hit him with the car, smack.' He smacked his fist into his other hand to emphasise his point.

'That was on the Black Track, right? On Sunday?' Deano clarified this for any others who didn't yet know the full story.

'Yeah, by the sub-station.' Jonah nodded.

Lewis spoke up next. 'So how the fuck did Welchy turn

up on Monday in Bedders Road?' He stood up and walked towards Jonah, who cowered back in his seat, looking nervously around at the others in the room for support.

'I dunno. He must have brought him here. I think there was two of them, yeah? Maybe three in the car. I think one had a shotgun, yeah? I couldn't do nuffin, man, honest.' Jonah was struggling now, torn between making a run for it and facing it out and risking Lewis's wrath.

Lewis stopped right in front of Jonah. 'So what fuckin' car are we lookin' for?'

Jonah looked around again, desperate now that his chance of escape had disappeared and Lewis was standing close enough to hurt him. None of the other Keepers were going to intervene, and no one wanted to take Lewis on. Some of them were grinning and looking forward to the coming entertainment.

'I, er, it was black. Yeah, black. Like a Hummer. But bigger.' He tried to squirm back into his seat.

Lewis leaned forwards and put his hand on Jonah's shoulder. 'Reg number? Anything else?' he asked Jonah, who was now almost at the point of wetting himself.

'Nah man, it happened too fast. I dunno.' As he tried to turn his head towards Deano, Lewis cupped the back of Jonah's head and struck him on the nose, causing blood to splatter across his face.

At the back of the room, Benton could hear the sickening crunch as Jonah's nose broke, but still he didn't flinch, showing neither encouragement nor disapproval for Lewis's violence. He felt sorry for Jonah as the young

Keeper always seemed to catch the brunt of any violence. Lewis pulled his hand back and struck Jonah again, this time with a fist to his right eye. The hand cupped around the back of Jonah's head ensured that no force was wasted and that all the inertia was absorbed by Jonah's face. Lewis let go of him and Jonah slumped to the floor, barely conscious and struggling to breathe through his flattened nose. Lewis lifted his leg, ready to deliver a crushing stamp to Jonah, but Deano intervened.

'Enough. Leave him. He'll be no fuckin use to us if you put him next to Welchy.'

A few of the gathered Keepers slumped back, disappointed that Deano had saved the hapless Jonah. Violence was entertainment, an extension of the brutal graphics of the computer games they had grown up playing.

Lewis spat on Jonah and resumed his seat, sipping from a beer can.

Deano spoke up again, louder this time. 'Right, get your arses out there and find out who these guys are, bring me the names. No one does anything else to them until me or Lewis says. We'll make them fuckin' pay. In blood and cash. Then we'll make a proper show of them on Flashpic. Nobody, I fuckin' guarantee, nobody is getting away with this.' He kicked Jonah in the ribs, eliciting a loud groan. 'Get up, you wanker, he's only fuckin' playing with ya. Get out there with everybody and bring them bastards back here.' He looked up at everyone else in the room. 'Fuckin' now!' he roared.

The room cleared in less than ten seconds, Keepers

leaving in groups or pairs, except for Benton. He picked up his bicycle from where he'd left it, casually strolled down the path, turned left up Bedders Road towards the edge of the estate and headed towards the main A34 road. He didn't rush and he didn't look back.

<u>Chapter 11</u>

Benton cycled briskly along the A34 Bloxwich Road, over Spratt's Bridge and turned onto the canal towpath. After a couple of hundred metres, he stopped under the next canal bridge and waited a couple of minutes, standing well back in the shadows. Looking both ways up and down the canal towpath and seeing no one, he concluded that he hadn't been followed so far. He carried on cycling for a few minutes until he came out on Harden Road bridge. From there he rode to the large crematorium at Ryecroft, where he took the back lane to the LMS waste ground, the Yellow Mess. Exiting that track on Mill Lane, he cycled into the Butts estate and stopped at a public phone box, one of the few remaining in serviceable, non-vandalised order. Dialling a number that he knew by heart, he waited for a reply. After two or three rings, the call was taken. There was no answer, no reply on the other end, just a pause as the recipient waited for him to speak.

Benton spoke clearly and slowly. 'UC-27. Sitrep for DS Tunstall.' His sitrep, or situation report, needed to be filed as soon as possible. Benton was UC-27, code for undercover officer number twenty-seven in the West Midlands Police Service.

Immediately there was a reply. 'UC-27, this is control. Verify code please.'

Benton replied without hesitation, 'Operation Finders. Code 63679A.'

'Thank you, UC-27. Please wait.'

Benton waited patiently, leaning against the side of the phone box so that he could see up and down the road. He had vision of at least a hundred metres in any direction, so he knew that he wasn't being observed, and a listening device would have to be fairly high-grade to pick up his speech from over a hundred metres.

'UC-27, this is DS Tunstall. How's things?' His operational controller, Detective Sergeant Tunstall, spoke to him.

'DS, I'm fine, no problems. Sitrep for you. Things are moving. Deano called a meeting. There were about twenty-five Keepers in attendance. He's put a call out to find someone, or a group of someones. That hit-and-run that we thought was inter-gang related? I'm not so sure now. I think it may be some sort of vigilante retaliation. There's been no contact from another gang, no bragging from anyone, and no demands. Typical gang MO would have been to use that incident to their advantage somehow, not just clam up about it. Otherwise what's the point?'

'I agree,' Detective Sergeant Tunstall replied. 'Any ideas who's behind it?'

'None yet. They're very twitchy though. They seem to

think there's possibly three men opposing them, travelling in some sort of four-by-four. One member thought it was a Humvee, but I can't see how something like that would go unnoticed around here for long. There's also bit of internal strife going on. Kalvin Lewis is off his leash, so we need to have eyes on him if possible. No telling what that maniac is going to do next.'

'Sorry, no can do.' DS Tunstall sighed. 'We haven't got any spare staff at present. There's two other operations going full steam right now, we're stretched as it is.'

'We live in interesting times,' Benton said. 'I'll keep you posted. I'm going to see if I can keep tabs on Lewis for a while, see if I can locate where the stash of pistols is hidden.'

'Well that was your primary objective. Don't let this other matter distract you. If some muppets want to take on a gang, that's their lookout. Our main concern here are three hundred Baikal pistols about to hit the streets.'

'Roger that, Sarge. I've heard no mention of them so far. Only Deano has a Baikal that I've seen. I haven't even seen Lewis with one. Are you sure that your snitch is right about this?'

DS Tunstall sighed again. 'My informant, as you so politely referred to him, is currently out of action and may well be unable to provide any further information, correct or not, for the foreseeable future. If ever.'

'Bloody hell, Welchy? He was the snitch? I'd never have had him for that. Didn't seem to have enough brain cells.'

'Didn't have much of a choice. Caught him red-handed selling kiddy porn DVDs. Don't think that would have done his reputation much good in Walsall, would it? We got good intel from him about his sources for that, but even so, we weren't planning on letting him off the hook so easily.'

'How is he doing, Sarge? Any news?'

'Plenty of news, all bad. Seems he had internal bleeding, which miraculously stopped before he got dumped but caused irreversible liver damage. The idiot also had a head injury that caused a bleed on the brain, though how we would have noticed the difference is beyond me.' Benton grinned on the other end of the phone. DS Tunstall continued, 'But the real spanner in the works is that his brain is completely fried. They're not sure if it was the electric current that caused the bleed on the brain, or the convulsions that followed, or the initial impact trauma, but either way, he can't breathe properly, he's in nappies, and he keeps slipping back into a coma. He hasn't spoken a coherent sentence since being in hospital. It appears that someone gave him the full beans from his own stun-gun that he was reputed to carry around. Very crude version of our own Taser, but completely illegal and way too powerful to be used on a human by the looks of Welchy. The police surgeon reckons it's an adapted cattle prod, but we don't know for sure as it hasn't been found yet. Anyway, the burns that the PS found were suggestive that Welchy sustained a prolonged and severe electrical trauma, causing irreversible brain damage. Almost makes you feel sorry for him, doesn't it?'

Benton thought of the two teenage girls that he had rescued last year after a taste of Welchy's stun-gun and a small dose of Rohypnol. He had found them in the back of an abandoned stolen van, dumped in Mill Lane, and alerted police before anyone came back to carry on where Welchy had left off. He knew it was Welchy, as the idiot had posted a ten-second clip of himself 'enjoying' the girls on Flashpic. Of course, that was no longer able to be used as evidence as it disappeared once deleted by the Flashpic account holder and couldn't be forcibly claimed for court evidence as the Flashpic server was in Russia. But Benton had heard enough bragging from Welchy about the incident. The two girls couldn't remember much, and even if they could, they were too terrified to testify against the gang. They were back home now, still living on the same estate as the Keepers.

'No Sarge, it doesn't make me feel sorry for him. Not by a long way. Right, I'd better get on, I'll keep you posted.'

'Roger that, UC-27. Check in forty-eight hours from now. Be careful.'

Benton hung up the phone, and once he had made sure there was no one observing him, he got back on his cycle and headed towards the Coalpool Tavern to look for Kalvin Lewis. Wednesday night was pool night, and Lewis liked to play the occasional game and then fight over the result. Benton was pretty damn sure that Kalvin Lewis knew where the stash of Baikal pistols was hidden. What he wasn't sure of was whether Deano knew about them or not. If he didn't then it opened up another avenue of investigation. Where did Lewis buy them from? Who were his contacts? Where was his funding coming from? Even buying them bulk would have cost tens of thousands of pounds, and Benton couldn't see where the Keepers would find that sort of money, not at the moment. He needed a lucky break and needed to get in deeper to get the intel, but he wasn't sure that he had the credibility with the Keepers yet to get that deep.

He had been working undercover now for almost a year. It was his first major UC operation since joining the team, and he didn't want to blow it. He had been chosen for this operation as he'd grown up in Coalpool and knew most of the players, or at least their reputations. After leaving school with a handful of mediocre qualifications he worked in some pretty crappy dead-end jobs and Benton had realised that if he didn't want to stay in Coalpool for the rest of his life, he needed to do something drastic, so he dropped off the grid, joined the police force and never looked back. After he had served for four years in Wolverhampton and Birmingham and had shown promise, especially when seconded to plain-clothes operations, he was redeployed as an undercover officer. So here he was at the pinnacle of his career so far. Back in Walsall on the estate he'd grown up on. The irony wasn't lost on him as he made his way to the Coalpool Tavern.

<u>Chapter 12</u>

From his vantage point in the bushes just inside Ryecroft cemetery, Dan saw a young man walk towards the Coalpool Tavern. He looked to be around twenty years old but his face showed evidence of a harsh life thus far. Cold eyes constantly checked out his environment. The young man's dark hair was cropped short and his coffee-coloured skin hinted at his mixed-race heritage. The way that he walked, strutting and arrogant, made people in the car park quickly move out of his way, subconsciously submitting to an alpha male. Dan sat up, stretched his arms and cracked his back as he tried to straighten out his joints after his three hours watching vigil. *I'm getting too old for this,* he thought. The last time he had done this sort of thing had been in Belfast in the early 1990s, and that hadn't ended well.

He had been a corporal on his first real reconnaissance mission in Northern Ireland, gathering intelligence on known Provisional Irish Republican Army terrorists operating near Crossmaglen. They were a four-man team and he was in charge, all of them seasoned veterans with four NI tours each under their belts. They had been laid up in some high woodlands overlooking two farms down in the valley. Weapons had been known to be hidden there, and recently an anonymous tip-off had suggested that there were surface-to-air missiles hidden there as well. These missiles would cause havoc for the Army Air Corps helicopters used all over the province, so it was vital to find them and disable them before they were used. Even if they only brought down one helicopter, the psychological advantage that PIRA would gain would be crucial at this period. They were fighting a losing battle of hearts and minds and they knew it. The mostly peace-loving people of Northern Ireland were sick of living in fear. Both sides had had enough of vitriolic rhetoric from Catholic and Protestant leaders alike, and they just wanted to get on with their lives and live in peace. PIRA needed a victory of sorts, something that they could claim justification for, and shooting down a 'helicopter gunship' would be just the thing to boost their rank and files' morale.

So Dan and his small team had the unenviable task of sitting in damp woodlands for a week, observing the two farms. They noted every coming and going, taking vehicle registration numbers, photographs and descriptions of people entering the farms. Also useful were the details of delivery vans and farm trailers as these were used to transport hidden weapons across the border from southern Ireland. So far, they had gathered a huge amount of intel, but not seen anything that could positively be identified as a SAM weapons cache. Until today. It was a typical Northern

Irish Sunday morning, pissing down with rain, misty and cold, and as the British squaddies at their observation post were having their cold breakfast, Dan saw a tractor and trailer pull in to the eastern-most farm entrance. Two young lads jumped out of the tractor and pulled a tarpaulin off the contents of the trailer. From his hidden vantage point, Dan fixed binoculars on the back of the vehicle and noted the registration number. Then he noticed the uncovered boxes stacked on the back of the trailer. Wooden, about four feet long, with Arabic script painted on the sides, these were surely what British Forces were looking for. He quickly called his team to action.

'Spriggs, get on the radio. Tell Delta 1 that we have goods in sight. Positive ID. We need feet on the ground ASAP before they're squared away.'

'Roger that. On it now.' Spriggs turned to his radio and called up Delta 1 at HQ to pass details. The other soldiers turned their full attention to what was going on, their cold breakfasts forgotten about for now.

'Denny, keep eyes on the other farm. Al, can you start squaring away? We might need to clear off sharpish once this is sorted.' Dan put his binoculars away and observed through his SA80 weapon sights instead. At a little over three hundred metres away, his SA80 sights were more than effective. As he watched the two young men uncovering the stash of weapons on the trailer, an older man came rushing out of the farmhouse, pulling on a raincoat and shouting at the young men.

'O'Halloran is out of the building and looks pissed off,'

Dan observed. He couldn't hear what was being said, but he could guess that the older man was bollocking the younger men for unloading the weapons in the open farmyard. He was pointing at one of the barns and shouting. Suddenly all three of them turned to face the farm entrance, and one of the younger men pulled the tarpaulin back onto the trailer, but in the rain, it just slipped off the other side as he pulled furiously at it. O'Halloran ran into the house and came out with what looked to be two AK-47 rifles.

'Switch on, lads, suspects now armed. Spriggs, radio it in.' Dan swung his sights around to see what had got them so agitated, just in time to see a Royal Ulster Constabulary squad car pulling slowly into the farm entrance. 'Shit. Denny, any movement at the other farm?'

'Zero,' came the reply. 'No sign of anything yet.'

'Right. Switch your sights to O'Halloran's farm. We've got RUC just turned up and two AK-47s with the boggies.' This wasn't part of the plan. As far as Dan knew, all RUC and Army units were supposed to be keeping clear of the two farms to let the terrorists get lax with their security and allow a glimpse of a weapons cache.

He watched the scene unfold with a growing dread. The two younger men crouched behind the trailer and pointed the rifles at the RUC car. The two policemen in the RUC car opened the doors and slowly got out, completely unaware of the threat. As they pulled on their uniform hats one of the men opened fire, shattering the windscreen of the car. The RUC men froze for a split second then scrambled around to the back of their car. The other young man started shooting now, peppering the squad car with bullets. O'Halloran produced a pistol from his raincoat and pointed at the police car as he slowly walked around the farmhouse outbuildings. Dan could see what was happening. The two younger men would keep the policemen pinned down until O'Halloran could creep around and shoot them from behind. They'd obviously blundered into the situation without knowing what was going on. They didn't stand a chance.

'Corporal. Orders?' came the request from Denny, the older and more experienced of his squad.

'Wait. Keep your sights on the two with rifles. O'Halloran will try to flush the RUC out into the open. If he starts shooting, the RUC will have no choice but to run. If that happens, take the riflemen out. Denny, you take the rifleman near the front of the trailer, target two. Al, you take the rifleman at the rear of the trailer, target three. O'Halloran is target one. Spriggs, sitrep to Delta 1. Everyone clear?' Dan swept his scope around as the others replied that they understood his orders. He was trying to locate O'Halloran. 'Anyone got eyes on target one?'

'Negative,' came the replies in unison.

For a few seconds, there was a pause in the shooting. One of the RUC stood up and fired two pistol shots at the riflemen. At best, he could only be hoping to scare them. He was fifty feet away and had no clear line of sight. As the two riflemen returned fire again, Dan saw O'Halloran emerge from one of the outbuildings behind the RUC car. The shotgun that he was now carrying was aimed roughly at the crouching RUC men but they were unaware of his presence as they were looking forwards, focussed on the perceived threat coming from the riflemen. Dan knew that from the close range O'Halloran was at, he would likely cut them in half with a shotgun blast. In the split second his mind took to process this new information, he weighed up the life-changing consequences of the actions he would have to take over the next few seconds. Wait for orders from HQ and do nothing, and the RUC men would surely die. Open fire without clear and direct orders, and he would have to take the legal consequences of shooting and potentially killing a civilian. Either choice would change his life irreversibly. People would die, no matter which choice he made, but there should be no collateral damage to innocent civilians. That was an accepted British Army rule of engagement in any conflict, but also a personal moral rule for Dan and most other British Army soldiers that he knew.

He didn't class O'Halloran or his two young thugs waving rifles around as innocent civilians any more. They had entered the realms of 'armed enemy forces in direct engagement'.

He fixed his SUSAT sight on O'Halloran and squeezed the trigger of his SA80. As far as he knew, he had not made a conscious decision to do this, but his training and his gut-reaction took the ethical and moral decision to kill the bastard. The SA80 round flew towards O'Halloran as Dan squeezed the trigger a second time. A double tap. Two 5.56 mm bullets travelling at between seven hundred and fifty and eight hundred and fifty metres per second, aimed at O'Halloran's plentiful centre mass, took only a fraction of a second to achieve their objective and hit their target. The first bullet hit O'Halloran squarely in the chest as he raised his shotgun to aim at the policemen hiding behind their squad car. The lead bullet shattered his sternum, simultaneously sending fragments of bone backwards through his body, having the effect of creating a dozen or so smaller projectiles that had the lethal result of making mincemeat of his lungs and his heart. It was very unlikely that O'Halloran knew anything about his death. As he was flung backwards by the energy of the impact, the second bullet struck his shotgun stock and ricocheted off towards the farmhouse.

Unfortunately, Mrs O'Halloran had chosen to stand at the farmhouse window to observe the excitement. She had presumed that she was safe at that distance and angle. Yet ricochets have an amazing ability to find safely hidden targets, and against incredible odds they have a knack of causing catastrophic and unwanted collateral damage. As the ricocheting bullet spun through the air, it struck the glass in front of her face, shattering it into hundreds of shards. The bullet went on to hit her in the throat, not with enough force to pass straight through her neck, but with enough unspent velocity to enter and split her carotid artery. She collapsed backwards and fell onto the shattered glass on the floor. As she struggled to breathe, and scrabbled around on the floor, the glass shards caused further lacerations to her body, hands and legs. After a few seconds, when she finally stopped moving, the scene looked like an abattoir.

Outside, the two younger men had seen O'Halloran

fall, and wrongly assuming that it was the RUC that had shot him, they stood up and walked towards the squad car, shooting as they advanced. They separated and moved to either side of the car, before one of them, undoubtedly the one that had slightly more brain cells, lay down and took aim under the squad car. Dan knew that if the man found his target, the RUC officers were done for.

'Fire on targets two and three,' he shouted calmly. Simultaneously Denny, Dan and Al fired at the two riflemen. At less than three hundred metres and out in the open, Dan knew that he was issuing a death sentence, but if he didn't, he would be as good as signing the policemen's death warrants. A split second later, after six 5.56 mm rounds found their targets, the two riflemen lay dying on the farmyard floor. Without needing to be told, the British soldiers stopped firing but kept their SUSAT sights trained on the riflemen, waiting for further signs of aggression. One of the injured riflemen rolled over onto his back and clutched at his belly, trying to hold in his unravelling intestines. The other lay very still as a puddle of blood slowly spread around him. The silence was deafening.

A few seconds later, the two RUC policemen cautiously stood up from where they had been pinned down behind their car. They were visibly shaking as they looked around them at the carnage, but they were both unharmed. One of them ran to the front of the car to get on the radio. The other drew his Webley pistol and aimed it at the men on the ground.

'Don't think there's any need for that, matey,' muttered

Dan. 'Spriggs, update Delta 1 with a sitrep, will you?'

Spriggs spoke on the radio to headquarters, updating them with a situation report. He listened for a few seconds. 'We're to move out from here, Corporal. Make our way to the extraction point and await evac. Do not make contact with RUC.'

'Roger that,' Dan replied as he watched the RUC policemen through his SUSAT sight. They were looking around, bewildered, trying to figure out where their saving allies were and also making sure that there were no other enemies in the farm buildings. One of them pointed at the wooden boxes on the back of the trailer and they slowly walked towards it to investigate.

'Well done, Sherlock,' Dan muttered as he watched them cautiously approaching the tractor and trailer. They stopped a few feet away, sensibly deciding to wait for the Army to come and check out their discovery for hidden booby traps. Both the RUC and the British squaddies had learned the hard way over the years of the Troubles that the PIRA loved to booby trap their contraband goods in case it was ever found by the authorities, and many men had lost their limbs and lives to these cowardly tactics.

As Al and Denny squared away their equipment and Spriggs made sure that there was no trace of their having been there, Dan crawled backwards away from the edge of the OP. A few minutes later they were jogging quietly through the dense woodland towards their extraction point.

That had all been a lifetime ago, but Dan could still remember the bitterness that followed as his team had been hauled over the legal and political coals for killing an 'innocent'. Mrs O'Halloran had undoubtedly known about what her family was doing, but she hadn't been holding a weapon at the time of her death and so had posed no immediate threat to anyone. Dan had often wondered how many other deaths she had played a part in by her silence. No one had commended Dan or his men for saving the lives of the two police officers, who had inadvertently stumbled into a live reconnaissance operation after seeing the tractor driving with defective rear lights and had only stopped to advise the driver to get them fixed. Eventually, after the Ulster Freedom Fighters had claimed responsibility, Dan and his soldiers were all found innocent of any wrongdoing, but not before Dan had been demoted to lance corporal. The British Army kept quiet about what had happened, leaving the UFF to proudly take the blame, and normal duties resumed in the province.

In those days, when he was in his early twenties, Dan had thought nothing of sitting still for hours in uncomfortable and cold surroundings, but after three hours of sitting in a bush in the cold May drizzle, he was feeling a bit worse for wear. He shook himself off, squeezed through the gap in the cemetery railings, and crossed the road towards the Coalpool Tavern. The tavern had been an estate pub of dubious reputation for as long as Dan could remember. It seemed a good a place as any to try and find one of the Keepers gang. As a child, he and his friends had sat on the wall outside, waiting for fights to erupt from inside so that they had something to watch on a Friday or Saturday night.

He would probably blend in OK now, he thought, dressed in scruffy jeans, a soaked black hoodie and workmen's boots. Just another one of the travelling roadworks crew staying locally, come in to quench their thirst after a day of digging holes and holding up traffic. With his local accent, if he could recall it, and his scruffy looks, he probably wouldn't attract much attention. If he did, his silence and thousand-yard stare was usually enough to deflect most problems. 'Just be the grey man,' he remembered one of his army training sergeants telling him. 'Blend in, keep your head down, don't make eye contact, don't attract attention. Keep your eye on the nearest exit and keep your back to the wall.'

As he remembered all this advice, given to him a quarter of a century ago, he found a quiet spot near the bar and pointed at the pump delivering Best Bitter. The pool tables were close by, and a dozen young men were clustered around them, watching the games play out, making bets, boasting of recent fights, lots of posturing going on. Three bored looking young women sat on a nearby table, all of them fiddling with mobile phones, not talking to each other or anyone else, ignoring the young men's bravado and banter, which was undoubtedly put on for their benefit.

Dan quietly scanned the room as he paid the vacant looking barman. Sipping at his pint, he saw Lewis emerge from the Gents toilet. As Lewis walked towards the pool tables, the banter suddenly quietened down. The other young men looked uncomfortable, not wanting to lose face in front of each other and the women, but noticeably uneasy in Lewis's presence.

'Alright, Kalvin?' one of the young men ventured, haltingly.

Lewis paused and looked at him for a couple of very tense seconds. 'Yeah, mate,' he said, showing a couple of gold-capped teeth in a sly grin. 'Busy. I'll be back in a minute, play a game of pool with ya, show ya how it's done. Yeah?' He disappeared through into the back room of the pub, ignoring the barman who had suddenly found a keen interest in cleaning the bar, for probably the first time that week. As the door to the back room and living quarters swung closed, the young men at the pool table took one look at each other and wordlessly made a hurried exit. Dan noticed that the young women had now looked up from their phones, and as soon as the others had left the pub, they swiftly downed their drinks and followed.

When Kalvin Lewis came out of the back room fifteen minutes later, there was no one in the bar except the barman, Dan and a stoned looking youth slumped on a bar sofa in the corner. Lewis looked around, shrugged and sauntered over to where Dan was now playing a solo game of pool. The barman, who himself had once been on the wrong end of Lewis's violence, made a discreet exit to the cellar, having suddenly realised that at least one of the beer barrels needed changing.

'Who the fuck are you?' was Lewis's greeting. 'These are my fuckin' tables. And I fancy a game.'

Dan didn't look up as he played his shot. A yellow ball slid into a corner pocket.

'There's two other empty tables. Help yourself, matey,'

he said in a friendly, nonchalant way to Lewis, who bristled and clenched his fists as he leaned on the table. He reached out and swept several of the pool balls onto the floor. Dan chalked the tip of his cue and looked down at the remaining balls. 'Well, Kalvin, if you keep up that childish behaviour you're going to find it hard to play a game with no balls on the table.' As Dan leaned down to line up his next shot, Lewis took a step back.

'How you know my name? What are you, filth or sumfin? You ain't safe here, man. You ain't got no friends here. No backup.' He grinned and reached into his inside jacket pocket. 'You is a nobody man here.'

As Lewis's hand slid out of his pocket, Dan played his shot, thrusting the long wooden cue straight into Lewis's solar plexus. Lewis doubled over as air whooshed out of his mouth. Dan swapped the cue around in his hands and calmly stepped around the table to where Lewis was kneeling on the floor, trying to draw in air, but his immobilised diaphragm wouldn't allow his lungs to expand. His mouth opened and closed like that of a fish as his eyes bulged. He looked up at Dan with pure rage and hatred.

Never in all of his eighteen years had anyone bested him, but right now he felt powerless. As Lewis's vision blurred due to the ensuing lack of oxygen reaching his brain, Dan swung the pool cue around and down onto Lewis's hand, which was clutching the pool table. There was an audible crunch as bones became splinters and Lewis collapsed to the floor, trying to scream but not able to breathe. Dan didn't hesitate but stepped forwards and swung the cue again, hitting Lewis on the side of the head. Dan stood over him and held the cue upright like a spear, ready to thrust straight down.

'It's incredible just how many enemies you have, Kalvin Lewis. One of them sold you out for the price of a packet of cigarettes, that's how cheap you are. Showed me a photo of you on his phone, told me where you live, told me where you hang out. You should stop picking on people, matey, show a little respect.' He jabbed the cue straight down, and as Lewis put his hands out to deflect the blow, Dan shifted his aim towards his groin, catching Lewis squarely in the balls. This time Lewis had got enough of his breath back to emit a cry, although it was more of a high-pitched squeal. As he doubled over in pain, Dan struck him on the back of his head just above his neck, not too hard, just enough to daze him. That part of the brain, the medulla oblongata, controlled many things, but was also the most sensitive part of the brain and was the easiest place to knock a victim unconscious.

Lewis slumped. Dan grabbed hold of his jacket and quickly searched him, finding a Baikal pistol in his jacket inside pocket. He shoved it in the waistband of his jeans, then satisfied that Lewis had no more weapons, dragged him out to the car park outside where his Land Rover was waiting, minus registration plates. He yanked the back door open and heaved Lewis up into the back of the vehicle. While he was occupied with trying to close the door on the groaning Lewis, he didn't see the blur of movement but instead felt something connect with the side of his head.

He stumbled away from the vehicle, trying to see who had attacked him. Someone grabbed him around the neck in a headlock and growled into his ear, 'You've had your fun, now fuck off.'

Dan was roughly shoved to the ground and he shook his head, trying to regain his senses and his balance. He realised he'd been hit on the ear, since it was ringing; this had the effect of disorientating a person without causing too much lasting damage. Dan's brain registered this fact and he tried to get his legs underneath him, staggering slightly as he did so. Then he saw that the youth he'd thought was stoned in the corner of the bar was dragging Lewis out of the Land Rover and across the car park.

Dan stood up and reached for the pistol tucked into his waistband. Lewis's rescuer looked at Dan with a dark stare and motioned at him to leave, then reached out to help Lewis, who was in danger of falling over again. Dan realised he was in no state to continue his mission, so left the pistol where it was and groggily slid into the driving seat of his Land Rover, started the engine and jerkily pulled away from the car park, speeding away and heading down towards Walsall town centre and the M6 motorway junction. Cursing himself as he drove, Dan slowed down to not draw any more attention to himself. Before long, he was on the motorway, cruising at a sensible sixty miles per hour as he tried to regain his senses. His ear was ringing and his pride was bruised, but apart from that he felt OK. He'd stepped into the lion's den, punched the creature on the nose and escaped in one piece, so things weren't so bad really. The only thing that stopped him enjoying all of this were the memories of what had started the whole escapade. Janice and his dad had done nothing to deserve what had happened, but Dan could almost feel them watching him, demanding justice.

As he pulled into his driveway and parked around the back of his garage, he felt suddenly sick. Just in time, he threw open the driver's door and vomited onto the gravel. He slumped back in the car seat, closed his eyes, and was unconscious in seconds.

Chapter 13

Deano was pacing back and forth in the front room of his house in Bedders Road. He looked calm, but Lewis knew that he was angry – though he was probably nearer to a rage. The gang boss was trying to think, to put this together, to suss out where this threat had suddenly come from. It didn't seem like it was from another gang, and besides, Lewis said it was an old guy. Not Eastern European either. A strange accent, neither here nor there, Lewis had said. Not posh, not Walsall, just strange.

Lewis lay on the sofa, eyes closed, with an ice pack on the side of his head where the pool cue had connected with him. Nausea came in waves but he fought it, refusing to let this man, this old guy, beat him so easily.

Benton stood leaning against the doorframe, silently watching Deano. Benton knew that this was his chance to get further in to the Keepers, to gain their confidence and maybe find out some intel on where the Baikal pistols were stashed or, if they had already sold them on, who they had been sold to. He now knew that Lewis had carried a pistol too, and that the man who had attacked him had taken it.

That man perturbed him as much as he perturbed Deano, but for different reasons.

Benton didn't see this man as a career criminal or a rival gangster, and he didn't have the bearing of a down-and-out. Ex-military perhaps? Certainly the calm precision of the attack on Lewis and the use of a Land Rover fitted that theory. But as far as Benton knew, there was no military involvement in trying to get hold of the Baikals, but that was something he would have to clarify on his next sitrep update. Could he have been a mercenary? Had the Keepers somehow reneged on the arms deal? Surely even they wouldn't be so stupid as to go head-to-head with an Eastern European backstreet arms dealer? And why was he trying to abduct Lewis? Was this the same man who had taken and beaten the other Keeper, Welchy? If so, he was a force to be reckoned with. If Benton hadn't taken the man by surprise, Lewis would now be at his mercy. But why was he doing all this? When he'd attacked Lewis, there had been no pre-amble, no argument, no questioning. He knew who Lewis was, wanted him subdued, neutralised and abducted, not just beaten up. There was no message passed on, no threats, no rationale, no posturing. It appeared to be planned and executed, simple as that, with very little wasted time or energy.

'So what the fuck, Lewis? How did this happen? A guy just walks into the Coalpool Tavern, empties the place, then kicks you around a bit? Since when did you get soft?'

Deano looked at Benton. 'What did you say your name was?'

'Benton.'

Deano nodded, barely remembering. 'Right, yeah, no offence.' He looked back at Lewis. 'If Benton here hadn't been around, he'd have had you. Like Welchy. What the fuck?'

Lewis gritted his teeth as he opened his eyes. Already angry and embarrassed, he didn't like being reminded of his shortcomings. But he had to admit that Deano was right.

'I didn't see it coming, alright!' he snapped. 'This old guy, he was just takin' the piss, playin' pool, like, on my table. I thought he was pissed or sumfin. Didn't realise he was waitin' for me. Next time, I'll kill the bastard. He's dead man walkin', a nobody man.' He closed his eyes and lay back against the sofa again.

'So what did he look like? White, black, what?'

When Lewis just shrugged, Deano looked at Benton, who had to check himself before reeling off a standard-format police description of the offender.

'About your height, Deano. Dark hair. A white guy. Not fat, not muscly either. Looked like he was fit though. And fast. I reckon he's a hard bastard from somewhere, the way he used that pool cue. He never even blinked when he smacked Lewis round the head. Could've killed him.'

Lewis looked over at him. 'So how come you was there? I didn't see you when I went in.'

Benton shrugged. 'Saw them slappers go in, fancied a pint and a chat with 'em, but they legged it when you came in. Ran off with the tossers playin' pool. You put the shits up them, you know how people are scared of you.'

Flattery worked on Lewis's ego, especially in his fragile state right now when his ego was probably more bruised than his body. He groaned and lay back down, holding the ice pack to his head again with his bruised and swollen hand, trying to cool both injuries at the same time. His hand hurt more than his head, and he wasn't sure which injury was making him feel sick.

'So,' Deano began. 'We need to find this guy, this *nobody man*, and sort him. Show everybody else they don't fuck with us. Nobody has before, not like this.'

'Yeah, right, man. And how do we do that?' Lewis snapped. 'We don't know him, nobody knows him. Ain't seen him before. Dunno what he wants, do we?'

'Well, we know he's got one of our fuckin' guns!' shouted Deano.

Lewis looked meaningfully at Benton, then back at Deano.

'So what?' said Deano. 'He knows already, saw this guy take it off you, like takin' it off a fuckin' child. Does this nobody man know about the rest?'

'Couldn't do.' Lewis shook his head, then instantly regretted it as nausea gripped at him and the room spun around. 'Nah, he didn't see nuffin. I was in the back, never came out the bar with anything.'

Deano nodded thoughtfully. Benton had pricked up his ears at this. So Lewis had gone through to the back room of the Coalpool Tavern for something to do with the Baikals, had he? Well, that narrowed things down a bit. A beer cellar would be an ideal place to store weapons. Cool, dark, away from prying eyes. Secure. Everyone knew that the Tavern was under Keepers' control, so it wouldn't get burgled or vandalised. Good intel to be passed on. Neither Deano nor Lewis had realised what they may have just let slip.

'Right. Send out a Flashpic message to all the Keepers. Tell them what happened and tell them to keep their fuckin' eyes open for this wanker.'

'Tell them what?' Lewis looked up at Deano. 'Don't tell anybody I got beat up.'

Deano looked incredulous. 'Are you serious? Every fucker on Coalpool will know by now, you dickhead.' Deano almost grinned at Lewis's discomfort. 'Forget it. No fucker will dare say anything to you, especially after what we're gonna do to this bastard.'

Lewis grimaced, but he knew that Deano was right. Again.

'If they see him,' Deano continued, 'I wanna know. I'll have him, I'll be ready for him. Just make sure none of them take him on before I get there. The bastard is mine.'

Benton looked from one to the other. Lewis didn't look like he was jumping to any commands any time soon. 'If you want, Deano, I'll do that. Messin' around with a phone screen will make Lewis's head spin.'

'Yeah, that's about right. He's so battered he can't even use his fuckin' phone!' Deano didn't look like he was amused. No, not at all. 'Give me your phone, Benton, I'll set you up on our Flashpic.'

Only Lewis, Welchy, Deano and Jonah had full access to the Flashpic messaging account. Everyone else was able to reply to messages and view images and videos but not send out messages in the first place. Benton would now be able to give his phone to the IT specialists back at HQ at some point to see if they could gather even more intel.

Deano finished what he was doing with Benton's phone and passed it back to him. 'Send the message out today, before this wanker tries it on again with us. I want this dealt with, soon as.'

Benton nodded and turned to leave.

'If this tosser messed up your plans with the ladies today,' Deano said to Benton, 'go see Mandy Prees in Cartbridge Crescent. Tell her I sent ya. She'll sort ya out proper!'

Benton flashed what he hoped was a lascivious grin at Deano. 'Right. Thanks, man. See ya later then.'

After sending the Flashpic message to all the Keepers, Benton grabbed his bike and pedalled away towards Cartbridge Crescent in case Deano was watching, but he had no intention of swinging by there just yet, if ever. He had a sitrep to send, and he made his way to a telephone box on Goscote Lane. Using the same phone box repeatedly was bad form, in case he was seen, and it was dangerous to use a mobile phone in case it got into the wrong hands and someone checked his calls list.

Pushing coins into the slot, ignoring the stink of piss and keeping his feet well clear of the pile of faeces in the corner of the kiosk, Benton held the phone away from his face so it wasn't touching his skin. He had already checked the inside of the handset to make sure that there were no razor blades or syringe needles attached by Blu Tack. It was incredible what people did for kicks these days, but Benton had no intention of ending up having to see the Occupational Health Dept for blood tests after spiking himself on these dodgy booby traps. When he had worked in Birmingham, the ambulance crews who had to respond to hoax calls in blocks of flats told him they would always push the lift buttons with a pen, as there were often needles wedged in there, waiting for an unsuspecting finger. The bannisters on the stairs would have razor blades stuck on the underside too. How people lived in those places was a mystery to Benton, but he supposed that you just got used to it.

After hearing the dead silence when the ring tone stopped, he gave his half of the code.

'UC-27. Sitrep.'

Immediately there was a reply. 'UC-27, this is control. Verify code, please.'

Benton replied without hesitation, 'Operation Finders. Code 63679A.'

'Thank you, UC-27. Please wait.'

Detective Sergeant Tunstall came on the line. 'You're updating late today. What's up?'

Benton wasted no time, passing on the details of the incident at the Coalpool Tavern, and the subsequent intel obtained.

'Do you think it's legit? Could it be their way of giving you misinformation to check you out? If we go raiding that place now and there's nothing there, you're compromised. They'd know straightaway that you'd given the info.'

'I know that, Sarge, but I think on balance it's good.

They were too wound up by Lewis getting beaten to try and be clever. The agenda was strictly on finding this guy and sorting him out. The guns only got mentioned because Lewis had his weapon stolen.'

'I'd have loved to have seen that bastard getting his comeuppance,' DS Tunstall said, and Benton could almost picture his smile. 'Not that I'm condoning vigilante violence, of course.'

Benton grinned. 'Course not, Sarge. But it was well worth seeing. This guy, whoever he is, just took him apart without breaking a sweat. Cool as a cucumber.'

'Any ideas who he is?'

'No idea, Sarge, but I got a really good look at him. I could have a photo-fit drawn up.'

'Not just yet, you're far more valuable there for now. The Detective Chief Superintendent is personally taking an interest in these guns and he's not happy that they're on our patch and unaccounted for. I don't think he'll be too unhappy about a couple of local ruffians getting slapped about a bit in the meantime.'

'OK, I get the message. But I reckon that you should check out the Tavern, Sarge. We don't know how long the guns are going to be there. I can't imagine that Deano will be arming his Keepers – they're mostly just thieves, and lots of them are still kids, technically. I reckon he's doing a deal with someone, either to curry favour with some big boys from Birmingham, or as part of a drugs deal. Some of the guns will probably stay in the local area though. It's worrying, especially now that the Keepers are all spooked.

They'll be shooting at shadows.'

'I agree. I'll speak with the boss, see what he wants to do. Final decision is out of my hands, but if I were you, I'd steer clear of the Tavern for the next couple of days. I'll let you know what's happening at your next sitrep.'

'Cheers, Sarge. Oh, by the way. Is there any mention of Special Branch or military involvement in the search for these weapons?'

'Not that I'm aware of. Why do you ask?'

'Just a hunch, I suppose. This guy was good. Drives a Land Rover with no number plates on it. I just wondered.'

'I'll bear it in mind, but as far as I know, no one else is out there looking for them, at least, not from our side. God only knows who else might be involved from the other gangs though. Be careful.'

'Will do, Sarge.' Benton hung up the phone, thinking that if he was being careful, he wouldn't be doing this job in the first place. After checking the area around the phone box, he picked up his bike and headed off towards Goscote.

He'd been sub-letting a room from another of the Keepers. Another welfare state scam. People get housing benefit, usually from some sort of disability benefit swindle, then they illegally sub-let rooms or entire properties to other people who can't get on the housing ladder, or who are trying to stay under the radar so don't apply for housing in their own name. Reputable landlords always want identification and references, but sub-letters generally couldn't care less. So Benton paid fifty pounds per week for a bedroom in a three-bedroom semi-detached house, unfurnished, shared access to a scabby bathroom with a drug addict rent boy and an alcoholic ex-convict. The kitchen was also shared, but as the alcoholic frequently puked in there, no one used it for preparing food. Neither asked questions, and the landlord got paid cash in hand monthly, in advance. No contracts, no references. If the rent was late, the room got re-let to someone else.

Benton headed there now, intending to grab a few hours of sleep before going out again for the night. He had a feeling that events were likely to heat up soon, and he didn't want to be too tired to react if they did.

Chapter 14

The day of Janice's death

A stolen black Yamaha R6 sports motorcycle pulled up next to the Hanford Sub Post Office. Jonah stayed on the bike as Deano jumped off the tiny rear seat and ran in, carrying only a rucksack and a pistol. To add a menacing air, and to avoid identification, he wore a black visor on his crash helmet. As he ran through the door, he fired two shots, one at the protective Perspex screen and one into the lower leg of the nearest customer in the queue.

There were about fifteen customers waiting in the Post Office, including a young woman with two small children. Deano threw the rucksack towards the counter clerk and then made straight for the woman and grabbed her by the ponytail. He pointed the gun at the nearest child and yelled at the counter clerk to fill the bag with money. The customer who had been shot in the leg was screaming and bleeding, people were shoving each other out of the way to escape, and an old man was pushed backwards into the sliding exit door. He fell awkwardly, gashing his face open.

As people panicked and tried to get out of the door, he was wedged firmly into the opening, hindering their escape. In the ensuing panic, the counter clerk, using her wits and training, started to fill the rucksack and keep the gunman focussed on her.

'I'm doing it, I'm doing as you say, don't harm her, it's not my money, you can have every penny, just don't hurt her or the kiddies. OK, I'm filling the bag.' She rammed notes into the bag, emptying the till. She reached for a large coin bag next to her seat.

'Just fuckin notes, you dumb Paki bitch!' Deano roared and fired off another shot at the Perspex. This time the bulletproof Perspex cracked, and the Indian clerk got the message. She shoved notes into the bag as quickly as she could. Tens, fives, twenties, fifties, even a load of euros. When the bag looked over half full, Deano shoved the young woman towards the counter, still gripping her ponytail and shaking her head viciously. 'Grab the bag off the fuckin' Paki and give it to me,' he screamed in her ear. Terrified, the sobbing woman did as she was told. By now, the children were also screaming and the whole scene was pandemonium.

Deano fired another couple of random shots and ran through the door, kicking out savagely as he went past the old man, his boot connecting with his frail ribcage. A random ricochet of Deano's last shot had embedded in the old man's back. He slumped unconscious onto the floor, thankfully never feeling the kick that fractured his ribs and punctured his lungs.

Deano jumped on the back of the Yamaha motorcycle, pulling on the rucksack as Jonah revved the engine hard and pulled into the mid-morning traffic. The whole episode had lasted less than a minute, in and out and away. They sped down the busy road. Just before the motorway junction, they pulled into a layby and stopped the bike. There was a Suzuki GSXR 750 in the layby with the ignition already hotwired. They had left it there only four minutes ago. As Deano started the still warm engine of the waiting bike, Jonah revved the Yamaha hard, pointed it at the hedge alongside the layby and dumped the clutch, falling off the back of the bike as it disappeared into the hedge. He jumped up onto the second bike's pillion seat as Deano roared away from the layby.

Within seconds they were doing eighty miles an hour down the M6 southbound motorway slip road. Minutes after that, they were rapidly filtering through the slowed traffic in the roadworks, having chosen this route to deter a police chase. After Junction 12, Deano eased off the speed a little and coasted into the left-hand lane. At Junction 11 they exited the motorway and were soon into the maze of housing estates of North Bloxwich. Deano pulled into a disused factory car park and stopped the bike just inside the loading bay, out of sight of the main road. Jonah jumped off the back and Deano put the bike on the side-stand, getting off and stretching his legs. At six feet and four inches tall, he was hardly the ideal rider for a Suzuki GSXR 750, but the lightweight, powerful and fast bike was ideal for his purposes that day.

'Right then, Jonah, let's just count this lot and you can scoot. Keep your eyes on that road.' Deano started to pull out the cash from the bag and loosely arrange it into piles. 'Fuckin' hell, the dumb bitch put euros in here. Do I look like I'm off to fuckin' Ibiza? Fucks sake.'

Jonah felt sick but still kept his eyes firmly on the entrance to the factory and the road beyond. It wouldn't do to let Deano down. He would be pumped up with adrenaline already, and he had a pistol in his jacket pocket, so Jonah didn't want any security guards or druggies looking for a quiet place surprising them. Deano quickly finished counting the money and shoved it all back into the bag.

'Not bad. There's twenty grand in there. Take it to Bedders Road, give it to the old man, tell him to put it in the safe and lock it. I'm going to see one of the bitches. Man, I'm pumped up! Feels fuckin' great, don't it?' He slapped Jonah on the shoulder and grinned, a wolfish leer that made him look more than a little unhinged.

'Yeah, Deano. I'm good man, good. I'll get this to the house. See you later then.' Jonah waited for Deano to slip quickly away on the Suzuki then ran into the shadows of the loading bay. He fumbled with his trousers and dropped them barely in time before his bowels unloaded in a rush of cramping fire. He felt sick. He used a five pound note from the top of the rucksack to wipe himself, then pulled his trousers up. He knew that Deano and the other Keepers got off on this sort of thing, but it just scared the crap out of Jonah, literally. He knew how to ride a motorcycle, that wasn't the problem. He enjoyed the rush of the speed and buzzing through the slow traffic on a stolen bike, but he hated the thought of what Deano had done in the Post Office. He had heard the screaming, and the shots. The first shot that had hit someone in the leg had splattered blood up the window, and he had seen Deano kick that old man on the way out. There was no need for that, he wasn't in the way, wasn't trying to stop Deano. The poor old bloke was just terrified and trying to escape. Jonah hoped the old guy would be OK, but he had a feeling that he would never be OK again.

As the nausea settled a bit, and his guts stopped screaming at him, Jonah picked up the rucksack and trudged off towards Bedders Road. He would have to deal with Deano's father now, and he was crazier than Deano. At least he could outrun that loony old fat bastard, Jonah grinned to himself. Old Man Dean had lost half a leg to diabetes a couple of years ago, wore a badly made prosthetic limb and was drunk most of the time anyway. He'd just leave the bag with him and go and find a quiet place to lie down for a bit.

It would be pointless going home to his family's house in Holden Crescent. Even if none of his elder brothers were home, which was unlikely, his mother would have him doing errands for her, fetching booze or cigarettes usually. At nineteen years old, Jonah was the youngest of five brothers. None of them had jobs, all of them liked either drugs or booze, and three of them still lived at home. He was either their whipping boy, errand boy or punchbag, depending on their mood and what sort of day they'd had. He decided that he would take a tenner out of the loot and go get himself some fish and chips and find somewhere quiet for a while. Deano would be occupied with one of his slappers for an hour, so he wouldn't be phoning Jonah. There was no one else who gave a toss enough to bother him, so he figured he could get some rest. He'd been up all night stealing the two bikes used in today's escapade and he had had to check them over too. It was shocking how some people didn't look after their bikes properly. The last thing he wanted was for one of them to break down in the middle of a job, Deano would beat the crap out of him for that. It was a pity he couldn't keep the Yamaha though. He'd enjoyed riding that. Stealing another bike wasn't really an option, as one of the other Keepers would only have it off him. Welchy was the usual culprit for that. Too lazy or stupid to steal his own stuff, he'd just take it off the younger or smaller members of the gang instead.

An hour later, still high on drugs and sex, Deano was sauntering out of one of the flats in Cartbridge Crescent, where he had been visiting one of his girlfriends. In truth, they didn't consider themselves to be his girlfriends, but what choice did they have really? The latest lucky lady had had to hide her boyfriend in one of the other bedrooms. If Deano had found out she had a boyfriend it wouldn't have gone well for either of them. She hadn't seen or heard from Deano for about six months, as he'd supposedly found himself a pretty young thing in Coalpool, but that one was pregnant now, so Deano had lost interest and had started paying visits to some of his old favourites again. Deano had left his jacket and shirt in the dustbin of the house he'd just visited as they were splattered with blood, so he rode the GSXR down towards the back of Ryecroft Cemetery shirtless. It was a warm enough day, and he'd built up a bit of a sweat.

The sweat made his false tattoos on his neck run and smudge. He rubbed at them to make them illegible. Should really have got rid of them before seeing that bitch, but no matter, she would keep her mouth shut. He had crudely drawn the number eighteen and a swastika on his neck to throw as a red herring. Both of those tattoos were known to be used by neo-Nazi gangs as the number eighteen signified the first and the eighth letter of the alphabet, AH, for Adolf Hitler, and the swastika was self-explanatory. Deano didn't have any allegiance or sympathy with neo-Nazis. He hated everyone with equal intensity, regardless of race or religion. In fact, he couldn't think of any one person that he actually liked. Some people he tolerated, some he openly disliked, and an unlucky few he actually despised. The police and the state benefits staff fell into the latter category.

He rode the Suzuki along the tracks of the disused railway of the LMS, intending to dump it, burn it and get rid of the last piece of evidence. He was thinking about the girl he had just visited, and the fun he'd had, when a dog's barking and lunging at him almost knocked him off the bike. Fucking dogs, he hated fucking dogs. He skidded to a halt and turned around to give the owner of the dogs some verbal abuse.

From where Jonah was lying half asleep on the steep

banks of the LMS waste ground, he sat up and watched the altercation. He recognised Deano of course, but didn't know the woman. 'Just say sorry,' he muttered to himself, giving silent advice to the woman. 'Just let it go.' He heard Deano shout something at her, but couldn't hear what he said over the noise of the bike engine and the dogs' barking. Seeing the woman turn and walk away, Jonah breathed a sigh of relief for her. He'd seen more than enough violence for one day. Then as disaster happened and Deano dropped the bike, Jonah tensed up again. 'No, no, fuckin' no,' he muttered. Deano would be embarrassed and Jonah knew how that would make him angry, but the savagery of what happened next both stunned and sickened Jonah and he turned and vomited his fish and chip lunch into the long grass next to where he lay.

When he turned back, the dogs had stopped barking, and the woman lay still on the track. Deano was nowhere to be seen. Jonah scrambled down the embankment.

The woman was collapsed half off the main track with her large black dog still lying across her chest. Kneeling down next to her, Jonah could see that neither of them were moving. The woman's eyes were open but they weren't staying in focus. Blood from both victims pooled around their inert bodies and, knowing it was no use, that he couldn't help here, Jonah carefully backed away, desperately trying not to leave any footprint or trace of himself. Not knowing what to do, he crawled off into the bushes and lay there sobbing for a while. Should he call for an ambulance? Police? What if no one found her before it got dark? He couldn't stand the thought of leaving the poor woman lying here overnight. The decision was taken away from him, mercifully, when he saw two men walking down the overgrown path. One of them broke into a run and shouted out a name as he saw the two bodies. Jonah sat in the bushes hidden from view, frozen to the spot for what seemed like an eternity before coming to his senses and making his escape to the other end of the Yellow Mess and away through the Cartbridge estate. He knew it wouldn't be long before the police would be all over the area. The Post Office robbery was bad enough, but this unprovoked and savage attack on an innocent woman was in a different league, and Jonah wanted no part of it.

Steven Jenkins

Chapter 15

Occasionally Dan and Janice argued. Not very often, but when they did, it was like a thunderstorm after a long dry spell, clearing the atmosphere and blocking out everything else for a short time. Wild, noisy, tumultuous and incredible to watch – from a distance. They stood in the front garden of their house having one of those arguments now.

Janice's green eyes flashed angrily. 'You can't do this, Dan, it makes you as bad as them. You need to forget this violence, go to the hospital, start your treatment and get better.'

'It's pointless, you know that. It'll just prolong things, give me maybe another year. And for what?'

'To live, you bloody idiot.' Janice hurled a piece of wood, fallen from the tree in their front yard, straight at Dan. It hit him on the shoulder but strangely it made his head throb. 'To live. Do you think you're God? Do you think you choose when you die? How many people would give anything for a second chance, for just a few more months? How many stillborn children would love a chance to live a while, to take first steps, say first words? Don't be so fucking selfish.'

Dan frowned. Janice never swore. This wasn't like her. He supposed it must be the anger, and the reference to the stillborn child …

They hadn't had any children, which was their joint choice. When they had first married, while they lived in Germany, Janice quickly fell pregnant, but at six months she miscarried. There had been no warning, no accident, no preceding illness, just a sudden terrible cramping stomach pain, torrents of blood and a rush to the German hospital near where they lived at the time. The doctor had told them afterwards that it was an 'idiopathic and spontaneous placental abruption'. In other words, Janice's body had just let go of the baby, kicked it out for absolutely no fathomable reason. She was distraught and decided then and there that she couldn't go through it again. Dan had felt powerless and helpless, unable to comfort her and knowing that there were no words to make it right, so instead he had just stayed silent and held her. They had discussed it afterwards, a couple of months after she was home from hospital, and decided that they wouldn't try for another baby. That had been when she was twenty-three years old, and time had slipped away so fast. There had never been another discussion, nor any contraception, but Janice never conceived again. Dan felt secretly guilty, as he wasn't that keen on having children anyway. He had been at first, had wanted kids to make their little family complete, and to make Janice happy, but as he grew older he came to the conclusion that this was no world to bring children into. Perhaps it was the careers he had chosen that made him cynical, but he preferred to think of it as realistic. Besides, he had seen how much the miscarriage had hurt Janice and he never wanted to be the cause of that hurt again. She had never spoken of it again, until now.

'Are you even listening to me?' She slapped him angrily on his arm, making his head throb with pain again. 'It's just bloody typical of you, to be so stubborn and pig-headed. Get yourself to hospital, Dan.' She stood there, eyes blazing, arms folded, glaring at him. 'At least have some treatment to slow things down a bit.'

Dan stared at her, puzzled. 'But, I haven't told you. When did I tell you?' His head hurt and he put a hand to his right temple. That slap from the young man who rescued Lewis must have been harder than he thought to leave him confused and nauseous like this. Looking up at Janice again, he saw that his father was standing next to her.

'She's right, son,' said Pete. 'She usually is.' He smiled at Dan. 'You have to wake up and get yourself to the hospital. You don't know what they can do for you these days, they work bloody miracles, these doctors.'

Dan stared, speechless, his head throbbing and his vision blurring. 'But you're ... I went to your funeral, I travelled in the ambulance with you to hospital. You're ...'

'Dead, Dan. Yes, he is. We both are, and you know it.' Janice was now sitting next to him in the front seat of the Land Rover, though Dan couldn't remember moving. Pete was sitting behind them, in the back, holding Bryn on a lead as if they were all about to go off for a drive and a walk. Janice reached across and gently shook Dan, her tone relenting. 'I know that you're angry, you want revenge, for you, for us. It's who you are. But it's not helping us, Dan, and it's making you more ill. Every day that you miss your treatment is making you more and more ill. Please, go and see your doctor. Now wake up.' She shook him again, more firmly this time. 'Wake up.'

She kissed him, and there is no more passionate a kiss between lovers than the last kiss of the brave man who is about to go into battle. The intense feeling of those few seconds must last a lifetime, must sustain him through the conflict, through loneliness, hunger and times of bowel-crushing fear. Going into battle was how Dan felt right then.

Dan tried to reach out to her, to hold her, but his arms felt like they were pinned to his sides. He looked around to the back of the Land Rover, but his dad and his dog weren't there. When he looked back to where Janice had been sitting, she was gone too. Tears blurred his vision as he heard her say, 'Wake up.'

'I don't want to,' he croaked through his tears. 'I'll stay with you instead.'

He heard Janice sigh. 'Just wake up, you stubborn idiot!'

Dan woke with a start, nausea ripping through him, and he reached for the door of the Land Rover, fumbling for the catch and opening it just in time to vomit onto the driveway for a second time. He felt like the worst hangover in the world was wreaking havoc with his head and stomach, only he hadn't had the pleasurable alcohol consumption beforehand. Looking at his watch, Dan realised that he'd been passed out in the Land Rover for more than twelve hours. Looking at his trousers, he also realised that he'd wet himself, and he'd bitten his tongue by the sore feel of it. The realisation dawned on his groggy mind that he must have had a convulsion while he was passed out.

'Rough night, mate?' came a voice not too far away.

Dan looked up to see the postman walking up his driveway, holding out a bunch of letters warily, which didn't surprise Dan, knowing how he must look.

'Yeah, something like that, matey, sorry. Just leave the mail on the bonnet there. Thanks.'

The postie put the letters down on the bonnet and retreated down the driveway. Dan walked unsteadily round his car and picked up the mail before stumbling into the house.

After a hot shower and a cup of tea, Dan felt recovered enough to open his mail. Junk, junk, he discarded the first two envelopes. Then seeing the NHS postmark on the third, he paused before opening it. It was from Dr Jeffreys' secretary. He read it through, then put it to one side as he made another brew. Jeffreys had sent a letter expressing concern that Dan hadn't arrived for his first two sessions of radiotherapy and hadn't returned messages left on his answerphone. Staring out of the kitchen window, Dan wondered if it was all worth bothering with. Remembering his … dream? Hallucination? Delirium? Whatever it was, Dan knew deep down that he should at least give it a go. It would have been what Janice and his dad would have wanted him to do, had they still been here.

Picking up his house phone, he called Jeffreys' office to make an appointment. What the hell, at least it might give him time to finish what he'd started. Knowing that blackouts and convulsions were definite signs that his condition was worsening, Dan had the sense that time was running out.

While he was on hold, waiting for the NHS machine to slowly answer his call, Dan thought about the situation. Letting the criminals get away with what they'd done was not an option. 'If it's the last thing I do, I'll have the bastards,' he muttered to himself. That thought made him sit down and think. The last thing he may well accomplish in his life would be a series of violent acts, revenge, retribution, anger, causing more grief to someone somewhere. Was that really what he wanted? Wasn't he bigger than that? Remembering his father, his dog, and his beautiful wife didn't clarify things at all.

He wanted revenge, and Dan knew full well that the British criminal justice system would not provide him with a shred of that. More likely, if he went to the police now, he would be the one in prison, and the Keepers would end up with compensation and sympathy. Should he just let it go? He'd put one of them out of action completely, the one who stole his father's motorbike and consequently caused his death. Shouldn't that be enough? But what about Janice, and his dog? What about the fear that these delinquents caused in the town that decent people tried to live in?

A voice in his head argued that he couldn't be responsible for all of this, that systems were in place to deal with these problems, but another stronger voice argued back that these systems were failing, that the British people were facing huge social problems. Violence, theft, gangs, drugs, extortion and massive abuse of the welfare system were rife in modern Britain, and gangs like the Keepers were only one small part of it.

'So what can you do about it?' one voice argued. 'Who are you, some comic book hero?' Dan knew that his inner voice was right, that he couldn't possibly right all the wrongs in society, but he also knew that he couldn't let his loved ones' deaths go unpunished. Sure, it may not be the right and proper punishment, but it seemed to Dan to be the only option available to him. Even if the police and Criminal Prosecution Service decided to pursue the matters, it would take years for the cases to finish in the courts. Clever solicitors and barristers would tie up proceedings in legal red tape and technicalities, dragging the court cases on for years, at more expense to the taxpayer, eventually ending up with paltry sentences to the accused, even if they were found guilty.

No, that wasn't an option any more. They started this. Dan and his family had done nothing to provoke any of this, had done nothing wrong to anyone, and they didn't deserve this. Once upon a time, Dan had been trained by the British Army, as a servant of the Crown and its government, to deal with transgressors and enemies with force. Surely, if ever there was a time and place for that force, it was now? Were these criminals any less of a problem than the Irish terrorists and religious extremists like ISIS? Some could argue that they were more of a problem, as they erode all that was good and fair in the country from the inside. They took advantage of British justice, or lack of it, and they took everything they owned from society while giving absolutely nothing back. Dan saw the Keepers, and those like them, as the weights that were dragging British society down deeper in the mire, and he knew that he wasn't the only one who felt like this.

His mind was made up. This was one last mission, which only he could complete satisfactorily, as far as he saw it. Justice to those that deserved it. He had worked at a bikers' festival a few years ago, providing medical cover over the weekend of the festival, and he had seen a tattoo on the arm of an Outlaws MC biker. It had read 'We only do bad things to bad people'. Certainly Dan had seen no evidence of any other type of violence that weekend. There had been no sense of intimidation, and as a paramedic, Dan had been treated with utmost respect, certainly more so than when working on a typical Friday night in the city. That was how Dan felt now, that he would be justified, as long as there was no collateral damage, as long as all of his retribution was carried out on the 'bad' people.

'Hello.' A voice on the end of the phone brought him back to the present. 'This is Clare, secretary to Dr Jeffreys. How may I help you today?'

Dan made the appointment.

Chapter 16

National Newspaper Tabloid

Elderly Hero Dies in Post Office Robbery

olice are appealing for witnesses to a violent and savage robbery that took place at a Post Office in Stoke-on-Trent yesterday. A helmet-wearing gunman shot two innocent customers before taking a young mother hostage. He escaped with an undisclosed amount of cash, but as he made his escape he violently assaulted an elderly man who it is believed was trying to stop him. The elderly man collapsed due to his injuries and was declared dead on the scene by paramedics attending the incident.

Neighbours of the elderly victim described him as 'a lovely gentleman who had served his queen and country in World War II.'

The other victim of the robbery, who was shot in the leg as the gunman made his dramatic and terrifying demands, is said to be in hospital with serious but stable injuries.

Police have issued a description of the gunman as about six feet tall, well-built, with a Black Country accent and neo-Nazi style tattoos on his neck. Police state that they are following several leads and are confident that they will apprehend the gunman and his accomplice who rode the getaway motorcycle.

Chapter 17

Although he was in his early fifties, Peter Crosslyn was still an intimidating looking character, standing over six feet tall, well-built and with close-cropped black hair that set off his dark eyes perfectly. Soulless and cruel was how his own wife had described him, before she had left him. Peter was accompanied by two of his younger brothers, Michael and Joseph. God help the person that shortened those names to Mickey and Joey.

Joseph thumped on the door of the flat in Cartbridge Crescent. 'Come out, we only want to talk to you,' he shouted in his coarse travellers' brogue. 'Just open the door a wee bit, you don't have to let us in. Just a quick word and we'll be on our way.'

The three brothers could hear adult voices inside, and a baby crying at full volume.

'Get lost, you're scaring my kid!' came the reply.

'I'll do more than that if you don't open the fucking door, you stupid—' started Peter, but Joseph interrupted him with an elbow in the ribs. Joseph was the ladies' man in the trio, dark hair, green eyes, in his late forties but slim and gentle looking. A real wolf in sheep's clothing.

'Mandy, love, come on. Really, we only want to ask you a couple of questions, then we'll be off. That's all, I promise. We don't have any argument with you now, do we? Why would we want to hurt you or your wee kiddie?' Joseph looked at Peter and motioned for him to step away from the spy hole of the front door. 'For fuck's sake, Peter, I wouldn't open the door either with you standing there looking like a bailiff. Give her a bit of space.'

'What's it about? Why do you want to talk to me?' Mandy shouted from the other side of the door. The brothers could also hear a male voice, pleading with Mandy not to let them in, not to open the door.

'We don't want to shout it in the corridor, love, it's private. Don't want any of yer nosey neighbours hearing our private business, do we?'

'I don't have any business with gyppos,' came the reply.

Peter lifted his foot and kicked the front door just below the door latch. It swung inwards, sending Mandy flying as it hit her. He took two steps into the hallway and grabbed Mandy by her hair, lifting her to her feet as she squealed. The young man standing further in the hallway put his hands up imploringly.

'Please, don't hurt her, she didn't mean it, you scared her, that's all. She was going to open the door anyway.'

Michael backhanded the man across the mouth as he walked past, knocking him into one of the bedrooms off the hallway. 'Should've opened it sooner then, shouldn't she? Who the fuck are you anyway?'

'He's my boyfriend, you wanker.' Mandy was struggling and trying to escape Peter's grip but he was dragging her towards her boyfriend in the bedroom. In the background the baby's screaming reached the point where glass would shatter. Joseph went into the other room and in a few seconds the screaming quietened down.

'What have you done? Bastard!' Mandy screamed and thrashed around in Peter's vice-like grip, trying to lash out at him with her feet and fists. Her boyfriend lay dazed on the floor, blood running from his mouth where his lip had been split open.

Joseph came into the room, cradling the baby in his arms, cooing and smiling at her. The baby was giggling and seemed comfortable. 'Calm down, I'm not going to hurt the kiddie. What kind of man do you think I am?'

Mandy was crying now. 'What do you want? I haven't done anything. Don't hurt her,' she begged.

'I told you, we just wanted to talk to you. That's all. It was you who started with the name-calling and upset Peter here. If you'd opened the door, none of this would have happened. Now,' he stroked the baby's soft hair, starting off a fresh bout of giggling, 'let's all calm down. OK?'

Mandy nodded, tears spilling down her cheeks.

'We hear that you're a wee bit fond of a certain young man we're trying to track down. Name of Deano. He runs the local gang, from what we've heard.' Joseph immediately noticed Mandy's pupils dilate. 'We wanted a chat with him, but we've lost his phone number and address. You know how it is when you change yer phone.' He shrugged and smiled. 'A bit of business to see to, that's all.' He stroked the baby's head again. 'It's important that we speak to him, in person like. So, where does he live?'

Mandy was visibly shaking now. 'I-I don't know. He always comes here. I've never been to his house.'

'Oh, come on. I'm sure you know where yer lover man hangs his coat at night. We're asking nicely, no threats.' Joseph glanced around at Mandy's boyfriend lying on the floor spitting blood and what looked like teeth into a tissue, and at the remains of the front door hanging off its hinges in the hallway. 'Well, that was a misunderstanding. You upset wee Peter here, calling us names. We're not gyppos, we're fairground people, and there's a bit of a difference, see. He gets sensitive about it.'

'He's not my lover man,' sobbed Mandy. 'I don't have much say in the matter, do I? Deano's a bloody nutcase. He don't come here that often now anyway, since I had Siobhan. Please don't hurt her.' She held out her hands to the baby, wiping the tears away from her face, trying to reassure her with a smile.

'Siobhan? That's a lovely name,' said Joseph, tickling the baby and making her coo with pleasure. 'We're not animals, love. We just want to know where Deano is. We've got some, well, some business with him.'

'I haven't seen him for ages,' Mandy sobbed.

'Ah, come on now.' Joseph smiled. 'See, we know for a fact he was here not long ago. There was a Post Office robbery in Stoke that the police think was done by some English Nazi group from up there. We think different. Was

Deano here on the third of May, bragging about having some cash? Riding a motorbike?'

'I don't know, I don't remember.' Mandy looked at her boyfriend. He simply shrugged and looked away.

'So what about you, sonny?' Michael asked the boyfriend, who was still lying on the floor. 'Do you remember?'

'I wasn't here, I-I don't know,' he stammered, then spat more blood into the tissue.

'Wasn't here when?' Michael persisted, leaning over him.

'When he came round. I wasn't here.' The young man cowered back against the wall. 'I don't know anything about it.'

'So he did come round?' Joseph looked right at Mandy, and she saw a change to the pleasant demeanour in his eyes. Suddenly they were cold, menacing and seemed to see right through her.

She glared at her boyfriend. 'You wanker. You was here. Now you've dropped us in the shit, proper.' Mandy looked back at Joseph. 'Yes, he was here. I don't know the date. It was the start of the month like, just after I got my giro, but he didn't want none of that. Usually he takes some of it, but he just wanted his way. He was hyped up, bouncing off the walls, a bit rougher than usual. Didn't take long, though. It never does with him. Then he left. That's all I know.'

'Good girl. See, that wasn't too hard, was it?' Joseph went to hand over the baby, but as Mandy reached out to her, Peter yanked her hair back viciously.

'Just a couple of details to clear up though, Mandy. Then we'll be gone.' Joseph settled back on the bed, cradling the baby. 'Did he have a motorbike that day?'

Mandy nodded. 'Yeah, I think so. I heard one pull up before he turned up, then I'm sure he left on one. I heard it rev up after he left. And he had a helmet, I think.' She looked to her boyfriend for confirmation and he nodded resignedly.

'Anything else you remember about him that day?' Joseph asked quietly.

Mandy nodded. 'Yeah, there was something. He had new tattoos. Well, I thought they was tattoos at first but they was smudged. Daft tattoos, like numbers, and a German war thing.' She shrugged. 'I didn't ask cos I didn't care, I just wanted him gone. He's a bleedin' nutjob. Please don't tell him you asked me, OK? Don't say I said anything. He'll kill me, and the little 'un.'

'So,' Joseph continued in a soothing voice. 'Where does he live?'

Mandy hung her head. 'Bedders Road. I don't know the number, I swear. It's a house in the middle of the street, black door and big black metal gates. I don't know any more, I swear. Please.' She sniffed hard. 'Please don't tell him I told you.'

Joseph handed the baby back to Mandy. 'I don't think he'll bother you, love. I think he's going to have his hands full. Don't bother yerself over him. We won't tell him anything, don't you worry your pretty little head.' He stood up and turned to leave, motioning for his brothers to follow him.

As they walked back to their car, Joseph spoke to his

two brothers. 'Right, so we know he had a bike that day. We know he had fake tattoos, so it was probably him that did the robbery. I don't give a shit about that, but it puts him here at the right time, with a nicked bike. The police found pieces of a motorbike next to Janice when she was killed, and it was bound to be a nicked bike. Let's put two and two together. I think we just confirmed this bastard is our number four.'

'It's a bit of a stretch, Joseph,' Michael said.

'Not really.' Joseph shook his head. 'Who else steals bikes round here except this gang – what are they called?'

'Keepers,' said Peter.

'Yeah, right. The Keepers. So they steal all the bikes. One of them is used for a robbery. We know it wasn't who the police think it was because cousin Liam already had a word with the local Nazi wankers about shooting on his patch. It's bad for the fairground business if people are getting scared of guns and robberies in the area. The Nazis are just as pissed off cos it brought down a lot of bother off the police. I don't think even they're stupid enough to shit on their own doorstep.'

'So how does it link in with Deano?' Peter asked.

'The gunman had a Black Country accent, according to people in the Post Office. That brings us to Walsall. There's no other gangs who behave like this in other parts of the Black Country. And the police reckon it was a Baikal used in the robbery, that's what came out at the inquest of the dead old bloke. Hit by a ricochet and kicked in the head. Everyone knows Deano has a Baikal. He calls it his "pit bull". He's the leader of this gang, so if it wasn't him who did the robbery, he'll know who it was. But he was definitely riding a stolen bike round here that day.'

'How do we know it was nicked?' Michael asked.

Joseph sighed. 'Cos who else would be riding motorbikes on waste ground? They're bloody expensive things, Michael. And he never buys anything, does he? Just steals anything he wants, then gets rid of it and steals something else.' He took out his car keys as he reached their car. 'No, it was him. I feel it in my water. Let's go home and have a cuppa with the family, see what they want to do about it.'

'What about Danny Boy?' Michael asked as he got in the car. 'Are we getting him involved? He was her husband after all.'

Joseph shrugged. 'Nah. He's too straight up nowadays. He was a bit wild in his younger days but not now. Could handle himself too, eh, Peter?' He grinned in the mirror at Peter, who was sitting in the back seat.

'Piss off, Joseph,' warned Peter.

'What's this?' Michael looked from one to the other of his older brothers.

'You wouldn't remember, Michael, you were too young then. But Peter here,' he nodded at the rear view mirror at the glowering brother, 'Peter decided to warn Danny off marrying Janice. Said she had to marry one of her own kind, and told Danny to leave her alone.'

'What happened?' Michael asked.

'Joseph,' Peter again warned, but Joseph was obviously enjoying his brother's discomfort.

'Well, Danny didn't agree with Peter. He said Janice was old enough to make up her own mind, so Peter hit him. Well, he swung at him anyway. Danny Boy danced all round him, like a monkey round an elephant. When Peter wouldn't give up, Danny hit him a couple of beauties, right on the chin. Danny Boy was half his size but he stood and fought for his woman. After we woke Peter up with a bucket of water, Danny apologised, said he didn't want to fall out with his fiancé's family. The old man made him promise to look after her and let her see her family when she wanted, and that was that. Sorted out the proper way, like men.'

'Except he didn't look after her, did he? Our sister's dead,' Peter growled from the back seat.

Joseph nodded, and was silent for a minute. 'Yeah, she's dead. But she wasn't just our sister any more, she was a grown woman, and I don't blame Danny for this. I blame that bastard that ran her over and then stabbed her and robbed her as she lay dying.' His grip tightened on the steering wheel. 'But don't you worry yerself, Peter, we'll have the bastard, and he'll beg to die before we've finished with him, you can bet on that.' He spat out of the open car window to reinforce his point. 'He'll fucking beg.'

Chapter 18

National Newspaper Tabloid

*P*olice are appealing for witnesses to a sickening attack on a pensioner that happened yesterday in a busy Walsall street, near the local Post Office. Thugs terrorised a 75-year-old woman as she left the Post Office with her small pet dog, setting a vicious dog onto the smaller helpless pet. The two hoodie-wearing brutes grabbed the pensioner's handbag as she was distracted and then made their escape, leaving their attack dog behind to carry on with its macabre mission.

The pensioner's pet dog was killed outright in the brutal attack. The pensioner suffered bite wounds as she tried to intervene and save her beloved companion, and she also sustained a fractured hip after being knocked to the ground as the muggers made their cowardly escape.

Police are urging any witnesses to this callous and savage robbery to call 101 or to report it to CrimeStoppers, which they reassure is an anonymous service.

The dog used in the attack has been located and

destroyed. It is believed to have been stolen from a nearby garden earlier yesterday and given street drugs before the attack to make it turn vicious. The owners are said to be distraught, but have declined to comment on the matter.

Robbery is thought to be the motive for this cowardly attack, but the elderly victim had not been to the Post Office to withdraw money. She had in fact been there to pay a utility bill and the thieves escaped with only small change in the stolen handbag.

Chapter 19

'One pound fucking twenty pence!' The Keeper threw the handbag to the ground and turned on his companion, prodding him in the chest. 'You said she'd be getting her pension.'

The other Keeper shrugged. 'Well how was I supposed to know?'

'She's your bloody gran. You said she always gets her pension today.'

'She must've changed her mind. I dunno, do I? Is there anything else in there we can sell?'

The older of the two Keepers turned the bag upside down. Tissues, perfume, a couple of pens, an address book and a set of house keys fell out onto the ground. He picked up the keys. 'These'll do.'

The younger one, almost nineteen years old, caught his drift immediately.

'Yeah, she'll be in hospital for a few days. There's no one in the house. C'mon, it's only down the road. We'll find sumfin in there and get some cash. Gotta get some Monkey Dust, man. I'm getting the shakes.'

The Monkey Dust he referred to was the latest craze to hit inner-city streets in Britain. A cheaply made synthetic drug, it caused its users to feel strong and invincible, which often resulted in people injuring themselves. It could be injected, smoked or snorted and was incredibly addictive. The two hoodie-wearing Keepers had been using it for days, but had now run out of both the drug and funds to buy more.

They made their way to the pensioner's empty house, hoping for a find that would prove to be an easy sell. On the way, one of them had another bright idea.

'Why don't we ask Deano for some Dust? He's always got a stash lately.'

'Are you still smacked up? We got no money. Do you think he'll just hand it over? Yeah, lads, help yourself, don't mind me, just take all my fuckin' stash.' He slapped the younger Keeper round the head. 'Fool. Let's just get to your gran's house, see what she's got for us.'

The younger man pouted. 'No need for a slap, man. Just trying to be helpful. And she's my gran, so I get first pick of anything.'

'Yeah, whatever. She hidden any cash in the house? They all do it, these old gits. They all got money from the war or whatever. They should share it, then we wouldn't have to rob them. It's their own stupid fault.'

The younger one shrugged. 'Dunno. Probably. She's always got money to spend though. Always giving it to the little kids in the family.'

'Well it's your turn for some now, innit? Only fair.'

They walked hurriedly down the street before jumping over the wall of Ryecroft Cemetery to take a shortcut to the other estate.

Behind them, Jonah watched from a distance. He'd done some bad things in his time with the Keepers, but he thought these two had hit an all-time low. He'd heard about the robbery and the dogs. Jonah loved dogs. In fact, he liked dogs more than he liked most people, and certainly more than these two Keepers. He felt angry with these two, but didn't know what to do about it, so for now he just followed them. He wasn't really sure what he wanted to do, but he knew that he wanted to get at them, pay them back for what they'd done to the dogs and the old lady. There was no need for that. They could've just broken into her house at night if they wanted money. What they did was cruel and pointless.

He scrambled over the wall and quietly followed them through the cemetery, keeping to the trees and bushes that lined the grounds. They made enough noise anyway to drown out his footsteps, even if he'd been walking on the gravel paths. What he didn't know was that he had a follower himself.

From a distance, Dan had watched Jonah come out of the Tavern earlier that afternoon. He recognised him from the Flashpic video where Welchy had torched his dad's bike, remembered that Jonah had told Welchy not to set fire to the motorcycle because Deano had wanted to ransom it. This youth was probably one of the Keepers, but if he was, why was he following the other two? They certainly looked like members of the gang. Even without the hoodies they looked shifty, and Dan recognised the jittery mannerisms and loud voices that meant they were probably suffering withdrawal from something. There looked to be a hidden agenda here and it intrigued Dan. Was it something he could use to his advantage? Looking at his watch, he realised that whatever it was would have to wait. He had an appointment at the hospital with Dr Jeffreys in an hour's time. Just long enough to get back to his Land Rover and drive to the hospital. Casting another puzzled glance at Jonah as he scrambled over the cemetery wall after the other two, Dan turned and walked back down Coalpool Lane to where he'd left his car.

As he drove along Coalpool Lane, negotiating the speed bumps and finally turning back on himself through the housing estate, Dan let his memory take him back to growing up here. There'd be football matches and street games going on in the estate streets, unmarked and unspoken territories, but each group of friends knew how far they could extend their play zones. Sometimes the boundaries could merge, temporary unspoken treaties forged. Now of course there were too many cars, vans and pickup trucks parked in every street to allow kids to play those sorts of outdoor games. Not that this or the previous generation would use the space anyway. Most of them seemed to Dan to be part of the zombie generation, as he had heard them nicknamed. Heads down, staring at mobile phones constantly. Unaware of what was going on around them. Easy pickings for streetwise gangs like the Keepers who would mug them for the very phones that lowered their guard. The phones would then be replaced either by an insurance claim or stolen ones bought from the gangs that stole them in the first place.

Dan looked at the houses as he drove past. They seemed more tired, more scruffy and unkempt now, even though people had more money these days. He'd heard all the social arguments by the bleeding-hearts liberals about inner-city poverty being worse than ever, but he didn't accept it. Looking around, he saw newer cars than he'd ever seen here as a kid. The standard car then was a beat-up, rusting old British car. Morris, Austin, Rover, Hillman, all held together by the local welder and hobby mechanic. Every street had one or two of these men, unqualified but handy with spanners and welders. Now, most of the cars were foreign, Japanese, Korean, German and some French. His dad would never have driven one of those. They were fine cars, these foreign machines, well-engineered, but Pete had always insisted on British cars. He looked after them and they lasted. Which reminded Dan, he should go and collect the old man's Rover 75 at some point, before it got stolen from the driveway. He'd probably give it to Christine, as her old Renault had sounded on its last legs when he'd had a lift off her last week. That also seemed to be the new order of things in Britain, that working people on minimum wages had the oldest cars and struggled with their bills more than people who didn't work at all. Dan had tried to get his head around it but had given up long ago.

After driving around in a big circle through the estate and coming back onto Coalpool Lane, he went over the railway bridges that only bridged over empty grass tracks now, the railway being long gone, and passed the new children's play area on what used to be called the Sandhole. Back then it was an open expanse of grass, mostly ignored by local kids as it was right on the border of two estates and always in territorial dispute. A football game there could end up as a gang clash and a big fight, so kids just didn't bother with it, especially after what happened to Dan's friend Alex Chambers. Now, the Sandhole had been developed into a large play area, with expensive looking, brightly painted swings and climbing frames, large enough to allow maybe a hundred children to play. Apart from one or two young mums and their toddlers, it was deserted. Old habits die hard here, thought Dan. It was still disputed territory.

As he carried on towards the road out of Walsall and the M6 motorway, Dan drove down Proffitt Street and then onto Stafford Street. The decline here was stark. Small shops that were once owned by proud independent shopkeepers of the Arkwright generation had been replaced by seedy looking Western Union shops that looked like they had never been cleaned. There were more off-licences and mobile phone accessory dealers than shops selling food. The pubs were mostly closed down, only a couple left open to allow local criminals to gather somewhere. The huge church of Saint Peter that once stood imposing like a silent sentinel overlooking the populace now looked derelict, and Dan wondered how many people attended Sunday service here any more. He was never one for religion, but he could definitely see the benefits to a community of having a church as a focal point and a support network. The grand old building was now covered in Arabic graffiti, the grounds outside strewn with litter and detritus.

As he drove on past the magistrates' court, he saw the same type of people hanging around outside it as there had always been. Overweight women smoking cigarettes and shouting at young children running around, there to support their errant boyfriends or husbands who were looking uncomfortable in suits that were either borrowed or saved for court, so didn't fit any more. Of course, they'd all be innocent, and it would always be someone else to blame. Still the same as when he lived here. He shook his head as he drove past. Does no one ever learn?

As he trundled up the Wolverhampton Road towards the motorway junction at a steady thirty miles per hour past the speed cameras, he saw that this side of town had also deteriorated. The houses were in a shocking state of repair, even though they were mostly privately owned these days. Dan knew from his time as a paramedic that violence erupted here on a regular basis. Sometimes between families, but also from far-right gangs coming here to stir up unrest among the predominantly Muslim populace. Belligerent and hostile faces stared at him from the side of the road, and he noticed that there were no fuel stations along this road any longer. There used to be two or three but crime had taken its toll and they had given up and closed down, now operating as Eastern European car washes.

Dan eventually joined the M6 motorway at Junction 10 and mentally let out a sigh of relief as he drove steadily away from Walsall. The town and its surrounding areas had become a depressing place, certainly for him, and he guessed it would be the same for a lot of people living there.

On the way to the hospital, Dan mulled over what else he'd seen today. He wasn't sure about this ginger-haired lad, Jonah, that he thought to be one of the gang. At first he'd intended to snatch him as another of the Keepers but had then seen him act deferentially to an old couple walking along the road, stepping off the kerb to let them walk past. That didn't fit in with the arrogance and violence of the rest of the gang. He looked to be the right age, late teens, but didn't have the brash swagger that Dan had seen in the others he had observed. And he had argued with Welchy about setting fire to his dad's motorbike in the Flashpic video. From Dan's observations, he was usually on his own and avoided hanging out with others in the gang. Yes, he was definitely an oddity.

Pulling into the hospital car park about forty-five minutes later, Dan put thoughts of the Keepers to the back of his mind for now. He had promised Janice that he would get some treatment. Well, he had promised his hallucination of Janice. It meant the same thing to Dan. It suddenly struck him that he hadn't grieved properly yet, for either his wife or his father. There hadn't been time since he had started down this road of vengeance, and Dan knew that sooner or later it would catch up with him. That was if he had enough time left. Oh well, after today's appointment perhaps he'd know a bit more about that.

The waiting room was almost empty when Dan sat down, and it wasn't too long before he was sent through to Dr Jeffreys' consulting rooms. Dan was half expecting to see one of the junior consultants in the team but he was met by Jeffreys himself.

'Dan, come in, come in. Glad you decided to make time to see me,' Jeffreys greeted him warmly with a handshake and a pat on the shoulder. 'I heard about your sad news lately, old chap. Terrible things to happen, and so close together too.'

'How did you hear about that?' Dan was taken aback.

'It's a small world, you know. Paramedics speak to nurses, nurses speak to consultants, and so on.' He gestured at Dan to have a seat. 'Coffee? We have a lot to chat about, so you've got time.'

Dan sat back in the chair while Jeffreys ordered drinks from his receptionist via his intercom. All of this seemed so surreal, but then, so did most of his life lately. Janice and his father's deaths, the action against the Keepers … if only Jeffreys knew what state of mind Dan was in, he might not want to start the treatment.

'So,' Jeffreys sat forwards and leaned on his desk, steepling his hands together. 'Let's make a start, shall we?' He picked up a few documents on his desk. 'These are your previous scans and the results of your biopsies. The cells we took from those have been used to create the vaccine that we discussed, and the biopsies have also given us more insight into your GBM.' Jeffreys went through the scans and test results in some depth as Dan listened.

'The tumour is benign, which is good news.' He held up his hand as he continued. 'Good, but not great. There's less chance of it metastasising to other parts of your body, but it could still grow and expand, which is not healthy for the brain. We still need to treat it. Surgery has limited success, as the tumour too intertwined with the cortex. We should consider that is a last resort. My recommendation remains the same as at our last meeting. Start the radiotherapy, now, today. And then start the experimental vaccine treatment tomorrow.'

'So soon,' Dan said. 'I hadn't realised you'd want to start today.'

'The sooner we start this treatment, the better the chance of a success. Do you have somewhere more important to be?'

Dan liked Jeffreys' blunt approach. 'No, of course. Sorry. It's all happening so fast. And with everything else that's been going on, you know. I haven't really had time to absorb everything yet.'

'Well, we could put it off for a week, but I really wouldn't advise it.' He leaned forwards on his desk. 'I'm pulling out all the stops here, old boy. I feel like I owe you an enormous debt, and I'd like to repay it. What do you say? Can I send you down to the radiotherapist?' Seeing Dan's nod of assent, Jeffreys continued. 'Good man, excellent. Finish your coffee and I'll have one of the porters come and get you. You're not advised to drive after the treatment, so you might want to call someone. There might well be side effects, but everyone is different. Some don't have the side effects for days after the first treatment, some people feel them immediately. Nausea, dizziness, vomiting, the usual suspects, I'm afraid. And some hair loss is probable. As your tumour is near the back of your head, it will likely only happen in that area. Still, with your locks, it will cover up fairly easily.' He looked at Dan's thick dark hair as he subconsciously smoothed back his own thinning hair. 'Any questions?'

Dan shook his head, feeling as if he were trapped inside a whirlwind and struggling to keep up with events as they sped by.

'Good man, excellent. Let's get on then, shall we? I'll put the requests through. Go and see Clare, my secretary, get the forms filled in, and make any phone calls you need to.'

Dan stood, shook Jeffreys' hand and left the room in a daze. As he filled in the numerous forms at the secretary's desk, he realised that he had only one person he could call. Christine answered the phone, and Dan told her what was going on, starting with his diagnosis. He apologised for not speaking to her in detail about it before.

'I didn't want you to worry about this. I wanted to deal with it. I was going to tell Dad and Janice, but things happened so fast, and now they're gone. I should have spoken to you, Chris, I'm sorry.'

'Oh, Dan, I'm glad you're getting treatment. We've been so worried. You haven't been in touch, and I've heard about, erm, things going on around here. Me and Malcolm didn't know what was happening, if you were alright or anything. We're here for you. What do you want us to do?'

Dan explained that he would need collecting from the hospital later the next day, and someone would have to drive his car home for him. Christine tried to insist that he stay with them, but he declined.

'I appreciate the offer, really I do, but I'd rather be at home. I don't know how this is going to affect me, and I don't want to put your girls through this. I'll call you more often, I promise. I'm sorry I haven't been in touch.'

Christine accepted his refusal of help with a sigh. 'You always were a stubborn bugger. We'll be at the hospital tomorrow afternoon, so don't worry about anything. We'll get you and your car back home.'

Dan muttered his thanks and hung up, feeling selfish. She was right. He should have been in touch before now. Christine was his only family and he really should think of her feelings too. He made a mental note to stay in more regular contact in the future as he followed one of the hospital porters to the Radiology Department on the next floor. He took a deep breath as he walked through the double doors.

'Oh well, here goes,' he said to no one in particular as he approached the smiling receptionist at the desk.

Chapter 20

While Dan was in hospital, things were not going well for Deano. His career (for crime was the closest he would ever come to having a career) was about to hit a very rough patch. Deano had never had a job. The very idea of going out to work, to actually contribute to society, was as alien to him as if someone had asked him to walk on the moon. Like his father before him, he was a career benefits claimant. Every so often he would go and see his GP and persuade him to sign a sick note for another few months. This persuasion was fairly easy after Deano had followed him home once to find out his address. Not long afterwards, the GP had come home to find a shirtless Deano sitting in his lounge with his teenage daughter, who was very drunk and not wearing much in the way of clothes.

'Hi Doc, how's it going?' the smug Deano had drawled as he lay back across the sofa. 'Me and Charlotte have been having a right laugh, ain't we, Charlie?'

She giggled and took another swig of her drink. 'Yeah. Dad, you should see your face! Don't be so stuck up!'

Dr MacFarlane had told Deano to get out or he would

call the police.

'Now, Doc.' Deano stood up. 'Before you do, just think on. She's seventeen, I'm eighteen. She invited me over. We've been chatting on Facebook. Ain't no harm in that, is there?' He took out his mobile phone from his jeans pocket. 'Now this, on the other hand, this could be really fuckin' harmful.'

He pressed a button on his phone and held it out to the doctor. Noises that sounded like a pornographic movie filled the air. Horrified, the doctor saw that Deano and another young man had been having sex with his daughter, and had filmed it.

'All consenting adults, Doc, as you can see. I like this little movie, but it'd be a real shame if it got put on the internet, or on your daughter's Facebook page. Wouldn't do her future career any good now, would it? Or yours?'

'You've drugged her!' Dr MacFarlane shouted. 'That's rape that you've filmed there.'

'Prove it,' challenged Deano. 'She looks pretty willing to me. More than willing, in fact. At one point, she's begging my mate to—'

'Alright, alright, I don't want to know.' The shocked doctor put his hands up, as if to stop Deano's words reaching him. The thought of that video reaching innumerable people via the internet horrified him. Dr MacFarlane would support his daughter, no matter what, but right now the important thing was to get this vile young man out of the house. Once he was sure Charlotte was safe, he would contact the police. Dr MacFarlane's brother was a solicitor; surely there must be something they could do about this? Whatever Deano had said or threatened to do, this incident was a serious assault. 'What do you want?'

Deano smiled. 'Well, there's the little matter of my sick note, and my benefits claim forms. If you sign them off as maybe depression, or mental health or sumfin, then I won't have the bastards from the dole office on my back. I don't like that. Your daughter, on the other hand, she loves it on her back. This video is amazing, Doc, you should watch it. I'll email you a copy if you like. Straight to your surgery. Better be careful I don't send it to the wrong person there, eh?' He leered at the doctor.

Dr MacFarlane looked ashen.

'I've left the forms with your receptionist. You know, the really nosey one? She's on Facebook as well. Just sayin.' He waved the phone at the doctor, then his demeanour changed like the flick of a switch. 'Just fill the fuckin forms in. And don't think about passing me off to any other GP, neither. If that happens, I'll send them the video.' He picked up his shirt and shrugged into it. 'See ya, Doc. See ya, Charlie. Maybe soon?'

Charlotte looked up at him with glazed eyes. 'Yeah, cool.' She looked around the room and belched loudly. 'Is that my dad? I don't know if I'm dreaming or not. I mean, I don't know you, do I? And I've got no clothes on and Dad's right there.' She put her hand to her head. 'I don't feel very well. I think I'm going to be sick.'

After that, Deano never had any problems getting signed off sick for his benefits claim, and now he claimed full disability benefit for a range of medical problems, none of which he actually had. The police had investigated Dr MacFarlane's allegations and had interviewed Deano several times. His mobile phone had been taken as evidence and the video had thankfully not been uploaded to the internet. So far, the investigation was still continuing, adding to the long list of allegations of Deano's crimes.

He had first discovered the advantages of persuading figures of authority when he'd been at school, not that he'd attended all that much. There was one teacher that thought she could save all the problem children of the world. Deano hadn't wanted to be saved. He wanted to see how much trouble he could cause, so he took full advantage of her kindness.

For most of his time at school, Deano had been a destructive and disruptive force. Rules were flouted, detentions ignored, teachers berated, threatened and undermined in front of the other schoolchildren. As he reached secondary school age, most teachers had learned that the easiest way to deal with Deano was to find an excuse to throw him out of the lesson early. Of course, this suited Deano, who then had the perfect excuse to simply leave the school grounds.

Mrs Gant, though, was convinced everyone had a good side and Deano just needed kindness and nurturing to bring out his finer points. Unfortunately for Mrs Gant, Deano's finest point was a cunning and cruel sadistic mentality, even at thirteen years old. She showed him patience and kindness and he lapped it up, pretending to be positively influenced by her. He even handed in a couple of homework projects, that he had 'persuaded' other students to do for him. Mrs Gant was elated as she thought she was getting somewhere with this rebellious and notorious student. When Deano asked for extra tuition one day, she thought that a miracle had truly happened.

'This is what I started teaching for,' she enthused to the other teachers in the staff room one day. 'To help students like young Andrew.'

'The only thing that would help that little bastard is a shotgun,' remarked one of the older teachers. 'He's past help, that one, you mark my words.'

'Nonsense,' Mrs Gant said vehemently. 'Is it any wonder he's the way he is when you all treat him like that?' She stormed out, leaving the other teachers shaking their heads.

'She'll learn,' one of them said.

Sadly, she did learn. After a couple of one-to-one extra tuition sessions, Deano's father made a complaint that Mrs Gant had touched his young teenage son inappropriately and made suggestive remarks of a sexual nature. Deano had fuelled the fire by spreading rumours to his classmates that Mrs Gant had given him a hand-job during one of these tuition sessions. He had told them to wait by the classroom windows to watch. While discussing his poor school attendance with Mrs Gant, he had pretended to bare his feelings to her about his terrible upbringing, erupting in floods of tears. She had responded as any kind person would and put an arm around him, pulling him closer to her as he sobbed.

From their vantage point, the other students could only

partially see what was going on as Deano and Mrs Gant had their backs to the window, but they heard Deano making strange noises and Mrs Gant's arm around him as they sat huddled together on the school bench. After statements were taken and the police had investigated, Mrs Gant never came back to school to teach. No official charges were made as there was no evidence to prove what Mr Dean had alleged happened to his son, but mud sticks in the teaching profession. Mrs Gant was rumoured to have suffered a nervous breakdown. Mr Dean claimed compensation for the alleged events and the local education authority paid an undisclosed amount before the case got anywhere near a court.

After this, Deano had free reign at school. He never had a detention, the teachers simply turned a blind eye when he bunked off school, and he had learned some very important lessons in life. If you're going to lie, make it a whopper, make it serious, and the more hurt you cause, the more enjoyable it is.

His notoriety had grown ever since then, and when he started to get a reputation as a vicious bully too, he was never reigned in. His followers quickly became feared by association, which only made Deano's position in the local community stronger.

Until now. When one of the Keepers ran into Deano's house in Bedders Road shouting that the police were all over the Coalpool Tavern, he didn't quite believe it.

'What the fuck you mean, pigs all over the Tavern? Why? What's happening?' He threw his dinner at the teenage girl who had brought it in to him from the filthy kitchen. 'What the fuck you still doin' here, bitch? I'm finished with you. Fuck off home.' He turned back to the Keeper. 'Tell me what you're on about.' Seeing the young man's hesitation, he grabbed him by the front of his shirt. 'Fuckin' now!' he roared in his face.

'Pigs with guns, man, they're all over the Tavern. Loads of 'em. Four vans full of 'em. Carrying boxes out of the Tavern. They arrested Duncan.'

'The barman? If he squeals, I'll kill him.' Deano pushed the young man away. 'Find Lewis, bring him here.'

The young man turned and ran out of the house. Before long, Kalvin Lewis sauntered in and slumped into one of the armchairs.

'What da fuck, man? How'd they know about that? Who grassed us?'

Deano was beyond rage. He'd also had a quick blast of cocaine, which didn't settle his nerves any. 'You tell me, Lewis. You fuckin' tell me.'

Lewis looked at him through slitted eyes and sucked his teeth. 'What? You think I'm a grass now? You getting as thick in the head as your ol' man?'

Deano went for him but Lewis was quick, jumping up to his feet and out of range just in time.

'What's up with you? I didn't grass nobody. I was lookin' to make some money on the guns, like you. Think the pigs would pay me more than that? You been sniffin' too much of that shit or sumfin?'

Deano had to admit he had a point.

'But there was only me and you who knew they were there.'

'And Duncan,' Lewis reminded him.

'Yeah but he's been arrested,' reasoned Deano.

'Right. That ol' trick. Man, you getting slow, Deano. He'll be out tomorrow, you watch. Charges dropped. No evidence. You see who the grass is then, man. You see.' Lewis walked towards the front door and turned as he reached it. 'Don't be callin' me no grass. You dis me like that, I'm gone. Fuck you, fuck your little gang. I don't need none of you.'

Deano watched him as he strutted down the garden path and got into a stolen black Audi saloon, then heard the engine roar as he sped away down Bedders Road.

For Deano, this was a major setback. The stash of Baikal pistols had been intended to be sold in the cities, to other gangs. Police in London had intercepted a huge shipment of illegal arms last year and arrested some major arms dealers, so supply was currently less than demand. Unfortunately for Deano, as well as losing this vast source of profit, he had also lost the assets he needed to pay for the Baikals in the first place. The gun dealers he had bought them from had taken a small deposit and were allowing Deano three months to pay for the rest of the guns, with a small interest charge of course. Deano hadn't the reserve of cash to pay the dealers now, and he knew that people like that always had serious heavy backup at their beck and call.

'Fuck.' He kicked the table over. 'Fuck! Fuck! Fuck!'

# # # #

Duncan was arrested and detained for questioning. Detective Sergeant Tunstall was present at his interview, which proved absolutely fruitless. After refusing to speak a single word until he had legal representation, Duncan then answered every single question with a 'No comment'. After twenty hours of watching him stare off into space and repeat this mantra, DS Tunstall and Detective Constable Benton discussed what to do next.

'There's no way he'll break down. He's shitting bricks already. He knows what Deano and Lewis will do to him and his family if he gives evidence against them. We can't offer him protection and he knows it. He'll keep his mouth shut and there's nothing we can charge him with. I'm sure our "learned friend" has already advised him of that fact. Bloody solicitors,' Tunstall said as they walked towards the coffee machine.

'They'll go for him anyway, Sarge, they won't know who else to blame.'

'Can't be helped. We've got the guns off the street and that's the result we needed. The raid on the Coalpool Tavern netted us nearly three hundred illegal pistols and four boxes of ammunition, and that's thanks to you, Benton. The boss will be very impressed. He'll have something to tell his commissioners and the press. It all makes him look shiny and competent.'

Benton shrugged, a little uncomfortable with the praise.

'So what now, Sarge? Do I stay in place for a while? We still don't know what Deano and Lewis had planned for those weapons.'

'Good point.' Tunstall sighed. 'I don't want you compromised though. Is there any chance that this will bounce back onto you?'

'I can't see how,' Benton replied, grimacing at the taste of the lukewarm brown liquid he had just bought from the coffee machine. 'God, that's foul.'

Tunstall grinned. 'You've gone native if you've forgotten how bad that stuff is. Seriously though, if you get any sense that things are going pear-shaped, you get out. Right?'

'Yes, Sarge.' Benton threw his coffee cup into the waste bin, where he noticed there was already a pile of half full cups. 'As long as they don't force-feed me anything like that, I'll be OK.'

'I reckon you'll have another week, ten days at most, before we pull you out anyway. There are other cases waiting. I don't think the boss will care about the plans for the guns. As far as he's concerned this one is closed already.' Tunstall turned back towards the interview rooms. 'Right, I reckon we'll be releasing the barman soon, so make yourself scarce. Don't want him seeing you here, do we?'

'No, Sarge. I'll check in as usual, twenty-four hours from now.' Benton made his way out the back of the police station and along Green Lane before heading to the canal, where he cycled lazily toward Coalpool, wondering what his next move should be.

# # # #

Deano and two other Keepers waited in a van in the car

park opposite the magistrates' court in Stafford Street. Guessing that the hapless Duncan would walk this way back to Coalpool, they had been waiting for two hours already.

'How much longer, Deano?' one of them asked.

'Shut the fuck up, Smudge. As long as it takes. He's been there nearly twenty-four hours now, so they can't hold him much longer.' Deano drummed his hands on the steering wheel.

Smudge and the other Keeper, Cowley, sat against the sides of the van in the back. They had been chuffed at first to be picked by Deano to come on this job, as it made them feel important, but the boredom was becoming intolerable. More used to sitting watching pirated movies or playing computer games when they weren't out burgling houses or taking drugs, the two of them found it very difficult to sit still for long. Both had been diagnosed with ADHD when at school, although more than one teacher had started referring to this as LSS. '"Little Shit Syndrome" is what they should call it,' remarked their form tutor on more than one occasion. Either way, this was torture for them, being confined in a closed space and keeping quiet in case they annoyed Deano, not even able to look out of a window.

'Here he is.' Deano sat up straight and opened the van door to get out. Duncan the barman was walking dejectedly along Stafford Street, hands in his pockets and head down. 'Cowley, get in the driving seat.' Cowley stood up quickly, glad of an excuse to move around and do something, but unfortunately he forgot that the van roof wasn't as high as he was tall. He smacked his head on the inside of the roof and let out a string of expletives, which made Smudge erupt into peals of laughter. The noise echoed in the van and Duncan looked up in alarm. He was about twenty paces from the van and Deano saw the decisions going round in his head.

'No need to leg it, Duncan, we've just come to offer you a lift home, that's all.' Seeing Duncan look around and weigh up his options, Deano took a step forwards. 'That wasn't a fucking choice, Duncan. Get in the van.' He opened the sliding side door and Duncan took a step backwards.

'I haven't said anything, Deano, not a word. I wouldn't, would I? I don't know anything anyway, do I?' He held his arms up, backing away.

'Well, you've got nothing to worry about then, have you?' Deano motioned at the open door. 'Stop pissing me about and get in.'

Duncan was shaking as he stepped up into the side door of the van. Deano jumped in behind him and snapped at Cowley, 'Drive. Yellow Mess. Nice and slow, we don't want no pulls, do we?'

On the journey Duncan looked around with wide eyes at the grinning Smudge and the now silent Deano.

'Why are we going to the Yellow Mess? I told you, I haven't said a word to them.'

Deano whipped out a clenched fist, hitting Duncan in the face. Smudge grinned as blood started to flow from the barman's nose. Deano leaned forwards, and seemed to fill all of the space in the restricted confines of the van.

'We're going there cos I fuckin said so. I wanna talk to you. Now shut up until I ask you sumfin, right?' He lashed out again and Duncan's head snapped back and hit the metal framework of the van. Smudge was making high-pitched eager noises as he watched, like an excited dog waiting to be let off its leash. Deano sat back. 'Loosen him up a bit, Smudge. Save me the bother.'

Cowley drove slowly towards Mill Lane, where he pulled into the rubbish-strewn car park at the edge of the LMS waste ground before turning around in his seat to watch the fun. Seeing Duncan getting his 'chat' took his mind off his recently bumped head, and he wondered how far Deano would go with this. He had seemed pretty wound up earlier, and Cowley knew that wasn't a good thing. He looked at Duncan as he spat out a mouthful of blood and a couple of smashed teeth onto the van floor. Nope, not a good thing at all.

Chapter 21

Two days later, Dan had received his second bout of radiotherapy and the experimental vaccine treatment and was feeling surprisingly well. No nausea or dizziness had plagued him, though he knew that not everyone suffered these crippling side effects. The worst problem he had faced so far was lethargy. He just wanted to sleep all the time but he also wanted to get on with his mission.

He was no nearer to finding out who had killed and robbed Janice, and he was no nearer to locating and taking out the leader of the Keepers, this Andrew Dean, or Deano as he was known. Dan was pretty sure that he'd known someone with the surname Dean when he was growing up in Walsall, and was also sure that particular person had been violent. Perhaps his son was a chip off the old block. He remembered that particular Dean trying it on with Janice once, and Dan had a really hard time extracting himself and Janice safely out of that confrontation. Dean … what was his first name? Dan felt like his memories were eluding him lately. Perhaps this was another side effect of his condition. He shrugged. Lost memories of growing up in Walsall would be no great loss at all. Robert! That was it. Robert Dean. A year or two older than Dan, cruel and vicious, he loved to cause fights everywhere he went, like so many of the lads on the council estates.

Dan pushed these memories away as he checked his Land Rover in preparation for his next excursion. The last thing he needed was for the old truck to break down in the middle of a Walsall housing estate. He also opened up one his outbuildings and brought his motorcycle out into the sunshine, started it up and left it ticking over while he checked it. Not trusting himself to ride it until he was absolutely sure he wouldn't suffer a dizzy spell caused by his treatment, he finished inspecting it, switched it off and put it back into the outbuilding, locking it securely with a heavy padlock and chain and setting the alarm. There was very little crime out where he lived, but old habits die hard, and it didn't hurt to be safe. Dan had never had a bike stolen, and he didn't intend for that to change any time soon.

Putting the keys back in his keysafe in the kitchen, Dan sat down to consider his next move. He wanted to rile the gang, to knock them off their guard and shake things up a bit. Dan wanted the lesser members to take a step backwards, disappear into the woodwork for a while, until he got hold of the major players. He was sure that a crime like the one that had taken his Janice wouldn't have been committed by a minor Keeper. They were all for thieving, intimidation, drugs and girls. They probably didn't think with any part of their body much higher than their waists.

Dan had identified three main targets so far: Deano,

the leader, who he hadn't yet seen; Welchy, who had been dealt with, as Dan held him personally responsible for his father's death; and Lewis, who was the next feared member after Deano. There were also another couple of Keepers that had intrigued Dan. The small, red-headed wiry one that had been polite to the old couple looked out of place in the gang. He was also sporting bruises around his face and a swollen nose, so looked a bit downtrodden. Was he even a Keeper? Dan couldn't work him out. The other one was the guy who'd intervened and rescued Lewis. Dan hadn't seen that coming and was relieved that he hadn't suffered more damage at this Keeper's hands, taken by surprise as he was. The more he thought about it, the more he was perplexed by this character. Why hadn't he done more than rescue Lewis? The way he had handled himself suggested to Dan that he knew how to, but he had almost seemed to use the minimum force possible to get Lewis away, which didn't follow the Keepers' normal pattern. Strange.

Deciding to stake out Deano's house again that evening, Dan thought that a few hours of sleep would come in handy first, so he went to bed, falling into a dreamless sleep within seconds.

# # # #

DS Tunstall was having no such relaxation period. He had been called to Walsall Manor Hospital's Emergency Department by one of the uniformed constables.

'Thought you might be interested in this one, Sarge,'

Constable Richards told him outside the hospital room. 'Duncan Hateley, barman at the Coalpool Tavern. Well, he was, until this morning. Apparently he's been sacked, which is the least of his current worries. He was beaten up pretty badly last night sometime and found unconscious over Mill Lane, near the Monkey Hills. He's still heavily sedated, but the doc doesn't think his injuries are life-threatening. Life-changing, he said, but not life-threatening.'

DS Tunstall raised his eyebrows. 'Life-changing how?'

Constable Richards grimaced as he looked at his notebook. 'Both arms broken, several ribs fractured, one lung punctured, head injury, hence the unconsciousness, and one other nasty injury.' He rubbed his temples and looked at Tunstall. 'He had his tongue cut in half. Doc reckons they can stitch it back up, but it's been badly hacked so they don't know if he'll be able to speak properly again.' He shook his head. 'What's the world coming to?' He put his notebook back in his pocket. 'Oh, one more thing. He had a capital "K" cut into his back. So no problem working out who did it. Cocky bastards.'

'Cocky, all right,' Tunstall agreed. 'But they know full well that if Hateley won't point the finger at whoever's responsible for those guns, then we don't have much hope of prosecuting them. What they've done to him, it's a warning to everyone else not to speak to us.'

Constable Richards shrugged.

Tunstall looked in Hateley's room but quickly decided that the drowsy and sedated man could tell him nothing, so went in search of his doctor instead.

'He's due to be transferred later today,' Dr Aslam informed him. 'He's stable now, so we'll get him across to the Queen Elizabeth Major Trauma Centre in Birmingham. They've got the experience and the facilities there to try and put this poor fellow back together again.'

'Have you taken photographs of the injuries, Doctor?' Tunstall asked.

'Of course. I'll ask my secretary to send them across to you when the patient is well enough to give consent.'

Tunstall sighed. 'Is there any way we can circumvent his consent? I'd really like to get to work on this case, and photographs would help me get extra funding for the investigation.'

'I'm sorry, Sergeant Tunstall, but only those medical professionals directly involved in his treatment have a right to see those photographs at the moment. If his condition worsens and he loses the capacity to give or withhold consent, then we'll speak again, but for now, I have to assume that he will soon be able to make that decision for himself.' He shrugged apologetically.

Tunstall knew that he was right. The medico-legal aspects of crime investigation grew more restrictive by the day. It seemed that the police investigators were held back at every opportunity.

'OK, Doctor, thank you. I'll be in touch.' He turned and walked briskly away from the department, keen to get the smell of disinfectant out of his nostrils. He hated hospitals.

# # # #

Jonah and two other Keepers were lazing in the late evening sunshine outside the Coalpool Tavern. The doors were closed until the brewery found someone to come in and manage the place. Unsurprisingly, after a video on Flashpic had appeared showing Duncan screaming and taking a frenzied beating in the back of a van, there were no volunteers. Not that any of this bothered the Keepers gathered outside. Alcohol was a poor and expensive substitute for street drugs these days. The Tavern was mainly a local meeting point.

Jimmy Austen was bragging to the others about a new kind of drug. 'Strong shit, man,' he said. 'Really fuckin strong.'

'So what is it? Monkey Dust? Spice? Don't be jack, man, share it out.'

'Nah, nah. There's only enough for me. I ain't sellin' or nuffin. Don't want Deano thinking that!' He laughed nervously.

'Screw you then. Laters.' The disgruntled Keeper slid off the wall they were sitting on and started his moped up. He rode off into the estate, helmetless on his stolen bike. None of the Keepers were worried about being caught on a stolen bike. Police drivers could potentially be prosecuted for dangerous driving if anyone was injured during a chase, so if anyone on a moped, scooter or motorcycle didn't immediately pull over when apprehended, which was improbable to say the least, the police were unlikely to give chase. The public were afraid but powerless to do anything about the spate of robberies, vandalism, acid attacks and mobile phone snatches carried out by riders on stolen mopeds, some as young as ten or eleven years old. Of course, if the police did try to chase them, the moped riders would inevitably crash due to lack of riding skill or experience, then the press had a field day reporting that police had caused the injuries and that the innocent children were merely playing pranks. The craze was spreading across inner cities in Britain like a virus, and videos were prolific on social media of these moped robbery incidents.

Jonah and Jimmy Austen watched him ride off, the noisy buzz of the engine soon receding.

'So where are your drugs then?' Jonah asked, his voice sounding nasal after his beating from Lewis. His face was bruised and his nose still swollen.

Austen tapped the side of his nose. 'Private, man. Private. D'ya think I got to nineteen years old by telling all my secrets?' He laughed as he got up and stretched himself. 'Might see if I can share them with one of them wenches down Holden Crescent later, see if they'll give me special treatment, know what I mean?' He grinned as he walked away.

Jonah knew that Austen referred to some of the young women who lived on the Coalpool estate. They liked to be associated with the Keepers. God knows why, but they seemed to bask in the glory and the violence, even though they were often treated badly themselves. Jonah watched Jimmy Austen swagger away from the Tavern, then jumped off the wall and followed at a distance as the sun started to set behind the tired houses on Coalpool Lane.

# # # #

Earlier the same day, Dan had woken with a start from his nap, thinking that he had heard a noise outside. Running out of the front door, he saw what had caused the commotion that had raised him from his slumber. A young deer was nudging at the wheelie bin, curious at the smells emanating from it. It didn't see Dan standing by the door, and he stayed perfectly still, realising that the young deer's mother would be close by somewhere. Sure enough he heard a muffled barking sound, more like a huffing, then the young deer looked up as two adult deer walked past the open gateway. It looked around lazily, then seeing Dan, it bounded off after the elder members of the herd. In seconds there was no trace of any of them.

Deer had become a familiar sight to Dan since moving to Shropshire. Janice would leave food out for them to encourage their usually nocturnal visits. Suddenly feeling guilty, Dan went back inside and fetched out a scoopful of the special deer food that Janice had bought. Leaving it around the edge of the driveway near the gate, he looked up at the Wrekin hill. When Janice's ashes were released, he would take a midnight stroll on the hill and scatter her remains there too. They had both fallen in love with Shropshire many years ago, and living so close to the hill and forest of the Wrekin had been a dream come true for both of them. Neither of them relished or enjoyed the trips back to Walsall to visit family. Thomas Wolfe wrote a novel titled *You Can't Go Home Again,* but Dan thought he could write one titled *You Shouldn't Go Back Home Again*. Every journey back to Walsall was full of trepidation, and the homeward journey was always overshadowed by a sense of depression after being in the town. He had frequently had a bad feeling about the place, and it had finally come true.

Dan sat down on the bench in the garden, feeling weary. He looked over at the Wrekin and wondered where all of this would lead. Would he feel better after finding out who had killed Janice? He doubted it. Maybe he would feel some closure, especially if he had his revenge, but did that not make him as bad as them? The moral dilemma was taking its toll on Dan and he knew it. Not just from the aspect of breaking the law so severely and the risk of being caught, but from his own personal viewpoint as well. Both he and Janice had abhorred violence even though Dan had used physical force in his past career. That was necessary, and for the good of the country, he argued with himself, thinking back to his time in the Army when it had seemed so much easier to identify and deal with the enemies. Right now, he felt as if the society that he and so many other soldiers had fought to protect was hell bent on self-destruction, either through the lawless actions of its latest generations or the inexcusable way that the authorities refused to deal with this upsurge in violence and crime.

The apathy of the public didn't really help either, although sometimes Dan could excuse that indifference due to fear. Why attempt to help when the chances were you would end up worse off as a result? Stories were in the press all the time about middle-aged men trying to break up a fight or stop a crime in progress, and being beaten to a pulp for their efforts. Or in some cases, ending up as the one in the dock, being prosecuted – like Tony Martin, the farmer who shot a burglar after repeated break-ins at his home. It was no wonder that the public usually buried their heads in the sand, simply looking the other way.

Dan felt suddenly overcome with the helplessness of fighting back. Was there any point, really? As he sat there thinking about what had brought him to this point, memories of his father and his wife flooded into his head. He had been crying silently for some time without realising it, and then he just let it all out. The grieving process had finally caught up with him.

His training as a paramedic had taught him that the five stages of grief started with denial, and he had certainly felt that when both Janice and his father had died, not forgetting his dog Bryn. That was an additional bereavement too. Next in the process was anger, and Dan knew for certain that he was in that stage right now, but his was a cold and calculating anger, not a wild and irrational thing. Bargaining was supposed to be the next stage, but Dan didn't think there would be any of that. The subsequent stage, depression, was the one he feared the most, as he felt he had very little to lose already, and he worried where that stage would take him before the final stage, acceptance, occurred.

Time slipped by as Dan let out his grief, sitting in the garden of the home that he and Janice had worked so hard for, and had planned on retiring to very soon. The injustice and unfairness of events only served to fuel his anger, and he welcomed this. He decided to make his next move, while the anger was fresh.

Chapter 22

Austen strutted along Coalpool Lane, heading to his destination. His older sister Tanya worked as a visiting care assistant in the local area, and he had heard her talking to their mother about someone they both knew.

'It's such a shame, Mum,' Tanya said. 'Old Man Dickerson, he's dying of cancer and there's only us and his wife there. And we're only there three times a day for fifteen minutes. The rest of his family don't bother with him at all any more.'

'Huh.' Her mother had shrugged, drawing on her cigarette. 'I bet they'll bother enough when the Will's read out. You watch, they'll all suddenly care then. Typical of them bloody Dickersons, that is. They couldn't care less. Is he suffering?'

'No, he's out of it mostly. He's got one of them pumps in his arm, keeps him full of morphine and midazolam and stuff. The district nurse comes every afternoon about five o'clock and changes it. It must be strong stuff cos she was late last week and he was screaming in pain when it ran out before she got there. Soon settled him though, when she refilled it. It's a shame, seeing him like that. I've been going

171

there for two years and they're both lovely people, him and his wife, always friendly and grateful.'

'Yeah, they've always been the same, them two. Always had sweets for the kids in the street. Never moaned at them playing football outside. The old man was never the same after he got mugged the once. Took all his pension, they did. Bastards.'

Austen had stayed quiet as a mouse in the kitchen as he listened to the pair of them gassing on about the old couple. He could never understand why his sister did that job anyway. Who wanted to go into old fogies' houses all the time? Wasn't as if she got paid much, and the daft cow never stole anything from the silly old sods. Not like they'd know anyway, most of them were demented or something. But the snippet about the drugs had grabbed his attention. He knew where the old Dickersons lived. All he had to do was wait until the district nurse had put a fresh load of drugs in the pump and he could have the lot. Listening to their conversation again, he picked up some more interesting information.

'The delivery driver from the chemist came the other day. You should see him. Right dishy, he is. Tall and dark looking. Ever so nice as well. He dropped off all Mr Dickerson's drugs for the district nurse for the week. I have to put them in the locked cupboard in the kitchen, cos the old lady can't be trusted with them, with her Alzheimer's and everything.'

So as Jimmy Austen strolled along Coalpool Lane he was full of sunny thoughts, even as the sun was setting. He'd have plenty of drugs tonight, and have a bit of a party with the girls from Holden Crescent. Not once did he spare a thought about the dying old man that he would be stealing them from, or the amount of pain and distress he would be in until someone could come and set up a fresh syringe driver full of pain relief. Such cares were for other people, not the Jimmy Austens of the world.

Jonah was following at a discreet distance, keen on finding out where Austen's fresh supply was. Not that he was that much into drugs, but Jonah always welcomed the opportunity to make a few quid. If he could steal half of Austen's stash while he was stoned, it would be easy pickings, and Austen probably wouldn't even remember. So intent was he on watching Austen that he didn't notice the black Land Rover that slowed down as it passed him on Coalpool Lane.

Dan saw Jonah walking along Coalpool Lane as he was driving towards the Keepers territory. He recognised the scruffy ginger hair instantly and automatically slowed to get a better look. Realising that he had slowed noticeably, he cursed himself for making such a stupid mistake, drove past the youth and glanced in his mirror to see if he had realised. No, he seemed too intent on watching someone else walking along the road. Walking with a brash swagger, arms swinging like someone in a comedy sketch acting out a parody of one of the Gallagher brothers, this young man looked every inch like a Keeper. He wore the classic uniform of a hoodie, tracksuit trousers and pristine branded trainers, and tattoo had been scribed around his neck.

Dan drove past the two of them and slowed down as he rounded the corner. Last time he had been here, he had noticed an empty house on the Lane that was having building work done to it. Seeing it, he slowed down and swung into the open driveway. Luckily the drive extended around the side of the house and out of sight of Coalpool Lane. Dan turned the car around to face the road so that he could drive away quickly if needed. Jumping out of the driver's seat, he had a momentary blast of pain in his head, like the shortest, sharpest headache he'd ever had, but thankfully it only lasted a second or two. He steadied himself against the wall of the house and watched the first Keeper swagger past. After Jonah walked past, Dan discreetly followed.

Before long they turned off the main road into the estate and walked along Holden Crescent. Dan knew this area really well, or had done in his younger days. There used to be an unofficial pathway that ran between the houses in this street and the one behind it, and after dark he and some of the other young kids used to dare each other to go 'fence hopping', to see how many back yards of the houses they could cross by any means, before they were caught by prowling dogs or watchful householders. The dogs were the preferable ones to get caught by.

He slowed down, not wanting to get too close to either young man ahead. He watched as the first one slipped down the alleyway next to the old people's bungalows. Jonah hesitated before sneaking a peek around the corner and following.

'What are you two up to?' Dan wondered aloud. He

waited a few seconds then risked a glance round the entrance of the alleyway. Seeing Jonah still standing in the alleyway, Dan turned back onto the road and leaned against the nearby lamppost. Making sure that no one was watching, Dan hoisted himself over the six-foot wooden fence bordering the alleyway. As he had hoped, it was still rough ground behind it. One of the local householders had long ago fenced off a portion of their own garden and had been dumping household rubbish into the gap over the years, creating an unofficial no-man's land to border their back yard, to deter thieves getting over the fence. Dan carefully picked his way through broken glass, burst bin bags, dog shit and discarded tyres. When he got to roughly where he had seen Jonah standing, he looked through a gap in the fence. He saw Jonah doing the same, obviously watching where the first young man had gone. Then quick as a flash, he hoisted himself over the fence and was gone from Dan's sight.

Cursing the young man's athleticism and his own advancing years, Dan scrambled over the fence into the alleyway. He couldn't see either Keeper now, but he heard a dog furiously barking just ahead. He jogged down the alleyway and peered through a gap in a fence. He could see the first young man running across the back garden of one of the old people's bungalows and a large black and brown cross-breed dog was barking at him as it strained at the end of a long chain. Without breaking stride, the young man kicked it square in the head, and as the dog staggered unsteadily, he picked it up and threw it over the wooden fence. Dan saw the chain snap taut, but it was fixed to a metal post in the back garden. Horrified, he watched as the young man opened the back door of the house and stepped inside. Dan ran along the alleyway, remembering that it went round in a large circle and came out on the other side of the fence where the dog was now hanging.

From his vantage point behind the shed, Jonah had watched as Jimmy Austen dealt with the dog. As soon as he was out of sight, Jonah ran across the garden and launched himself over the fence. The large dog was kicking furiously as he hung on his chain, strangled by his own collar, claws scrabbling wildly at the fence. Jonah grabbed the dog, taking his weight and holding him next to his body as he fumbled with the collar.

'Hold still, hold still,' he muttered as the dog thrashed about. After a couple of seconds he unclipped the dog's collar and let him slip to the ground. Dazed and angry, but otherwise seeming none the worse for his misadventure, the dog shook itself and sprinted off down the pathway. Jonah scrambled back over the fence a second before Dan rounded the corner, almost getting knocked over by the escaping pooch.

Dan assumed the collar had broken under the dog's weight. 'Lucky escape, matey,' he murmured after the retreating dog, who was making a bid for freedom.

Jonah slipped back behind the garden shed where he could observe the back of the bungalow and wait for Austen to emerge. What he hadn't expected was to see a man climb over the fence and cautiously make his way up to the back door of the bungalow and peer through. In the retreating daylight, Jonah thought he recognised the man from the back, but he wasn't sure where from.

# # # #

Jimmy Austen approached the old lady, who was sleeping in her chair next to an old man lying in a bed. The old man had an oxygen tube positioned under his nose, and the rhythmical sound of the oxygen supply machine created an eerie soundtrack to the old man's lingering death. Creeping slowly past the slumbering old lady, Austen stepped into the kitchen and started looking for the locked cupboard that stored Mr Dickerson's medications. Finding it, he made quick work of yanking it open. It wasn't designed to be secure, just a deterrent to Mrs Dickerson opening it by accident. Jimmy quickly scanned the medications to find what he wanted.

'Hyoscine,' he read the label and threw it onto the floor. 'Midazolam.' He grinned and put that box in his pocket. 'Diamorphine. Yes!' Into his pocket with that box. 'Levomep … levomopr …' he stumbled over the pronunciation. 'Fuck it, it's free.' He decided to take it and find out what it was later. Quickly rifling through the rest of the cupboard's contents, he also found a couple of boxes of Tramadol, a potent opioid painkiller, which he pocketed, taking a couple of pills first, just to loosen him up. Everything else was run-of-the-mill tablets that old people took so he threw them on the floor. Right at the back of the cupboard was a small glass bottle. 'Easy, man,' he muttered with a grin. 'Oramorph.' He reached in and grabbed it, unscrewing the lid. 'Come to Daddy!' He took a generous swig of the liquid morphine, then shoved it into his bulging pockets. Turning around, he was confronted by old Mrs Dickerson.

'Who are you?' she demanded in a querulous voice, pointing her walking stick at him with shaking hands. 'You're not a carer. What are you doing?' She looked at the floor, which was now strewn with tablets and boxes.

'Chill out, love, I'm from the carers. Just delivering some tablets for you.'

Mrs Dickerson looked at him through narrowed eyes. 'No, you're not. I wasn't born yesterday.' She started to shout at the top of her reedy voice. 'Bill! Bill! We're being robbed! Bill!' She was waving her stick at Jimmy Austen, resolute and defiant.

Austen pushed past her, ignoring the stick that bounced feebly off his arm. Mrs Dickerson stumbled, tried to grab the doorframe but missed and fell to the floor, striking the hard linoleum with the side of her head. She scrabbled around, trying to get up. Austen ignored her as he stepped into the other room where Mr Dickerson had now woken. He looked at Jimmy Austen through rheumy eyes as the young drug addict leaned over him, looking for the syringe pump that was supplying the strong medication that would allow the old man a peaceful and pain-free last few days.

'Gotcha,' Austen said, finding the small machine under the old man's pillow. He yanked it away from the bed, pulling out the drug supply cannula from Mr Dickerson's arm. He looked at the old man. 'It's wasted on you, Grandad.' He grinned. 'You'll soon be dead anyway.'

The old man stared up at him from what would soon be his deathbed.

'Curse you, you piece of filth,' he uttered in a coarse whisper, full of venom and hate. 'I'd rather be dead than live in a world with the likes of you.' He tried to lift his arm up to shake his fist at the grinning youth, but he was too weak. Closing his eyes, he sighed as his arms fell back on his bedsheet. In his formative years, Bill Dickerson, now aged ninety-six years old, would have wiped the floor with Jimmy Austen and five more like him all at once. The old man was a decorated World War II veteran, having fought for his Queen and country and survived the carnage and terror of the D-Day landings. He had worked hard all his life after the War, and had never spoken of the horrors he had seen during the conflict. Truly, he would be glad to be rid of this modern world that he could never understand. He could hear his wife shouting for him in the background as he lapsed into blessed unconsciousness again.

Austen, caring none for the old man or his wife, stepped through the sliding patio doors into the garden, straight into a flat-handed strike to his right ear. Dan had arrived at the window in time to see Austen rip out the syringe pump from the old man's arm. His anger and disgust at the callousness he had just witnessed was boiling over. As Austen staggered from the blow, Dan struck him again on the left ear, flat handed. Dan knew that neither blow would leave a mark, but the instantaneous massive increase in pressure to the eardrums would render Austen disorientated and off-balance for a good few minutes. As the inert young man dropped to his knees on the paving slabs outside the patio doors, Dan grabbed him and dragged him over to the garden shed.

Jonah shrank back out of sight, having witnessed this man disable Jimmy Austen in about two seconds flat. Jonah didn't like Austen very much, especially after seeing what he did to the dog, so he certainly wasn't going to Austen's aid. As he crouched out of sight, Jonah suddenly realised where he had seen this man before. The woman that Deano had stabbed over the Yellow Mess! This guy was the one that had come looking for her and found her as she had lain dying. Shit. Now it made sense. The one that Deano had told them all to be on the lookout for, this was him, and Jonah now knew why. It was all Deano's fault. He had gone too far, overstepped a boundary and brought this man here for revenge. He stood up and risked a peek into the shed through the dusty and cracked shed window.

Dan had dragged Austen into the shed. The door lock had long since been broken off, and the shed was virtually empty inside, all items of any value already stolen from the old couple. The youth was lying on the floor, groaning and holding the side of his head. Dan struck his right ear again for good measure, further incapacitating his victim.

Austen moaned and turned onto his back, vomiting from the severe vertigo he was experiencing. He tried to cough away the vomit and turn onto his side, but he couldn't work out which way was up. He could see which way was up, from the dim light in the shed coming through the window, but his internal balance sensors in his ears were telling him a different story.

Dan grabbed the syringe pump from where it was lying on the floor outside the shed. He threw it into the shed and stepped back in, pulling the door shut behind him. The syringe pump outer case was now smashed, and Dan pulled the syringe full of drugs off the machine, noticing that it was virtually full. The label on the syringe told Dan that it was filled with a high dose of Diamorphine and Midazolam.

Rifling through the young man's pockets as he lay moaning on the floor, Dan found what he was looking for. A small Tupperware container, storing the addict's kit of syringe, spoon, lighter, needles and tourniquet, for injecting street drugs into his veins. He opened one of the needle packets and secured it to the syringe full of drugs taken from the old man.

'Was this what you wanted?' Dan growled at his struggling opponent on the floor as he hoisted him up by the neck of his hoodie. The youth tried to lash out at his attacker, but couldn't co-ordinate his arms properly. Dan hit him again with an open-palm strike to his ear. As the youth slumped back onto the floor, Dan pulled up the sleeve of his hoodie and attached the tourniquet to his right bicep and yanked it tight. Within a second or two, a vein stood out prominently in the crook of the right elbow. Dan didn't hesitate and plunged the needle straight into the vein. He drew back slightly on the plunger, saw blood coming into the syringe so he knew for certain that the needle was in the vein, and then he depressed the plunger all the way in, pushing the powerful dose of strong drugs straight into the vein. He yanked the tourniquet off to allow the drugs to enter the circulating blood system, and rolled his victim onto his back. Dan knew that this would be a fatal overdose of strong drugs. He watched the youth grow weaker, his pupils widely dilating as the drugs took hold, and allowed him to slump onto his back on the shed floor.

Dan looked around the shed interior. There were no tools, no lawnmower, nothing of value. The old couple had lost all of their gardening implements to thieves years ago, giving up on gardening when the replacements were also stolen. The years that they should have been able to spend happily sitting in a well-tended garden were taken from them as they watched the small garden grow into a wild and unkempt patch of wasteland. The only item of any interest to Dan was a small canister of petrol, kept for a lawnmower long gone.

Hoping for some left over fuel, Dan unscrewed the lid and smelled fumes. Enough liquid sloshed around in the can for what Dan needed. He overturned it next to the inert youth and watched as the small amount of petrol spilled onto the wooden shed floor and Austen's clothes. Standing back, he flicked on the lighter he'd found in the drugs kit and touched it to the spilt petrol. There was a whoomph as the petrol burst into flames and Dan ran towards the fence. He scrambled over it as the fuel and fumes left in the canister ignited and caused a small explosion, blowing out the remains of the glass window.

As he jogged away from the scene, Dan knew that someone would have heard the explosion and would call the fire service. Calls to the police were few and far between, but no one would be persecuted for a call to the fire service. Hopefully what the police and firefighters would find was a thief who had stolen and taken too many drugs and managed to set fire to the shed with his own drugs kit. It wasn't a solid case, but Dan hoped it would buy him enough time to find out who his nemesis was before the authorities did. Meanwhile, the world would not be any the worse after losing someone like the Keeper Dan had just killed. Hopefully when the full facts of the robbery came to light, someone would have the common sense to call for paramedics and get the old man's medication replaced.

Dan slowed his jog to a brisk walk as he turned the corner onto Coalpool Lane. No need to draw unwanted attention to himself. He quickly found the house where he had left his Land Rover and without turning around or breaking his stride, he walked up the drive as if he had every right to be there. He strode around the back of the empty house and approached his vehicle, which was thankfully still there and in one piece. As he reached out to put the key in the door, his arm twitched and he dropped his keys. Cursing, he bent down to pick them up and felt a searing pain in his head. It felt like his head was going to explode. The pain was incredible, white-hot pressure inside his skull. Somehow he manage to grab the key and open the door with shaking hands. He dragged himself up onto the seat, pulled the door shut and collapsed.

Jonah, who had followed Dan along Coalpool Lane, saw him slump in the front seat, and after turning around to make sure there was no one watching, hurried up the drive to the Land Rover and got in.

Chapter 23

National Newspaper Tabloid

*P*olice, ambulance and fire service were called to a tragic scene in a house in Coalpool last night. A source within West Midlands Police told this reporter that a member of a local gang had broken into an old couple's home where the elderly husband lay dying in bed. The heartless drug addict proceeded to assault the helpless eighty-eight-year-old wife of the dying man before ripping out his medication pump and then stealing all of his prescribed palliative care medication, leaving the bedridden old man in pain. The drug-addicted robber then proceeded to break into their garden shed to take his fill of the stolen drugs but unfortunately took a fatal overdose of the strong painkillers, and in his delirium is thought to have set the shed and himself on fire. He was dragged from the blazing shed by firefighters but pronounced dead at the scene by responding paramedics.

The elderly gentleman and his wife were treated by the paramedics before a doctor was called to the address *to arrange further painkiller medication. The ageing victim of this heinous crime, a ninety-six-year-old D-Day World War II veteran, sadly passed away within an hour of the terrible episode.*

His wife, who was a nurse for most of her working life, praised the paramedics and the doctor who came to her assistance. 'They were lovely. They helped my Bill when he really needed it. He was a war hero and he didn't deserve to die in pain. I don't know what this country is coming to when young men can do things like this.'

She was also reunited with her pet dog, who had escaped after having been thrown over the fence by her attacker but was returned by kindly neighbours.

Our police source added that they will fully investigate the details of the failed burglary, but they are not looking for any other suspects at this time.

# # # #

Christine put the newspaper down and wondered if Dan had been involved in this latest event. It seemed that the Keepers, if that was the gang this young man belonged to, were suffering from accidents quite a lot lately. She wondered if it would help matters, or just stir up a hornets nest. Either way, if she knew Dan, things would play out right to the end. He had never been one to leave a job half done, and she didn't suppose that he would change now.

# # # #

At that very moment, Dan was being dragged along the floor from his bedroom to his bathroom by one of the Keepers. He mumbled and groaned as he tried to regain his senses, feeling disorientated and weak, but at least his headache had dulled now. Feeling hands under his arms and around his chest, and recognising his own home, he tried to remember what had happened. Last thing he could recall was getting to his Land Rover in Coalpool, then fragments of the drive home while slumped in the passenger seat. Trying to raise his hands to rub his aching head, he felt clumsy and awkward. Both of his hands were working together even though he only wanted to move one of them. Struggling to lower his left arm, he suddenly realised why his arms felt so strange: his wrists were bound tightly together with gaffer tape! Coming to his senses in a rush, he tried to twist around to see who was dragging him but was overcome by a wave of vertigo and nausea.

'Let go of me, you piece of shit! Put me down.' He struggled against his wrist bindings with all his strength and kicked out with his legs to free himself, only to find himself unceremoniously dropped onto the cold slate floor of his hallway, next to the bathroom door.

'Alright, mate, calm down. Easy. Just lie still.'

Dan rolled over onto his front, trying desperately to get to his knees and stand up, but the vertigo fought against him, even as his captor stood back and watched.

'Just stay still, mate. You've been out all night. You still don't look so good either.'

'Fuck you.' Dan tried to focus on his captor as he struggled against the gaffer tape holding his wrists together, but he lost his balance and slid down the wall to the floor again. He looked round groggily and saw the young man approaching him with a knife in his hand.

'Seriously, mate, hold still, will ya? I only put the tape on your hands to stop you waking up and beating the crap outta me like you did to Welchy. If you promise to calm down, I'll cut the tape off.'

Dan slumped back against the wall, eyeing the young man warily. He recognised him as the ginger-haired Keeper, Jonah.

'OK, OK. Just get rid of the tape and we'll talk. What do you want?'

'Nuffin, mate, nuffin. Well, I want you to promise me you're not gonna beat me up, but apart from that, nuffin.' Jonah shrugged.

Dan held out his hands cautiously, noticing that they were shaking despite his best efforts to control them. Jonah carefully reached out and sliced the tape. He folded his knife blade away and put it into the back pocket of his trousers, then held his hands up in front of him.

'Easy now, easy. I ain't no threat to you. I was just tryin' to get you into the bathroom to get you sorted. You, er, had an accident while you was passed out. You're starting to stink.'

Dan flexed his wrists and arms and looked down at his trousers, noticing for the first time that he was soaked through. 'Oh,' he mumbled, then staggered to his feet, swaying as he leaned against the wall. Reaching out with shaking hands, he opened the bathroom door, stepped inside and closed the door behind him. He realised that he was taking a big risk allowing the young man to stay where he was, but he also realised that in his current condition he didn't have a lot of choice.

A few minutes later, after taking a cold shower to wake himself up, and dressed only in a bath robe, he stepped out of the bathroom into the hallway. The Keeper was nowhere to be seen so Dan went to his bedroom and hurriedly got dressed into jeans and t-shirt. Reaching under his bed, he found his hidden pistol, the Baikal that he had taken from Lewis. He racked a round into the chamber and shoved it into the back of his jeans before walking down the hallway towards his kitchen, where he found the Keeper coolly making a cup of coffee.

'Feel better?' the young man asked Dan without turning around. 'I made you a coffee, thought it might wake you up a bit. Made myself one an' all, if that's alright?'

Dan didn't reply, but sat down on one of the stools next to the breakfast counter. Jonah put the coffee in front of him. Dan ignored it and fixed his gaze on the young man. 'So what's the story then?' he asked angrily. 'Why the sudden urge to help instead of rob?'

'Keep your hair on,' Jonah replied. 'If I'd have left you there, they'd have found you. You would've been fucked.'

'They don't scare me,' retorted Dan, 'if you mean the lowlife gang you hang around with.'

'Yeah, them,' said Jonah quietly as he sipped at his coffee.

'The Keepers,' Dan said, more as a confirmation than a question.

'Yeah. Keepers.' He fidgeted as he stood. Looking around, he saw that the only seat was a stool opposite Dan. 'Look, mate, I helped you, yeah? So can you chill a bit, and at least let me sit down. It's been a long night and I'm knackered.'

Dan thought for a second or two, then nodded at the stool.

'Help yourself. Why's it been a long night? Hang on.' He looked at his watch. 'What time is it?'

Jonah shrugged. 'Dunno. I ain't got a watch. But it's morning. You've been passed out all night, fitting and puking and fuck knows what. I kept having to turn you on your side so you didn't choke.'

Fitting? Morning? Dan realised what had happened with a heavy dread. *It must be progressing,* he thought. 'Who taught you to do that?' he asked.

'My sister's little 'un, she's got the epilepsy, and we all was showed how to sort her if she had a fit.' He shrugged again. 'My sister's not always around, so the little 'un gets looked after by everybody in the family.'

Dan nodded, recognising how these dysfunctional families tried to help each other out. The poor kid would be passed from pillar to post while the errant parents partook of whatever vices they struggled with, be it drugs, booze, prostitution, or spells in prison or borstal. But the fact that this young man had learned how to help in an emergency showed that it wasn't all bad. Sometimes the children were better off looked after by well-meaning and responsible relatives, rather than ill-equipped, addicted or dysfunctional parents.

'How did you know where to bring me? How did you know where I live?' he demanded.

Jonah grinned. 'Your satnav in the glove box. It's got "home" programmed into it. You shouldn't do that, you know. Makes it easy for car thieves to come and rob your house if they've nicked your car. Just programme somewhere nearby, not your own house.' Jonah shook his head in disbelief. 'How come people don't know this stuff?'

Dan was amazed. Of course, it all made sense, people making it easy for thieves with their own technology. He'd never touched the satnav, he preferred maps and A-Z map books, but Janice had probably programmed it for him and left it in his Land Rover. To be honest, he'd forgotten it was even there, but he made a mental note to change the settings, or leave it at home.

'What's up with you anyway?' asked Jonah. 'How come you passed out like that? You got the epilepsy as well?'

'Something like that. So, you're Jonah, aren't you?' Dan asked, picking up his coffee.

Jonah looked surprised. 'Yeah. Richie Jones, but everybody calls me Jonah. How did you know that?'

'I saw you on one of those Flashpic videos.'

Jonah cringed.

'I'm Dan. Are you one of the Jones's family then? From Holden Crescent?' Dan asked.

Jonah eyed him warily. 'Yeah, but how'd you know that?'

Dan looked at him carefully. 'I recognise the family resemblance.'

'What?' Jonah asked.

'The resemblance, the way you look. You look like Carol Jones. She your mum?'

Jonah stared at Dan. 'Yeah. How do you know her?'

Dan finished his coffee and walked over to the kettle to make another one. He hadn't realised how thirsty he was.

'I knew the whole Jones family when I grew up around there.' Seeing Jonah's reaction, he carried on. 'Yes, I was from there. I got out, hated the place. Still do, even more so now, since … Since recent events.'

'Yeah, about that,' Jonah said hesitantly. 'I want to tell you, I had nuffin to do with that, alright? So don't come after me. I know you probably did Welchy, and I seen what you did to Austen, but they was wankers anyway. Probably deserved it.'

Dan turned to face the young man. 'Nothing to do with what, exactly?'

Jonah sighed. 'Your missus, weren't it? Over the Yellow Mess? I seen you, when you found her. I went to help, before you got there, but … there was nuffin I could do.' He shrugged and wiped at his eyes.

Dan had started to lunge forwards at Jonah in anger, but hesitated when he saw the young man's obvious remorse. 'You were there?' Dan swallowed back his emotion. This was important, he needed this information.

'Yeah, I was. I mean, it weren't me on the bike or nuffin, but I saw what happened. I'm sorry, mate, she didn't deserve that. She didn't do nuffin wrong, or her dogs. Just in the wrong place at the wrong time. Deano was wrecked, man, off his face on Monkey Dust and speed probably.'

'Deano?' Dan snapped. 'It was Deano that killed them?'

Jonah suddenly clammed up and looked at the floor. Dan rushed round the breakfast bar and grabbed hold of the young man, who offered no resistance but just kept looking down at the floor with tears in his eyes. Being grabbed and used as a punchbag had become such an everyday event for Jonah that it was as natural as walking or talking. He simply remained submissive in Dan's grip.

'It was nuffin to do with me. Honest. I tried to help. Then you turned up, so I ran off.'

Dan couldn't speak. He was so angry he felt sick.

'It's so fucked up,' Jonah continued quietly, ignoring the fact that Dan was gripping his t-shirt by the neck. 'He's out of control, always high on sumfin or other. He's got guns, drugs, everybody's scared of him. Lewis is just as bad, always batterin' me. He hates me, but he hates everybody so it ain't personal.'

Dan let go of him and leaned against the kitchen counter. His head was pounding again, and he couldn't think straight. *I've been wasting my time*, he thought angrily. *I've been trying to find this Deano because I thought he was the gang leader and he'd know who did it, and it was right there in front of me all along. It was him. Bastard.*

'You filmed Welchy, didn't you?' Dan demanded of Jonah. 'When he set fire to that old motorbike?'

'Yeah. It was a shame, that. I didn't want him to, but he

was high on something, and even when he ain't, he's just plain stupid sometimes. It was a nice old bike. Deano had seen it and he knew it worth a few bob, so he told us to put it on Flashpic and ransom it. Reckoned it would get a couple of grand, but that wanker set fire to it.' Jonah shrugged despondently. 'If he weren't already fucked, Deano would kill Welchy for wasting money like that, and not doin' what he'd been told to do.'

Dan stared at Jonah, then broke the silence. 'You do realise what you did? That old bike was my father's pride and joy. When he found out it was stolen, he had a heart attack.'

Jonah looked up, startled. 'Really? Fuck. Is he OK now?'

'No,' Dan replied quietly, looking hard at Jonah for some sign of guilt or remorse. 'No, he's not. He died. Never regained consciousness after the heart attack. I found him as he lay dying on his driveway.'

Jonah looked down at his hands. He sat there for a long thirty seconds, then raised his head to look Dan in the eye.

'I'm sorry. It was never meant to do that. I didn't know it would. It's so messed up.' He wiped his eyes again. 'I wouldn't blame you if you beat me up anyway. I suppose I would if it had been my dad it happened to.' He shrugged. 'Not that I know who he is, but, you know, I get it.'

Dan thought about it, he really did, but he couldn't quite bring himself to strike the unfortunate Jonah, who offered no resistance, or even an excuse. He had fully accepted his part in the proceedings, shown remorse, and seemed genuinely sorry. Dan thought back to his own youth, and some of the things he had got up to. Had he ever truly considered the consequences then, or how others would be affected? How did he know that his actions then had never upset anyone so much that they'd become ill? He could forgive this kid. He was merely a product of crap surroundings and a terrible upbringing, but Deano? That was different. From what Jonah had told him, Deano's actions were cold, brutal and unnecessary. Dan doubted that Deano would show genuine remorse, but he'd make sure he would know regret before Dan was finished with him.

He turned around, looking for his car keys, but the room spun slowly and he couldn't focus. He knew that he was standing up and holding tight to the kitchen counter in front of him, but his brain was sending different messages to his limbs. He felt a strange sensation in his nose, and putting his hand shakily to his face, he felt blood trickling from his nostrils. As he slumped forwards, on the verge of collapse, he felt Jonah grab him and lower him to the floor.

'Thanksh, Jonah,' Dan mumbled, hearing his speech come out slurred. 'Ged an ambulansh?'

Before he could do anything, Jonah heard the front door slam open and angry voices carried down the hallway. He recognised the traveller twang in the accent immediately. 'Shit, now what?' he muttered as he gently let Dan's head rest on the floor.

'Danny Boy! Dan! You in here? It's about time we had a wee chat now, don't you reckon?'

Jonah was torn. Should he stay where he was and try to bluff his way out of it, or make a run for it? But he could see how this would look. A scruffy youth standing over an unconscious man on the floor of his own home, and to make matters worse, Dan's nose had started to bleed everywhere. Shit. He made his decision. Pulling the patio doors slowly open so as not to make a noise, he slipped out into the garden and ducked behind a garden shrub just as two big men appeared in the kitchen. He watched as they saw Dan on the floor and heard one of them shout to the other.

'Fer fuck's sake, Michael, call an ambulance. Now,' Peter Crosslyn barked to his younger brother, who took one look at the unconscious Dan on the floor and grabbed his mobile phone out of his pocket.

'Not on yer own phone, fer fuck's sake,' Peter snapped. 'Use the landline. It won't be traced back to us then, will it?'

Michael nodded and looked around for a landline phone, finding a cordless one on the kitchen windowsill. He made the call, watching as Peter rolled Dan onto his side and checked for a pulse and breathing. Peter nodded when he located both of these vital signs.

'What the fuck have you been doing, my lad?' muttered Peter, as he looked uneasily at Dan. 'What's going on here?' To his surprise, Dan's eyes fluttered open and he looked up at the older Crosslyn brother. Recognition dawned in Dan's face, and he tried to say something, but Peter didn't catch it. 'Say that again, Dan, yer speaking terrible quiet. Speak up now, tell me again.'

Dan closed his eyes, screwed up his face in concentration and spoke again, louder this time. 'Deano. Ish Deano.' He slumped a little as Peter held his head, and his eyes closed. 'Janish. Deano did it.' Dan said no more. Peter lowered his head back to the floor and satisfied himself that his brother-in-law was as comfortable as possible. As Dan slipped back into unconsciousness, Peter noticed the Baikal pistol sticking out of the waistband of Dan's trousers. Without even pausing, he slipped it into his own jacket pocket, thinking that he might need something 'for the weekend' if this went the way he thought it might.

'I'll look after it for yer, Danny Boy. Wouldn't want you taken off to hospital with that in yer trousers now, would we?'

Michael put the phone back in its charger and wiped it with some kitchen roll. 'They're on the way. Let's get out of here. We'll only get the blame.'

Peter nodded. 'Yeah. I dunno what's going on here, but he's OK for now. We'll just let them deal with it. We can go see him in hospital if we need to. I don't think he's gonna be up to helping us much anyway.' He stood up and stepped out of the kitchen. 'Make sure you wipe anything you've touched, Michael. Don't let people be getting the wrong idea now, eh?'

As quickly as the Crosslyn brothers had arrived, they slipped quietly away, leaving the front door wedged open.

Jonah had watched the whole episode from his hidden vantage point in the garden, and satisfied that Dan was OK for now, he too decided that discretion was the better part of valour and that it would be best if he wasn't there when the emergency services arrived. He could hear sirens in the near distance. He ran out of his hiding place and walked briskly along the road, dodging into the woods surrounding the Wrekin hill when he saw the approaching ambulance.

'Fuck's sake, I'll have to hitch a lift now,' he muttered to himself, as he made his way towards the motorway that he had driven along yesterday. He half thought of going back to Dan's after the ambulance had left and 'borrowing' one of his cars, but he soon decided that he really didn't want to piss the guy off even more than he already was. *Shit, he lost his missus and his dad? When he wakes up, someone's gonna be in the crap,* Jonah thought. He put his hands in his pockets and ambled off towards the motorway, guided by the relentless hum of the traffic. Before long, he was standing at the eastbound entry ramp of the motorway with his thumb out, and not long after that, he had got a lift with an Irish lorry driver who didn't ask any questions but loved to talk. A lot.

Chapter 24

Deano sat in his ripped and faded leather reclining armchair in the house in Bedders Road. He absentmindedly played with a folding butterfly knife while mulling things over. Recent events had shaken him. Someone, or some gang, was invading his territory and taking out Keepers, then disappearing into thin air. No one had any idea who was behind it. No one had recognised anything or anybody. Of course, not seeing anything would be a standard response to enquiries made by the police, but Deano expected people to talk to him and the Keepers. In his own deluded mind he expected a form of fealty, if not loyalty, from local people, although he had no idea what either concept actually meant.

This morning one of the younger Keepers had come running in to tell him about Austen. Deano had almost liked Austen. He was vicious, shameless, unethical, liked women and drugs and would steal for Deano when occasion demanded. There was no way he would have accidentally overdosed. He knew what he was doing. No, this was another one of these unnerving incidents. Someone had taken Austen out of the picture. Deano was fuming, but he had no idea how to deal with this threat. A threat it was, of that he had no doubt. But from who? And why?

He looked around at his surroundings as he deliberated. The house was looking tired, scruffy, chavvy. He remembered seeing the houses occupied by the Albanian-Serb gang in East London that he had visited last year. They were opulent, oozed money, had loads of rooms where gorgeous Eastern European women lounged around, waiting for the gang foot soldiers to visit them and be entertained. Or so it had seemed to Deano's increasingly drug-addled brain. He had aspirations to live in a house like that, with a powerful gang at his disposal. But he was stuck in this flea-infested council house in shitty Walsall, with muppets for gangsters. His old man still lived with him, for Christ's sake. And now some bastard, or bastards, Jonah had mentioned three of them, were taking the piss and knocking off members of his gang whenever they felt like it. It wasn't right.

Deano felt that he was destined for greater things, and this problem was holding him back. He needed to figure out who was behind this outrage. The obvious culprits were the Albanians, as he still owed them fifty grand for the Baikals. The three months' loan for the outstanding payment was up next week, and if they'd heard that he had been raided and lost the guns, they would be all over him, both for the unpaid debt and to ensure he kept his mouth shut about where the guns originated from. The attack on Welchy had happened before the weapons raid though, so that didn't make sense. Who else?

One of the Wolverhampton gangs had been sniffing around earlier this year, Deano had heard. Trying to get a foot in the door with the Monkey Dust trade, but Deano had found a source and spread some cheapened MD around, cut with speed, so it became very popular very quickly and the Wolves lads had lost their customer base. That had happened easily though, without any confrontation or loss of face, just supply and demand really, so Deano didn't think it would be them.

Gypsy gangs hadn't been an issue for a while. They tended to move around so much that they never permanently staked out territories. When they arrived in an area, there was always an open confrontation as they were all about showing off their strength, being big hard fighting men. Usually by the time they'd got what they wanted, they were ready to move on anyway. Deano didn't see the point. Besides, they usually ran the illegal dog-fighting rings and bare-knuckle bouts that drew the rich gamblers, which Deano had nothing to do with. They were also expert thieves, but there were enough pickings to go around, so Deano couldn't see that they would go to all this trouble just to claim a territory like Walsall.

To calm his nerves, or so he excused it to himself, Deano took another snort of cocaine. He would never admit to being an addict, but then again, he never thought about his cocaine habit as anything out of the ordinary so he didn't really care. Already jittery and wound up, when a movement at the hallway door flickered in his peripheral vision Deano spun sideways in his chair and flung the knife in that direction. It stuck firmly in the doorframe, inches away from where his father was standing after entering the living room.

"Fuck's sake, Andrew, you're gonna kill somebody with that!' Old Man Dean yelled at his son. He pulled the knife out of the doorframe with some difficulty and flung it back in the general direction it had come from. It bounced harmlessly off the wall and landed with a clatter on the floor near Deano's feet. 'What the fuck's up with you, you bleedin' idiot? You sniffing that shit again?' He gestured at the line of cocaine on the coffee table next to Deano's chair. 'It'll mess your head up, it will. Never needed that shit in my day.' He wandered towards the kitchen.

Deano reached down and lazily picked up the knife before taking aim and throwing it at the kitchen door as his father reached out to open it.

'Fuck's sake!' the old man spluttered, yanking his arm back and staggering backwards, almost tripping over some clutter on the floor.

Deano calmly walked over and retrieved his knife.

'We're not in "your day", old man.' He looked his father up and down, as if seeing him clearly for the first time. He took in the shambling gait, the scruffy few days' worth of grey beard still stained with last night's alcohol-induced vomit, and the piss-stained pyjama bottoms. 'And you've got no room to talk about being messed up, you fuckin' wino. How many bottles of wine you had this week? You stink.' He squared up to his father, trying not to get so close that he had to breathe in his stale, acrid smell. 'It's about time you fucked off. I'm sick of seeing you round here.'

'It's my bloody house, you cheeky bastard. My name's on the rent book. If anybody's going, it's you!' He prodded Deano's steroid-developed muscular chest with a shaking finger.

Deano slapped the old man across the side of his face, sending him reeling and sprawling on the floor.

'Wrong. My name's on the book. You put me on the book last year. You was pissed so you don't remember, but you signed it. Now get your stuff and fuck off before I have you put in a home. They won't let you drink in there.' Deano grinned at his father. 'It's up to you. Either fuck off, or I'll have you put away. I could always tell social services and the police about your stash of kiddie porn under your bed.'

'I haven't got any porn! Not like that anyway,' the old man said, trying to get up off the filthy floor.

'So what?' Deano replied. 'That can be easily sorted. Your choice.' He waved at the door leading upstairs. 'You've got half hour, then I'll make the choice for ya.' He went into the kitchen, leaving the old man spluttering with rage and struggling to get up.

'You're a piece of shit, Andrew,' the old man mumbled, not quite loud enough for his son to hear. 'The best part of you dribbled down your mother's fucking legs.' He shuffled upstairs, trying to think where he could go for a while. He had no illusions about his son's threats – he knew he'd go through with them. Best to leave, lay low for a bit and let him calm down for a few days. Still, he'd need some funds to tide him over.

Meanwhile, Deano was far from calming down. He'd taken another snort of coke, and had decided to go and find some of the useless bastards in his gang. Stuff needed sorting, and soon. That's what they were there for, after all. It wasn't all up to him. He picked up his phone and put a message on Flashpic: 'Coalpool Tavern. Now. Deano.'

Not wanting to walk the few hundred yards to the Tavern, Deano drove his stolen BMW there and parked in the deserted car park before remembering that the Tavern was closed and locked up.

'Fuck, fuck, fuck.' Deano jumped out of the car in anger, opened the boot and grabbed a crowbar. He made short work of opening a side door and went inside to wait for his gang.

They arrived in dribs and drabs, some of them actually laughing and joking with each other still, whether out of stupidity or false bravado Deano didn't know or care. When the bar area was full with a good preportion of his gang members, Deano decided he didn't want to wait any longer. Listening to the amassed idiots bragging about their cars, mopeds, motorbikes or girls was starting to make him really agitated. Looking around at the gang, he chose one member at random: the loudest, brashest gobshite he could see, or hear in this case. Striding over to him, Deano punched him before the hapless gang member had even registered the incoming threat, knocking his head viciously sideways and splattering blood from a torn lip all over the face of the young man sitting next to him.

As the dazed young man slid down the back of the bar

seat, the one next to him jumped up and stepped quickly backwards, away from the livid Deano.

'What da fuck, man?' He spread his arms wide. 'What? What'd he do?'

Deano stepped menacingly towards the whining young man, who instantly regretted his outburst. 'I'm sorry, Deano. I didn't know he had pissed you off, man. Sorry. I didn't know ...' His voice tailed off as he backed up against the wall and looked down at the floor, hoping that a show of submissive body language might defer or deflect his punishment for speaking out.

Deano grabbed hold of him by the ear, his own animal instincts overruled and over-fuelled by the man-made substances floating around in his bloodstream. He leaned right into the terrified young man's face and snarled something unintelligible before pushing him sideways onto one of the torn and stained bar benches. He turned around to face the rest of the gang, who were now completely silent and watching events unfold.

'Listen to me. Now. Shut the fuck up and just listen.' Deano stared around to ensure he had everyone's full attention before continuing in a low voice, grinding out each word as if he couldn't relax his jaw enough to speak. His fists clenched and relaxed repeatedly at his sides as he walked around the room, making those sat nearer the front of the group more than a little uneasy. No one dared make eye contact with him. They had never seen Deano this angry, ever. He was a cruel bastard, but usually calm, deliberate and calculated. This new state of fury was a terrible sight to behold and no one wanted to be the next punchbag.

'Someone is fucking with us, with me, and with you stupid bastards, and you come in here laughing, joking and clowning around like baby fucking monkeys!' His voice rose to a shout as he spat out the last few words. 'Welchy – fucked. Lewis – knocked out and nearly taken. Austen – fuckin' dead!' He screamed this last word, although there was no need. Everyone assembled had got the message now. They were listening, finally. 'Who's next, huh?'

Deano slapped the nearest Keeper round the side of the head, hard enough to make the unfortunate youth's ears ring.

'You? If you think that fuckin' hurt, how do you reckon Welchy felt when these cheeky bastards ran him over then tortured him with his own fuckin' weapons?' He stared around the room. 'We don't know what information they wanted from him, do we?' Carrying on without waiting for an answer he yelled, 'We don't even know how many of them there actually are, or even what colour they fuckin' are. Why is that?' He slapped out backhanded, barely noticing as the young man nearest to him ducked underneath the swipe, leaving his unlucky mate sitting next to him to catch the brunt of the blow. 'WHY IS THAT?' Deano roared, spittle flying. He was met by silence.

After a few seconds, he continued, 'It's because you lazy wankers are too busy looking out for the next fix, the next steal, the next girl. Stop thinkin' with yer fuckin' dicks and wake up. We don't know what they want, we don't know who they are, and we don't know where they're from. So tell me.' He prodded one of the seated Keepers in the chest. 'Just fuckin' tell me how we're supposed to see it coming, huh?'

Deano saw that he had finally got his message across.

'We are all on dodgy ground here. Nobody is safe until we find out what the fuck is going on, why is it going on, and who is doing this shit. So get yerselves out there. You've a job to do for me, and until it's done, no whoring, no thieving, and no pissing about. Got it?'

He received a few mumbled replies and nodding of heads, and just as he was about to dismiss them all in his usual expletive fashion, the barroom door opened and Kalvin Lewis sauntered in. All eyes turned towards him, then back to Deano expectantly. Now this would be interesting. What was Lewis doing strolling in so long after everyone else? Lewis looked around at the silent group, noticing one blood-spattered young man barely conscious in his seat, propped up by the man sitting next to him. The aura of fear and intimidation in the room was difficult to ignore, but Lewis felt no such feelings personally.

'What did I miss then?' he enquired nonchalantly as he leaned against one of the pool tables in the room. Faces looked from him to Deano, wondering how their leader would react to this show of indifference.

Deano ambled over to Lewis, the group parting around him like the Red Sea before Moses. 'Not much really. You didn't miss hardly anything. Just having a chat, like, about how some wanker comes into our fuckin' place, takes out Welchy and Austen and knocks you about like a tosser, right in the middle of our own territory. So what do yer reckon, Lewis? Anything to say about that?'

Lewis's face froze as he registered the insult. There were a few ways this could pan out, and Lewis calculated his chances in all of them as he faced Deano down. He knew there would be no support from the rest of the gang. If anything, they would back Deano. His Baikal had been stolen, and his only other weapon was a knife, which he silently cursed himself for leaving in his car outside. As Deano approached further, standing only a couple of steps away now, Lewis reached across the pool table and placed his hand on top of the cue, not gripping it, not lifting it off the green felt, but the message was clear. He would fight, not submit, if the need arose.

Without breaking his stare away from Lewis's eyes, Deano spotted the subtle gesture and grinned. 'You want to do this, Lewis?' he challenged.

Lewis stared back. 'I didn't know I'd become the enemy, but whatever.' He shrugged, still not breaking the staring match that lasted for a long thirty seconds more before Deano laughed and turned away.

'Yeah, whatever. Whatever.' Deano picked up a can of soft drink from one of the Keepers and took a long swig before turning back around to face Lewis, the increased distance between them diffusing the tension, although Lewis's hand stayed firmly on top of the pool cue. 'So where you been?' Deano asked.

'Trying to keep you out of the hospital, if you must know,' Lewis replied, drawing the attention of everyone in the room.

'Hospital? Me? What the fuck you talkin' about?' Deano frowned.

Lewis dragged the moment out a while, turning the balance of power back towards himself. 'While you've all been havin' fun in here, I've been out lookin' for this wanker. Seems that the Crosslyns have been lookin' for you. What you done to piss them off?'

Deano looked perplexed. 'Crosslyns? Who da fuck are they? Never heard of 'em. How do you know this anyway?'

Lewis continued, enjoying being the one with the answers in front of Deano and his little gang. He had come to think of himself as outside of the Keepers lately, as Deano seemed to sense the developing threat from Lewis and both knew there was a conflict coming. So Lewis was playing the long game, avoiding the conflict, getting ready to make a wedge of cash, enough to get out of Walsall and start over somewhere else. His plan had been working until the police raided the Tavern and stole his nest egg. Lewis had been negotiating a nicely lucrative deal with a gang from Birmingham, and had planned to steal and sell the whole cache of weapons from under Deano's nose before getting away.

'The Crosslyns are gyppos. Travellers. Whatever. They've been knockin' on doors askin' 'bout you, man. Knocked Mandy Prees and her boyfriend about the other day, askin' where you lived, what you've been up to. They said they never told anything, but the boyfriend looked shit scared. You ask me, they know where you live now, and it's them causing this shit. You got to watch your back, Deano.

There's lots of these bastards, you know what the clans are like, all stickin' together and that shit.'

'Gyppos? What the fuck?' Deano looked up to the ceiling as he thought. 'No man, you're wrong. I ain't pissed off no gyppos. They ain't been around for ages anyway.'

'That's where you're wrong,' Lewis continued. 'They live around here, don't they? The fairground travellers up at Bloxwich and over Slackey Lane site. They're different to the usual gyppo gangs we get, but they're all related. And they sound mighty pissed off wich you, man!'

Lewis looked around the room at the other Keepers, noticing and enjoying the apprehensive looks on most of their faces. No one wanted to get mixed up with the gypsies, whether they were fairground travellers or Irish or whatever. The result would be the same – carnage, gangs in greater numbers. These people were not to be fucked with by a gang of mostly opportunist bullies, young layabouts and kids, which was what the Keepers essentially were. The only thing they had going for them was fear in lawless local housing estates. Lewis thought that Deano should know this by now, but he had delusions of grandeur and somehow he had obviously overstepped his mark and brought this shit down on them all. The rest of the Keepers knew it now too. Whatever had happened to Welchy, Austen and Lewis was somehow Deano's fault, and they were all at risk if they identified as Keepers.

'Nah, man, that's bullshit,' Deano argued. 'Where's Jonah? He saw them. Did they sound like gyppos, Jonah?'

Jonah answered from where he was sitting, still sounding

nasal after his nose had been broken by Lewis a few days ago. 'Nah, I only seen them a bit, but they didn't sound Irish. Might be English gypsies though, I dunno,' he lied smoothly, convincingly, never letting on that he knew the real culprit now and that there had only ever been one man all along.

'You're fuck-all use, Jonah.' Deano looked around the room. 'Where's that guy, the one that rescued your sorry ass, Lewis? Benton?'

'Back here,' the undercover policeman replied from somewhere at the back of the room, near the fire exit.

'Yeah, you got a good look at the one of them. Did he look gyppo to you?'

Benton thought it over for a couple of seconds, not wanting to cause an inter-gang war on the estate but not wanting to give anything else away either.

'Not really.' He shrugged. 'Sounded English. And he was on his own. Since when do they come and fight on their own?'

'Yeah, right.' Deano warmed to this reply. 'They never come on their own, do they? Always in gangs, van loads of the fuckers, when they come for trouble. Nah, it ain't them, Lewis, you're wrong there.' He smiled at the room. 'Still, I appreciate you trying to do something to find them. More than these tossers have been doin'!' He laughed, trying to make light of it and bring the gang back around to his way of thinking. 'So, you heard what I said. Get your lazy tosser arses out there, find out what the fuck is going on, and let me know. I want a phone call the second you find anything out, yeah?'

The gang quickly left, glad to be out of Deano's unpredictable wrath zone, and most of them wondering if it was worth just lying low for a while. No one wanted to end up like Austen, or worse, like Welchy. Rumour had it that he was wearing nappies now, couldn't even go to the toilet on his own. Cowardice had its benefits, and these Keepers were none too keen to prove their valour against a hostile enemy that hit back.

Lewis left in the middle of them, bad-temperedly shoving anyone out of the way who slowed him down as he left. Jonah sauntered away to make his way home, or to find something to eat, and Benton slipped away like the shadow that he strived to become, to make another sitrep. This needed looking into before there was an open war on the estate.

# # # #

Lewis pulled his Audi over to the side of the road after he had driven for a couple of minutes. He knew that he needed to calm down and think. What the fuck was Deano playing at? Deano was losing his grip on reality if he thought that this bunch of losers and scumbags were going to war for him. No, the stark reality that Lewis foresaw was that the Keepers would all slip away into the woodwork for a while until this was over. They would all claim that they were out looking for the enemy, but Lewis knew better. He also wondered if he should do the same. Screw the Keepers.

Lewis knew they were going nowhere anyway and he had already decided to leave them behind.

He reached under the driver's seat and pulled out a padded envelope that had been taped to the underside of the seat. Inside the envelope was a Baikal pistol that Lewis had lifted from the stash in the Tavern before it was raided. Deano had already given him one, but that cheeky bastard had nicked it from Lewis when he had got lucky in the Tavern. He still seethed over this. Next time, the guy wouldn't be so lucky. If there was a next time. Lewis wasn't scared of anyone, but he realised that some enemies were best avoided if possible, if avoiding could be done without losing face. He made up his mind that he wouldn't search too hard for this nobody man, but if they came face-to-face again, Lewis would be more than ready.

He was glad that he'd stolen the Baikal and stashed it before all of this shit had started. He only had fifty rounds and one magazine, but it was the eighteen-round capacity mag, so Lewis figured that would be more than enough. He wasn't planning on using it for anything other than intimidation and as a last resort to help him escape any nasty situations that might arise. Feeling that this type of situation was getting more likely with every day that this unknown enemy hadn't been found and put down, Lewis took the gun out of the envelope, quickly checked it over, and loaded a full magazine before slipping it into the specially made inside pocket of his hoodie. He didn't intend to find this guy for Deano, but if the guy found him, he was damn sure he'd make him regret it.

Putting the Audi into gear, he drove away from the estate.

# # # #

Benton made his sitrep call to DS Tunstall shortly after leaving the Keepers' meeting.

'It's all getting a bit out of hand, Sarge,' he reported. 'Deano has sent all of them out to look for this adversary that none of them have a description of and none of them know anything about. It's a recipe for disaster, if you ask me. Half of them are high on drugs, and the other half are either plain stupid or full of testosterone and steroids. There will be collateral damage, I'm afraid to say. Any innocent bloke who happens to be in the wrong place at the wrong time will suffer consequences, and if this chap is half as good as I think he is, they won't find him. He'll be holed up somewhere well away from here, planning his next move. It seems that he's only after Deano, for whatever reason. Have the team go through any recent info on incidents where Andrew Dean was suspected to be involved, whether proven or not. It could be that Deano has picked on the wrong family or organisation and someone has gone vigilante on him. I can't see any other explanation for this right now.'

'No hint of a rival gang being involved?' DS Tunstall asked.

'It doesn't seem that way to me, Sarge,' Benton replied. 'It doesn't fit the usual method of response. It would be all posturing, drama and showing off rather than these cloak-

and-dagger guerrilla-warfare attacks. I get the impression that this assailant is ex-military. He plans, executes the strike, then disappears. He seems to know the area pretty well, certainly as well as I do, and I grew up round here. Can you cross-reference any records of ex-military personnel in the area to our man? He's about forty-five to fifty years old, white, and I would suspect that he has a clean record, which will make it more difficult to trace him.'

'I tend to agree. It's very strange, but as whoever it is has only hit back at the gang members so far, we'll keep it on a back-burner for now while we investigate the guns problem. I just don't have spare staff at the moment. Any idea who Dean was planning to sell the weapons to?'

'None, Sarge. I don't even know if he had any idea himself. He seems off the rails at the moment. He's alienated himself from his second-in-command, Lewis.' Benton went on to describe the confrontation between the two at the earlier meeting. 'My main concern is that if any of the gang decide to try and curry favour with Deano by catching this vigilante, they'll pick up any man that may have put a foot wrong or said anything against the Keepers, which could be half the men on the estates round here.'

'Yes, agreed. It's a real concern, but I don't see what we can do to eliminate that threat at the moment. I'll ask uniform if they'll increase visible presence in the area slightly. It might just force the gang to hold back for a while. If we increase it too much, it'll just inflame the situation.'

'Right, Sarge. Do you think it might be worth running this past our NCA contact?' Benton referred to the National

Crime Agency, set up to combat organised and gang crime in the UK.

'It wouldn't hurt,' DS Tunstall agreed. 'It might throw up some intel on what Andrew Dean has been up to in other areas.'

Benton signed off and headed back to his bedsit. He had a bad feeling about the situation in the area, but he was stumped on how to respond. He thought that this 'nobody man', as the Keepers had started to name their adversary, would make another move, and another, until he got to Andrew Dean. Benton didn't have a lot of compassion or sympathy for the Keepers, and as long as it was only them that got hurt, it would have to suffice to wait for the nobody man's next move, then react and investigate further.

Chapter 25

Dan and Janice were walking along the track through the old shooting ranges on the Wrekin. The sun was low in the winter sky and Bryn was running around up ahead, sniffing after rabbits or squirrels or whatever it was that interested dogs so much. Janice held Dan's hand and was talking to him in a low voice, what Dan called her 'lecturing voice'.

'You have to take care of yourself, Dan. This problem won't just go away, and you can't control it. For once in your life, you have to trust someone else. Just let the doctors do their job.'

'I trust you, Jan,' he replied.

'I know, honey, but this is a problem I can't help you with. If I could, I would, you know that. Let Jeffreys try to help.'

'That's just it though. He can only try. It's not a guarantee, is it?'

Janice sighed and squeezed his hand. 'Nothing's guaranteed, Dan. Nothing. We know that, don't we? But you have to at least try.'

'Dan stopped and took both of Janice's hands, noticing how cold they were.

'Why? Why do I have to try? Can't I just stay with you and Bryn? It's so nice here, it's so peaceful. I've had enough of fighting, struggling, hurting.'

'That's what life is like sometimes, Dan. Then there are other times where life is happy walks in favourite places, with loved ones.'

Dan squeezed his eyes shut in frustration. 'But there won't be any more of those, will there? You're all gone, and I'm left here on my own.' He put a hand up to his head, which had started thumping with pain. He turned to Janice but she was standing a hundred yards away, Bryn sitting next to her. They both looked at Dan. Janice waved and they both turned around and started walking away.

'Jan!' He tried to run, but his legs wouldn't move. His head pounded mercilessly and his vision blurred into darkness. He could hear someone shouting his name, the sound echoing all around him, becoming louder and louder.

'Dan! Dan! It's OK, you're safe. Try to lie still for us.' The light became brighter and his eyes tried to focus. 'I think he's coming round. Go and fetch one of the nurses, would you?'

Christine held Dan's hand as he waded through the treacle in his head to get back to full consciousness. He tried to speak but his mouth was dry and all that came out was a croak.

Christine passed him a cup of water from the bedside tray and helped him to sip it.

'Where am I?' Dan asked.

'Hospital. You were found unconscious at home. Someone called an ambulance and you've been out of it for nearly two days. What happened?' Christine looked worried.

Trying to remember, Dan shrugged his shoulders. 'I've no idea. Can't remember.' He lay back against the pillow as one of the nurses came in, followed by Joseph Crosslyn. The nurse reached over to feel Dan's pulse at his wrist. She looked at his eyes, gauging his pupil reaction, and smiled.

'Back with us? How are you feeling now?'

'Er, fine, I think.' Dan frowned as he tried to recall the nurse's name. 'Becky, isn't it? Am I in the High Dependency Unit?' He knew quite a lot of staff at the hospitals.

Becky smiled. 'Nothing wrong with your long-term memory then. I'll fetch the doctor. He wanted to speak to you as soon as you woke up.' She glanced at the monitoring equipment, made a note on the clipboard at the end of Dan's bed, then left, closing the door softly behind her.

Staring up at the Crosslyn brother, Dan looked puzzled. 'What are you doing here?'

'Joseph came to fetch me,' Christine interrupted. 'He told me you were in hospital, then brought me here. We've taken it in turns to sit with you. The doctors said you'd wake up, there was nothing life-threatening, but your brain needed to rest first.'

'Oh, right.' Dan sat up in bed, feeling a bit like Bambi trying to stand up on ice. 'Thanks, Joseph, I appreciate it.'

'That's alright, Danny.' Joseph smiled. 'It seems we have

things to talk about anyway, so I'm glad ye've woken while I'm here.' He looked across at Christine. 'Would yer mind fetching us a cup of that brown stuff they call coffee, love?' He opened his wallet and handed Christine a twenty pound note. 'That café by the main entrance sells the best stuff. D'yer mind?'

Christine looked from one man to the other, shrugged and stepped outside the room.

Joseph sat on the chair next to Dan's bed. 'Now, firstly, Danny, I've not come to cause ye any bother, old son. It looks like yer've enough of that. I know we've had our differences in the past, but y'looked after our sister, and she always seemed happy. She had a nice place to live, never had to worry about a drunken bastard laying hands on her in temper, and was free to come and go as she pleased. She came to see us sometimes, and none of us have any problems with how things turned out for her.' He held out a meaty hand. The tattoos covering it were blurred nowadays but the grip was still strong as Dan shook it. 'Let bygones be bygones, what d'yer say?'

Dan nodded. 'Fine by me. I never had a problem with you or your family in the first place.' Joseph Crosslyn leaned back in his chair, his bulk making it creak a little.

'I know, old son, I know. We all do. We was young, stupid. Stuck in the old ways.' He sighed. 'And now this. We've got to deal with this, so we're obliged to slip back into those old ways for a little while longer, if yer get my meaning.'

Nodding, Dan remained quiet, letting the big man say his piece.

'None of us blame you for what happened, Dan. Christine told me that's what y'think, but yer wrong. We blame whoever did it, and we want to find out who that was. We know she was hit by a motorbike, and we reckon it was nicked. There was a robbery earlier that day, and it comes back to this gang round here. The Keepers?' He noticed Dan nod, and continued. 'I see yer've heard of them. Well, the leader of this gang is a tosser called Deano, so we tried to find him, to see if he knew who the rider of that bike was. Only he's gone to ground on that shitty estate and we can't get near him without getting caught in the middle of it. You know what they're like, they spot a stranger in seconds and let everyone know. We'd be trapped. So we have to be absolutely sure before we go in mob-handed. Then we pop round to ask if you know anything and we find you on the floor. So here we are.'

'What makes you think I know anything?' Dan asked quietly.

Joseph sighed. 'We didn't think you'd just sit back and ignore what happened to Janice. You grew up round there. You know people. We knew you'd start poking your nose in. And you told Peter that Deano did it.' He paused. 'Peter and Michael came out of your house like their pants were afire. At least they'd got sense enough to call an ambulance for yer first. I fetched Christine, she's yer next o' kin now, ain't she?'

Dan nodded. A vague memory was surfacing of speaking to Peter Crosslyn just before he passed out.

'Anyway,' Joseph continued. 'Christine told us about yer problem here.' He tapped his head. 'We're sorry that's happened, Dan, really we are.' He leaned forwards and lowered his voice. 'We know that a few of these Keepers have had … accidents. We're OK with that, but we want Deano now. We reckon you do too, but yer in no fit state to deal with it.'

Dan started to argue, but sank back in his bed as the room spun out of control, making him instantly nauseous.

'It's alright, old son.' Joseph grabbed Dan's hand to reassure him. 'It's alright. I know yer'd like to do it yerself, but yer can't, not being like this. Don't worry. We'll sort it. For Janice and for you.' He stood up as Christine came back into the room, followed by a doctor who was carrying a hospital file.

She looked from one man to the other. 'Everything OK?' she asked.

'Fine, love, fine.' Joseph smiled. 'I was just on me way now. I'll leave you and Danny to catch up, and let this fine young man sort my brother-in-law out.' He slapped the doctor on the shoulder as he walked past, causing him to wince a little.

'I'll be in touch, Danny, you take care now, and rest up. We'll look after things for yer.'

The doctor stood next to Dan, unconsciously rubbing his shoulder as he spoke.

'I'm Dr Richardson. So how do you feel, Daniel? Any headaches or blurred vision?'

Dan shook his head, then instantly regretted doing so. He grabbed at the side of the bed, trying to will the room to stop spinning.

'Ah, I see you have a little vertigo problem. Not to worry, we can get you some medication for that. I have some good news and some bad. The good news is that while you were unconscious yesterday, we did CT and MRI scans of your brain, and the treatment you've had so far seems to be working, at least in respect of shrinking the tumour. It's smaller than when you had your first scans.' He shuffled the file, opening it at one of the scans.

'So what's the bad news, Doc?' Dan asked.

'Well, we're still not entirely sure what is causing you to have these episodes of convulsion and loss of consciousness. We'd like to monitor you for a while, try some additional treatment and medication, see if we can prevent it, or at least reduce the negative effects.'

'Yeah, fine,' Dan replied. 'Just let me know when the appointments are and I'll make sure I'm here.' He slowly sat up in bed, the room having slowed down its spinning motion for now. 'I'll have some of that medication for the vertigo though, to take home with me if I can.'

'No, you misunderstand,' the doctor said. 'We need to keep you in here for a few days, run more tests. I've spoken to Dr Jeffreys and he will be popping over this afternoon to review your case with us and the MDT.'

Christine looked puzzled. 'MDT?' she asked.

'Multi-disciplinary team,' the doctor explained. 'So that we can do our best to co-ordinate Dan's treatment options, and get the best results possible without transferring Dan to another hospital. It saves us wasting time passing letters and test results between departments if we can all sit round a table and discuss it together. Dr Jeffreys is keen for you to have some oncology treatment here, rather than be transferred back to his hospital. It seems like a good idea until you're more stable, so that's been agreed.' Dr Richardson smiled. 'It seems Dr Jeffreys has a fair bit of pull and he gets things done, so I'd be glad of that if I were you. This way is much better than staying here for a few days then being transferred to another hospital to start again.'

'Can't I go home while you do that?' Dan asked. 'I've got stuff to be getting on with.'

'No, Dan, you don't,' Christine said firmly. 'This is more important. It's what Janice would have wanted, and so would your dad.'

Realising the futility of arguing while he felt so weak anyway, Dan held up his hands and sat back in bed. 'OK, OK, you win. A couple of days, then we'll reassess. Deal?'

The doctor smiled at him. 'Of course. You're not a prisoner, you know that, but I have to give you my best advice and recommendations. I'll have the nurses pop in to check up on you regularly and I'll come back in when the MDT has had the meeting. Now try to rest.' He nodded at Christine and left.

'I'm glad you've seen sense, Dan,' Christine said as she sat next to him. 'Just for a while, huh? Let them do their thing. I don't even want to know what Crosslyn was talking about, but let them deal with whatever they're dealing with. We all just want you fighting fit again, OK?' She patted his hand and passed him a cup of coffee.

Dan smiled at her and sighed. 'OK, I give up. Just a

couple of days though, and I'll be back home, you'll see.'

Chapter 26

Cowley was strung out, desperate to get high. Anything would do, but he had no money and nothing to trade with any of the other Keepers. Ideally he would have liked some Monkey Dust, but Deano controlled all of the local supply, and no one who had any spare would dare give some to one of the Keepers in case of the misconception that they were dealing on Deano's turf. Cowley had scrounged some diazepam off his mother from her prescription earlier that day but the effects had worn off and he was jittery now. As he sat on the low wall outside the still-closed Coalpool Tavern, his legs bounced up and down rapidly, keeping time with his fingers as they played a staccato tune on his thighs.

Man, he hated being like this. He couldn't concentrate at the best of times, but when he was seeking a fix, his mind was all over the place, racing, stumbling thoughts tripping over each other as they fought for dominance in his brain. Images of Duncan Hateley flashed through his mind and he grinned at the memory, then flashes of Deano and Lewis arguing, then the two girls from Holden Crescent after they saw that Flashpic video of the barman getting beaten up.

That had made them hot, and the ecstasy that Cowley had taken with him to visit them had made them even more eager to please.

That had been a good afternoon, but today was torture. He jittered and bounced on the wall, trying to come up with a scheme to get a score. Asking Deano was a definite no-no, especially the mood he was in lately. A sweetener was what Cowley needed, and what would help to keep Deano sweet right now? Lewis and Deano were both after this creepy guy that had picked off a couple of the Keepers and almost got Lewis. Cowley had no idea who he was, but then again, neither did Lewis or Deano. An idea began to form in Cowley's drug-starved brain. Not the best idea he'd ever had, but in truth, there hadn't been many good ideas in his brain for a long time, if ever. In his current state, any idea was bound to be a bad one, but this one was venturing right out into disastrous.

His eyes focussed on a point somewhere in the distance as he quickly mulled over the finer points, then he jumped off the wall and made his way to Bedders Road. Before long he was knocking on the back door of Deano's house. A young girl opened it and, recognising Cowley, she let him in.

'Where's Deano, bitch?' Cowley was in no mood for hanging around. The sooner he could speak to Deano, the sooner he'd get his fix. Hopefully.

The young girl, no more than sixteen or seventeen years old, looked up at Cowley with a glazed look on her face. Her skin was sallow and she was rake thin, the crystal meth having taken its toll on her body over the last year or so since she had taken up with the Keepers.

'Hmm? Who?'

Cowley slammed her against the kitchen door frame.

'Deano! The main man. Where? Is? He?'

She rubbed the back of her head where it had hit the door frame. 'OK, OK, no need to get stressed. He's upstairs in bed.'

Cowley released her and stood back.

'Well, fetch him then.' When she didn't hurry herself, Cowley slapped her round the side of the head. 'Fuckin' now!' As she swayed past him, Cowley muttered, 'And have a fuckin' shower while you're up there.' He wondered why Deano put up with the skanky wenches he seemed to prefer. There were decent slags on the estate, and they'd all put out for Deano. Cowley shrugged. Each to his own.

A couple of minutes later, Deano came down the stairs and walked through the front room into the kitchen, ignoring Cowley. After picking a can of lager out of the fridge, he spoke to the younger Keeper. 'The fuck you want?'

'I got some news for ya, man. Some good stuff. Info, like. I know who's causing us this grief.'

'What grief?' Deano stopped drinking his lager and stared at Cowley, his eyes narrowing.

'Welchy, Austen, Lewis. These blokes who beat them up. I know who they are.'

Deano advanced on Cowley, crushing his empty beer can and dropping it in the kitchen sink. 'And how da fuck do you know this?' he demanded.

Cowley backed up against the wall. The idea didn't seem so good any more, but he'd started now, and he needed his fix. Really needed it. 'I saw them. Three of them in a black Jeep thing, like Jonah said. They was in Halfords Crescent. Talking to people, like, and I heard them asking about you.'

'When?' Deano glared at Cowley.

'About half hour ago.' Cowley noticed Deano's fists clenching and unclenching and suddenly his fix seemed even more important. His jitters got worse and he could barely stand still.

'Half a fuckin hour, and you've only just told me!' Deano spoke in a low voice, but it was even more terrifying than if he'd screamed it in Cowley's face.

'Well, it might've been only quarter of an hour, I dunno like,' Cowley stammered. 'I tried to follow them a bit, but they got back in the car and went off. I came straight here then.'

'Who was they talkin' to?'

'What?' Cowley hadn't formed this part of the idea yet. He hadn't anticipated being asked specifics.

'Who was they talkin' to? You said you heard them talkin' to people, asking about me. Who?' Deano jabbed a finger at Cowley's chest.

'Old Man Hildicks, top of Halfords Crescent,' Cowley said.

'Fuck's sake, he's pissed out of his head most of the time, and when he ain't, he's got dementia.' Deano looked Cowley right in the eye. 'So what did he say? Did he tell them where I live?'

Realising he had bought himself some breathing space, providing a witness who couldn't remember his own name most of the time, Cowley continued to embellish his story, figuring in his own mind that the better the story, the better the reward.

'He couldn't understand them, they was foreign. He hates foreigners, don't he? He told them to piss off!'

'Foreign how?' Deano asked.

'I dunno. Like Polish or Russian, I think,' Cowley lied.

'Polish? Russian? Were they white?'

'I, er, I dunno. White?'

Deano sighed in exasperation. 'Yeah, white. Like us. Or were they dark-skinned, dark hair?'

'Oh, right. Yeah, they were white.' Cowley was getting into the swing of things now. 'Short cropped hair, and black leather jackets. Big fuckers. One had a scar right down the side of his face.'

Deano looked up sharply. 'A scar? Were they Albanian?'

'Albanian? Fuck knows, man. I dunno like. They just sounded like the Terminator.'

'Shit.' Deano leaned against the grubby kitchen work surface. 'Shit, shit.'

'Why, Deano? You know who they are?'

Deano stayed silent, thinking. He recalled that one of the Albanians he had bought the Baikals from had a prominent scar on his face. He was a big, nasty looking bastard as well. It must be them that were causing all this grief then. But why? They hadn't asked him for any money, not that he had enough to pay them back yet. Maybe they were muscling into the area? Well fuck 'em. If they thought Deano was a soft touch, they'd find out different.

'Yeah, I think so. Now fuck off, will ya. Get as many Keepers here as you can, on bikes or scooters. We're gonna pay somebody a visit.' Deano turned around to step into the toilet by the back door.

Cowley started to panic. This wasn't how he'd imagined it would turn out.

'Deano, I wondered if I can scrounge some stuff, like? Y'know, as payment for the info?' He listened to Deano taking a piss in the toilet, then listened to the silence that was his reply. 'Deano?'

Deano came out of the toilet, looking at Cowley in surprise.

'You still here?'

'Er, yeah, I'm just off. I'll get as many as I can, quick, like. But, er, can I, er, have some …?'

Deano laughed at him. 'You're really squirming, ain't ya?' Opening a kitchen cupboard door, he fetched out a small bag of white powder, which he tossed to Cowley. 'Here. Coke. Now fuck off.'

Cowley dropped the bag and scrabbled round on the filthy floor to find it. Before he'd even stood up, he'd opened it and was snorting it straight from the bag and rubbing it around his gums, trying to get the quickest hit possible.

'Don't fuckin' kill yourself, I need some numbers today, you fuckin' idiot.' Deano kicked him up the backside. 'Now, fetch me some bodies here. Or I'll come lookin' for you first.'

'Yeah, Deano, thanks man. I'm going.' Cowley ran out

of the back door and headed off towards the other end of Bedders Road. He knew where at least five of the Keepers would be. That would do for a start. If he brought a good number back, he might get some Monkey Dust next time, and he could mong out for a few blissful hours while Deano went and paid his visit with his gang. Cowley had no idea who Deano thought he was going to visit, but then again, he planned on being stoned out of his mind at the time, so who cared? He couldn't be blamed if Deano went after the wrong people, could he? He was just doing what Deano had asked, trying to find out who was causing all the grief.

Chapter 27

Benton was talking to DS Tunstall, updating him on the developing situation.

'Andrew Dean has called members of the gang to the house in Bedders Road. Apparently he's planning to stir up some Albanian gang, but I don't know any more details than that. Can we get some sort of surveillance ready? If this kicks off, it could be carnage.'

'I can request the eye in the sky to be on standby,' DS Tunstall said, meaning the police helicopter. It would be the easiest way of tracking a number of vehicles without the drivers being aware of it. 'Weather's OK today so there shouldn't be any problem. We can ask them to stay high and just monitor, see if we can work out Deano's destination, then send in local units to control it if needed.'

'Sounds like a plan. I might be able to keep you updated en route. I'll need a bike, though. Deano has called in Keepers who have two wheels, but I don't trust any of them not to kill me if I go pillion.'

'We were thinking of pulling you out of there,' DS Tunstall replied. 'We have other more pressing cases that we may need you for, but it looks like this situation is escalating so you'll have to stay put for now, just to give us eyes and ears on the ground. The last thing we need is an all-out turf war in the Coalpool estate. Andrew Dean may think he's in charge there but he has no idea what he's doing if he's trying to stir up one of the Eastern European gangs. They will tear him and his ragamuffins to shreds, which admittedly no one will cry many tears over, but the risk of civilian collateral damage is too high if this kicks off. Get yourself to the incident but keep well back, stay on your bike and do not get involved in any firearms confrontations. Go to the vehicle compound in Bloxwich and I'll make sure there's a bike there ready for you.'

'It'll have to be quick, Sarge,' Benton replied. 'He's already put the call out, and I don't know how long they'll wait.'

'Make your way there. I'll have it ready for you within the hour.'

'Roger that, Sarge. Thanks. I'll stay in touch.'

'Make sure you do, Benton, and pull back if there are firearms involved. Pull back and request Tactical Support immediately, OK?'

'Will do.'

Benton put down the phone in the public payphone kiosk, jumped on his bicycle and made his way towards Bloxwich. He reckoned it was about fifteen minutes to the secure lock-up, so he would have time, as long as the mechanics had a bike ready for him.

# # # #

Already there were several riders outside the house in Bedders Road. Most of them were on stolen scooters, but there were a couple on higher-powered motorcycles. A few years ago, any wannabe biker riding a scooter or moped would have been mocked for their vehicle's lack of power and street credibility, but now these machines were earning a reputation as the tools of violent street criminals. Gangs in the big cities were using the manoeuvrable and lightweight scooters as hit-and-run getaway vehicles, their agility making up for the low power. Their pillions often carried weapons like baseball bats, knives and hammers – or bottles of acid. The savage effects of acid evoked terror, and people were less likely to put up any sort of fight if a criminal simply carried a water bottle, which could be just filled up with tap water. It was impossible to know the difference unless used, and of course there was no law against carrying a bottle of water, if the criminal was unlucky enough to get caught and arrested.

By the time Benton arrived on a stolen-recovered Honda 250cc trail bike, the Keepers were about ready to leave. Deano rode at the front, on a stolen Triumph sports motorcycle, and the others, numbering about twenty by now, rode behind. Deano had told everyone that the intention was to cause a little trouble on another gang's turf, stir up a reaction from one or two of their heavies, then put them out of action in retaliation for Welchy and Austen. Their destination was Caldmore, Walsall, which had a reputation for being a red-light district up until the local

Asian populace forced a police clean-up in the late nineties. Nowadays the prostitution was run by Eastern European gangs, mainly an Albanian gang ruthless enough to silence the locals.

The demographics of the area had changed over the last ten years or so. For decades it had been a run-down area, mainly inhabited by Asian families who had their own communities, their own ways, and usually kept themselves to themselves. Then the influx of Eastern European immigrants in the late nineties changed everything. They went to areas like Caldmore because it was cheap and the Asian landlords weren't too bothered about references for tenants. Before anyone realised what was happening, the new immigrants had ousted the established migrant communities and taken over a lot of the shops and local businesses. Car washes sprang up on every abandoned car park, usually as a front for some other illegal business, laundering money through the books and transporting drugs from one town to another in sparkling clean cars.

In the background, the Eastern European gangs grew stronger, their territories growing ever larger against weak opposition with the police helpless to intervene due to Crown Prosecution regulations and lack of resources or funding.

This was the hornet's nest that Deano was leading his Keepers into. He had no real idea what he was going to do when he got there, but he figured if he didn't know, then the Albanians sure as hell wouldn't have a clue what was going to happen either. And that, Deano rationalised, would make him harder to beat. His vague plan was to get in there, show that he wasn't to be messed with, then melt back into the shadows of Walsall. He wasn't going to make a big deal of saying who he was or identifying the Keepers as a gang in case he was wrong, but if it has been this bunch coming after him, they'd guess pretty quickly.

He had given the Keepers a stirring speech worthy of a scene in Braveheart before they left. Benton had arrived too late for it, but he understood that the gist of it had been to stir up some racial hatred against the Albanians, getting the Keepers to believe they were doing their country a favour by kicking some foreigners' arses. Of course, this had also been fuelled by the drugs that Deano had shared around. A few of the Keepers had taken some old-school Angel Dust, or phencyclidine to give it the pharmaceutical name. It had mind-bending effects that could be unpredictable, but it gave the person taking it immense strength and made them violent beyond reason. It could also be hallucinogenic, which was not always a desired effect in a fight, but Deano had a stash that was cut with amphetamine, which reduced this hallucinogenic side effect while keeping the violence-inducing properties. Angel Dust was feared by police as it made the users less vulnerable to Tasers. The police would often be injured by the super-human strength and violence that Angel Dust invoked. Deano thought it would give his gang a subtle edge in the ensuing confrontation, although he was careful to only give it to pillions. He didn't want anyone wrecking themselves in a road accident before they had travelled the fifteen or so minutes to Caldmore.

As the motorised rabble pulled up into Caldmore from the Birmingham Road direction, they started beeping horns, revving engines, throwing bricks and other missiles at shop windows, riding up onto the pavements to intimidate pedestrians, and generally causing mayhem. The sight of such a large gang on scooters and bikes soon cleared the streets, but had locals reaching for their mobile phones to call for backup and protection, which was what Deano hoped would happen. Less than two minutes later, a black BMW X5 SUV with blacked-out windows pulled into the main street where the Keepers were making merry. It stopped just short of where Deano was standing. As he was the tallest of the gang, Deano stood out figuratively and physically. And the fact that he was only standing and watching while all the others were riding around like lunatics told the two large men in the BMW all they needed to know. Deano stared straight at them through the tinted windshield, but made sure to keep his crash helmet on to prevent identification.

Almost in a choreographed move, the two large men stepped out of the SUV, both of them wearing black leather boxer jackets and sunglasses. They stood by the side of the car for a moment, then walked casually towards Deano.

They stood either side of him and looked at the youths riding around the Caldmore square, pulling wheelies, revving engines and shouting. Deano watched them both, never taking his hands out of his hoodie pockets, where his right hand was cradling his 'pit bull', the Baikal pistol.

'Tell your little children to stop making nuisance,' one of

the heavies said to Deano in a thick, guttural accent. 'You can all go home now, ask Mommy to put you to bed.'

Deano stared at him and without saying a word, pulled out the Baikal and pointed it at the big man's chest. From a distance of about three feet, he couldn't miss.

The other Albanian shook his head incredulously at Deano, as the Keepers started to gather in a group around the three standing men.

'You do not want to come here pointing your guns at people. You will upset some very nasty men. If you go now, you may get away, but you have no idea how much trouble you are in already.' He stepped towards Deano and pointed in the direction of Birmingham Road. 'Go. Now. You are making me angry.'

One of the Keepers was revving his scooter engine and spinning the back tyre, holding the machine stationary with the front brake, just a couple of feet away from the big man that Deano was pointing his gun at. Smoke was coming from the tyre, and the smell of melting rubber rose in the air.

The big Albanian grinned lazily. 'Go away. You are like little bee, making so much noise. In my country, old ladies ride these machines to go shopping.' He turned to his colleague and said something in what Deano assumed to be Albanian, and they both laughed.

The Keeper on the revving scooter let go of the front brake as the engine revs hit the redline. The rear wheel, which had only been spinning against the pressure of the front brake, suddenly found grip and the bike lurched forwards like a missile. The rider let go of the handlebars and rolled off the back of it as it flew at the big Albanian, front wheel at waist height. It may have only been a low-powered bike, but it weighed around a hundred and fifty kilograms and it hit the big man like a sledgehammer, knocking him backwards against his BMW. The rear wheel, still spinning in a frenzy, ripped against his clothing and the front wheel slammed upwards into his jaw, whipping his head back violently. As he collapsed to the ground, already unconscious, his friend reached into his jacket, stepping backwards and trying to find cover behind the BMW.

Without warning, Deano lowered his aim and calmly shot the big man in the leg. At such a close distance the damage was colossal. Fragments of bone and tissue erupted out the back of his knee as he fell to the floor, blood splattering against the side of the BMW. As the Albanian howled with pain, he tried to reach inside his jacket again, but stopped when Deano held the gun inches from his face. He bent down to speak to the man.

'Well, you ain't in your fuckin' country, are ya? And I bet that little bee fuckin' stings now, don't it?' He nudged the Albanian's nose with the muzzle of the Baikal, then turned away and got back on his bike. A couple of the Keepers, high on Angel Dust and spurred on by the sight and smell of blood and violence, ran over to the prone Albanians and started to ruthlessly attack them. The unconscious man fared the worst, not being able to defend himself at all. Kicks and punches rained down on him, disfiguring his face and limbs. The young Keepers stamped on his head and arms as he lay unconscious on the floor. The other man managed to curl up into a defensive ball to deflect the blows, but couldn't stop them from kicking his shattered leg. His screams of rage and pain pierced the air, which together with the effects of the drugs, made the vicious Keepers laugh manically as they dealt out their violence. Finally the downed Albanian managed to pull out a pistol from the inside of his jacket but a sharp kick sent it flying to the pavement before he could use it to defend himself.

As Deano started his bike's engine, a few of the Keepers began to ride away, and Deano quickly followed, leaving the two men at the mercy of his drugged-up Keepers who were still kicking at their prey. From his vantage point near the rear of the pack, Benton had seen the whole incident. Before setting off with the others, he looked upwards and could just about make out the shape of a helicopter as it tailed the group of riders speeding back towards the other side of Walsall. He hoped that backup and an ambulance wouldn't be too long, or there were going to be two dead bodies to account for.

He rode over to the group doing the beating. 'Leave it, come on! I heard sirens, the filth are here!'

The gang members looked around in a daze, but through the drug-induced rage they could barely understand what Benton was saying.

He shouted at them again. 'Police! On the fuckin' way, c'mon!'

One of them left his victim and he pulled at another Keeper's arm, trying to get him to come with him, but he just turned round and punched his fellow gang member in the face. As they started to fight with each other, Benton saw two police cars swerve around the corner of the street and skid to a halt. A black van was seconds behind them, which Benton knew contained the Armed Response Unit. He kicked the bike into gear and sped off down the street, skidding the bike into an alleyway and coming out the other side onto the main Birmingham Road, where he executed an illegal U-turn and made his way to Walsall town centre, reducing his speed and blending into the regular traffic. Now was not the time to be Tasered by one of his own team or for his cover to be blown. He needed to make an urgent sitrep. The violence had blown up out of all proportion and Benton knew that this was the time to pull Deano in. He was clearly out of control, and there would be too much collateral damage if he was allowed to continue using the Keepers as weapons. With what he had seen, his evidence in court should be enough to put Deano away for a good few years, even taking into account the ridiculous leniency of the bleeding-hearts-liberal British justice system. He'd also noticed that the area where the incident had occurred was covered by CCTV, if it was working of course.

Benton hoped so, as that would make damning evidence in court, with his own identification of the culprits involved. He rode through the congested town centre traffic, looking for somewhere to make his report.

Chapter 28

One of the Keepers had filmed the Caldmore episode on his phone, or to be more accurate, on the phone that he was currently using, which he had stolen the week before. Within an hour of the incident, he had posted the video online with the description *'Keepers sorting out the foreign fukkers. Freedom fighters!'.*

The video clearly showed the whole incident, from the initial anti-social behaviour through to the savage beating that almost killed the two Albanians. A lot of background noise made it sound like it was being recorded on a toaster, as tinny sounding mopeds raced around, but the images were crystal clear. Thinking only that it would enhance the Keepers' violent reputation, there was never any thought that he was inadvertently providing damning evidence for the police and for gang retaliation.

Unbelievably, in the few hours that the video was live online, before the site providers were forced to remove it, the clip received over two thousand 'likes'. Comments were varied, but most of them seemed to support the Keepers.

Bruv21 – Fuck, yeah. giving the Polish sum stick!!

Simmo – R they Polish? How do u kno?

Bruv21 – whatever. Russions, poles, all the same

Simmo – hardly the same mate. Lol. Where did u go 2 skule?

Bruv21 – piss off wanka

Simmo – pmsl

Nashfrunt – whatever they r, they got sorted. Nice 1

Bruv21 – proper sorted!!!

Nashfrunt – u can hear bones braking, I swear.

Bruv21 – fkin hope so. Did u c that big wanka fly backard wen the moped hit him? Sick!

Nashfrunt – mayb they'll fck off home now

Patriot – not til theyv spent sum NHS money 1st. If I was in ther country theyd leve me 2 die in the road. Wudnt be free 4 me, like it is for them over here Ther police wudnt giv a shit either cos they don't like foriners

Simmo – how do u kno? U been there?

Nashfrunt – piss off

Patriot – u shud go and c wot happens 2 u over there simmo

Simmo – over where? U don't even kno wer they from

Patriot – wish Id been ther Id luv to hav helped out, giv the bastuds a kickin

Nashfrunt – yeah, me 2

Patriot – them lads shud av a medal, sortin out th terorists like that

Simmo – wot terrorists?

Nashfrunt – ther all terorist bastuds, all th forin fuckas

Patriot – 2 fkin rite
Simmo – fucks sake. R U 2 4 real?
Patriot – fkin heros they r
Nashfrunt – yeah. Like resistuns fiters
Patriot – wer do I join up?

# # # #

National Newspaper Tabloid

Police have made a number of arrests following an altercation in Caldmore, Walsall, yesterday. Two men are reported to be in police custody and are alleged to have been charged with firearms offences following a brutal assault, which was thought to be racially motivated. The arrested men are part of a local gang who are reputed to be involved in drugs and extortion, although the region of Walsall that the incident took place is not in the same area that these thugs usually ply their evil trade.

A local shopkeeper, who wishes to remain anonymous, told our reporter that a large gang of young men on motorcycles and mopeds 'just turned up and started creating mayhem'. A number of parked vehicles were damaged and several shop fronts were damaged and sprayed with graffiti, which included racial abuse and 'gang tags' that have been identified as those belonging to a gang known as the Keepers, who hail from the nearby estates of Coalpool, Blakenall and Goscote.

A police spokesperson told us that the investigation is ongoing and that they are determined to 'stamp out this terrifying and unacceptable anti-social behaviour'. Police have assured residents in Caldmore that they will increase police patrols in the area to safeguard local families and businesses. Some Caldmore residents and business owners have replied that it is 'too little, too late' and that this notorious gang of young hoodlums have been allowed to get away with their crimes for too long already.

The two victims of the vicious assault were both taken by ambulance to the Queen Elizabeth Hospital Birmingham's Major Trauma Centre, where their injuries are described as severe but stabilised. Both victims are thought to be Eastern European immigrants who tried to intervene and stop the gang from causing further trouble. Police have confirmed that the two victims were unarmed and had shown no signs of aggression or threat to the thirty-strong gang before they were pounced upon in an unprovoked and deadly attack.

Police have confirmed that the investigation is ongoing and they will endeavour to bring this unruly gang of young men to justice.

# # # #

'Fuck's sake, Deano, what the fuck was you thinkin', man?' Lewis shouted as he threw the newspaper to the floor in the

Bedders Road house.

Deano merely shrugged his huge shoulders and grinned. 'Wanted to stir the bastards up, didn't we? Now they know who they're fuckin' with.'

'Yeah, they know all right. Which fuckin' idiot tagged the front of the shops? What fuckin' moron put the video online?'

'Dunno,' Deano answered. 'Who cares?'

'Are you off your fuckin' head, man?' Lewis roared. 'They're Albanians! They were a hard-man gang over there for years before they came here. A proper gang, not a bunch of loser kids. It wasn't an Albanian who had a go at me in the Tavern, was it? He was fuckin' English! You've made an enemy where you had no business. You fuckin' nutcase.'

Lewis looked around at the few Keepers dossing in the front room of Deano's house. They were sprawled out on sofas or on the floor, mostly fiddling with mobile phones, some watching a couple play a PlayStation game on the large plasma-screen TV.

'Fuck this, and fuck you, Deano. You've lost the fuckin' plot. I'm done with this shit.' Lewis turned to leave, then froze as he heard the unmistakeable sound of a pistol being cocked behind him.

'You're done when I say you're done, Lewis. Turn your chicken shit around and sit down.'

Lewis turned around, his face full of rage, and saw that Deano held his 'pit bull' loosely aimed in his direction. Deano gestured towards one of the seats and the two younger Keepers scurried off to avoid being in the line of fire. When Lewis didn't immediately move, Deano shouted, 'Sit the fuck down.'

Lewis stood his ground, then slowly took a step forwards, not towards the sofa but straight towards Deano. 'What ya gonna do, man? You gonna start shootin' your own now?' Lewis sneered at him. 'How fuckin' long before there's none left, Deano? Huh? Then you gonna have to start shootin' at yourself.'

Lewis looked around at the wide-eyed young men in the room. 'Look at them, they're shitting themselves. How much use they gonna be to you when the Albanians come after you? If I was you, and thank fuck I ain't, but if I was, I'd be on the motorway out of here. Or else,' he gestured at the Baikal in Deano's shaking hand, 'that's gonna be your only way out. You'll need to save one last bullet for yourself though, cos if the Albanians catch you, they'll make you fuckin' pray for death. They're serious shit.'

Lewis turned around and calmly walked out of the door. Deano stared at Lewis's retreating back, his hand shaking as it held the Baikal still pointing at where Lewis had been standing. His drug-addled brain refused to acknowledge the truth in what Lewis had said and he turned on the young men in the room.

'Get out there!' he shouted, waving his 'pit bull' around wildly, causing the youths to duck and scramble for the doors. 'Watch the fuckin' streets and let me know when the bastards are coming. I'll have a fuckin' surprise for them.' He beat his hands on his chest. 'This is my fuckin' estate, my fuckin' house! I'll kill every one of the bastards.'

The Keepers scarpered, heading off in different directions as they escaped Deano's wrath. As they took off on whatever mode of transport they had arrived on, they all had a similar thought process going on. Get the hell out of there, screw Deano's instructions, make themselves scarce for a while.

Later that evening, a number of the Keepers had gathered in the car park of the Tavern, choosing not to go inside the shuttered-up building for fear of becoming trapped.

Smudge, a shaven-headed delinquent who had known Deano for most of his life, was speaking to the others gathered around.

'Lewis was right. Deano has lost it. He's mad. He's gonna get killed, either by the filth or the Albanians, or whoever has been picking us off one by one.'

Jonah, who had been sitting quietly near the back of the group, now spoke up. 'It weren't the Albanians.'

'How do you know, knobhead?' Graham Alton, known just as 'Gray', sneered at him.

'Cos I saw them, remember? When they took Welchy.'

'Yeah, an' you did fuck all,' one of the others muttered.

'There was three of them. They took Welchy like he was nothing. What would you have done?' Jonah knew that keeping the lie going was a good bet, especially at the moment. He didn't want any of these idiots thinking that the Albanians had been to blame, though. Probably best to not stir up any more bad feeling towards them. They would be coming to Coalpool for a little visit soon, everyone knew that, but it was Deano's mess and he could clear it up.

'They was English, not foreign,' Jonah continued. He hadn't been at the incident in Caldmore, having deliberately avoided the whole sorry mess.

Gray carried on. 'Yeah but that don't matter. We can't leave Deano on his own. He'll fuckin' kill us.'

One of the others, a mixed-race young man called Mosey, shook his head. 'I don't think Deano's gonna be around to fuck with us. You heard Lewis, the Albanians are serious shit. What was you all thinkin', going into their place and doing that stuff? They're gonna come after us. Fuck this, I ain't getting the blame for it, I weren't even there.' He walked off, leaving his stolen scooter behind. The red 'K' spray tagged on the front panel of it identified it as a Keepers bike, and he wanted no more part of the gang, not if the Albanians were out looking for them.

Benton sat on the low wall of the Tavern, watching these new developments with interest. This was probably a good outcome, meaning that the gang would disperse, at least for a while, allowing the police to mop up any of the others that were at the incident in Caldmore without serious resistance. Benton had been able to provide a list of names of most of the perpetrators, and there was a series of raids already planned to detain and arrest them. They could all be held on serious charges as they were involved in a firearms incident. He had no doubt that most of them would sing like canaries to try and reduce their own sentences.

'Fuck you anyway, you black bastard!' Gray shouted after Mosey. 'Fuckin' coward!'

'Shut the fuck up, Gray,' hissed Jonah, looking around. 'If

Lewis hears you shouting that crap, he'll rip your head off.'

'Yeah?' Gray postured, spreading his arms wide. 'I don't see him, do you? He's a fuckin' black coward as well.'

Several of the other Keepers sitting around had heard enough. It was bad enough worrying about Albanian gangsters coming after them, but most of them were more frightened of Lewis. He was a real and visibly violent nutcase, whereas the Albanians were stuff of legend and movies. They stood up and walked away, also leaving their 'K'-marked bikes and cars behind.

Benton made a mental note that these vehicles should be collected before they got torched, to collect prints and God knows what else that had been left inside them. That could be the first part of the series of planned raids.

Gray watched the Keepers deserting the car park. Before long, there was only Jonah, Gray and Benton sitting there in the dwindling evening light.

'Leave it, Gray,' Jonah advised. 'Just keep your head down for a bit, yeah?'

'No fuckin' way!' Gray was almost in tears. 'Keepers is all I've got. They'll all come creeping back, you watch, when Deano's sorted these bastard foreigners out. They'll beg to come back.' He stood up and jumped on one of the abandoned bikes. 'I hope Deano kicks their chicken fuckin' heads in.' He started the engine on the stolen dirt bike and roared away down the road, back towards Bedders Road. Jonah and Benton watched him go.

'What about you, Jonah?' Benton asked quietly.

'Dunno.' Jonah shrugged and looked at Benton,

recognising him from several of the Keepers meetings in Bedders Road.

'You're not going back to Deano, are you?' Benton asked incredulously.

'No.' Jonah shook his head emphatically. 'No way, he's dead meat. I saw the Albanians get one of the dealers in town once.' He paused, recalling the events. 'They're cold, mate. Like ice. They broke his legs and his arms, never even broke sweat. Didn't smile, didn't speak, nothing. It was just like work to them. Scary shit.'

'Fuck,' Benton said. 'When was that?'

'Last summer, when the Food Festival was in Walsall town centre. I was hanging about by the Wharf, know where I mean?'

Benton nodded. The Wharf was a recent development of housing apartments and small businesses, restaurants, pubs and the like. It was previously a derelict area next to the canal, home only to rats, dodgy backstreet lock-ups and homeless people sleeping in decrepit remnants of factory buildings. At least one homeless man had been beaten to death there. That particular incident had drawn a lot of negative national attention to the area, especially when the offenders were caught. The oldest of them had been only thirteen years old and they admitted they had done the crime for a dare. Nowadays it looked very different and almost everyone in the town agreed that this development was an improvement, even as they turned a blind eye to the insidious takeover of ownership of the businesses by the less than honourable.

'What were you doing there?' Benton asked.

'Looking at a nice Ducati. Always parked up there, cos the bloke who owns it works in one of the restaurants and he leaves the padlock and chain round a lamppost. I superglued the padlock so when he leaves it next time, he can't use the lock, and I'll have the bike. I was waiting for him to turn up when I saw a couple of the Albanians drag this lad out of one of the pubs. They took him round the back, right where I was hiding. He'd been selling drugs in their pub.' He shook his head at the memory. 'Fuck, they made a mess of him. He was in so much pain he couldn't even scream. He kept passing out and they just waited for him to wake up and started again. He was from out of town, a Scouser, I think.'

'What happened to him?' Benton asked.

'Dunno.' Jonah shrugged. 'I snuck off before they saw me. He's probably in the cut behind the pubs.'

Benton made another mental note to check whether any ambulances were called at that time to that area for a serious assault, or they were going to have to dredge the canal to look for a body.

Jonah stood and stretched. 'I'm off home, I suppose. I'm laying low for a bit. What about you?'

'Yeah, the same,' Benton said. 'Got some family up in Manchester. I might go and see them for a while.'

'Yeah, sounds like a good idea. See you around, mate.'

Benton watched Jonah walk away and decided that now was a good time for any UC operative to go back to base. He wasn't briefed or prepared for evading Albanian gangsters out seeking revenge. Pity that he never got to the bottom of who it was that picked an urban-guerrilla style fight with the Keepers, but it seemed almost irrelevant now. Whoever it was would have to get in quick, or there was going to be nothing left to pick on except bones, and there might not even be any of those left to find, if the Albanians did what they normally did and made any evidence disappear.

Chapter 29

Jeffreys walked onto the ward where Dan was unsuccessfully trying to get some rest. The incessant beeping of the machines monitoring his heart rate, blood pressure and oxygen levels was driving him crazy and he had already got out of bed to switch off his own monitor, much to the annoyance of the nurses. There weren't enough nurses on the ward to deal with every patient's needs and they had long ago learned to tune out alerts and alarms, meaning they had fewer jobs to do. Before Jeffreys had even arrived, Dan knew that he would be leaving the hospital today, if only to get a few hours of silence and sleep.

The only good thing about being in hospital was that it was somewhere neutral where Dan could gather his thoughts. Did his acts of revenge make Dan as bad as the Keepers? Wasn't he acting in a criminal way, using revenge to justify taking lives and injuring others? All his life, Dan had believed in law and order. To not believe in it meant only anarchy, and he had never subscribed to that school of thought. Serving in the armed forces was mostly about upholding peace and human rights, wasn't it? So what was so different about what he was doing now? The truth was that he had ceased to care about or have faith in the law. So no, he wasn't acting within the law, but as long as no innocents were involved, Dan decided that he was at peace with his conscience regarding the personal vendetta and all of the consequences.

As Jeffreys sat down next to him, Dan sat up straighter in bed, ready to discuss the next step of the treatment plan.

'Sorry I didn't see you yesterday afternoon,' said Dr Jeffreys, 'but I was waiting for the test results to come in. So, how are you feeling this morning?'

'Apart from tinnitus caused by these bloody machines beeping all the time, I'm feeling fine,' Dan muttered. 'Whatever meds you've put me on are working. The vertigo and nausea have gone now and I feel a bit of a fraud still being here.'

'Good, good, I'm glad that you're feeling more like your old self. You were quite poorly when you were brought in to the Emergency Department. I don't know if you remember but your paramedic colleagues had to give you twenty milligrams of diazepam intravenously before you would stop convulsing on the way here. You didn't wake up for over twenty hours, which admittedly could have been down to the diazepam, but it was still concerning.' Jeffreys opened a folder that he was carrying and looked at the contents. 'However, the scans that my colleagues have done so far are more reassuring. The alternative treatment seems to have worked well alongside the more conventional therapies, and the results are quite progressive. However, it's almost impossible to give you a guaranteed prognosis at this point, Daniel, as I'm sure you know.'

Dan nodded.

'But the size of the tumour appears to have reduced slightly, which is always a promising sign. The alternative cell transplant treatment is causing the surrounding brain tissue to reject the growth of the cancerous cells better than we had hoped. As long as that continues to happen, I am fairly confident that we can keep this under control for an indeterminate time.'

'But not cure it?' Dan asked.

'Cure is a difficult word in oncology. We can hold tumours at bay, sometimes for years, or we can operate and remove them and they mysteriously return, and we still don't always know how or why. Since surgery isn't a viable option with the type of tumour you have, the alternative therapies are your best option – and they seem to be working.'

'For now,' Dan added cautiously, not wanting to get his hopes up too much.

'Yes, for now.' Jeffreys sat back. 'Like I said, there are no absolute guarantees, but with careful monitoring, continuing your treatment, rest and a bit of luck, we can hold this at bay for a while.' He spread his hands. 'How long that while will turn out to be, I couldn't hazard a guess. But you are in a much more positive place now than you were at diagnosis. Physically, anyway.'

Dan nodded. There was a time bomb ticking away inside his head. He understood that was the best he could hope for, and hopefully it would continue ticking long enough for him to get this Keepers business over and done with.

'Well, thanks for all you've done, Dr Jeffreys. I really appreciate your hard work, and this alternative treatment that you've tried. Let me know when you want me to come back in and I'll make sure I'm here.'

'We'd like to keep you in for a while yet, Daniel. At least another forty-eight hours, maybe longer. That last convulsion you had came out of the blue and we couldn't find a clear cause.'

Dan swung his legs out the side of the hospital bed, pleased that this movement didn't cause any vertigo symptoms.

'Doc, listen. I am genuinely grateful. I know that you only want to do the best for me but it's stressing me out lying here in this ward. All this noise.' He swept his arm around and both Dan and Jeffreys couldn't help but listen to the continual beeping of machines and general hubbub of the ward activities. 'This noise,' he continued, 'is making me feel worse than if I were at home relaxing. I can continue to take my medication and I'll keep any appointments you call me in for. But right now, I really need to be at home. Please.'

Jeffreys looked at Dan for a couple of seconds, then shrugged and stood up.

'You're probably right. If this environment is bothering you that much then resting at home might well be the best option. I suppose you feel like you're still at work. I know I did when I was in hospital after my heart attack.'

He reached out his hand to Dan, who took it in a firm and steady handshake. 'Good luck, old chap, and stay in touch. I'll have my secretary arrange all the follow-ups.'

'Thanks, Dr Jeffreys. I'll see you soon.' Dan watched as the consultant walked to the nurses station, briefly stopping to confer with the sister in charge and fill in a prescription, then strode purposefully out of the ward. Dan walked steadily to the same nurses station to arrange his discharge.

Steven Jenkins

Chapter 30

After Dan had discharged himself from the hospital, he had gone home and dragged himself straight to bed. He felt exhausted and knew that events would have to wait until he was rested and better prepared. Any soldier, past or present, knows the six 'P's: Prior Preparation and Planning Prevents Poor Performance. Part of that preparation included rest, and after a few hectic days in hospital, Dan was in dire need of peaceful sleep. He briefly considered taking one of his prescribed diazepam to knock himself out for a few hours but was reluctant to dull his senses more than necessary. Before collapsing on his bed, he drank a large glass of water so that he didn't wake up with a headache and he set his house alarm so that no one would surprise him by entering his home as he slept. Dan was under no disillusion now. The Crosslyns had visited, and at least one of the Keepers knew where he lived. Dan was inclined to trust Jonah, but since he'd only known him for a brief time, it didn't hurt to be cautious.

About six hours later, Dan awoke with a start. Had he heard something outside his window? No alarm had sounded, so he knew that no one had broken in, but that didn't mean no one was trying. He slowly rolled out of bed, staying low beneath the window, and crossed to the bedroom door. He slipped soundlessly into the hallway and walked through to the bathroom. As he peered through the small window that overlooked the part of the rear garden, Dan saw what had disturbed him. A deer, maybe the same one that he had seen recently, was munching on the grass under his bedroom window. Dan watched as the graceful creature ate the grass then lifted its head up to eat some of the offerings on the bird table for dessert. Quietly moving away from the window, so as not to disturb the gentle animal, Dan made his way to the kitchen to make a coffee.

As he sat at the kitchen table sipping his fresh filter coffee, Dan contemplated his next move. Should he continue with his quest for revenge now that he knew exactly who was to blame for Janice and Bryn's deaths? He had already avenged his father's death, and he didn't think that Welchy would be leaving hospital anytime soon, at least not in one piece. He certainly wouldn't be terrorising any more people.

Now that Dan was able to sit and reflect on recent events, he was struggling to raise the anger that had previously fuelled his actions. There was no doubt in his mind that Andrew Dean was his wife's killer, yet he was unsure how to proceed. The police would probably not be able to prosecute Deano without more proof, and Jonah would undoubtedly refuse to go to court out of fear of retribution or being outcast in his community, seen as a 'grass' and someone not to be trusted. His already miserable existence would become more isolated. Jonah was the only proof that Dan had, but it wasn't enough. And even if Deano were imprisoned, he'd probably adapt well, continue living to an acceptable standard, surrounded by like-minded criminals. Also, knowing the British justice system, Deano would be back on the streets in five years or so, and Dan might not be around to deal with that.

No, the only acceptable ending to this unplanned journey would be to fully avenge Janice himself. Dan knew he would be miserable and restless for the rest of his life if he stopped now. Trouble was, how far was he prepared to go? Going into the middle of a Walsall housing estate with all guns blazing would be a recipe for disaster and would undoubtedly involve collateral damage. The estate was a rough place, full of thugs and miscreants, Dan knew that, but there were also innocent people living there. A lot of people on the inner-city sink estates were good people. Unfortunate circumstances, poor education, or lack of jobs or opportunities kept people living in places like that, despite their best intentions and ambitions. The last thing Dan wanted was to damage anyone else's life the way his family's life had been blown apart.

As Dan mulled over this moral dilemma, knowing nothing of the events in Caldmore or the structural breakdown of the Keepers gang, he knew that there would be no straightforward answer. Dan always did his best thinking while on his motorcycle, and he found himself unconsciously preparing for a ride. He went out to his garage, and after disabling the alarm and removing the high-security padlocks and chains from his Triumph Thruxton, he pushed it out into the sunlight. Janice's bike, an older classic Honda, stood under its cover in the corner of the garage, chained to a high-tensile steel ground anchor. Growing up in Walsall had made both Dan and Janice paranoid about security. Removing the cover, Dan took a moment to admire the gleaming finish on the old Honda 750. He and Janice had rebuilt this bike a few years ago and spent many happy miles touring around Britain and Europe together. He grew angry at the thought that he would have to sell the Honda soon. If he didn't sell it himself, it would no doubt be auctioned as part of his estate and end up being sold for a fraction of what it was worth when he died. All the proceeds of his estate would go to Christine as she was his only surviving relative, and Dan wanted her and her family to have every penny possible. These thoughts made him suddenly acknowledged the fact that he was very likely dying. Not imminently, although that wasn't impossible, but certainly within the next five years and perhaps within the next two, according to the literature he'd read since being diagnosed. The research about the new treatment he was having was still in its early days, and although results so far made for positive reading, it wasn't a done deal by any stretch of the imagination. He made a pledge to himself to put his house in order as soon as this Keepers business was over. Prior to Janice's death it wouldn't have mattered as he already had a will that left everything to her. Yet another aspect of these circumstances that Andrew Dean was to blame for.

After preparing his bike, Dan locked the garage, set the alarm and put on his helmet and jacket while the Triumph sat ticking over in the sun as the engine warmed up. Dan favoured more old-style motorcycle clothing and he wore blue jeans, army combat boots and a waxed-cotton Belstaff jacket. His helmet was black and had a distinctive paint job that Janice had done for him, with the Triumph logo on the back. Black leather gloves completed the ensemble. He swung his leg over the bike and settled into the saddle, reaching forwards to the handlebars. It seemed like months since he had ridden the bike and a part of his mind worried about his recent symptoms of vertigo and convulsions. Making a promise to himself that he would pull over and stop at the first sign of any untoward symptoms, Dan pulled away and rode down the lane that paralleled the Wrekin hill, opening the throttle a bit more when the lane opened onto a wider road.

Before long he turned onto the B-road that used to form part of the old A5. Accelerating briskly through the gears and grinning as the speedo spun round to the one hundred miles per hour mark, Dan felt more in control of his mind, thoughts and body. He had originally decided on a route down through Buildwas and Wroxeter, past the old Roman fort and towards Bridgnorth, but his subconscious seemed to have other ideas and before long he found himself on the back roads running parallel to the M54 motorway, heading east. Towards the sprawl of Walsall.

Heading down towards North Walsall, Dan formed a plan. Jonah had described Deano as a big lad, strong and violent. But he also described some important aspects of Deano's character that Dan intended to take full advantage of: he was reckless and tended to lose his temper easily. Deano's size didn't worry Dan too much. He had taken on big opponents in his younger days and lived to tell the tale. The Crosslyn brothers were a prime example of that. As long as he used his own strengths to his advantage and let Deano lose his cool, he might be OK, despite the fact Dan wasn't as fast or as competent in hand-to-hand combat as he had been in his prime. So, first and foremost, he needed Deano to be angry. Angry opponents made hasty mistakes. Dan figured that another hit on a Keeper would push Deano that bit further. According to Jonah, he was already furious at the sheer brazen cheek and lack of respect shown by someone daring to strike at the Keepers, so this seemed a good way to start the final offensive.

Sweeping the Triumph around a large roundabout, foot pegs scraping the ground, Dan knew where to go to next. Back to where it all started. The Yellow Mess.

# # # #

Gray rode the stolen motorcycle along the Black Track, behind Borneo Street. He was angry, frustrated and couldn't understand why the Keepers were deserting the gang now, when they needed to be strong and fearless. So what if a few foreign blokes were pissed off with them? So fucking what? Deano would sort them, of that Gray had no doubt. He revved the Yamaha dirt bike hard and hoisted the front of the bike in a wheelie, narrowly missing a couple out walking their dog, but to be fair to Gray, their existence didn't even register with him. Like the person he had stolen the motorcycle from in the first place, they didn't count. Had their bike stolen? They could easily buy another, couldn't they? They had jobs and stuff, loads of money, so it didn't really matter to them. Pet dog run over? Same. Didn't matter. There were loads in the rescue kennels, weren't there? That queer bloke on telly was always going on about them. There were thousands – they could just get another. Gray didn't see what the fuss was about. Seemed like people were generally selfish, in his opinion. So what if he wanted to ride their bike, drive their car? When he grew bored of whatever vehicle he'd stolen, or, as was usually the case, crashed and wrecked them, he would leave them where they stopped, for the next person to have the scraps. Sharing.

He turned along the track that would take him to the hills and jumps on the Yellow Mess and wound the throttle on hard, spinning the back wheel and almost losing control of the bike alongside the electricity sub-station. As he crested a small rise on the track, he saw a motorcycle travelling up to the bridge on Mill Lane. His natural curiosity and 'I see, I want' attitude kicked in, and he thrashed the bike along the Yellow Mess to come out onto the road behind the bike. He accelerated up to the bridge, skidding around the tight corner, to see that the motorcyclist had stopped, alighted from his bike and was looking over the bridge parapet at the Yellow Mess and the Black Track.

From his vantage point riding over the Mill Lane bridge, Dan had seen the rider of the dirt bike narrowly miss the young couple and their dog and knew it would only be a matter of time before he looked up towards the bridge and noticed another motorcycle, so he had ridden over the bridge a few times, trying to attract his attention. From his younger days, riding older versions of the dirt bike (called scramblers then, before the imported American dirt bike nomenclature) on the same tracks, Dan knew that only a rider of a stolen bike would come off the track and onto the road. Riders on their own bikes would try to avoid reports to the police, who would confiscate their bikes, but riders on stolen bikes would revel in the ensuing chase.

The fact that this rider had followed him up onto the bridge told Dan all he needed to know. At the very least, he was a bike thief. Hopefully he was one of the Keepers, and the lure of a shiny Triumph would no doubt be enough to get him to stop. Sure enough, as the young man on the noisy motocross bike pulled up, Dan saw the tell-tale 'K' roughly spray-painted on the fuel tank, warning other bike thieves to keep their hands off it.

Gray stopped the Yamaha next to the old bloke and his Triumph. He didn't know much about that sort of bike, but it looked valuable, probably worth a few hundred to the right buyer, of which there was an abundance. Various motorcycle breakers would turn a blind eye to paperwork and proof of ownership for the right bike. Online auction sites were another easy way of selling spares and generating easy money. It would certainly be worth more than the

Yamaha bike he was on.

Dan turned around as Gray leaned the dirt bike against the bridge parapet. The cast iron sections of the bridge hadn't been painted for decades and on the other side of where they both stood was a spray-painted *'Dan + Jan'*. Faded now, but still legible, Dan remembered hanging over the bridge while Janice had held his legs. They were only kids at the time, but he recalled using a whole can of paint on the two words, wanting to ensure that the graffiti lasted.

'Nice bike, mate,' Gray said, looking greedily at the Triumph and noticing that the keys were still in the ignition. *Easy. Slap the old bloke down, jump on, ride away. Seconds.*

'Reckon you could ride it?' Dan asked.

'What?' Gray said, puzzled.

'They're not as easy as that scrambler. You need skill and finesse to get the most out of these,' Dan explained.

'Gis a go, and I'll show ya,' Gray chanced, reckoning that he wouldn't even have to slap the fool.

Dan paused, appearing to consider the challenge. 'Put my helmet on first then. You don't want to get nicked.'

Gray couldn't believe his ears. Greed and stupidity naturally overrode any thoughts of caution. 'Yeah, alright then. Gis it here.' He held out his hand for the helmet, thinking that it would probably fetch another fifty quid online.

Dan passed it to him and waited until Gray slipped it onto his head before snapping out his right hand to grab the chin piece and pushing it sharply up and backwards, simultaneously twisting it to the left. This had the desired effect of leaving Gray completely off-balanced and momentarily disorientated as the twisted helmet obscured his view. He tried to brace himself by locking his legs, and Dan took full advantage of this by driving the heel of his combat boots straight into the locked knee of Gray's left leg. The resounding crack and piercing scream told Dan that his aim had been perfect, and he let go of the helmet and watched Gray collapse to the floor, clutching his broken knee. Gray fumbled to get the helmet off, dropped it on the floor and yelled out a stream of expletives and threats at Dan, who calmly picked his helmet up and hung it on the handlebars of the Triumph, tutting at the scratches. He turned and grabbed hold of Gray's left ear, twisting it and pulling his head to the side.

'A message for your mate Deano,' he said calmly into Gray's other ear. 'I'm coming for him now.'

Dan pulled Gray painfully up into a standing position. 'Your ear takes about twenty-five pounds of force to rip it off, matey, and I reckon I could twist and pull double that, so do as you're told.'

The pain in his knee and ear, and the calm demeanour of his attacker, put real fear into Gray. Struggling to stand on only his good leg, he realised this was the guy they should have been looking for, the one who had attacked Lewis, Welchy and Austen. But he wasn't foreign, so what was all that about in Caldmore? As Gray's brain struggled to assimilate this new information, Dan spun him around, grabbed hold of his left arm and twisted it behind his back, then propelled him sharply forwards, lifting him at the same time. Gray's chest struck the hard edge of the parapet and the air rushed out of him. Before he had the chance to collapse, he felt his feet leave the ground as Dan hoisted him forwards, then he was falling, briefly and bizarrely wondering who had written the graffiti on the wrong side of the bridge as he plummeted head-first towards the train tracks under the bridge, unable to scream as his lungs had yet to recover and draw breath.

Dan jumped onto the Yamaha dirt bike and kick-started it into life. He rode it to the edge of the bridge where the chain-link fence had been damaged for years, and turned to aim at the bridge, revving the bike hard. As the front wheel hit the gap, Dan leapt off the back of the bike. It sailed through the gap, struck the brickwork of the bridge and started to somersault into freefall. Dan threw his head back and yelled as loud as he could for about a second. Stepping down onto the road again, he rolled his Triumph back towards the end of the bridge, jumped on and coasted soundlessly down towards Coalpool Lane. Somewhere near the bottom of the dip, he started the engine, and without even a glance back, he rode calmly off towards Walsall town centre and then joined the motorway back to Shropshire and home.

Chapter 31

National Newspaper Tabloid

A young man was seriously injured yesterday in a motorcycling accident on Mill Lane, Walsall. The motorcycle that he was riding, which had been reported stolen the week before, appears to have left the bridge on Mill Lane, travelling through a gap in a broken fence, before plummeting almost fifty feet to land on the train tracks below.

Luckily two members of the public, who had themselves narrowly missed being run over by the man on the stolen motorcycle just minutes earlier, heard a scream and saw the motorcycle fly from the bridge.

West Midlands Police have said that they are investigating the incident, stating that it appears to be a tragic accident at this time. They urge any other witnesses to come forwards. The injured young man has not yet regained consciousness. West Midlands Ambulance Service attended the incident and they issued a statement saying that a young man suffered serious injuries in a motorcycling accident and was treated at the scene by an ambulance paramedic crew before being transferred by helicopter to the Major Trauma Unit at Birmingham Queen Elizabeth Hospital.

The rider of the stolen motorcycle was not thought to be wearing a crash helmet and suffered serious head injuries and multiple fractures in the accident. His family have issued a statement this morning, through their solicitor, saying that they will be seeking compensation from Walsall Council as the damaged fence has been in this state of ill repair for many years. They feel that the Council are partly responsible, as had the fence been complete and serviceable, he would not have been able to fall over the bridge from the road.

<u>Chapter 32</u>

The Crosslyn brothers were in a black Mitsubishi four-by-four and heading towards Coalpool. Peter, the driver, was leading the discussion.

'So what's the plan when we get there, Joseph?' As usual, Peter and Michael deferred to the middle brother. Over the years, Joseph had become accepted as the calm thinker of the three of them. It was usually Joseph who got the best deals for the travelling fairground clan, finding them the best sites and sorting out all the paperwork with the local councils.

Historically, travelling fairgrounds had always utilised the same pieces of land around the country, but now a lot of those areas were no longer available. Local fairgrounds used to be a seasonal event, providing a place teenagers could meet boyfriends and girlfriends, parents could take youngsters for a treat, and local communities could celebrate the changing seasons. Nowadays, new housing estates were being built on the land previously used for fairs, with no thought given to leaving open spaces for recreation. Even so, somehow Joseph always managed to find a site and keep the family business going. Other travelling fairground families around the country respected Joseph, often asking him to intervene on their behalf with difficult councils and landowners.

Travelling fairground communities were often labelled as gypsies, with all of the attached biases and ill-feelings, but they didn't class themselves as gypsies at all. They were culturally different to most people, as travelling around the country had an impact on many aspects of family life, but they were not ethnically different. And they would argue that the quality of their lives was better in many ways. Their sense of family history, of belonging and of self-sufficiency, were qualities to be admired and revered.

The Crosslyns were an example of this. Their family started in the showground business in the late 1800s, after one of the Black Country Crosslyns decided he wasn't going to spend the rest of his life 'down the pit'. As the showground business developed, more of the family became involved until eventually there were more Crosslyns on the showground circuit than there were living in the mining community. Their children grew up in a strong, insular community where they looked after each other and only met outsiders at the shows – where they viewed them as customers or 'marks'. Over time, these families became very strong-willed and almost tribal in some aspects of their lives. They educated their children, they had their own beliefs and values, and they looked after their elders when they became too old to work. They took very little from the state but were still obliged to pay taxes, of course.

Reputation was everything. If you were late arriving on the grounds, your pitch was lost. If you didn't maintain your equipment, it broke down and you lost money.

And of course, as in any self-contained community, justice was generally dealt with in-house, without the need to involve strangers who didn't understand the family values.

So the bond between these three brothers was as strong, if not stronger, than any between soldiers or gang members. Joseph thought for a minute before answering Peter.

'Let's just take things easy at first, alright. No heavy-handed shenanigans until we know the score. We're almost sure this Andrew Dean is our man, but I want to be absolutely certain.'

'Then what?' Michael asked.

'Then we deal with him,' Joseph answered. 'He'll pay for what he did to Janice, then he'll disappear. I doubt the police will look very hard for him, and from what we've heard he hasn't got many friends that'll miss him.'

Peter and Michael nodded, satisfied that their brother hadn't gone soft after years of living, mostly, on the straight and narrow.

'The old man would have torn him limb from limb,' Peter growled.

'The old man would have got caught or outnumbered,' Joseph countered. 'He'd have marched right into the house and wanted a man-to-man fight to sort things out.'

'What's wrong with that?' demanded Michael, defending their father.

'Nothing,' said Joseph. 'As long as both sides agree to fight the same way. But these modern thugs have no sense of honour, of what it's like to be a man and stand up for your family. Everything is easy come, easy go for them. What they don't steal, the state gives them on a plate. They don't work, they have no family, no values. Yeah, the old man would have taken them on and beaten them easily in a fair fight, no matter how big they are, but it would never be a fair fight. This Deano sounds like a dirty scheming bastard, so we've got to play him the same way. Agreed?'

Both brothers reluctantly nodded their agreement. The car was silent again for a couple of minutes as they drove slowly along Coalpool Lane and past the Coalpool Tavern, still shuttered-up and closed.

'We'll go in softly-softly, ask him about buying some drugs,' Joseph mused. 'See the lay of the land, how many of them are with him, how easy it'll be to take him then and there. If it's not possible today, we'll set up a meeting with him for the drugs thing and take him at a place outside of this shithole estate, away from his little fucking empire.'

'We don't know anything about buying or selling drugs, Joseph,' warned Peter.

'Exactly,' Joseph continued. 'He'll sense that, and he'll think he'll get an easy deal with some idiots who don't know what they're selling, and he'd be right.'

'So how will that work?' asked Michael warily.

'He's greedy, reckless and stupid,' explained Joseph. 'We'll tell him that we came across a drug deal at one of the fairgrounds, ran the dealers off and they left a bag of stuff behind. They were too scared to come back for it, and we just want to sell it. We think it's cocaine, but we're not sure. Let him show some interest and then we'll say we'll show it to him once we know he's interested. If we can't get him today, that's the bait to bring him out of this place some other time.'

'Sounds lame,' said Michael.

'It does that,' agreed Peter.

'You're right,' said Joseph. 'But it's only a backup excuse, in case there are too many of them for us to take today. If that turns out to be the case, we'll tell our little story and get out. But if we can get him now, that's what we'll do. Knock him down, tie him, chuck him in the back and take him somewhere quieter so we can have our private chat.'

'That's more like it.' Peter nodded grimly.

# # # #

'Richie! Get down 'ere!'

Jonah was sitting up on his bed, playing on his PlayStation. He heard his mother shouting up the stairs but decided to ignore her. She'd likely only want him to run some shitty errand that she was too lazy to go on herself. He turned up the volume of his game.

'Richie Jones! Get your lazy arse down here! Somebody here to see you,' his mother shouted.

'Fuck's sake,' Jonah muttered as he threw his PlayStation controller onto his bed. 'Alright, I'm coming,' he shouted in the general direction of his bedroom door.

'Well hurry up,' his mother shouted back. Although it would have been quicker to go up the twelve stairs to speak to him directly, like most people Jonah knew, families tended to communicate by shouting rather than moving closer to each other.

He slipped on a pair of trainers and ambled down the stairs, taking care not to trip over the loose and frayed carpet. Stepping into the front room, he saw his mother's sister sitting on the edge of the sofa.

'Aunt Joyce, how's things?' said Jonah.

'Not good, our Richie.' She sounded on the edge of tears.

'Why? What's up?' he asked, looking from his aunt to his mother.

'Your bleedin' mate Andrew bloody Dean, that's what's up,' his mother snapped. 'Our Cheryl is round there with him. And you can bloody well go and get her back. She's only fifteen, she don't want to be hanging round with him. God knows what he's got her doing.'

'Calm down,' Jonah said. He turned to Joyce. 'Is that right? Is Cheryl with Deano?'

Joyce nodded, staring at the floor. 'Yeah,' she said quietly. 'I found some stuff, I think it was drugs, in a bag in her room. I asked her what it was and where she got it, and we had a massive row. Now she's stormed out and said she's gone to live with Deano.' She looked up at Jonah expectantly. 'He's a friend of yours, Richie. Can't you go and fetch her back? Talk some sense into her? Please?'

Jonah could see that she was near to tears, but he felt hopeless. If Deano had taken a shine to Cheryl, and that was very likely, given that she was a pretty, impressionable teenager, then he'd have a hard time trying to persuade him to let her go home before he'd used her and grown bored of having her around. He shuddered at how he'd seen Deano treat other young girls at his house. He would sweet talk them, offer them drugs, then take them upstairs. Sometimes they'd stay a few days, sometimes only hours, but they always left in a worse state than when they arrived. If they decided they didn't want to do what he wanted, Deano would get scarily aggressive very quickly. More than once, Jonah or one of the other Keepers had to take one of the girls home after Deano had finished with them and beaten them. Of course, the girls and their families were too scared to contact the police so he always got away with it. One girl's father had stormed round to sort Deano out and had ended up in intensive care at the Manor Hospital after a good kicking by Deano and several Keepers.

'Well go on then.' Jonah's mother pushed him towards the front door. 'Get round there and get our Cheryl back, or you tell bloody Andrew Dean I'll be round there to sort him out.'

Jonah sighed. He knew as well as his mother did that her words were just that: words and empty threats. She would no more go round and tell Deano what's what than would his aunt. They were both terrified of him, but at least Joyce wasn't ashamed to admit it. His mother continued her high-pitched tirade, a cigarette dangling from her mouth as she shoved Jonah out the front door.

As he walked along the pavement, Jonah hung his head

low. Right now, the last place he wanted to be was anywhere near Andrew Dean. He was losing it, big time, using more of his drugs than he was selling and getting more violent and unpredictable with every passing hour. Jonah knew that he would at least have to try to get Cheryl home. If he could talk to her, she might listen to him, if she wasn't already stoned on whatever Deano had given her. He liked his girls vulnerable and stoned; he said they were more fun that way.

Jonah felt angry and sick of living in this environment. When had this become a normal way to live? Rescuing your child cousin from a sexual predator and vicious bully that everyone knew about but was too frightened to stand up to? How had things got so bad?

As he walked along Bedders Road, Jonah became more and more apprehensive. Trying to talk Deano into letting one of his pretty playthings go, just because she happened to be Jonah's cousin, was going to be risky. *Risky?* Jonah thought to himself. *More like bloody suicidal.*

# # # #

Meanwhile, Cheryl was also having second thoughts. At first when she'd told her mum she was going to stay at Deano's house, she had only half meant it. She was just trying to get back at her. How dare she go looking through her stuff? Anyway, that bag of stuff wasn't hers. She was looking after it for her friend Debbie. Debbie's stepdad was always checking her room, making sure that she wasn't up to anything she shouldn't be. Debbie reckoned he just liked to look through her clothes and stuff, but Cheryl didn't believe her. The guy seemed OK. He was always nice to Debbie and her friends, and he was always talking about Debbie going to college and university. Of course, Debbie didn't want to go to college and university. She said she was sick enough of school, let alone doing the same crap for another five years!

Cheryl often wished she had someone to talk about college and university. She wanted to go to uni, but hadn't got a clue how to go about finding out how to get there. It seemed to be out of reach for girls like her, from places like Coalpool, with friends like Debbie. Debbie just wanted to waste her life, it seemed to Cheryl.

Now she was in Andrew Dean's front room because of her stupid mate Debbie and her bloody bag of cannabis. She had thought there would be lots of people here and she could just blend into the background for an hour to make her mum sweat a bit, before everyone calmed down and she could go home. But she was on her own with Deano and he wasn't like she'd seen him before. In fact, he was scaring her half to tears.

'Just try it, sweets,' Deano cajoled, offering Cheryl a drag on a joint. He'd forgotten her name, if he'd ever known it in the first place. Before he showed his true self, the girls were always 'sweets' or 'darlin'', then when he had them hooked, their names invariably changed to 'bitch' or 'slag'. He offered the joint again. 'It'll make you feel chilled.'

'I'm fine, honest, Deano. I'm chilled already.' Cheryl tried to push the joint away from her lips as Deano leaned into her on the grubby sofa.

'Yeah?' Deano asked. He put his hand on her leg, sliding it up the hem of the short skirt Cheryl now regretted wearing. Why hadn't she worn jeans? She put her hand over Deano's, trying to halt its progress up her leg, but to no avail as he just pushed her hand out of the way. 'You don't seem chilled to me.' He pushed the joint towards Cheryl's mouth again. 'Just have some, don't be fuckin' stupid.' He relaxed a bit, turned his snarl into a smile. 'Then we'll go upstairs and have us some fun, yeah?'

Cheryl realised that she was way out of her depth here. She was still a virgin, although like most of the girls in her class, she always bragged that she wasn't. Losing her virginity to someone like this hadn't been how she'd imagined it, but she couldn't see how she was going to escape. Having seen the Flashpic videos of Deano beating people up, she knew how violent and crazy he was. Tears sprang unbidden to her eyes.

When Deano saw this, it only served to excite him more. 'C'mon, bitch, just have some of this, then you won't feel bad. You'll just go with the flow and enjoy it. I promise.' As he tried to shove the joint into Cheryl's mouth, he pinched her nose shut and his grip was like a vice on her face. Struggling was useless – he was much bigger and stronger than Cheryl. She could feel his excitement through his trousers as he pressed against her and she began to panic, squirming under his grip and breathing rapidly through her mouth, inadvertently inhaling the smoke from the crack joint. After some time doing this she started to feel light-headed and detached from reality, and she slumped back on the sofa.

'Yeah, see, I told you it would chill you out, didn't I?' Deano said as he easily picked Cheryl up. He turned to carry her up the stairs, just as someone pounded on his front door. 'What the fuck?' he snarled. 'Fuck off!' he shouted. 'I'm busy, yeah?'

# # # #

From his vantage point peering through the grimy front window, Michael nodded to Peter and Joseph as they stood at the front door.

'He's on his own,' Michael said. 'No, wait, he's got some girl with him, but she looks out of it.'

Peter didn't hesitate, but put his foot against the door and kicked as hard as he could. Unfortunately, what he didn't know was that the front door had been reinforced with steel plates and bolts on the inside to protect against police raids, so his kick proved futile. He bounced back, grimacing against the pain shooting up his leg.

'Fer fuck's sake, Peter,' Joseph said. 'You not had yer breakfast today?'

As Peter lifted his leg to try again, Michael ran past.

'Forget it,' he said. 'The curtains are blowing about inside. I reckon the back door's open.'

The other two brothers followed him around the back of the house, carefully avoiding all the junk and dog shit strewn across the path. A chained up and scrawny looking

Staffordshire bull terrier barked loudly at them as they ran past, but it had tangled its chain around some of the junk and thankfully couldn't reach far enough to stop them getting to the door. As Michael had suspected, it had been left open.

The three brothers entered the house. Joseph cautioned both of his brothers back with an open palm. As he approached the door leading from the kitchen to the living room, he could see it was slightly ajar but not enough for him to see into the next room. Standing still, he motioned to his brothers to stand either side of the door. If anything nasty was going to come through the door, there was no point it taking out all three of them. He tensed himself, then launched at the door, knocking it flying open, and ducked as he ran through into the next room.

# # # #

Jonah saw the black four-by-four parked outside Deano's house. At once his thoughts raced to all sorts of improbable scenarios. Had the Albanian gangsters come to fetch Deano? If Cheryl was there, what would happen to her? Imagining all sorts of people-trafficking plots, he broke into a jog to get to the house quickly but he noticed that there was no one waiting in the car, which seemed strange to him. Surely if someone from another gang had turned up with bad intentions, they would at least leave a lookout in the car? Something seemed really wrong with this picture, and he slowed down as he approached the house. Heart racing and adrenaline flooding his body, he peered around the gateway down the side of the house. Seeing no one and hearing nothing, he crept towards the back door.

# # # #

After hearing the door slamming downstairs, Deano dropped Cheryl unceremoniously on the floor just inside his bedroom, which overlooked the front of the house. He ran to the window and glanced out, keeping as much of his body out of sight as possible. There was a black four-by-four parked right outside his driveway, the cocky bastards. They hadn't even bothered to sneak up on him. Fucking Albanians and their black four-by-four cars, he thought. Well, screw the lot of them. He'd show them.

The Baikal pistol, his 'pit bull', lay under his pillow where he always kept it as he slept. He snatched it out, quickly checked the magazine and positioned himself next to the bed, getting as much cover as he could from the mattress. He'd read somewhere that blankets and a mattress could deflect bullets enough to decrease most of their impact, so now seemed a good time to try the theory. Not that he had much choice. He rested the 'pit bull' on the mattress and took careful aim at where he thought the first Albanian's belly would come through the door. One good gut-shot would stop the first guy, he reasoned, and the screaming would make the others think twice.

As he waited in the silence, beads of sweat formed on his forehead and cheeks, but he barely noticed it. His focus was on the door and whoever would come through it.

# # # #

Joseph stood up in the living room and seeing that no one else was in there, he whispered to his brothers to come in.

'Jesus, it stinks in here,' Peter said as he came into the room, wrinkling his nose in disgust at the aroma of sweaty bodies, stale washing up and discarded takeaway food wrappers. A waste bin stood in the corner of the room, its contents spilling onto the floor.

Michael brought up the rear, looking back towards the door they had just come through in case anyone sneaked in behind them. 'Let's just find the bastard and get out of here, OK?'

Joseph nodded and pointed at the door leading to the stairs. 'He must've gone upstairs. There's nowhere else for him to go. Michael.' He looked to his younger brother. 'Grab that.' He pointed to a baseball bat leaning against the back of the sofa. 'If anyone comes in that door, hit em first, don't wait to ask questions. If anyone comes down the stairs except us, same thing goes.'

Grabbing the bat, Michael nodded. Joseph pulled a small but heavy leather cosh out of his jacket pocket and turned to Peter. 'I'll go first. We know he's got a gun, so be bloody careful.' As he turned to take the first step up the stairs, Peter grabbed his arm.

'Wait.' He pulled out the Baikal from inside his jacket. 'I'll go first.'

'Where did you get that?' Joseph hissed.

'Danny Boy had it on him when we found him collapsed. I took it. Figured I'd help him out so the police didn't ask too many awkward questions. Kept it just in case.'

'It's not a fuckin' fairground air rifle, you idiot,' Joseph said. 'Do you even know how to use it?'

Peter shrugged. 'Point it at the wanker, pull the trigger. How difficult can it be?' He stepped past Joseph and took the stairs two at a time.

'Fer fuck's sake,' muttered Joseph, taking off after him.

Peter stopped on the top landing, looking around at the doors to the rooms. One obviously led to the upstairs bathroom so he glanced in there first, figuring it wouldn't be the first place to hide since there wasn't much cover. Catching a full blast of the rank smell coming from inside, he quickly pulled his head away from the door.

The other three doors must be bedrooms, he figured. Two doors were closed fully, and one was open slightly, as if tempting him in. As he stood deciding which one to go through, Cheryl chose that moment to let out a muffled groan as the effects of the joint started to wear off. She was lying right behind the door that was slightly ajar.

Peter turned to Joseph and nodded towards the door.

'You hear that?' he whispered. 'Bastard's still with his girly. He doesn't even realise we're in here!' He grinned incredulously. 'Let's disturb his fun, shall we?' He took two rapid steps towards the door and burst straight into the bedroom. The ensuing loud bang from the gunshot happened simultaneously with the image of Peter flying through the air before hitting the floor.

Chapter 33

Dan was unsuccessfully trying to get some rest after discharging himself from hospital. He was only managing to snatch short, light naps, which were punctuated by vivid dreams that invariably woke him. Usually he didn't dream all that much so he supposed it was the effects of the drugs he'd been given in hospital, or maybe it was the tumour, reminding him it was still there, lurking in the background, fighting a silent fight. As his latest scans had shown that the tumour was shrinking, he concluded that the strange dreams were definitely caused by hospital drugs. Knowing they would wear off eventually, he tried several times to sleep through the effects, but to no avail.

Whenever Dan had bad dreams, they would invariably be about his time growing up in Walsall. Memories from his years in the British Army had never bothered him, though he had reflected on these experiences over the years, trying to make sense of them. Even so, they didn't cause him any anxiety. His years in the Ambulance Service had shown him more of what suffering could be about, and also how resilient people could be, but again none of these events had really bothered him. He had been accused by several colleagues of being emotionally numb, but he argued that it wasn't that he didn't care, just that he never showed it. In truth, he rarely felt upset by the more objectively distressing incidents, but conversely he always felt a pride in doing the best he could for every single patient. If they survived whatever emergency they had suffered, then great, it was a job well done. But if they didn't survive, or didn't make a full recovery, Dan would reflect on what he had done to clinically treat them, and as long as he knew he had done his best, there was no point beating himself up over it, was there?

His solitary nature was another aspect of his personality that people seemed to struggle with, but Dan never saw it as a problem. Janice was always there for him, and she seemed to intuitively know when it was best to leave him alone or when to offer some company. Other people would ask him what was wrong when there wasn't anything wrong. Just because he was introspective and quiet, preferring his own company, that didn't mean he was depressed or antisocial, did it? The way he saw it, everyone had different ways of being, and his way was more independent and isolated.

It seemed to him that just because he had served in the Army and as a paramedic, everyone automatically assumed that he suffered with post-traumatic stress disorder. Dan knew that if he did show any signs of the condition, the source of the problem began with his experiences of growing up in Walsall. He absolutely loathed the place and its associated memories. Dreams about events there always left him feeling down and angry without being able to identify exactly why. He never had a happy dream about the place or his childhood.

In contrast, if he had dreams or memories about his time in the Army, they were usually abstract or even funny. Not being able to find his kit was a common theme, or recalling banter and camaraderie. Even recalling the conflicts seemed straightforward to Dan. He remembered the friends he had lost but knew that it was their choice to join up, and he also knew that they would all do the same again, despite knowing the risks. Such was the eternal optimism and fearlessness of young men of that calibre.

No, Dan refused to believe that he had a problem with PTSD, but he did acknowledge that his formative years were spent growing up in a rough, deprived, violent and lawless environment. He accepted that this would almost certainly have an effect on how he acted and reacted to certain situations, and that he could sometimes be perceived as cold and angry, when in fact he wasn't. That was life. He dealt with it. He'd left Walsall and the memories were just that – memories. They could no more harm him than could the idea of ghosts.

So for the third time that morning, Dan woke after an elusive dream and he decided that it was pointless trying to have a lie-in. He may as well get up and get on with his day. Rest would come when his body needed it and couldn't be forced.

After an enjoyable breakfast, Dan took a cup of coffee out into the garden to decide what to do next, regarding his plan for the Keepers, and Deano in particular. Sitting in his garden in the early June sunshine, he remembered happier times. Bryn bouncing around, trying to catch birds in the trees as he and Janice laughed at him, watching him bark furiously at the birds then lose interest and become completely incensed if he saw a squirrel. They had fetched Bryn from a rescue kennels two years ago after their previous dog had died of old age. Bryn was a strange cross-breed of indeterminate ancestry, looking like a jet-black genetic mish-mash of an Alsatian, Collie and Labrador, but they had both seen potential in him. The rescue centre didn't know much of his history, just that he had been brought in by police after a drugs raid on a house. He was thought to be around twelve months old when they adopted him. At first he was timid and withdrawn but after plenty of daily exercise, some training and a peaceful environment, he had grown into a strong, healthy, protective and loyal dog, thriving in the surroundings of the Wrekin area where Dan and Janice lived.

Dan could clearly recall how he and Janice had taken Bryn on a walk the day they had brought him home, before he was allowed to enter the house. Janice wanted to take him down to the reservoir for a bath first, to get rid of the scent of the kennels. Bryn hadn't known what to make of the large expanse of water and refused to get in. Not wanting to throw him in and risk traumatising him, Dan had stripped down to his shorts and gone in first and Bryn had followed without a second thought. The barn conversion where the three of them had lived happily for the last two years seemed suddenly empty and too quiet.

Looking around the garden, Dan appreciated just how much care and love Janice had lavished on this small corner of Shropshire that they had called home. It was looking bedraggled already, and she had only been gone a month. He knew that he didn't have the natural flair or patience for gardening that Janice had possessed. She had been a quietly spiritual person, not overtly religious, and not following any strict religious order, but instead she seemed to have come to her own conclusions about life, the universe and its intricate workings.

Small clay ornaments lay half hidden around the garden. Cernunnos the Green Man, the Celtic god of fertility, hung from one of the trees. Epona, goddess of horses and dogs, stood behind the bird feeder. A strange figurine leaned against the damson tree in the far corner of the garden. Janice had told him that this one was the darkest of all the Celtic deities, the White Lady. Although the colour white was universally seen to be positive and good, this particular deity was associated with death, revenge and annihilation. Sometimes also known as Andrasta, she was reputed to be the goddess that Boudicca had called upon before charging against the Roman army in that last desperate battle to overthrow the foreign oppressors. Dan was never sure just how much Janice had actually believed in these deities and mythology, but he had always liked to hear the legends and stories behind them. If there ever was a deity who represented revenge and annihilation, Dan thought that having her support over the next few days might not be a bad thing. He knew that Janice had sometimes gained solace from her beliefs and wished that he could do the same, but he had never truly shared her faith. He had never subscribed to any religion at all.

Dan felt his anger rising. Anger that both Janice and Bryn had been taken from him in such a violent and pointless fashion, and anger that the person responsible for it was still at home, free to do as he pleased with his violent and pointless life. *Andrew Dean*, he thought, *you are a dead man walking*. Throwing the dregs of his coffee to the ground, he rose and went back into the house, his mood darkening with every step.

Chapter 34

Benton was riding around the Coalpool estate on his Honda motorcycle, looking for any Keepers. He had seen plenty of evidence of their activities in the form of abandoned vehicles. Every street seemed to be littered with discarded cars, motorcycles, scooters or bicycles, easily identifiable as Keepers' property due to the spray-painted 'K' on them, which usually kept them from being re-stolen. Someone might have chanced stealing a tagged bike, if the marking could have easily been covered up, but no one seemed to want to risk touching anything associated with the Keepers right now. Word had spread like wildfire that Deano had taken on an Albanian gang from the other side of town, personally shooting one and leaving two severely beaten and lying in the street for their overlords to find. Most, if not all, reckoned that he had overstepped his mark and that vengeance would surely follow. The last thing anyone wanted was to be caught using one of the tagged vehicles and to be mistaken for a Keeper by a rival gang seeking revenge.

Benton's own bike didn't have any such marking,

thankfully, and the registration number would show up on the police ANPR database as a Home Office registered vehicle, and thus shouldn't attract any undue attention from local police. Not that there would be many police patrol cars around here, Benton thought, as he cruised along Goscote Lane. He turned into Hildicks Crescent and passed yet another burned-out car. Probably another one of the Keepers' abandoned flotsam. He hadn't seen a single recognisable gang member all morning and he was beginning to understand the full implications and difficulties in policing this type of urban gang. They simply melted into the background and were swallowed up by the communities that they terrorised. Many of the families of the members of street gangs had no idea that their relatives were involved.

After riding around the few streets on the Goscote estate, Benton rode the Honda over a broken fence and onto the canal towpath that would take him to Dartmouth Avenue in Coalpool. There, he would leave the canal and try his luck on Bedders Road. If there were any Keepers to be found, surely they would be there?

As he plodded slowly along the canal towpath on his motorbike, he thought about his assignment. It had yielded far more information than he had originally been tasked to find. The main players in the Keepers gang, their drug dealing, their extensive criminal and antisocial activities had astounded his superiors. There had not been the slightest suspicion of the widespread effects of this gang of young men, youths and children. The success of their terror tactics was shocking. Whole communities clammed up when police appeals went out for information regarding crimes in the area. Not even anonymous replies were received. This cycle of fear and subsequent secrecy needed to be broken, and Benton thought that Andrew Dean had inadvertently broken it himself by taking on more than he could possibly handle with the Albanian gangsters. Surely his disorganised band of young villains couldn't take them on? From what he had seen so far today, it looked like the Keepers had made the decision for Deano and had all disappeared. If that was the case, then the inevitable fallout and damage to their street credibility would surely lessen the fear factor of the group. Benton hoped so.

He approached Bedders Road at the furthest end from Deano's house, so he could see the lay of the land before making another sitrep. He had the feeling that he would be extracted in the next few days to go into a different undercover investigation in Birmingham. Pity, as it seemed that things here would probably be getting interesting very soon. As he turned into Bedders Road, Benton was brought sharply out of his thoughts as a black four-by-four almost ran straight over him. It swerved past him, engine screaming, wheels mounting the kerb as it roared away down Holden Crescent. Benton had to take instant evasive action, throwing the Honda motorcycle up onto the kerb and narrowly missing a lamppost.

He came to an abrupt stop and looked back at the car that had almost killed him but it was too far away now to read the number plate. Shaken, Benton slowly pulled away and headed towards Deano's house. As he approached, he saw one of the Keepers, the red-haired young man he knew as Jonah, walking along the pavement, supporting a stumbling young woman that looked really drunk. Benton thought Jonah looked worried and concerned rather than lustful, so he didn't have any immediate concern for the young lady's welfare. Besides, they were heading away from Andrew Dean's house, not towards it, so that could only be a good thing.

As Benton passed the house, he saw no signs of activity and certainly no sign of any other Keepers hanging around. Perplexed, he rode on and decided to head into the police station to make a sitrep in person rather than by phone. Something didn't feel right at all.

# # # #

Peter burst through the bedroom door. Cheryl saved his life. As the bedroom door swung open, it hit her as she lay on the floor and rebounded straight back into Peter, knocking him off-balance and sending him to the floor. The bullet that came from Deano's Baikal pistol would have hit him in the belly if he hadn't stumbled. Instead, the bullet grazed his left buttock, sending a searing pain up his side and down his leg, but doing no serious harm. As he fell, Peter fired haphazardly in the general direction of where he thought the shot had come from. The shot missed Deano completely and went straight through the wall.

The two extremely loud gunshots in such a confined

space had a concussive effect and disorientated Joseph, who had been close behind Peter, for a second. He paused and stared at his brother Peter, who was sprawled on the floor, clutching his leg, blood starting to stain his trousers.

Deano took advantage of the big man's hesitation and shot at him, hitting Joseph in the left arm. The bullet passed straight through the bicep muscle and continued on into Joseph's chest, ripping aside the pectoral muscle before exiting just in front of the sternum. Joseph spun around and hit the floor like a sack of potatoes.

Michael had heard the first gunshot and sprinted towards the stairs. As the second shot sounded he was halfway up the stairs, and as the third gunshot echoed in the hallway Michael drew level with the bedroom door, in time to see his brothers on the floor, one writhing in pain and the other lying in a pool of blood and not moving at all. He stopped just outside the bedroom door.

Peter was waving the pistol around loosely aiming it at the other side of the bedroom and yelling curses. Michael could see that he was squeezing the trigger but no shots were forthcoming. Through the gap in the doorjamb Michael saw a large young man stand up on the other side of the bed raise his right arm. In his hand, Michael saw another Baikal pistol and it was aimed at Peter, who had nowhere to hide. Without thinking, Michael whipped his body sideways through the bedroom door and flung the baseball bat, hoping it would distract his opponent long enough for him to get close enough to him to attack him, hand to hand.

Deano turned his head at the rapid entrance of a third

opponent. As he aimed the 'pit bull', the baseball bat spun through the air and hit him on the side of the head from a distance of about two metres. He heard a sound inside his head that resembled a loud bell, then he sank to his knees, the pistol forgotten in his hand. Michael jumped onto the bed and brought his right foot up in a vicious kick that caught Deano under the chin. Unlike in the movies, there was no getting up from a blow like that and Deano slumped backwards against the wall, already unconscious.

'Quit screaming, yer big girl, and help me with Joseph,' Michael shouted at Peter.

'I've been fuckin' shot!' replied Peter.

'Yeah, but yer screaming, so you'll live. Joseph isn't even moving. Get over here before that lunatic wakes up.'

Peter scrambled up onto his knees and crawled over to his brother who was lying face down on the filthy carpet in a pool of his own blood. Michael grabbed Joseph under the arms and pulled him into a sitting position.

'Grab his legs, Peter. Let's get out of here. He needs a hospital. Come on.'

As Peter struggled up and grabbed his brother's feet, Michael heard footsteps hurrying up the stairs.

'Shit. We've got company.'

Peter dropped Joseph's legs and lifted his pistol.

Jonah appeared at the bedroom door, out of breath and red-faced from running up the road and through the house. He saw the pistol aimed at him and the blood on the floor and raised his arms above his head.

'Shit!' He stopped dead in his tracks. 'Don't shoot. I ain't got a gun. I've only come to get Cheryl. She's my cousin. There.' He pointed his left hand to the sobbing young girl lying in a foetal position, wedged between the bedroom door and the bed. Neither brother had noticed her, and with the gunshots still echoing in their ears, they hadn't heard her.

Michael ignored Jonah and turned back to what he was doing. 'Peter, pick his legs up. Let's go.'

Peter kept a watchful eye on Jonah as they struggled past with Joseph. As soon as they had left the bedroom, Jonah jumped in and shook Cheryl.

'Chez, wake up, it's Richie. Come on, get up.' He shook her roughly and yanked her hair to get her attention.

'Ow,' she whimpered. 'That hurts.'

'Good, it means you're awake. Come on, let's get out of here. Where's Deano?'

'I dunno, he was here.' She shrugged as she tried to stand on shaky legs. She smoothed her skirt back down and looked around the room, seeing Deano lying slumped against the other side of the bed. 'Shit, there he is.' She looked at Jonah and started to tremble. 'Is he dead?'

'Fuck knows,' said Jonah, grabbing her hand. 'Let's just go before anybody else comes.'

They staggered down the stairs, Cheryl barely able to keep her balance while Jonah tried to support her. At the back door, they heard the black four-by-four roar away down Bedders Road. As Jonah and Cheryl reached the front gate, Jonah saw the large black vehicle narrowly miss a motorcyclist as it sped away.

# # # #

'Jesus fuckin Christ, Michael,' Peter muttered as he cradled the unconscious Joseph in his arms across the back seat of the Mitsubishi. 'There's blood everywhere.'

'Try to put pressure on the wound,' Michael advised as he drove the car at speed along Coalpool Lane. They flew past the shuttered-up Coalpool Tavern at about eighty miles per hour, almost treble the speed limit.

'I'm trying, but there's no little bullet hole,' Peter snapped. 'His chest looks like minced steak.'

'Take yer jacket off and bundle it on top of the mess, then press hard. He'll bleed to death in the car if we don't do something,' Michael told his brother.

As Peter yanked off his jacket, Michael sped straight across the junction onto Stafford Street. He was heading towards the Wolverhampton Road and the Accident and Emergency Department.

'What are we going to tell them when we get there?' Peter wondered aloud. 'If we say he's been shot we'll have the police all over us. If they go back to that house they might find a dead Deano. You hit him pretty hard, Michael.'

'I had to,' Michael countered as he swerved around a bus and straight through the traffic lights on the Wolverhampton Road junction. 'He was just about to shoot you again, and I doubt he'd have shot you in your fat arse a second time.' He suddenly hit the brakes and swung left onto Pleck Road. 'Shit, shit.' He swung the Mitsubishi to the side of the road and turned to Peter.

'What are you doing? Why have you fucking stopped?' Peter yelled.

'The gun, you idiot. Do you still have the gun?'

Peter scrambled around in his jacket pockets as he held the blood-soaked coat on Joseph's chest. He fetched the gun out of the side pocket and sheepishly handed it to Michael, who stepped out of the car and calmly walked over to the canal bridge.

Unzipping his coat and looking like he was going to undo his trousers and take a piss, Michael stepped down onto the canal towpath. Once out of sight he dropped the Baikal into the murky water where it would soon be swallowed up in the silty mud that lined the canal bed. Stepping quickly back up onto the street again, he made a show of zipping up his fly, in case anyone was watching. He wouldn't be the first to use underneath the canal bridge as a toilet, and he doubted that anyone would worry unduly about seeing him. As he jumped back into the driver's seat and pulled sharply away into the traffic, Joseph stirred and moaned but didn't open his eyes. Peter looked up and met Michael's eyes in the rear view mirror.

'That's a good sign, isn't it?' he asked hopefully. 'Do you think he's coming round?'

'Better hope not, not just yet,' said Michael. 'That's gonna hurt like billy-o.' The Mitsubishi screeched to a halt in the ambulance parking bay outside the Accident and Emergency doors and Michael jumped out and ran over to the nearest ambulance, where the crew were leaning against the side of the vehicle, each of them sipping a coffee. They saw the blood on the big man's clothing and were instantly on their guard. Michael stopped a few feet away from them.

'Can you help, please?' He pointed back at the black four-by-four. 'It's my brother. There was an accident at the fairground and some machinery exploded. He's really hurt.'

One of the paramedics rushed over to the car to have a look and the other grabbed a stretcher and a kit bag from the back of the waiting ambulance, calling it in on her radio as she worked. They grabbed the motionless Joseph from his brothers and manoeuvred him onto the stretcher. One of them strapped a trauma dressing across Joseph's chest, putting firm pressure on the wound. A paramedic from another waiting ambulance came over to help. They pushed the stretcher through the 'Staff Only' double doors and told the two brothers to go to reception and book their brother in.

As the doors swung shut behind them, Michael turned to Peter and told him, 'It was exploding hydraulics, OK? They won't know any different. Your wound was caused by the same explosion. Like shrapnel. OK?'

Peter nodded. The adrenaline was wearing off now and his buttock hurt like hell, but there was no way he was going to admit that to his brother. The piss-taking wouldn't stop for years. He limped after Michael and made his way into the bedlam of the Accident and Emergency Department waiting room, dripping blood and muttering curses as he went.

Chapter 35

As Dan was making early morning preparations to carry out a final recce prior to going for Deano, he received a phone call from Christine.

'How are you doing?' she asks hesitantly.

'I'm OK. Feeling well, all things considered,' replied Dan. He took a seat near the large patio windows and gazed out at the view of the Wrekin hill. 'How are you and the family?' Dan felt the familiar pang of guilt that he hadn't been in touch, but he had wanted to keep Christine, Malcolm and their daughters out of what was happening.

'We're all well, thanks.' With the pleasantries out of the way, Christine got straight to the point. 'We heard that there was a fight of some sort yesterday in Bedders Road. Guns fired, cars racing up and down the street. Blood splashed on the pavement.'

Dan was listening, his interest piqued.

'I hadn't heard. Do you know any more than that? Was anyone injured?'

Christine paused on the other end of the phone. 'Really?'

'Yes, Chris, I was at home all day yesterday. I had some

blood tests done at the doctors surgery, then stayed home all day.'

'Oh, right.' Christine sounded relieved. 'Well, it seems that Andrew Dean has upset a lot of bad people. Rumour is that he took a load of his gang up to Caldmore and stirred up a nasty fight with some Eastern Europeans. Then the next thing we hear is that guns are fired near his house. No one has seen him since.'

'What about his gang?' Dan asked. 'Haven't they been around?'

'That's the odd thing,' Christine continued. 'It's like they've suddenly just … gone. They've left cars and bikes all over the estate, either burned out or just left standing. Nobody's being bothered by them. Nobody's seen any of them. It's a bit strange, but sort of nice as well.'

Dan sat back in his chair, thinking about what Christine had just told him. How would this affect his plans? If Deano had got himself into strife with some heavy duty people Dan wouldn't shed any tears for him, but he needed to know for sure, otherwise he knew that he'd never find closure.

'Are you still there, Dan? Is everything OK?' Christine asked, sounding worried.

'Yeah, sorry. Just thinking.' Dan tried to sound reassuring. 'Well, with any luck, they'll make him disappear for good, and take his gang out of the picture too.'

Christine paused for a couple of seconds, then continued. 'Dan, will you let things drop now? Hopefully it's all sorted and you can concentrate on getting better. You don't need to get involved any further, do you?'

'Not if he's out of the picture for good,' Dan replied. 'But I need to know for sure, so if you hear anything, just let me know, OK?'

'Alright.' Christine didn't sound convinced, but she didn't see what else she could say to Dan to make him let things be. 'But keep in touch. Call us now and then, and if you have to go into hospital, let us know and we'll come and visit you, OK?'

'OK,' Dan appeased her. 'I will, I promise. I have to go back in a week's time for another round of treatment. I'll see you then.'

'Right.' Christine sounded relieved. 'Oh, and by the way. If you're at Walsall Hospital, check in on Joseph Crosslyn. He's had some sort of accident on the fairground and he's in a bad way apparently.'

Dan frowned. 'An accident? When was this?'

'Yesterday. Something exploded on the fairground site and he got hit by bits of flying metal,' Christine explained. 'Peter was hurt as well but not as bad. My friend is a nurse in A&E and she recognised the Crosslyns as soon as they arrived. She said Joseph looked a right mess at first, but they think he'll be OK.'

Dan considered this news. 'I might go and see how he's doing. It won't hurt to keep things on a good footing with them.'

'Well, be careful. And pop in to see us if you're coming to Walsall. Malcolm and the girls would love to see you.'

'I will,' Dan promised as he ended the phone call. And he meant it, but first, he had to finish this business once and for all. Too many factors and too many other people were involved now. First the Crosslyns – and Dan didn't buy the story about a fairground accident for one moment – and now there were other gangs involved too. Dan knew his limitations, and he had no desire to start a fight with the Eastern Europeans. If Deano hadn't yet been dealt with, he needed to get in there quickly if he wanted to be the man to deal with him.

One small problem nagged at Dan. He didn't know what this Andrew Dean looked like. As he pondered this problem, his mind wandered and he pictured the letter he had found in his dad's garage. He didn't see how it would help ... but of course! Social media. No doubt Andrew Dean would have a profile somewhere. Dan had never even seen a Facebook profile, but how hard could it be? Children did this sort of thing all of the time, right? He went upstairs to retrieve Janice's laptop, switched it on and made himself a cup of tea, ready for the long journey through unfamiliar territory.

Surprisingly, Dan found that creating a social media account was easier than he had thought. Giving all sorts of personal information didn't sit well with him, so most of what he input was fictional or vague, including a stranger's photographs, which he copied from the internet and uploaded to his profile as his own. Within half an hour, he had his own account and had tracked down Andrew Dean's Facebook account. He quickly skimmed through the profile, shaking his head at Deano's narcissistic account of himself. Under the 'occupation' section, Deano had described himself as 'hard bastard'. Various photographs showed him with gang members, hoods or balaclavas covering their faces, in a number of pseudo gangster poses. Lots of young women seemed to want to hang off his arm and be photographed with him, a fact that Dan couldn't understand. He thought about printing off a clear photograph, but decided not to. If he was caught with it on his person, it could be argued that he had gone hunting for Deano. Revenge was the main objective now, but if he could get away without being prosecuted, Dan would at least try to do that. Better to just memorise the face, and trust his judgement when the time came.

After shutting down the laptop, he went into his bedroom and grabbed a holdall from the top of his wardrobe. From inside it, he fetched out a thick dark grey combat jacket, a pair of high-leg army boots, leather gloves and a pair of dark cargo trousers. While he was trying on the clothing to ensure it still fitted, he carefully considered his next move.

Rushing in and getting himself shot would do no good to anyone, and he didn't have the Baikal any more. He knew that the Crosslyns had taken it when they'd found him in a collapsed state the previous week, which he knew was a good choice on their part. The last thing he had needed was for the police to be asking awkward questions about illegal possession of a firearm. After leaving the Army, Dan had vowed never to own or shoot a gun again, and up until this mess, it hadn't been a difficult vow to keep. Although neither he nor Janice had been vegetarians, they didn't hunt despite living in the countryside. So keeping a gun would have just been a pointless expense. He did have some other equipment that might be useful though.

A few years ago, after some high-profile attacks on paramedics, the Ambulance Service had trialled stab-vests. Dan had one, although he had hardly ever worn it. Despite knowing it would be next to useless against a bullet, he quickly tried it on, then took it back off again and shoved it into the holdall with the rest of his clothing. He also had a Kershaw boot-knife from his army days. It was black, lightweight, and fitted snugly into a sheath that could be concealed inside the high-leg combat boots. Dan preferred to wear it on the outside of his boot though; it was more comfortable and easier to grab quickly and he didn't need to use the sheath as the handle had a built in grip-clip that would keep the weapon secure on his boot. He put the knife into the holdall.

So, his strategy was going to have to be a recce followed by a rapid dynamic assessment, evolve a definitive plan of action as the situation developed, and then extraction to a safe location. In other words, poke his nose in, see what he found, hopefully deal with Deano once and for all, and then leg it. Without getting caught. Or shot. Or beaten to a pulp by a vicious foe that was half his age.

Piece of cake.

But first, he would put his usual civilian clothes back on and go and say hello to the Crosslyns.

# # # #

Deano woke up with a splitting headache. His mouth felt parched and as he tried to sit up he felt suddenly nauseous. Grabbing the side of the bed and pulling himself up to a half standing position made the room spin and he retched a couple of times. Closing his eyes made things a little better so he stood still with his eyes squeezed firmly shut until the nausea and the spinning ceased. Sitting carefully on the edge of the mattress, he gingerly touched the side of his head, feeling a gash surrounded by crusted blood and a swelling the size of an egg. Picking up his 'pit bull' from the floor, he vaguely remembered shooting at someone then being hit on the head. After that, nothing. His jaw hurt like hell and he could also feel swelling there, so he guessed that he'd been punched or kicked as he went down. But by who? Surely, he reasoned, if it had been the Albanians, they would have done worse?

Tucking the 'pit bull' into the back of his jeans, he realised he couldn't think straight with his head pounding like this so he staggered to his feet and went downstairs. The dog was barking furiously outside the open back door and the sound was piercing his brain like a red hot poker. Before he fetched himself a drink, he unclipped the dog from its chain and with a sharp kick up the backside that almost had Deano toppling over, he sent the dog on its way to freedom. Or to get run over in the street, he didn't really care which.

The silence that accompanied the dog's departure was soothing to his thumping head and he turned and went back into the house, opening the fridge door as he entered the kitchen. The only things in there to drink were some cans of strong lager and a few energy drinks. Deano opened one of each and cautiously made his way to sit down in the front room. As he slumped on the sofa, sending dust spiralling up into the air, he vaguely recalled having a piece of sweet stuff here with him. Short skirt, nice legs. He couldn't remember her name, or where she had come from, or where she had gone. Frankly he didn't really care all that much. There would always be others. Perhaps his attackers had taken her as payment? That would be fine with him. No problem at all. In fact, it seemed like a good deal. They had had the drop on him and he knew that they could have done a much worse job on him than leaving him with a sore head and jaw.

Sipping his drinks, he considered what to do next. He looked at his mobile phone and was surprised to see that he had been unconscious for almost twenty-four hours. What? No wonder he felt parched. But how come none of his gang had found him? Surely at least one of them had been here in that time? It didn't make sense to him at all. Some coke, he thought. That would make everything seem a lot clearer. Finishing his drinks and tossing the empty cans to the grubby floor, he fished out a small stash of cocaine from behind the DVD player next to the huge (stolen, of course) plasma-screen TV. Spilling a short line of the white powder onto the window sill, he snorted it back and sat down on the floor to let it do its magic.

The subsequent pounding that it created in his head made him regret his decision immediately. As the coke coursed through his system, causing blood vessels to constrict, his heart rate to accelerate and his blood pressure to raise even further, the pulverised blood vessels around his brain pulsated like a bass drum. The sharp jolts of pain that every accelerated heartbeat caused were enough to make Deano curl up into a ball and cry out with pain, his arms and hands wrapped around his head, trying to prevent it from exploding. Less than two minutes later he slipped into blessed unconsciousness again as the dangerously raised blood pressure in his head caused his brain to temporarily shut down.

The house in Bedders Road was silent again, except for the deep resonating snoring coming from the sole occupier. As Andrew Dean lay on the floor, to either recover or suffer a brain haemorrhage, the wheels of fate spun lazily on, unconcerned and unwilling to intervene.

Chapter 36

Inside another house on the opposite side of Walsall, two brothers were making a decision that would cause the wheels of fate to spin just that little bit faster for Andrew Dean.

'We have no choice. We can't put up with this. Two of our men are in hospital. One has brain damage and the other has broken arms and has been shot in the leg, and all of this in public! We must take revenge on these people.' The big man slammed his fist down on the table, making vodka bottles and shot glasses bounce.

'Calm down, Frenk.' Another man put his hands up, palms outwards, to placate the irate speaker. 'Of course we will avenge our brothers. Of course. But there were guns involved, and the British police do not like guns. They are frightened of them and it makes them very curious. We must be careful.'

'Careful!' Frenk snorted. 'We do not need to be careful, Abdyl. We need to be vicious. They are not even fully grown men and they have no respect.' He thumped his hand on his chest. 'I will teach them respect.'

A third man who had been silently observing his two friends spoke up.

'Frenk, you are right, my friend.' The big man smiled at this, glaring at Abdyl. 'But you, Abdyl, as always, are also correct. We must be careful. This is an unusual situation. We do not know why these young men came here, why they have made such a stupid mistake. Have you thought of this, Frenk?'

Frenk shrugged his huge shoulders. 'I do not care why, Zamir. I only know that they have done these things to our brothers.'

Zamir smiled at him. 'You are a loyal man. We are fortunate to have you, but please, sit down and let's talk about this some more before we act. I promise you and our brothers who have been disrespected that you will all have your vengeance.'

Frenk paused, took a deep breath and sat on one of the chairs around the table. It creaked under his weight.

'All right, all right.' He looked across at Abdyl and reached out his right hand. 'I am sorry, Abdyl. I did not mean to offend you. I am angry, that's all.'

Abdyl shook his hand and smiled at Frenk. 'I am not offended by you, I am offended by those mongrels, and I am also angry.' He sat back in his chair and looked at Zamir, who took this cue to take charge of the discussion.

'I happen to know that our cousins in London also have an interest in these people,' Zamir continued. 'They come here, wearing balaclavas and helmets, thinking that we do not know who they are, but they have gang signs on their motorbikes.' He shrugged. 'That seems to show how stupid they are. But,' he said, wagging a finger at his two friends. 'But, we do not know why they came. Are they being used by someone else to lure us into a trap? We do not know. So, I made a couple of phone calls and I know a little bit about them now.'

The other two leaned forwards in their chairs, eager to hear what Zamir had to say.

'The tall one who shot Guzim, he is their pack leader. He is an enemy who fights only the weak. A common drug-taker who likes young girls. So, he is no threat. Our only problem is the location and the numbers.'

'Go on,' said Abdyl.

'He lives in the middle of a shitty estate. They all stick together and they will know as soon as we enter any roads there that we are strangers. They do not like strangers. Also, his gang is numerous. Many of them are nothing more than overgrown children, but they are stupid and they are not afraid to use weapons.'

'This is not a problem,' argued Frenk. 'We have weapons. We have numbers.'

'Yes, we do, my friend,' Zamir said. 'But we would be entering an unfamiliar place. It is like a rats nest and we do not want to get trapped.' He sat back and grinned. 'But we may not have to even go there at all.'

'Why not?' Frenk demanded. 'We must teach them some manners, some respect.'

'They must be taught these things. You are correct, Frenk. But must it be us who take this bait? We live well here. The locals accept us, mostly. We have good businesses here. We are left alone by the police. If we get drawn into this strange battle, how do we know that we are not simply following someone else's plans for us? There are many people and groups in this country who do not like us. It would serve them well if we get caught by police in an open gang war, or even suspected of this. We do not want the police sniffing around here. It is not good for our businesses.'

'So what do we do?' asked Abdyl. ' You said that our cousins have an interest.'

'Yes, they do. Guzim was shot with a Baikal, he is sure of this. Our cousins sold a number of Baikals to a gang here, and they haven't yet been paid for them. And one of our friends in the police tells me that an equally large number of Baikals were confiscated from this gang very recently. The fools kept them all in one place, so one raid happened and they lost everything.'

'How does this help us?' Frenk asked.

'If they have no guns, they have no assets. But they still have a debt to our cousins and I doubt that they have any other means to pay it.' He grinned at the others. 'And you know how angry our cousins can get about money. All we have to do is to let them know that their customer has lost his means to repay his debt. If we add a little spice to the story, maybe say that he is still walking free as he is collaborating with the police, well, they will not want him walking or talking freely.'

'How does that help us though?' Frenk wondered aloud.

Abdyl laughed, understanding Zamir's plan. 'They will

do our work for us, my brother. If he has lost their guns to the police and they think he will give up information in return for his freedom, they will not allow that risk. They will come and find him and deal with him. Brilliant, Zamir. I like it.'

Frenk nodded his agreement. 'As long as someone teaches the runt a lesson, I don't care who it is.'

'I'm sure they will, Frenk.' Zamir reached for his mobile phone. 'I'm sure that this runt may never grow to be a full sized mongrel.'

He made a call to one of his associates, who in turn passed some information on to another, and within twenty minutes an important figure in an East London gang had made a decision that this unpaid debt and potential police informant required 'looking into'. Within an hour, three cars filled with Eastern European gangsters were travelling north on the M1 motorway. Destination: Bedders Road.

Chapter 37

As Dan drove along the M54 motorway towards Walsall, he hoped that this would be the last time he did this journey, at least as far as Andrew Dean was concerned. Travelling to see what was left of his family was one thing, but he was sick to the core of dealing with the Keepers now. He had the feeling that time was running out, whether that was for himself or for Deano he wasn't sure, but Dan knew that the conclusion had to come soon, if not today.

His headache was returning. Since making up his mind to come to Walsall again, and preparing all of his equipment and making his plans, he'd been experiencing a dull throbbing headache. Nothing like the ones that had previously incapacitated him, but worrying all the same. His treatment had shown nothing but positive results so he shrugged it off as nerves or stress, but still …

First destination today was to be the Manor Hospital to see how Joseph was recovering. His new found alliance with the Crosslyn clan was unexpected but Dan believed it to be a genuine truce. As Joseph had said to him when he'd visited Dan in hospital, they were all a lot older and wiser nowadays. Dan grinned ruefully. Wiser? So why was he acting like a vigilante from a bad Steven Seagal movie?

He thought about the Crosslyns. If Joseph had been shot by one of the Keepers, there would be hell to pay. The Crosslyn family were a large, insular and unforgiving community that had a well-earned reputation of not being messed with. Dan had heard plenty of stories from Janice about revenge, family feuds, fairground thieves and troublemakers caught and dealt with. Dan couldn't even guess how the reaction would be to a shooting of two of the clan, but he didn't think there would be much in the way of forgiveness.

As he approached the junction of the M54 and M6 motorway, he considered stopping off to see Christine after the hospital visit, but he knew that she would try to talk him out of what he planned to do next. No, he would make time to see Christine and her family afterwards, if the outcome allowed.

He looked ahead as he joined the M6 motorway and groaned as he saw the traffic grinding to a halt as usual. The next two miles would take him at least twenty minutes, he knew from past experience. Pulling into the inside lane, he settled in to a steady crawl and let his mind wander. He went through different scenarios in his mind, trying to anticipate any possible developments before he arrived in Walsall.

As he exited the M6 at Junction 10, three black Range Rovers cut in front of him at the traffic lights on the roundabout. Dan shrugged it off. Arrogant assholes would always be arrogant assholes, and no amount of horn beeping or hand gestures would change that. Besides, he didn't want to draw attention to himself. No doubt the police would find the contents of his holdall very interesting if he were to be pulled over. He watched as the Range Rovers cut a swathe through the almost gridlocked traffic and had to admire their skills in getting through without actually hitting anyone.

'Someone's on a mission,' he muttered to himself as he sat patiently in the traffic.

# # # #

Jonah had managed to get Cheryl home without any further drama and her mother had been really grateful. Cheryl broke down in tears when she told them both about what had happened, but Jonah knew full well that she had had a very lucky escape. He was seething inside, angry for Cheryl, hating Deano, despising the place he lived in, frustrated at the way that no one could change things.

Jonah had grown up quite close to his aunt Joyce as she had looked after him on many occasions when his mother had been busy with other things. When Cheryl came along, they had been like brother and sister, until, he realised with a sinking heart, he had started to hang around with the Keepers. Was that why Cheryl had done what she did? Was she trying to emulate her older cousin? The realisation that he had been the possible cause of what almost happened to Cheryl made Jonah incredibly angry. He felt ineffective and powerless to help any further, but he knew that whatever had happened with those men had inadvertently given Cheryl a reprieve. But if Deano had set his sights on his young cousin, she wouldn't be safe. He felt suddenly guilty that he had stood by and ignored it when the same had happened to other girls that had fallen into Deano's trap. Some of them were now hooked on drugs, some were emotional wrecks, but none of them had escaped undamaged.

Jumping up off the sofa, Jonah made for the door.

'Where are you going, Richie?' his aunt asked him, concern written all over her face. 'Please don't get involved any more. You brought her home and we're grateful, but don't go getting yourself in any bother now. You know what he's like.'

Jonah knew that she was referring to Deano's violent reputation but he was past caring. The thoughts of what he had seen and ignored had made him angrier than he had ever been in his life. He wanted it to stop: the violence, the fear, the cruelty, the drugs, all of it. He was sick of it.

'I'm just going out. I won't be long, Aunt Joyce. Keep Cheryl in for a few days. The effects will wear off, she won't need anything else. She'll be OK.' He smiled at his concerned aunt, hiding his anger. 'I'll pop in later, see how she is.'

Almost running out of the back door and along the path, Jonah felt a rage building and he knew that if he didn't confront Deano now, he never would, and he would be forever stuck in this depressing rut. He made his way towards Bedders Road, no plan in his mind except to tell Deano to leave his family alone and then to forget all about the Keepers and their mindless existence. There was more to life. Wasn't there?

# # # #

Benton was at the police station, speaking to DS Tunstall about the Keepers' sudden withdrawal.

'They've gone to ground, Sarge. I tried using the Flashpic account to bring some of them to the Tavern, but no one showed up. The only one that had been adamant that he would stand by Andrew Dean was the unfortunate lad that had the accident off the bridge in Mill Lane.'

'Yeah, strange coincidence that,' mused DS Tunstall. 'Still, we've no evidence to the contrary to say that it was anything but an accident. Those two witnesses were quite sure that he was riding like a lunatic only a couple of minutes before, and they didn't see anyone else in the vicinity.'

'But even apart from that,' Benton continued, 'they have all gone to ground. There's an atmosphere on the estates. It's hard to describe, but it's like an expectation, as if something is about to happen and no one wants to be around. I know that doesn't make sense.' He shook his head.

'It's because you've been so immersed in the environment,' Tunstall said. 'You've got much more of an intuition about the place and the people than we have because you've lived there for so long. What's it been? Six months now?'

'Eight months,' Benton said. 'You're right, I can just feel it, like the people that live there, even though most of them have nothing to do with the Keepers.'

'Perhaps now is the time to pull you out then,' Tunstall said. 'We don't want you getting too personally involved or going native on us.' He smiled, knowing full well that Detective Constable Benton was the most motivated officer he had in his command. There was no chance that he would 'go native' at all, and they both knew it.

'It's up to you, Sarge. You know I'll go along with whatever you decide, but I really think we should give it a couple of days. If we can pick Andrew Dean up on any little offence and get him in to the station for questioning, I think it might open the floodgates. I reckon he's in a weak position right now, and he knows it. He might get cocky or make a mistake, and we'll have him. We can tie him to those attacks in Caldmore with CCTV and my statement, and if we can provide a solid case, we may find that other informants or witnesses will appear. Seriously, Sarge, he needs putting away. He's like a rabid dog.'

Detective Sergeant Tunstall weighed up what his officer was telling him. He knew that Benton was right, but he felt responsible for sending him back out into the field when the situation was clearly reaching a critical point.

'Alright. Twenty-four more hours, Benton. That's all. Don't take any chances. If you get something more, then all well and good. If not, we'll bring him in on the assault charges and throw in the firearms charge as well. He had a helmet and balaclava on, the clever bastard, but he's not invincible. Somewhere, he'll have made a mistake. If we can get hold of that Baikal he likes so much, I'm pretty sure that forensics can match it to the bullets we recovered from

Caldmore. Just go in, find Andrew Dean and report straight back.' Tunstall had made his decision. 'We'll bring him in on what we've got already. It'll have to be enough. I don't want a full-scale turf war on those estates. Now get yourself some lunch and see me before you go back out again, OK?'

'Yes, Sarge,' Benton replied. Making his way towards the staff canteen, he smiled to himself. He never thought he'd actually look forward to a meal in the canteen, but compared to the junk he'd been eating for the last few weeks it would feel like a meal from a Gordon Ramsay restaurant!

# # # #

The hospital receptionist directed Dan to where Joseph Crosslyn was being treated. He could see the imposing forms of Peter and Michael Crosslyn standing by the bed and a couple of women sitting down that he vaguely recognised. Feeling slightly intrusive, he almost turned around, but Peter Crosslyn looked up and saw him. Pushing himself away from the wall that he was leaning against, he limped over to Dan. As he got within a couple of feet of him, he stretched out his hand, which Dan shook, glad that the welcome was going to be amicable.

'Danny Boy, glad to see you,' Peter said quietly.

'How is Joseph?' Dan asked.

'He's asleep right now, but he's on the mend. The piece of metal from the machinery that exploded tore across his chest, ripping his chest muscle away, bounced off his breastbone and out the other side.' Peter gestured at Dan to say they could talk more freely outside.

As Dan followed Peter out, he noticed how the big man was deferential and courteous to the hospital staff, making a point saying hello to the cleaners as he passed them on the way out of the main entrance. Peter saw that Dan had noticed.

'Doesn't hurt to be polite, does it? They're working people like us. And they've done a good job of stitching Joseph back together again.' He wiped his hand across his face. 'Me and Michael thought he was a goner, Dan, I'm not ashamed to tell you. He was pale like a ghost. There was so much blood. I'm sure it's easy for you, you've seen it all before, but we haven't.'

Dan nodded. 'It's never easy, Peter. So what happened? Machinery exploding? Really?'

Peter shook his head. 'It's the best we could come up with. We couldn't come in here telling them he'd been shot, could we? The police would've been all over us. Believe me, it's a bit of a nightmare now. We've had to phone back to the grounds and have a couple of the lads rig up a hydraulic ram and over-pressurise it so it shattered. Now the bloody Health and Safety Executive will be running around with clipboards and fluorescent vests checking all the equipment. You know what those bastards are like.'

Dan nodded in agreement. Although the fairground rides were generally safe, the HSE always gave the travelling community a hard time.

'At least we can say it wasn't in a public fair and it was only in testing.' Peter shrugged. 'It won't be so bad, I suppose. The main thing is that Joseph's OK.'

'Yeah,' Dan agreed. 'So what really happened?'

'We went to Deano's house. He was upstairs with some wench – drugged out of her skull, she was. He must've seen us coming. When I went through his bedroom door I tripped over the wench, luckily, and I only got a glancing hit. Joseph caught a full hit to the chest, but then Michael saved the day. Hit the bastard with his own baseball bat, then we legged it. Some ginger-haired kid showed up as we were leaving and got a good look at us, though I don't think he'll be a problem. He said he had only come to get the wench.'

Dan nodded thoughtfully. 'Was he a skinny looking runt of a kid? Busted nose?' Peter nodded. Skinny, ginger-haired lad with a broken nose trying to rescue a girl? It could only be Jonah.

'I've come across him recently. As a matter of fact, he helped me out. I don't think he'll be a problem. You can forget about him.'

Peter grunted non-committally. 'If you say so, Danny. As long as he keeps out of our way, we'll keep out of his. But that bastard Deano.' He slammed a meaty fist into his open palm. 'He's gonna be sorry. A few of the lads are thinking of paying him a visit, and me and Michael will be right there with them.'

'When?' Dan asked, without trying to sound too interested.

'As soon as the Lees cousins arrive from up north. Should be here later on today. We put word out as soon as it happened, and you know how we stick together. If we don't look after ourselves, nobody else will.'

Dan nodded thoughtfully. Did he want to involve the Crosslyns and Lees in this? He knew that he'd always operated best in a small team when he'd been a soldier, but that was when he wore a younger man's clothes. He took a breath and decided that he would still rather take his chances on his own, but some firepower would be useful.

'By the way, I never got the chance to thank you for removing that pistol from my house when you found me collapsed.'

'Oh, that.' Peter shook his head ruefully. 'Wouldn't have done you any good, Danny. I took it with me to see Deano, and I only fired off one shot before the bloody thing jammed. It's in the cut now, out of harm's way.'

Danny was disappointed. He had been hoping to ask for it back. Real life wasn't like the movies and Dan knew that he couldn't just walk into a shady pub somewhere and buy a firearm. He would be more likely to be mugged for his cash or arrested by an undercover Police officer. So he would have to take his chances without a gun. He had his boot-knife, so that would have to suffice.

'OK, Peter. Look, I won't disturb your family now. Joseph's probably still asleep anyway, so there's no point me hanging around. When he wakes up, can you pass on my regards? Tell him I called in to see him.'

The big Crosslyn brother shook Dan's hand again. 'I will, Danny, I will. And thanks for coming, it means a lot to us. We'll have that bastard, don't you worry, old son. Then we'll get together and celebrate with a few beers and a tub of whiskey! Alright?'

'Yeah, of course. Thanks, Peter. It's a shame it's taken something like this for us all to bury the hatchet but I'm glad that we have.'

Peter looked embarrassed. 'Yeah, well. Our Janice always spoke highly of you and we know you looked after her.' He looked away but not before Dan noticed his eyes moistening. 'She was lucky to have you, Danny, and that's no lie.' He reached out and patted Dan's shoulder before limping back to the ward and his waiting family, leaving Dan standing in the car park.

'She wasn't that lucky,' Dan murmured to himself. 'I should've been there, but I wasn't. I can't make that right, but I can make the bastard pay.' He turned on his heel, pushed his hands into his pockets to stop them from shaking in anger, and strode to his car.

Chapter 38

Andrew Dean was not in a happy place at all. He had sent out Flashpic messages, rallying his troops, and not had one reply. Not one! Where were all his Keepers? Stupid bloody name anyway, it was never his idea. One of the louder gang members came up with it, and in a drug-addled mood, Deano agreed with it. After that, it just sort of stuck. That had been two years ago. He reckoned there were about forty or forty-five Keepers out there, so why was no one replying or coming to the house? Of course he didn't yet know about Gray, who would have been his only loyal ally. Lewis was long gone, Deano thought. Well, good riddance to him. He didn't need him and his attitude anyway.

Deano pondered over the immediate problems. First and foremost, he assumed that the Albanians were out to get him after his recent foray into their territory. He hadn't reckoned on being abandoned by his troops though, and that definitely put a different light on the whole situation. With his gang around him, spotting them coming onto the estate would have been child's play. Literally, as his spotters were mostly children. Then he could have utilised his gang to spread the Albanians out, disrupt their plans, harass them from the outside and prevent them making any headway into the estate, let alone get to his house. Now, there would be no stopping them. They could just wander straight in. Those clowns that turned up while he had his little plaything ready and waiting were definitely not Albanians. Gypsies? Irish? Who knows, but they certainly got more than they bargained for and Deano reckoned they wouldn't be in a hurry to come back. He thought he'd shot two of them before one of them hit him in the head and ended that little battle. His head still hurt, but the coke had probably done more damage than the knock, although he would never admit that.

His second problem was, of course, the lack of Baikal pistols, or the means to repay his debt. That was definitely a problem. Unfortunately for Deano, when he had thrown his father out of his own home, the old man had compensated himself by clearing out what was in the hidden safe, including the cash from the Post Office robbery, or what was left of it. Deano himself had squandered a lot of it on drugs that he had intended to sell on at a profit but had either not got round to doing so yet or had taken himself. He desperately needed the means to repay the debt for the guns. How had the filth known where to go for the guns stash? As much as he had enjoyed pulverising and torturing Duncan, the hapless barman, Deano didn't think he had grassed. He had denied it right up until he had sliced his tongue apart. No one would have been able to resist that much of a beating and not give up. So who else knew?

Lewis knew, of course, but he wouldn't have grassed, would he? He had made a sharp exit afterwards and no one had seen or heard of him since, but what would he have gained? He stood to make almost fifty grand from the sale of the guns, and Deano doubted that the filth pay their snitches that well. No, he didn't think Lewis was the snitch, but he did miss having his violent acquaintance nearby, especially at a time like this when he needed foot soldiers around him. Who else knew? Who? He racked his brains. Only he and Lewis had been there for the delivery of the weapons, and they had unloaded the boxes themselves from the back of a beer delivery truck. To be honest, even Duncan hadn't known what was inside the boxes. So no one else knew, except … Wait. Who was that guy that saved Lewis from that nutcase vigilante? Deano hadn't seen him around much, but he had provided a couple of stolen high-end motors for selling on, so he had thought he was safe. Lewis had blurted out about the guns when he and Deano were arguing, and that guy had been in the room. What the fuck was his name?

Deano slammed his fist down on the kitchen work surface. Shenton? No, it was Benton. That was it. It must have been him. There was absolutely no one else that knew. Maybe he was in with that vigilante bloke? It was funny how he managed to sort him out when neither Lewis nor Welchy nor Austen could manage it. He didn't look that handy. Maybe it was all a setup? But why?

Which brought him back around to problem number three. Who the hell was the guy doing the vigilante thing?

Lewis had said he was English, not Eastern European, so why had they gone to Caldmore? Whose dumb idea had that been? Deano shrugged his powerful shoulders. He honestly couldn't remember. Didn't matter now anyway, he thought ruefully. God knows who the vigilante weirdo was, but Deano wasn't too worried about him. It was only one bloke. He'd handle him if he showed up.

He slumped forwards over the kitchen sink. His head still throbbed and he felt a bit dizzy, not quite with it, but he knew what to do to sort that out. Fuck all these problems, fuck the gangsters, whoever they were, fuck the guns and fuck the Keepers. They'd abandoned him, but he didn't need them. When this was over, he'd hunt them down, one by one, screw their sisters and make them watch. Then beat the living shit out of every one of the cowardly wankers.

Bending down, he opened a grubby kitchen cupboard door and reached under the pipework to fetch out a plastic bag full of prescription pills. Not from his prescriptions, of course, but some of them, in the right quantity and the right combinations, produced very entertaining effects. He swallowed a couple of codeine, some diazepam, a couple of paracetamol and some gabapentin. That should help him to sleep off his headache so he could think a little more clearly. As soon as he woke up he would go and find this Benton wanker and ask a few questions, with the help of his faithful 'pit bull' and a good strong dose of Monkey Dust. He patted his trouser pocket where he had stashed the Baikal pistol and went to lie down on the sofa in the front room. A few minutes snoozing would give the drugs time to work, then he'd be ready for a chat with Benton.

# # # #

Meanwhile, most of Deano's problems were already heading in his direction, although chatting was not on any of their agendas.

Chapter 39

Dan left the hospital car park and headed towards the Coalpool estate. After swinging into Mill Lane, he pulled in to the car park at the old dog pound and changed his clothes. After putting on the dark cargo pants and the pair of high-leg army boots, he then put on the stab-vest, a hoodie and combat jacket, and finally his leather gloves. He slipped the Kershaw boot-knife into place on the outside of his left boot. The purpose of placing his weapons on his left side was an old trick taught to him by a combat instructor, many years ago. If he needed to grab a hidden weapon, it was best to reach across the body with his right hand and draw from the left. That way, the weapon was at a ready and balanced position as soon as it was drawn. Dan figured he would need every trick in the book in the coming fight.

That there would be a fight, he had no doubt. Leaving Walsall today without a final showdown with Andrew Dean was not an option. Dan needed this closure while he still had the physical strength and the anger to carry it out. It may still not be enough, he was aware of that. Age was no longer on his side, and it had been a long time since he had entered into physical conflict of any note. Grapples with drunks in the back of an ambulance were hardly in the same league as a head-to-head fight with a vicious, drug-crazed gang leader who was probably at least twenty years his junior. Dan hoped that his cool head and previous experience would balance things out. If not, well, he didn't see what choice he had.

After changing his clothes, securing his weapons and stashing his civvy clothes under the back seat, Dan drove a short way to Borneo Street in the Butts estate. This had always been a less volatile part of Walsall and Dan reckoned he could safely leave his Land Rover here for a few hours before it attracted the wrong sort of attention. It was a ten-minute walk or a short jog across Mill Lane to Coalpool estate and Bedders Road, which Dan used to warm himself up, mentally and physically. As soon as he crossed Coalpool Lane and onto the estate, he slowed his jog down to a walk, not wanting to draw attention to himself. His dark and grey clothing didn't appear too out of place, especially as it was starting to settle into evening.

Although Dan had kept his personal fitness up to quite a high standard, his recent illness had taken its toll and he felt a little out of breath as he walked along Bedders Road. He slowed his walk down further to catch his breath. As he approached Deano's house, he saw a large young man exit the front gate and look up and down the street. Dan leaned against the nearest lamppost, swaying and singing tunelessly as the young man stared at him. Seemingly satisfied that an old drunk was of no interest to him, the young man turned and strode purposefully along the road in the opposite direction to Dan. He sniffed loudly a couple of times, then spat forcefully at a passing car as he strutted down the road.

Dan watched him go. If that wasn't Andrew Dean, it was someone who looked a lot like him and obviously felt in charge of the area. Not wanting to place his bet on the wrong horse, Dan quickly slipped into the garden of number 20 Bedders Road and ran around the back of the house. Finding the back door swinging open, Dan stepped briskly through the building, clearing each room silently and efficiently as he had been taught all those years ago at the Army urban combat training house in Warminster. Satisfied that there was no one at home, he exited the way he had come in and took a deep breath. Confirming that the young man who had left the house a couple of minutes ago was his adversary, Dan hurried after him, not wanting to lose sight of his quarry now that he was so close.

# # # #

Deano had woken up feeling a little refreshed but drowsy. A good dose of Monkey Dust had sorted that out and now he felt up for anything. Right then. Next job was to find Benton and deal with the fucking grass.

Deano thought that he lived somewhere along Dartmouth Avenue, but he wasn't positive. Never mind, he'd soon be able to find him. He sent out a Flashpic message telling Benton to meet him by the canal bridge just off

Dartmouth Avenue. If he was around, he'd get the message. If he was the snitch, Deano would soon get the truth out of the bastard. If not, well, no great loss.

He stretched his legs along the length of darkening Dartmouth Avenue. He felt invincible, his heart racing. He could feel every beat of it and it felt strong and powerful. Flexing his muscles as he walked, he envisioned himself as he thought others would see him – hard, dominant, mighty. Untouchable. This was his territory and he'd be damned if any fucking Albanian or Russian or whatever they were, was going to cause him any bother. He'd rip their heads off. No matter how many of them. The Monkey Dust was coursing through his veins, well and truly taking effect now. He shadow-boxed along the pavement, thinking to himself that he moved faster than Tyson Fury. Let this little bastard snitch try to take him on tonight. He was going to pummel the truth out of him.

As he moved along the street, lost in his own diminishing field of reality, he was watched by a few unseen pairs of eyes.

Dan watched the spectacle from the shadow of an empty house. Wondering what was wrong with him, but guessing it was drugs that caused the impromptu solo boxing show, Dan was prepared to wait until Deano moved out of public view. He knew that a lot of street drugs, especially the synthetic ones, would create the self-image of invincibility, but the truth was quite often the opposite. Although they gave spurts of incredible strength, sometimes in almost super-human quality, the amount of energy that it depleted from the body, and the immense strain that it put on the cardiovascular system, especially the heart, would be the undoing of his opponent. All Dan had to do was keep Deano raging and keep out of his grasp for about five minutes and Deano would probably collapse. Keeping out of the way of punches and kicks would be fairly simple as the drugs invariably caused poor co-ordination. Dan hoped that he would be able to outmanoeuvre his adversary long enough to take him down.

# # # #

Unaware of Deano's departure, Jonah was banging on the back door and shouting his name. Dan had pulled the back door shut and wrenched the door handle till it broke, hoping to stop his opponent returning easily to his lair, and it was now locked firmly. After he had been shouting for a couple of minutes, the next-door neighbour furtively popped his head up over the broken fence that divided the two back yards.

'He ain't here. Went out, five minutes ago. Up towards Dartmouth.'

Jonah looked after the retreating figure of the neighbour. His anger was starting to dissipate and his resolve was weakening the further he got from his own home. Was he wise to take Deano on? Jonah knew that he was a lunatic, and a violent one at that. Well, perhaps he'd just try to find him, follow him for a bit, see if there was a chance for a sneak attack. He jogged along Bedders Road towards Dartmouth Avenue.

As he rounded the corner at the junction of the two streets, he could see a figure up ahead in the gloom, dancing or something. Stopping under a streetlamp, Jonah watched the figure for a minute. Deano! What the hell was he doing? Must be stoned again, Jonah figured. Well, that might work in his favour. He slowly crept along the road, stopping a couple of hundred yards from the crazy sight of a shirtless Andrew Dean boxing with no one, yelling and cursing, in the middle of an empty street. He waited.

# # # #

Benton had been hiding in the shadow of a disused garage of an empty house a little way along from Andrew Dean's home in Bedders Road. First he had seen a shady looking character walk past him, his face partially hidden by a hoodie but wearing good quality combat fatigues and real high-leg combat boots, not internet copies. The man walked slowly but purposefully, then suddenly stopped and acted drunk. What? Then Benton saw Deano come out of his house and stare at the man and understood what was happening.

This man, whoever he was, didn't want Deano to take any notice of him. But why? Was this the vigilante who had been taking on the Keepers? Benton had come across him a few weeks ago when he had rescued Lewis. He couldn't make out his facial features now, but he thought the build was similar, although with the bulky jacket this guy was wearing, Benton couldn't be certain.

As soon as Deano continued walking and the man ceased to act drunk and disappeared into Deano's house, Benton knew for certain. It had to be. After waiting a couple of minutes more, he saw the man come back out of the house and head after Deano.

As Benton was about to step out of the shadows to follow them both, his phone buzzed. Opening it up, he saw that Deano had sent him a Flashpic message asking to meet him at the canal bridge on Dartmouth Avenue. He didn't care for the 'Or else' at the end of the message. Subtlety was obviously not one of Andrew Dean's strengths.

As Benton weighed up these new developments, he saw another one of the Keepers, Jonah, also go to Deano's house. After a minute and a quick conversation with a neighbour, Jonah emerged and followed the vigilante and Deano. Benton hung back in the shadows, trying to work out what was going on. Why would Deano have ordered Benton to meet him, away from the house? And were the other two involved? Had they received similar messages? It seemed unlikely that the vigilante had, but perhaps he had hacked the Flashpic account? And Jonah was just one of the minions, but not one that Benton would have thought of any significance to Deano. As far as Benton recalled, he had only ever seen this Jonah on the receiving end of violence, never being an initiator of it. So what was going on?

As he ruminated on the events and decided what to do, three black Range Rovers crawled along Bedders Road. As they passed his hiding place, Benton saw that they each contained four large men. He didn't need to be an undercover police officer to know that these were definitely bad guys. They slowed down as they approached an old man walking along the road and Benton could hear the unmistakeable Eastern European accents as they asked where Andrew Dean lived. The old man shrugged, put his head down and walked away as briskly as his legs would carry him. This was getting bizarre now, like the plot of a bad movie. Benton made a decision. He would grab a quick look at these guys, go to the meeting with Deano, but call for backup on the way. Then he was done, out of here. He had a feeling that his cover was blown.

He stepped out from the garage and sauntered down the road towards the Range Rovers. Putting his head down and his hands in his hoodie pockets, he saw that the brake lights flashed on the nearest car. As he drew level with it, a rear window whirred down and a rough voice, with a heavy accent, asked him for information.

'Hey. You. We are looking for a friend. You know where he lives?'

Benton played the part, sniffing, looking jittery and glancing over his shoulders as he warily approached the car. 'What friend?'

'Andrew Dean. Where does he live?'

'If he's your friend, how come you don't know?' Benton asked. Giving information too freely would look plain dodgy, so he stretched it out.

The man in the car turned to one of his companions, muttering something in a guttural language, then turned back to Benton.

'He is business friend. We need to speak to him.'

Benton looked up and down the street, then back to the car. 'I ain't a public information fuckin office. If it's business, what do I get for helping you?'

The man threw a twenty pound note to the floor and Benton snatched it up and put it in his pocket.

'Number twenty. Other side of the road,' he mumbled, then pulled his hood further over his eyes and hurried off. After a hundred yards or so, he ducked into a gateway and looked back. He could see the cars stop outside Deano's house and about eight or nine men got out, opened the boots of the three cars and pulled out short stubby guns that looked like Uzis, or cheap copies. Cheap copies or not, Benton knew he had to report this. Ducking back out of sight, he fished out his mobile phone. He didn't have time to get to a neutral phone box but this sitrep had to go immediately. He dialled 999 and asked for the police. After getting the usual greeting from someone in the general public emergency call centre, Benton gave his ID details and asked to be put through to DS Tunstall as an emergency.

'I'm sorry, sir,' came the call-taker's reply. 'I just have to verify your ID with one of my supervisors.'

'What?' Benton was incredulous. 'No, wait—' He heard the unmistakeable sound of being put on hold. The Casio concerto coming over his phone speaker meant that no one was listening to him. After a long minute, a voice came on the line.

'Sir, Detective Sergeant Tunstall is in a meeting. Can I take a message please?'

Benton looked up to the heavens in frustration.

'Yes. There is an emergency. I can't go through usual undercover procedures, there isn't time. There are at least ten armed men in Bedders Road, Walsall. They are about to enter 20 Bedders Road. I have positively identified at least eight firearms. I need immediate backup and an ARU.'

'Sorry, sir, a what?'

'For fuck's sake!' Benton exclaimed. 'Are you new or just stupid? An ARU, an armed response unit!'

'I'm sorry, sir, but I must ask you to calm down. Stop swearing at me and let me help. If you think there is an emergency, I need to take some details.'

'Are you serious?' Benton was incredulous. 'I'm an undercover police officer, reporting a firearms incident in progress, and you're asking me to stop fucking swearing?'

'Sir, I won't ask you again. If you continue to use abusive language I will terminate the call,' came the reply.

'Look. I've given you the address, the details and my ID. Please make sure that you pass this on to someone who knows how to do their job, OK?'

'I know how to do my job, sir. I'm just asking you to be calm.'

Benton heard more cars in the road and as he looked out of the gateway he was hiding in, he saw another four cars screech to a halt and a bunch of swarthy, rough looking men get out and head towards number twenty. He spoke into the phone again.

'Listen to me. I am calm. I am an undercover police officer. I am reporting a firearms incident in progress. There are now at least twenty men in Bedders Road, converging on number twenty. No shots fired as yet but I have seen firearms. Do you have all that?'

'Twenty men? You just said there were ten men, sir.'

'Well, more have arrived while you have been fucking me about!' hissed Benton down the phone. He was met with a dial tone. The call-handler had terminated his call.

'I do not fucking believe this.' Benton decided that if the men found that Deano wasn't home there would be no need for shots to be fired just yet, so he would get out of the firing zone and try again for backup. Hopefully he wouldn't get the same moron on the phone. He dashed out of the gateway and sprinted off down the road.

Chapter 40

The Crosslyn brothers waited in the car park and met the Lees cousins.

'I haven't seen you in fuckin' years and now you tell me some bastard has shot Joseph? What's happening?' Martin Lee asked Michael Crosslyn.

Michael clapped his arms on Martin's broad shoulders. 'Peter got his arse clipped with a bullet, too, but he's OK.' He gestured up to the main hospital building. 'Joseph caught a nasty hit though. He's sedated for now.'

Martin Lee looked deadly serious. 'Well, let's go and sort this bastard out. Jump in the car with me. Peter can go with Damien in the second car. There's ten of us, so we'll deal with this wanker right now. You can fill me in on the details while we drive.'

The Crosslyns and Lees got back in the four cars and headed away from the hospital, towards Coalpool and Deano. As they drove, Michael Crosslyn told them all he knew about Deano. Peter did the same in one of the other cars.

As they swung into Bedders Road, they saw the three

Range Rovers parked outside Deano's house.

'I thought you said they were low-end scumbags?' Martin Lee asked, gesturing towards the expensive cars.

'They are low-end. Just thieves and druggies mostly. They steal a lot of cars though. At least we know there are a few of them home,' Michael said. 'What do you reckon? Go in now, or wait until there's less of them?'

Martin Lee pondered on the plan, while the four cars idled at the end of Bedders Road. 'No, fuck it.' He shrugged his huge shoulders. 'We came up here for a fight, and a fight is what we'll fucking have.' He tapped on the shoulder of the driver. 'Go and let Jimmy and the others know. We're going in, fists flying. Try and get this Deano character out alone if we can. If not, just crack some heads.'

The driver nodded and walked over to the other waiting cars, relaying the brief orders to the others.

# # # #

The gangsters had kicked the front door, but couldn't get it open. The steel reinforcing plates had done their job. Instead of wasting more time, one of them merely smashed a window and climbed in, letting the others in through the obstinate door. They quickly went through the house and ascertained that no one was home. They re-grouped in the lounge, looking around at the peeling wallpaper, the filthy and frayed carpets and the sagging sofa.

'Why do they live like this?' one of them wondered aloud. 'They are like peasants back home.'

The leader, a large man in his thirties replied, 'Yes. Peasants. But peasants back home know their place. These peasants need to be taught.' He gestured towards the door. 'They're not here. Let's find them. The English do not know how to keep secrets and be loyal. We will pay for the information and find this little peasant.'

As they streamed back out of the house, they noticed a large group of men getting out of four cars at the front of the house. The waiting Albanian drivers had got out of the Range Rovers to confront the newcomers, but found themselves outnumbered and were glad to see the rest of their group coming back out of the house.

'Fucking hell, Michael, these are big lads,' Martin Lee said as they took in the size of the group of heavies coming towards them.

'Deano isn't with them,' Michael said. 'Perhaps he's still inside?'

'Well,' Martin Lee said, cracking his knuckles and rolling his shoulders. 'Let's go and get him then.' He grinned wolfishly at his cousin and let out a loud bellow as he rushed at the nearest gangster. The other Lees and Crosslyns followed suit, charging at the surprised Albanians.

A fight broke out in the middle of Bedders Road. Neighbours peered through lace curtains as the large group of fierce men grappled with each other, landing huge punches and kicks, splitting lips, losing teeth and sending each other sprawling senseless in the road. Knives and coshes were pulled from both sides and vicious injuries quickly followed before one of the Albanians decided to put an end to the brawl and fired two shots at the travellers. One hit Martin Lee in the shoulder, sending him flying backwards over a car bonnet, and the second shot hit Peter Crosslyn in the thigh, dropping him like a stone.

Immediately the two groups of men stopped what they were doing and stepped back from each other, warily sizing up their options. The bigger Albanians were not as effective fighters as the travellers, but they had firearms. Only one of the travellers had a firearm, and it was an old sawn-off double-barrelled Winchester shotgun. Two shells, no magazine, and likely to get the traveller cut in half by opposing automatic gunfire from the gangsters before he had time to get both shells fired off.

As the stand-off stretched out for a few seconds, a shout was heard from behind them. In their preoccupation with their immediate enemies, neither group had noticed a group of police vehicles pull up a short distance from them, either end of Bedders Road, effectively blocking their exits.

'Armed police. Stand still,' came the shout, through a loudhailer. 'Drop your weapons and raise your hands. Stand still!'

The travellers had the sense to immediately raise their hands. The one with the shotgun dropped it to the floor as they edged away from their opponents.

The Eastern European gangsters' leader, a huge man with a fearsome reputation, sporting a swollen eye and a spilt lip, turned and looked at the police. He saw one of his opponents grin at him.

'You're fucked, mate,' said Martin Lee.

Martin Lee had been the one to split the big man's lip and black his eye, and now he was laughing at him. In front of his men! 'Bastard!' hissed the Albanian as he dragged his heavy leather coat to one side to draw his pistol. He didn't get the pistol out of the holster before one of the police bullets hit him full in the chest.

His men, split in their decision-making abilities, floundered without a leader. Some of them turned towards the police and raised their weapons, immediately being hit by bullets. The others dropped their weapons and tried to run but were taken down by police dogs and their handlers waiting on the peripheries.

The travellers stood still, hands on their heads. A couple of them had the forethought to drop to the floor to avoid stray bullets. As the police officers closed in to arrest or detain the fighting groups of men, picking on the most dangerous targets first, a couple of the travellers managed to slip away behind neighbours' gates, quickly making their way to back yards and alleyways.

Ambulance crews on standby were making their way into the fray to try to patch up the injured, and chaos quickly ensued. Neighbours from houses in the street came out to watch proceedings, despite police warnings to stay inside. Most of them were hoping that Andrew Dean had been killed as he was a constant thorn in their sides. Some local kids thought it would be fun to throw stones and bottles at the armed police from behind fences and hedges, and in the space of just a few minutes, the police ARU sergeant in one of the Response Unit vehicles was ordering a tactical withdrawal before it turned into a riot. Bystanders were now jeering and shouting abuse at the police and he didn't want any of his men to retaliate. It was always a possibility when adrenaline was surging and men were under pressure, even with highly trained police officers.

Paramedics had managed to quickly load up the injured and were trying to make their way out of the road in the ambulances, sirens blaring, blue lights flashing as the emergency vehicles were allowed through the police cordon. Police officers had eight armed criminals in custody and four in the ambulances on the way to hospital. That would have to do for now, the sergeant decided, as his men and dogs made their tactical withdrawal. His officers had done a good job, he thought, stopping the armed threat without civilian injury. They would still have to go through a full investigation though, and that would mean at least four of his team would be out of operational duties until all of their actions had been deemed necessary and within the law by shiny-arsed officers who never saw the sharp end of police work. He sighed, not looking forward to the mountains of paperwork that this incident would generate.

# # # #

Not too far away, the brief exchange of shots was heard across the estate by Jonah, Dan, Benton and Deano, although it barely registered in Deano's drug-addled brain.

Jonah heard it, had no idea what was going on but was just glad he was nowhere near the sounds that he knew were gunshots.

Benton heard the unmistakeable sounds of gunshots, quickly followed by the unmistakeable sound of controlled MP5 return of fire, some vague shouting, then nothing. At least, he thought, his second phone call for backup had been effective. When he got back to the station he intended to find out who had taken his first call and have a quiet word with them. For now, he had other more pressing matters to deal with. Jonah was just ahead of him but he was jittery and kept looking round, so Benton had to keep a good distance between them. Of the vigilante's whereabouts, Benton had no idea, which worried him slightly. He didn't want to get on the wrong end of any rough justice before he had a chance to identify himself.

Deano was pacing up and down the canal towpath, underneath Dartmouth Avenue bridge. A few of the local kids had seen him and wisely scarpered before he gave them a smack in the mouth. His reputation was spread across all of the local estates. Kids were generally disrespectful of their elders, but not of Deano. They knew that whereas most adults were bound by the law to some degree and could be verbally abused and backchatted, this particular adult would reinforce his alpha male seniority with undisguised and unrestrained violence, especially when he was high, which he obviously was now.

As Deano paced, he ground his teeth, muttering to himself about being betrayed by one of his own. He held his 'pit bull' in his hand and waved it at imaginary opponents. Imagining all sorts of gangster scenarios, in which he invariably came out on top, he let the Monkey Dust take its full effect on his brain, feeling pumped up and ready for action. Looking along the canal towpath, he thought he saw a familiar face, and he shouted incoherently at the young man, who instinctively turned and ran away, dodging down the alleyway to Dartmouth Avenue.

# # # #

Jonah had lost sight of Deano and was walking warily along the canal-side towpath, which was growing darker as evening wore on. Suddenly from under the shadows of the bridge, Deano loomed, larger than life and waving a gun around. Jonah didn't hesitate but turned on his heel and ran full pelt, sliding on the loose gravel, into the alleyway, where he ran headlong into someone, sending them both to the floor. He stood up and dusted himself off.

'Shit, Jonah, what are you doing, running around like a fucking lunatic?'

Jonah recognised the guy as one of the Keepers. 'Yeah, sorry.' Jonah reached out and helped the man up. 'You all right?'

'What's the matter with you? You look like your arse is on fire.'

'Shit, it's Deano,' Jonah said. 'He's under the canal bridge, raving on drugs, and he's got a gun with him. He looks well wired up. I wouldn't go up there.'

Benton edged towards the end of the alleyway and cautiously peered round the corner. 'Where? I can't see him.'

'He's under the bridge, in the shadows. It's getting dark. I didn't see him until I nearly walked into him, for fuck's sake.' Jonah looked shook up and unnerved.

'OK mate, calm down. You sure he's carrying?' Benton asked.

'Definitely,' replied Jonah. 'He was waving his "pit bull" around like a madman.'

Benton thought for a moment. 'Have you seen anyone else with him? An older guy in dark clothes?'

'No, why?' Jonah asked.

'Nothing.' Benton replied, wondering where the supposed vigilante had gone. Perhaps he'd been mistaken? He'd been sure that the guy in the dark combats had been following Deano.

# # # #

Dan had heard the gunshots and the loudhailer voice in the distance, then nothing. Whatever was going on back there was nothing to do with him, he thought. Keeping his eye on the prize ahead, he picked up his pace as Deano turned into the alleyway that led to the canal. As he hurried to make up some distance, a part of his operational brain that he hadn't used for many years admonished him. *Rushing into contact without watching your back? Are you getting old? Or just over-eager?* Kicking himself, Dan glanced back over his shoulder as he turned into the alleyway, and sure enough, there was a young man about two hundred yards behind him, familiar, but too far away to recognise.

One of the Keepers?

Dan bolted along the alleyway, listening to Andrew Dean up ahead as he shouted and raged at no one in particular. He wanted to catch up with him before the effects of whatever drug he'd taken wore off. But he didn't want to get caught between two Keepers. Cursing his lack of vigilance, Dan thought of his options. Next to the alleyway was an infant school, with a playground that ran parallel to the canal. It was bordered by a dense hedgerow, and Dan knew that it would have a very secure fence, even in this area. Squeezing into the hedgerow, he peered through the mesh fence. The building adjacent to the playground was boarded up and looked disused. Local education cuts, probably, Dan thought. Bad luck for the local children but good luck for him. The fence surrounding the playground obviously hadn't been kept in good repair since the school had closed and he quickly found a gap where he could squeeze through.

Running along the edge of the playground, parallel to the canal towpath, he soon passed the bridge where Deano was waiting. When he reached the other end of the playground, Dan saw that it opened out onto the main Harden Road, so he scrambled over the broken fence and stepped out. After hurrying across the road, he ran down the steps leading to the canal towpath on the other side of the bridge to where he had last seen Andrew Dean. Leaning against the wall of the bridge, he peeked around the corner and waited for his adversary to catch up. While he waited, he steadied his breathing. *Not long now, matey*, he thought. *Not long, and you'll pay for what you did.*

He needed a plan. It was clear Deano was waiting for someone, and Dan had already seen another young man approaching. Whether he was one of the Keepers or not, Dan didn't really want any witnesses stumbling across the confrontation. Stepping away from the towpath again, he risked a glance over the bridge and along the canal where he'd seen the other young man. There was no one there. It was strange, and Dan didn't think that whoever had been there would follow the same route he had, not if he was meeting Deano. They would have simply walked along the towpath. After a second check, he reassured himself that no one was there.

Shrugging, he stepped back down to the canal, just as Andrew Dean launched himself around the corner of the canal bridge with a roar, fists clenched, huge muscles pumped up around his arms and shoulders, coming straight at him.

Steven Jenkins

Chapter 41

Benton looked around the corner towards the canal bridge, but he couldn't see Deano, or even hear him shouting any more. 'Shit.' He leaned back against the wall of the alleyway.

'What?' asked Jonah. 'What's up?'

Benton knew that his cover was about to be blown. There was no way he could risk leaving a drugged-up Andrew Dean rampaging around in a public place with a loaded firearm. If any innocent civilian happened to bump into him from the other direction, Benton knew there would be injuries. Of that, there was no doubt in his mind. But he couldn't rush him because Deano had the upper hand. He was hidden in shadow, he could see the towpath for a hundred metres in each direction, and besides, Benton was unarmed. It would be suicide. Reaching into the inside pocket of his hoodie, Benton fetched out his mobile phone.

'What are you doing? Who are you calling?' asked Jonah.

Benton looked at his phone screen. 'Shit. No one, by the looks of it. No bloody signal.'

'It's the canal.' Jonah shrugged. 'I reckon the water does

funny things to mobile phones. I can never get any signal here either.'

'Do you have any weapons on you?' Benton demanded, stepping towards Jonah.

'Weapons? Me?' Jonah shook his head. 'Nah mate, it's not my thing. I'm just your everyday common thief. I'm no good at violence.'

Weighing up his options, Benton realised that he was quickly running out of time. There was a psychopath with a gun, about a hundred metres away, in a public place, and unless he did something right now, someone was going to get hurt.

'Right.' He turned to Jonah. 'You want to stop him, right? You don't want anyone else to get hurt, do you?'

'No,' Jonah replied. 'If you must know, I came up here to have it out with him, cos he nearly raped my cousin. Only …' Jonah looked down at his feet. 'Only, now I've calmed down a bit, I'm crapping meself. He'll rip me apart.' As he looked up at Benton, he felt tears forming in his eyes. 'It's hopeless. I'm fuckin' hopeless. No one can stop him. He does what he wants, he always has, the fuckin' nutcase.'

Benton made his decision. He had to trust someone, and this young man was the best option he had right now.

'Listen, Jonah.' Benton put both of his hands on the younger man's shoulders and looked him straight in the eyes. 'I'm a police officer.'

Jonah's eyes widened in shock. 'What? But you're a Keeper?'

'No.' Benton shook his head. 'I'm not. I was undercover,

trying to find the stash of guns that Deano had. Now we've got them, but he's got the last one, and I'm really worried he's going to hurt someone. I can't get a signal, and I can't leave. I've got to keep eyes on Deano. I need you to go and make a call for me. Will you do that? I promise you, I'll do everything I can to get Deano off the streets.'

'I dunno,' Jonah mumbled. 'Undercover police? Fuckin' 'ell.'

'Jonah.' Benton shook his shoulders. 'Listen to me. We have to stop him, right now. We have no weapons and I think he's already on to me. That's why he sent me a Flashpic message and told me to meet him here. I need backup, but I can't risk letting him out of my sight. I'm going to walk slowly up there, as if I don't know he's hiding under the bridge. That'll buy you some time. Here.' He passed Jonah his phone. 'Just call 999, tell them that UC-27, on operation Finders, needs armed backup, and give them the location. Then just drop the phone down a drain and run, OK? You don't need to get any more involved than that, I promise.'

Jonah nodded and looked at the ground. He took the offered phone and repeated what Benton had just told him. 'UC-27. Operation Finders. Like Finders Keepers?'

'Yeah.' Benton grinned. 'Lame, huh? Go on then, Jonah. Thanks.' Watching the young man sprint away down the alleyway, Benton prayed that he'd done the right thing in trusting him. If he just tossed the phone in a bin before making the call, there would be no backup, no reprieve. Even worse, he could betray him to the other Keepers, but Benton was fairly certain that wouldn't happen. For one thing, he hadn't seen sight nor sound of any of the gang all day, except Jonah.

Taking a deep breath, and crossing his fingers inside his hoodie pockets, Benton stepped out of the alleyway, onto the canal towpath and ambled lazily towards the canal bridge, to face whatever fate had waiting in store for him.

# # # #

Andrew Dean had other things on his mind at that precise moment. He had realised that someone had slipped past him and onto the canal on the other side of the bridge after he saw them run along the old playground in the closed school. Being high hadn't made him completely lose his senses, and he was hard-wired for street survival. Seeing someone run past him like that had woken him up and sharpened his senses, and as he crept under the canal bridge to see who had tried to sneak past and where they would go, he saw the man in dark combats – who didn't look so drunk any more – clamber up onto the bridge to look along the other side of the towpath. That told Deano all he needed to know. He could tell when he was being stalked.

As the man climbed back down and tried to slip under the canal bridge unnoticed, Deano pounced. The yell that Deano let out was to unnerve and disorientate his opponent, and it worked momentarily as Dan recoiled back in surprise, slipping on the loose shale of the towpath. Deano followed through with a vicious downward punch to his opponent's head, but luckily for Dan, his slip meant that he wasn't quite where Deano had anticipated him to be and the blow glanced off the side of Dan's head. It was still hard enough to send his senses reeling for a few seconds though. Deano was twenty-five years old, high on drugs and naturally strong anyway. Dan felt all of Deano's fifteen stone of muscle transfer through the punch and into his skull. Dazed, but still in control of his faculties, he rolled with the punch as best he could and scrambled backwards away from Deano, trying to buy himself some time to recover. Deano pounced on him, grabbing Dan's jacket by the lapels and smashing his forehead into Dan's face.

The sound of his nose breaking preceded a lightning bolt of pain that made Dan almost lose consciousness. Putting his arms up in front of his face, he managed to deflect the next headbutt coming his way. For a precious few seconds, Dan managed to block every punch and headbutt with his arms as he tucked his head into his body. Suddenly the blows stopped and Dan heard the unmistakeable click of a gun being cocked, the metal parts sliding together to create that very unique and terrifying sound.

Dan knew that his opponent had potentially made a serious mistake. He'd had the upper hand and he was winning the fight. Dan was double his age and about three stone lighter and nowhere near as physically strong, especially lately. Unless he shot him, which he accepted could happen, Deano was unwittingly giving Dan time to recover.

'Get the fuck up, old man.' Deano pointed the pistol at Dan, sideways, like he'd seen gangsters in the movies hold

371

theirs.

Again, Dan saw another mistake. Holding a pistol like that made it extremely inaccurate. Military marksmen use a similar technique called Flash Sight Picture, but Dan knew from experience with a 9 mm Browning, and hours on a firing range, that it was a difficult technique to master. As well as making it inaccurate, it also made the pistol easier to snatch from an opponent.

'What's up?' Dan said, through a mouthful of blood. 'Can't you take me without that? I thought you were supposed to be a hard man, Deano?'

Deano was jittery as he stood facing Dan on the towpath in the slowly disappearing daylight. He cocked his head to one side slightly.

'How do you know my name, old man?' He stepped closer to Dan and shoved the pistol forwards at him. 'Who da fuck are y—'

As he stepped within range, Dan took his chance. He knew there might not be a second opportunity, so as Deano thrust the pistol forwards, Dan turned his body sideways, away from the line of fire, simultaneously bringing his right hand upwards in an uppercut, as fast and hard as he possibly could. As his hand made contact with Deano's thickly muscled right forearm, he brought his left hand up to grab the pistol muzzle and snapped it viciously downwards against Deano's thumb, using the weakest part of the hand to loosen its grip and allow Dan to snatch the gun away.

As Deano reflexively tried to maintain his grip on the pistol, his thumb was forced through an unnatural angle and they both heard the sharp crack as the bone snapped. Deano let out a howl of pain, disbelief and rage as the Baikal pistol dropped to the floor, bounced once and then discharged a round from the muzzle.

In the tight confines underneath the low canal bridge, the report from the shot was almost deafening. Neither of them had time to dive out of the way as the bullet ricocheted off the bridge brickwork. Dan felt a hammer-like blow to his chest and was knocked sideways, almost toppling into the murky water of the canal. As he hit the floor, his legs thrashing around as he tried to suck air into this chest, his left boot struck the pistol and sent it skittering towards the canal. As Deano made a desperate grab for it before it disappeared into the canal, Dan curled up into a foetal position on his left side and lay motionless, his breaths coming in short, rapid bursts.

# # # #

Benton was only about twenty metres from the bridge when he heard the shot and saw a body hit the floor, jerk violently for a few seconds, then lie still. He dived to the ground and rolled into the brambles at the edge of the towpath. Peering into the gloom under the bridge, he could see the still body on the floor and could hear some weird breathing sounds from the casualty, but he couldn't see any sign of Andrew Dean.

'Shit.' Benton slowly stood up and tried to see into the shadows under the bridge.

# # # #

The police sergeant in charge of the Armed Response Unit received a call via his Airwave radio. It informed him that there was another firearms incident, within five minutes of his team's location. They were currently liaising with a section of unarmed uniformed police officers about half a mile from Bedders Road and had handed over the detained gunmen. They were about to get back in their own vehicles after securing the prisoners in locked police vans. The sergeant rallied his team, bringing them over to his vehicle, and quickly briefed them on what he knew.

'Right, it seems we have located a suspect that's absconded after the raid in Bedders Road. The suspect, Andrew Dean, is reported to be armed, high on drugs, and in a public place, namely the canal near Dartmouth Avenue.'

'Where's the info from, Sarge?' asked one of his team.

'Undercover ops, requesting urgent backup via a third party,' the sergeant replied. 'So let's get a move on.'

Within thirty seconds, the whole team, consisting of five armed police officers, were travelling at high speed towards the specified location. They used blue lights but no sirens. The officers from the first raid who had discharged their weapons in the confrontation had already left for headquarters to begin writing their statements, and the sergeant was furious at the ridiculous legislation that had split up his team at such a vital time.

As they sped towards their destination, the sergeant

spoke to his team through their radios.

'Situation update just received. Shots heard fired at our destination.' He checked his own weapon's safety catch. 'This is classed as a live zone, lads. Stay focussed.' He received a couple of affirmatives over the radio, then heard only silence as his team concentrated on what lay ahead. They were less than a minute from their target now.

# # # #

After making the phone call to the police, Jonah was in a quandary. Leaving the unarmed police officer to face Deano on his own was part of the dilemma, but Jonah also felt emasculated. His anger had spurred him on, made him ready to stand up to Deano but then he had run away. In truth, he was still petrified of the violent gang leader, but if that police officer was going to challenge him, unarmed and alone, Jonah knew he had to put his own fear aside and help if he could, otherwise his conscience would never be clear. So he had come up with a plan. Sort of.

Sprinting along Harden Road, he jumped over the low fence that led to Goscote Fields, which would bring him up to the same canal that Andrew Dean and his opponent were on from the opposite direction. With the setting sun behind him, Jonah hoped that he could surprise Deano without being seen.

# # # #

Andrew Dean cradled his injured right hand with his left, then bent down to pick up the Baikal pistol. Holding it in his left hand felt alien to him, but better that than losing it into the murky depths under the bridge. He forcefully pushed the muzzle into the back of his opponent's head, receiving only a vague grunt in reply. The Monkey Dust he had taken over an hour earlier was wearing off now, and his adrenaline was on its last reserves. He slumped down and sat leaning against the wall of the bridge. Sitting in the dark shadow, he couldn't fail to notice Benton creeping towards the bridge.

'Bastard,' Deano hissed. 'Come and fuckin' get it, you grass.'

As he raised himself to a kneeling position and aimed the pistol at the approaching man, a flash of movement to his left caught his eye, but too late. Dan had retrieved the knife from his boot and hit his target. The sharp tip encountered little resistance at Deano's thigh and continued deep into the flesh, passing through the quadriceps muscle as if it were butter. The delicate and life-sustaining femoral artery was sliced clean through as the blade penetrated to its full depth. Deano squeezed the trigger of the pistol as he fell backwards. A single shot was fired, then Deano dropped the pistol and screamed as he grabbed at the knife, buried to the hilt inside his thigh.

# # # #

The ARU officers were getting out of the vehicles that were

parked only fifty metres away in the entrance to the old infants school when they heard the shot, and the scream of pain that followed it. They moved into a rapid tactical approach and fanned out as they reached the bridge, all traffic screeching to a halt as the drivers on Harden Road saw five armed police officers, clad in black, running up the road towards them.

# # # #

Deano's shot had hit Benton. The searing pain in his right upper arm told him he was hit, but as he rolled on the floor in agony, with his left hand over the injury, he couldn't see any gushes of blood – there didn't appear to be any significant trauma to his arm. Still, it hurt like hell. He stayed down and watched as Deano grunted and pulled at the knife sticking out of his thigh. Blood had made the handle slippery and he couldn't get a grip on it.

Unbelievably, the other injured casualty was getting up, first to his knees, then trying to stand. Benton was incredulous. He'd seen him shot, hit at point-blank range and knocked to the floor.

Dan stood up on shaking legs, drawing in painful breaths. Deano was sitting on the floor, legs splayed out in front of him, with his back to Dan, and concentrating only on the knife jutting out of his thigh. Dan positioned himself behind the injured enemy and struck him a savage blow, slamming both open palms to Deano's ears to disorientate him. Then he dropped to one knee and clamped his arms around Deano's neck in a vice-like stranglehold, cutting off the blood flow to his already muddled brain. As his incapacitated nemesis struggled feebly in his arms, Dan spoke calmly into Deano's ear.

'You killed my wife, you piece of shit. You stabbed her to death and you robbed her as she lay dying. You killed my dog, and your gang caused the death of my father. For them, and for all of the people whose lives you've ruined, I'm going to help you, one last time, before I hand you over to the police.'

With that, Dan reached down, grasped the bloody hilt of the knife and yanked it free, removing the only obstacle that was preventing the blood from leaking out of Andrew Dean's femoral artery. Deano screamed and tried to stem the flow of bright red blood as it gushed out in great spurts, soaking the ground around him in seconds. His blood volume rapidly diminished, plunging his blood pressure to a dangerously low level, starving his vital organs of oxygen and causing his brain to start shutting down. As he lost consciousness and his hand slipped away from the femoral wound, he feebly grabbed at the Baikal pistol lying on the ground next to him.

Jonah had arrived on the towpath on the opposite side of the bridge to Dan and Benton. He hadn't seen the fatal knife injury, but he saw Dan staggering to his feet, covered in blood and then Deano pointing a gun at him from only a metre or so away. Neither had Jonah seen the police marksmen take up position on the other side of the bridge, just as he leapt forwards to snatch the pistol out of

Deano's faltering grip and run towards Dan with it. His intention had been to get it as far from Deano as possible, but the police officers were unfortunately unaware of his good intentions. Jonah raised the pistol in the air to show Dan that he had grabbed it, the threat resolved. One of the officers shouted a warning. From their position, it looked just as if Jonah was raising the pistol to shoot at an injured man, already covered in blood and staggering weakly. It was an impossible situation to read correctly.

Benton saw the situation unfold but from too far away to intervene. As Jonah raised the pistol and he heard the shouted warning, Benton shouted out 'No!' but whether he was heard or not, he had no idea.

# # # #

National Newspaper Tabloid

Police have sealed off an area along a canal in Walsall following a shoot-out between armed police and an unknown young man from the local area. The armed young man was said to have died following the shooting but it is not known whether he died from gunshot wounds or other causes. A police spokesperson said last night that the young man had attacked a passer-by and shot and wounded an off-duty police officer who tried to intervene. The young man was reported to be high on the street drug 'Monkey Dust', which gives users a feeling of invincibility.

An anonymous caller had alerted police to the fact

that the man was walking along the canal brandishing a hand gun and they were already responding to the call when he attacked the passer-by.

The innocent passer-by was taken to hospital immediately afterwards but his injuries are not thought to be life-threatening. The heroic and unarmed off-duty police officer who was shot and wounded was also taken to hospital and his condition has been described as stable.

At another incident just minutes before this one, and less than a mile away, a large number of men were detained by police after a street brawl. Several of these men were also charged with illegal possession of firearms.

These are the latest in an escalating series of gun-related crime in the area of Walsall. Chief Inspector Roberts of West Midlands Police has issued a statement telling us that police have recently impounded three hundred hand guns and a large amount of ammunition from the area, following an intense and thorough investigation, involving police teams from across the country.

Chapter 42

Social Media Chat

ThugLife – Deano was a fkin hero man. I heard it took six SWAT team coppers to kill him

Good1 – Theres no such thing as SWAT in Britain ThugLife u muppet!

ThugLife – Yeah ther is. They just dont tell us about it. They have to have SWAT to deal with hardcases like Deano.

LuvDrugs – yeah, that's rite. My bruv was on Harden Road when it happend, he said ther woz about ten SWAT runnin down the road, then he herd machine guns going off all over the place. Hundreds of bullets he reckond.

ThugLife – It would of took that much to kill Deano. He was legend man

Good1 – He was a hooligan. A bully. Thief. Druggie.

ThugLife – You wanna watch ur mouth Good1. He woz a hero

Good1 – Hero???? How do u work that out?

ThugLife – He died for a cors

Good1 – Cors?? He died for a yankee beer?? U mean a

cause? Haha!!

ThugLife – whatever. He did tho.

LuvDrugs – yeah, he did. Died fighting the pigs.

WalsallBest – bullshit. He was stoned. Walking up Dartmouth, boxing with himself like a muppet. Went past my mums house, they was all watchin him and laffing at him!! Probly shot himself by axident!!

ThugLife – if I find out who you are Im gonna fkin box you, WB

WalsallBest – yeah right. You boys don't have your big hard bullyboy to back you up any more. Watcha gonna do, little gangsta? Who's gonna hold your hand? ☺

LuvDrugs – piss off WB, and you Good1. Wel see whos gonna box who. Keepers are still here. Waitin for the pigs to get lost, then we r comin back

Good1 – that's funny, I heard u all ran away when the big nasty foreign men came to sort u out. Wher was u all then? Left your m8 Deano to look after himself. That's wot I heard.

WalsallBest – So? ThugLife? LuvDrugs? U there? Whatcha got??

Good1 – they ran away again!! Lol. PMSL. ☺

WalsallBest – Probly. Cowerds.

Good1 – I heard there was somebody else in it as well. Some shadow man, like a govument agent or military or sumthin. Takin out the Keepers 1by1. Loads of em hav disappeard or had axidents. Even Lewis is gone! Nobody knows wot happened to them all.

WalsallBest – yeah, Iv heard that as well. I hope its rite. Id help him if I saw him.

Good1 – And me. We could do wiv a few of them govument agents like that! Its about time.

Epilogue

Two weeks later

Dan and Christine were driving to Cline Hill Rescue Kennels in his old Land Rover, her two daughters sat in the back seats, enjoying the scenery and the unique experience of being passengers in what was basically a farm vehicle. It had survived a three-day stay in the side street that it had been left parked in while Dan had gone after Deano and ended up in hospital afterwards, with no damage at all. A minor miracle indeed!

Dan had been taken by ambulance from the scene of his showdown with Deano straight to the Emergency Department. Luckily for him, the ricocheting bullet that had hit him in the chest had been deflected enough by his stab-vest that it didn't cause serious injury. It had already lost the majority of its velocity after ricocheting off the brickwork underneath the bridge, and the stab-vest absorbed even more kinetic energy as the bullet passed through it, leaving Dan with only a couple of broken ribs and a small scar where the bullet had been removed. It had gone through his skin, bounced off two ribs and come to rest a few millimetres away from his left lung, causing mainly bruising. The breathlessness he had suffered at the time was simply the feeling of being winded, thankfully. After a couple of days being kept in for observations on his chest and head injuries, he spent a further day in a different ward having the next bout of his experimental treatment for his cancer. At the end of his stay, the consultant, Dr Jeffreys, came to see him.

'Well, Daniel, I hear that you've been in the wars again, old chap.' He sat down next to Dan's bed. 'Aren't you getting a bit old for all that shenanigans?'

As he shifted uncomfortably in the bed, his ribs hurting with every small movement, Dan couldn't help but agree. 'Yeah, I think you're right. But some things just have to be done, you know?' Dan looked at the photographs of his lost family on his bedside table that Christine had thoughtfully brought in for him. 'At least I can try and move forwards now. I can start to grieve properly for them at last.'

Jeffreys nodded quietly. 'I can't even imagine what you're going through. But if you feel that you can try to get on with your life in a positive way now, it will certainly help with your treatment.'

'How is it looking?' Dan asked. 'Any more news from the scans?'

'To be perfectly truthful, I've been very impressed with this treatment and the good results we're seeing. I cannot thank you enough for your bravery in trying it. I really think it's a major breakthrough for the treatment of this type of cancer, and I intend to present your clinical case at the National Oncology Conference later this year, if that's all right with you?'

Dan nodded. 'Of course. I'm just glad that it's worked so far. I'm suffering very few side effects now, apart from a dull headache.'

'Well.' Jeffreys smiled. 'That might be something to do with your hand-to-hand combat! At your age, Daniel, really.' He smiled again as he stood up. 'I'm going to discharge you today. Go home, get some rest, take the painkillers I'm going to prescribe for you, and if those symptoms come back, or that headache doesn't go away, you must get seen. I'll see you again in a month for your next treatment anyway. Try and stay out of trouble this time?'

Dan nodded and grinned ruefully. 'I'll do my best, Doc. Can't promise, though.'

After being discharged from hospital, Dan had immediately presented himself at the police station in Green Lane, Walsall, to voluntarily make his statement, after receiving advice from Constable Benton, who had been to see him while he was in hospital. They had enjoyed a long, interesting and off-the-record discussion about the Keepers and the events of that day that had ended Andrew Dean's rule of terror on the housing estates of Coalpool, Goscote and Blakenall. A transfer and possibly a promotion was on the cards for the young police officer, and Benton said that he had been transferred to a different area within the force, although he didn't say where and Dan knew well enough not to ask.

Benton had told Dan that Deano had died before an ambulance arrived, suffering rapid and catastrophic blood loss due to a severed femoral artery, according to the preliminary post-mortem findings. Strangely, his funeral had been well-attended by local adolescents and young men from the estates. Many of them had already elevated the dead Andrew Dean to a legendary status. Social media was split over this level of tribute. Some social media users were arguing that he was merely a hoodlum, a criminal who'd paid the ultimate and well-deserved price for his sins. Notably, these people almost always used an anonymised account to discuss Andrew Dean, to prevent retaliation and repercussions. Other people openly paid tribute to him instead, revering him like some modern-day Robin Hood, even though he had never given any of his spoils to anyone, least of all the poor. In reality, he had always been more likely to rob the poor and the weak but this detail was largely ignored by his followers. A photograph of Andrew Dean that had been digitally altered to look like Che Guevara had bizarrely received more than eighteen thousand 'likes' on one social media page. People who lived in the same area that he had terrorised in his short but violent and disruptive life silently breathed a sigh of relief that he was gone for good.

Dan had been kept waiting for only a short time before being taken to an interview room where a pleasant but efficient pair of police officers had taken his statement and recorded the interview.

'Do you think there will be any charges?' Dan asked, as

they all signed the statement.

'Not sure, sir,' was the brief reply from the older of the two officers, the one who had introduced himself as a CID constable. 'This will go to the investigating officer, who is compiling a case for presentation to the Crown Prosecution Service. At the moment though, you're not under arrest and are classed as "helping with enquiries", so you're free to go.' He shuffled the paperwork and switched off the recording equipment. 'I'll walk you to your car, sir.'

As they walked across the public car park outside the police station, the CID constable spoke quietly to Dan. 'This is unofficial, and I'll deny ever saying it, of course.'

Dan nodded, remaining silent.

'You've done everyone a bloody huge favour.' The officer grinned conspiratorially at Dan. 'That bastard has been a pain in the arse ever since he could walk. The rest of his mates have always relied on him and Kalvin Lewis to provide the fear in the community, so that they could get away with their thieving, bullying, drug running and God only knows what else. Now Andrew Dean is out of the picture. Permanently. And Lewis seems to have done a runner, so the monster has lost its head, so to speak. No one is stepping up to the mark to take their place, yet. Let's hope we can keep it that way.'

They reached the Land Rover, and Dan unlocked the driver's door.

'I reckon, and this is only a rumour, you understand,' the officer continued, 'public opinion being what it is, and the huge amount of social media interest that this case is attracting, I reckon your argument of self-defence will be justifiable, at least for that incident on the canal with Andrew Dean. We found his finger prints on a knife and a pistol . He shouldn't have been carrying those weapons with him, and it's lucky that you managed to disarm him before he used them further on you or anyone else. And there's no law against wearing a stab-proof vest, not yet. Some might say it's a sensible precaution in this day and age!' He looked around the car park as Dan started his car engine. 'Add to that the fact you probably saved the life of a police officer who had already been shot by Dean, and I can't see how it would be "in the public interest" to prosecute you. And I haven't heard that anyone is looking at you for any other incidents, if you know what I mean.'

Dan stared at him for a few seconds.

'Well, thanks.' He offered his hand, which the police officer shook warmly. 'But can I ask, what's your particular interest in Andrew Dean?'

'I grew up on that estate,' the officer said. 'Some of my family still live there. They're good people, salt of the earth, just skint. They can't get jobs anywhere else that will pay them enough to up sticks and move. My grandad lived there too, until he died recently.'

'I'm sorry to hear that,' Dan said.

'You grew up there as well, didn't you? Perhaps you've heard of my grandad? Bill Dickerson? He was a war hero. Wouldn't let any of the family visit him after he was diagnosed with cancer, as he didn't want us to remember him like that.' He shrugged. 'Anyway, it seemed that some thieving bastard broke in and stole his pain-relieving drugs before he died. Silly bastard burned himself to death in the old bugger's shed after taking the stolen drugs though. I'd told the old man about keeping petrol in there. Oh well. That's life, eh? You take care of yourself, sir. Let's hope our paths don't cross in the future, not professionally anyway.' He grinned. 'But if I ever see you in the pub, I owe you a pint or two.' Raising his hand in farewell, he turned and walked back towards the station.

# # # #

'Here we are,' Dan said to Christine as he turned the Land Rover onto a muddy dirt track that led up to Cline Hill Rescue Kennels.

'So what are we doing here, Dan?' Christine asked. 'I mean, it's been great catching up with you, and the kids have enjoyed the drive through Shropshire, but why are we here?'

Stopping the car at the entrance to the kennels yard, Dan switched off the engine.

'I've decided to get another dog. The company will be nice, and I like to think I'm helping a waif and stray. And Maisie is settled in with you and your family now.'

'Oh. Right,' Christine said. 'That's a bit unexpected, but I'm pleased. It means you're looking forward, and it'll stop me worrying about you so much.'

Dan smiled at her. 'Right then, girls, let's go. You have to help me choose a new dog.'

Christine's two young daughters grinned with delight.

'Really? We can pick one?' the eldest daughter asked.

'Not just like that.' Dan smiled. 'But you have to help one of them find me, so that we all know it's the right dog for the right owner.'

They all jumped down out of the Land Rover and walked along the muddy path into the kennels yard, where they were met by a young man with a shock of red hair. He opened the main gate for them and introduced himself as they walked towards the metal cages of the kennels where the dogs were all on parade, barking and jumping up at the mesh to attract attention. The girls were in front, and the young man explained the rules to them.

'Try to be calm around them, don't put your fingers through the cages, and walk all the way around before you ask to take one of the dogs out, OK? It's too easy to pick the first cute dog, and the ones at the far end get left behind. Here.' He pointed at a quiet dog in one of the first kennels. 'This one is new. She's had a rough time, but she's doing OK. She's a bit shy, but if you sit by the door, she'll come and sit with her back to you. It means she wants to say hello, but she's nervous.'

As Christine and the two girls tried to entice the nervous dog to come to them, Dan stood next to the young man.

'So what about you, Jonah? How are you getting on?'

The young man looked at the shy dog that was struggling to overcome its fear as it sat with its back to the girls.

'I'm OK, thanks. I love it here.' Looking around at the kennels, he continued quietly, 'Never thought I'd have a job, not really. I can't read or write, see. But this suits me. I'm all right with dogs, always have been. We sort of understand each other. And the kennel owners have sorted out a room for me in the workshop at the end of the yard. They said I can live there until I get something sorted, but I like it here, so I might stay a while before I move out. They pay me as well, and I sometimes eat in the house with them at lunchtimes and in the evenings.'

He looked really proud of himself. 'Makes me feel good, you know? That I'm working for my money, not stealing it. And they don't judge me, the owners. They're really nice people. Thanks for sorting this out for me, Dan, I really appreciate it. Honestly, I love it here. I would never have had this chance if it wasn't for you and that copper.'

'Well I reckon you earned the chance, matey.' Dan smiled at him. 'You phoned for backup. You helped me out as well, don't forget that. I don't know if Deano would have had the strength to pull the trigger one more time, but if he had, I'd have been done for. You snatched the gun away from him before we had to find out.'

Jonah laughed. 'Yeah, nearly got myself shot an' all, didn't I? I never expected the coppers with guns to get there so quick! Good thing you was staggering round the canal like a drunk, or they'd have shot me. One of 'em told me afterwards that he thought I was pointing the gun at you but he couldn't aim at me cos you kept gettin' in the way. Lucky for me.'

'Lucky for all of us,' Dan replied solemnly. 'I don't know how I would've lived with myself if you'd been hurt while trying to help me.'

'Yeah, well, I wasn't, was I? Did you know they wanted to give me a commendation or something?' Jonah looked amazed. 'I daren't have it though. Imagine me going back home, with everyone knowing I helped the police! They'd string me up.'

'Will you go back home?' Dan asked.

'Nah, I don't think so. Not for a bit anyway.' Jonah shook his head. 'Why would I? I bet my family haven't even noticed I'm gone yet.' He wiped his eyes angrily and continued resolutely. 'Besides, you've got me a chance to do something good. I only got mixed up with the Keepers cos I was bored, skint, had no mates. I know it's not an excuse for thieving an' that, but it didn't seem so bad at the time, you know? I never thought about what I was doing. Then things got really bad.' He looked sideways at Dan, feeling uncomfortable. 'Really bad. And then I knew, Deano and Lewis were like a poison spreading round the estates, making everybody as bad as them, bit by bit. When I think back, it's like I'm a different person now.'

He shrugged. 'I know it's only been a couple of weeks, Dan, but honest, I'll make things up to you. I'll show you. I won't let you down, really I won't. I don't want to lose this.' He gestured around at the kennels. 'I know it don't seem much to most people, walking the dogs and cleaning up the mess an' that, but it's more than that to me. It's hard to explain.'

Dan put his hand on the young man's shoulder.

'You don't need to explain, matey. I get it. And you

don't have to make anything up to me. You don't owe me anything. What's done is done. It's all in the past. Let's just look to the future, eh? Anyway,' Dan straightened himself up and looked to Christine and the girls, 'I've got to choose a dog to take home. Come and help me. You know them all by now. The girls will pick a fluffy lap dog, and I can't take that for long walks on the Wrekin, can I?'

They walked along the lines of kennels, speaking softly to each dog, encouraging the nervous ones while ignoring the barks of the larger, more aggressive ones. Both Dan and Jonah knew that the loud barking was just noise and posturing, and that all of the dogs deserved a second chance, regardless of their histories and past transgressions.

<u>Acknowledgements</u>

My heartfelt thanks to the late and unique Colonel William Flood, my headmaster for eleven years at Hydesville Tower School.

To Mrs Denley, my English teacher. (Any grammatical errors are mine and not due to her incredible teaching skills.)

Finally, to Consuelo and Victorina Press, who all believed in me and encouraged me to write.

Thank you all.

<u>About The Author</u>

The author was born and bred in Walsall, England, where this book is set. Some of the places mentioned do exist. The urban forest behind Ryecroft Cemetery is called the Yellow Mess by most of the locals, although few of the younger locals know why any more. The Monkey Hills really are called that, and the name stems from the reason explained in Chapter 6. Some poetic licence has been utilised for other places. The Coalpool Tavern, for example, no longer exists, but it did when the author was growing up, living in a council house just down the road from that notorious public house.

Some of the horrific incidents in the book are based on true stories, although all the names in the book are fictitious. One of the author's childhood thirteen-year-old friends did get his head bashed in by a gang for playing football on the wrong field. Burglars did throw a pet dog over a fence to leave it hanging while they ransacked the house, but unfortunately there was no one to rescue that poor animal. Instead, its owners found it dead when they returned home and found the house burgled and vandalised. An old man did get robbed for his pain-relief medication as he lay dying, although that happened many years later when the author was working as a paramedic.

The author was a Corporal in the British Army and served in Northern Ireland in the late 1980s and early 1990s, but all events and places mentioned in the book relating to that conflict are fictitious.

The social problems, crime and violence mentioned in this book exist all across Great Britain and they cause suffering and deprivation to the majority of good people of all nationalities who just want to live in peace, go to work and enjoy the fruits of their labours, and watch their children grow up in a safe place.

Finally, this book is a work of fiction, and the author does not necessarily condone vigilante violence. Although, if you were in Dan's position, and events had affected your family, what would you do? Makes you think, doesn't it?

Thanks for reading this book and please feel free to leave a review or contact me via Victorina Press.